PRAIRIE HEAT

"I'm not sleeping off by myself with those Indians roaming around."

"Cassandra —"

"And I don't care what you say." Her lower lip was thrust out stubbornly, and Alex found himself staring at it with hunger as she continued. "I realize you're doing the gentlemanly thing, Alex, observing the proprieties and all that, but this isn't a civilized situation and —"

"You're damned right it isn't," he muttered angrily. How much control did the girl think he had? She was playing with fire. "What is it you want, Cassandra?" he asked harshly. His tone caused her eyelids to flicker uncertainly and her mouth to close. She took a half step back. "Changed your mind? I thought you wanted to sleep with me."

ELIZABETH CHADWICK

BRIDE
FIRE

LEISURE BOOKS NEW YORK CITY

For Bill,
who suggested that I try writing novels

A LEISURE BOOK®

July 1992

Published by

Dorchester Publishing Co., Inc.
276 Fifth Avenue
New York, NY 10001

Special thanks to Joann Coleman for her encouragement and her editorial skills and Marion Coleman, whose expertise in period weaponry was invaluable; to Dr. Homer Jacobs for information on pregnancy and childbirth; and to all those helpful librarians at the University of Texas at El Paso and the El Paso Public Library.

Book I
The
Mustangers

May 1844 to
January 1845

Chapter One

She regained consciousness slowly, goaded by pain so intense that it saturated the upper left half of her body. *I'm going to die*, she thought but could hardly believe it. As dangerous and unconventional as her life had been in recent months, Cassandra had never expected to die. Seventeen-year-old girls from Massachusetts didn't die—not in agony, not as a result of Indian attacks out in the middle of nowhere. That must be why young men dreamed of war. Because they expected adventure, not death.

The second thing she noticed—after the pain—was the silence. Only the long grass, windswept and restless, whispered over the empty plains. The absence of other sounds told her that she was the only one left alive in the clearing. *How far from home am I?* she wondered. *A thousand miles? Two thousand? Three?* Not that it mattered. She wouldn't be going back.

The third thing came when she opened her eyes. Through a mist of tears like winter condensation on a glass pane, she saw the scalp lock flapping above her, a macabre banner at the end of the Comanche lance that pinned her to earth.

And last, above the scalp lock, above the dark etched branches and curled May leaves shivering against a spring sky, the vultures circled. How long would they wait to swoop down? Horror-stricken, she raised her hands and clasped them one below the other on the lance. With a strength born of desperation, she wrenched upward, trying to lift her impaled body away from the earth that held it. She failed, and a quick flood of agony swept her into darkness.

"Vultures," grunted Nicodemus Pelt. He halted the pack train and squinted into the westering sun.

"Probably some animal died," said Alex Harte.

"Yep, or some human. This is Comanche country." Pelt yanked an ancient hat lower on his forehead. "Maybe we better make tracks."

"We need water for the horses, and that's where it is." Alex was studying the knoll with its sparse crown of trees. It sheltered the only reliable spring in the area.

"I'm for movin' on," said Pelt.

"Look, Nico, it's a long way to the next creek. Better let me scout ahead. Then if I find Indians, I can get away faster than you." Nicodemus Pelt was a giant of a man, six foot six at least, and burly. No horse made good time with Pelt in the saddle. "You hang back with the pack train and bring them on if I signal."

"We'll flip to see if we scout or ride on."

Alex agreed reluctantly. If Nicodemus won the toss and they hit a dry creek the next day, they'd be in trouble. He fished a Mexican gold piece from his pocket and flipped. It was understood from long association that Pelt chose tails, Alex heads. The coin came up heads. Satisfied, Alex turned his horse toward the knoll.

"Watch your scalp," Pelt muttered.

Although he was willing to take the risk that there might be Comanches in the area, Alex was a careful man. He'd campaigned against both Mexicans and Indians during the twelve years since his arrival in Texas and had lost, in the process, the recklessness of youth. Therefore he searched for track as he approached the knoll, and he found it. Eight men had ridden in from the northeast with three of the horses shod, five not; eight horses had come off the knoll, but only five carried riders. Alex had a fair idea of what he'd find on top, but still he circled up cautiously, studying the horizons in all directions, just as the Comanches must have done when they approached the spring.

Nothing stirred on the undulating prairie in any direction other than the one from which he had come, and nothing stirred in the trampled clearing under the trees. He found the first man, arrow-shot and scalped, fifty feet northwest of the spring, a Kiowa by the look of him and far south of his usual hunting ground. The second man, a white of sixty years or so, had been knifed and scalped. He lay in a bloody heap by the dead campfire. To the north was a slender, fair-haired youth pierced by a Comanche lance. He'd been a handsome boy with fine, strong facial bones marred by a dark bruise along the left side from cheek to mouth. Odd that they'd leave the lance, Alex thought, puzzled. Even stranger that they'd pass up that scalp with its silver-gold hair.

He leaned forward to feel for a pulse at the throat artery in case the boy still clung to life. Surprisingly, Alex felt a stirring beneath his fingertips. Bastards! Had they deliberately left their young victim to be torn apart by vultures? "Someone hated you," he murmured as he slid a hand into the buckskin shirt to feel for a heartbeat.

Alex went motionless with shock, then edged his fingers to the left. "God damn," he muttered. "A girl!"

Cassandra felt the touch on her breast and heard the soft oath, but as if from a distance. Wherever she was, this new consciousness excluded pain. If the voice and hand were part of some dying dream, then she still lay alone and helpless, abandoned by the Comanches like camp refuse. On the empty Texas prairie where every mile looked just like the last. Her heart contracted in sadness at the prospect of dying by herself in this alien land. But her grief was only momentary and drifted away.

Then another thought crept in, insubstantial as mist on a gray winter's morning. If the voice and hand were real, she was at the mercy of a stranger. And there was the pain. If she came back, she'd feel that searing pain again.

"Can you hear me?"

Cassandra heard, but didn't answer. Why respond to a ghost whisper?

"Poor child," it muttered.

She could tell that it had touched the lance because pain shivered through her body. But she wasn't inside and didn't mind.

"This needs Pelt," the ghost muttered.

Pelt? An enigmatic thing to say. Her spirit puzzled over the words until a new aloneness told her that the ghost had moved. Perhaps it was leaving. Fear replaced indifference. If it was a real man, he could rescue her. He represented the only chance at life the real Cassandra had. Which meant she had to speak. To open her eyes. To repossess her own body with all its potential for agony and terror.

She heard the body moan, and evidently he noticed, for he came back. She could sense his presence.

"You're coming around," he murmured. "I signaled Pelt. Between the two of us, maybe we can get you loose."

She raised her eyelids and looked at the man kneeling on one knee beside her. Then she panicked because he was dark. Dark skin, black eyes and hair, *long* hair.

"Here now," he soothed, his voice deep and rich, a slow, comforting drawl. "I mean you no harm, child."

He spoke English, not Comanche, but he looked a dangerous man, dark and hawk-featured, tall with a deep, muscular chest showing through the loosely laced shirt, and his hair was long. But not braided like an Indian's. Whatever he was, she feared him.

"Don't strain against the lance, child."

Too late. The rich voice faded as agony washed her consciousness away once more.

"This here's a girl," said Nicodemus when he had studied the young body in its buckskin breeches and shirt.

"I figured that out," Alex replied.

"Girls are nothin' but trouble."

"You want to leave her out here to die?"

Nicodemus shifted his big frame uneasily.

"If she lives through us getting the lance out, we'll drop her off at a settlement," Alex promised.

"There ain't no settlements, an' none of the others'll wanna cut short the expedition—least not till we git us another good-sized herd."

"What choice do we have?" Alex argued.

"An' how we gonna git her to camp? Say she lives. She won't be able to travel, an' they need the supplies." Nicodemus Pelt nodded toward the pack horses loaded with ammunition and staples enough for another three months.

Alex studied the girl, then the situation. "Travois, I reckon. We'll rig one and tie her to it."

"That ought to kill her if we don't do it gittin' her loose. An' say we haul her to camp an' she recovers. Then we got more trouble—five men an' one girl. That's—"

"She's a child."

Pelt snorted. "Looks beddable to me. You kin be danged sure young Pinto ain't gonna see her as no child."

"Then Pinto will just have to look again," snapped Alex.

"Trouble," muttered Pelt.

"So what are you saying, Nicodemus? Kill her and be done with it?"

"Oh hell, I ain't sayin' that, Alex. Ain't never killed a woman yet." He stared pessimistically at the girl. "Had a few die on me."

"Well, this one may die too. How many men with an arrow in them lived that you know of?"

"Lance," corrected Pelt. "That head could be thirty inches long, an' we'll have to git it out if it's in her body 'steada the ground." He knelt beside her and cut through the shaft fifteen inches above her shoulder. "I'm gonna lift her up while you push down on the lance," he explained. "If I kin, I'll lift her right off it."

Maneuvering with difficulty, the two men freed her. "I'd like to know how come they didn't just kill her an' take the scalp," Pelt murmured as he laid her body down in the grass. "They scalped the other two." Her long, pale gold braid had fallen free. "That hair would be a prize."

"Pure meanness," said Alex.

"This is their territory," said Nicodemus. "They didn't invite none of us here."

The short, paunchy one with the barrel chest and narrow eyes wanted the paper her father used for his notes, and Papa was trying to tell him how important paper was to a scholar. But the Indian would never understand, and Cassandra wanted to plead with Papa to give it to him, just give him the paper. Please ... please. She wanted to tell him, but she couldn't speak. And the pain was so bad.

Her whole body on fire, she awoke from the dream. She was being dragged behind a horse, and the bumping hurt. If only the dark man, the Indian, would let her be still. If she could be still, it wouldn't hurt so much.

They'll never let Papa refuse. He'd said himself that they considered generosity so important. And the fat one wanted the paper. Just because of the paper, he shouted

14

and, drawing a knife, leapt upon Papa, catalyzing a wave of violence across the camp. Their Kiowa guide shot the Comanche who carried a lance and was in turn dropped by an arrow. The fat one plunged his knife into Papa. Pulled it out. Gathered the thin, white hair into his fist. He meant to scalp Papa.

Seeing this, Cassandra forgot how frightened she was and scooped up the Bowie knife that had belonged to their guide. She slashed it across that broad, cruel face before he could make the first scalp cut. Turning, a thin, red line from his forehead to his chin, he knocked her to the ground and held her there with a gritty, moccasined foot as the blood welled, thick and red, on his cheek. He leaned his weight upon her chest, pressing her against the earth until her ribs seemed to be collapsing and she could hardly breathe. Blackness crept in around her.

Gasping, she woke.

"You're burning up," said the man with the soft, drawling voice. "Here, try the water again."

She drank greedily, relieved to see that he wasn't an Indian, after all. His skin showed white beneath the laced shirt. She closed her eyes, trying to remember how many days of pain and fever had passed since her rescue.

She knew only that she was traveling with two white men and that her world was circumscribed by the tall grass through which the travois passed and an occasional glimpse of sky. And she was so hot. They had rigged a canopy to keep the sun from her face, but the heat burned inside her.

She couldn't breathe, and now he had the lance in his hand, holding it high, eyes blazing with malice, and she thought, "Oh no, please..." because she knew what he meant to do. And then he drove the lance down through her shoulder and into the earth, and the pain, oh God, the pain.

"I know it hurts, girl," said the one named Nicodemus, "but I gotta keep the wound clean."

Nicodemus and Alex. The one who had found her was Alex. Indian brown features, but a white chest. Still, with his long black hair and haughty face, she thought half the time that he was a Comanche who had come back to finish her off. When those fears assailed her, he seemed to understand, and his voice, rich and slow, soothed her. Alex was a mustanger, on his way with Pelt to meet others of his kind. *Mustang* meant wild horse, but she wasn't sure what a mustanger was.

The giant called himself Nicodemus. Cassandra remembered a Nicodemus in the Bible, a Pharisee who helped Joseph prepare Jesus for burial. This Nicodemus made her drink things—meat broth that caused nausea, water as cool as a gift from heaven, and something so bitter that she tried at first to refuse it. Nicodemus had to force it on her until she learned that it brought sleep and relief from pain. Sometimes she thought Nicodemus might be preparing *her* for death. Mostly she didn't think at all because the bitter stuff made her dream good dreams. Of Sunday tea in Mama's parlor in Cambridge, where Papa's colleagues and students came to call. Of school days at Mama's school, where everything was peaceful and safe.

Nicodemus was also called Pelt—perhaps because he was a *shaggy* giant, his heavy black hair and beard shot through with iron gray. He looked menacing and seemed to dislike her, yet he had gentle hands.

"Lost a lot of blood," said one.
"Fever's worse," said the other.
She couldn't always tell which was which.

"Damned if that wound ain't startin' to heal."
"Think she's dreaming about what happened, poor child?"
She wanted to explain that she wasn't a child. Had

she been crying when the pain got bad? She tried not to. She hoped that, if she was good and didn't cause them too much trouble, they wouldn't abandon her.

Throughout the day Cassandra had been wakeful because Pelt was giving her less of the bitter tea. The wound ached with a dull, continuous presence to which she had become accustomed, and today there had been distractions to take her waking mind from the miseries of her body.

Wildflowers grew all about her in the grass. She had only to turn her head, and they flowed by. Some were pert, weedy little things she had to look down on because they had hidden themselves; some had dark eyes peering out boldly at her from amongst their petals; and some waved above her head as if she were a tiny ground creature and they slender flower trees. Enchanted, she watched all day.

Also she could study her companions from beneath the canopy if one or the other happened to be riding nearby. She had yet to speak to either man, afraid that if she did, her words might break the spell and bring an end to the strange journey and her recovery. The two men might even abandon her or just disappear, having been hallucinations created by her fevered mind.

She liked it best when the one named Alex talked. He had a husky voice, and his words were marked by soft, elongated vowels that brushed pleasantly along her nerves. She had never heard anyone with an accent quite like his. Could it be the mark of the Texas frontiersman? Nicodemus Pelt didn't sound that way; he strung error on grammatical error until Cassandra thought him the perfect example of untutored English. Alex, on the other hand, seemed not only soft-spoken but educated.

Certainly he had neither resided nor been educated

in New England. At the thought of her home in Cambridge and her parents, Cassandra's spirits plunged. The house stood empty, her mother dead, the ladies' seminary, of which Jessica Whitney had been headmistress and owner, sold. And her father, who had been away from Cambridge pursuing his Indian research for nine years, was now dead as well, killed by the people he had been studying—or was he? Since she had survived the attack, perhaps he had too.

Startled into speech, she pushed herself up onto an elbow and asked, "What happened to my father?"

The two men turned to her, as surprised as if the hickory tree under which she lay had suddenly addressed them. Nicodemus Pelt, who had been whittling by the campfire, rose, tossed his stick away, and padded over to stare down at her. Lord, the man was big, she thought, wishing that he'd back away.

"Was you with your pa back there at the Indian camp?"

Cassandra nodded.

"Old fella, sixty or so?"

"He had white hair," she whispered.

"He didn't have no hair when we seen him," Pelt replied bluntly. "He was wearing a preacher's suit. That him?"

Cassandra wouldn't have called it a preacher's suit, but perhaps anyone in a suit looked like a preacher to a man named Pelt.

The giant studied her face somberly. "There was him an' a Kiowa, both dead," he added, not unkindly.

Cassandra closed her eyes.

"We give 'em burial. Alex spoke a few words from the Good Book."

She nodded, wondering why she had thought, even for a minute, that her father might have survived.

"You got a name, missy?"

"Whitney," she replied. "Cassandra Whitney." When he seemed about to turn away, she asked impulsively, "Are you called Pelt because of your hair?"

The giant frowned, and Cassandra, who had asked out of loneliness and a desire for the reassurance of human conversation, now saw her question to be impertinent. No doubt Pelt was his real name, and she had offended him, for which he could easily take revenge by walking away from her, he and his friend and their pack animals.

The chuckle of the one named Alex, who still lounged beside the campfire, took her by surprise. How long had it been since she'd heard good-natured laughter? The Comanches had laughed among themselves, but she'd always been afraid that their mirth signified some plot against unwanted guests.

"His name's *Van* Pelt, but he can't be bothered with the *Van*. It's a Dutch name. Am I right, Nicodemus?"

The giant grunted noncommittally and hunkered down again by the fire.

"And I'm Alexander Harte—late of New Orleans but *gone to Texas*, as they say when a man's debts mount or his feet itch to move on."

So that was the origin of the accent. He was a Southerner. Had he been a debtor or just a wanderer? Certainly the last, given his present location. And New Orleans—Cassandra had heard of New Orleans, a hotbed of French decadence and self-indulgent Southern luxury, home of slave markets and much disapproved of in Puritan, abolitionist New England.

She studied the younger man with surreptitious interest, trying to imagine him dressed as a Southern gentleman instead of clad in buckskins and boots. He was attractive in his way—soft-spoken, hard-faced, and quite handsome. The only males Cassandra had known heretofore were young students and their professors from Harvard, a few stiff-necked male relatives of her mother's, some Congregationalist ministers, and Comanches. Alexander Harte was completely outside her experience, but she remembered her mother

Elizabeth Chadwick

speaking of men who were too handsome and charming for their own good—*ladies' men* she'd called them. Cassandra had never met any in the intellectual circles frequented by her scholarly parents.

Was this Alexander Harte a ladies' man? Probably not. Else why would he be traveling in Indian country with a giant named Van Pelt and a train of pack horses? He was unlikely to find many ladies out here. Perhaps he had done some woman wrong and been driven out of society for his sins. She'd read that Southerners even fought duels. Perhaps he'd killed someone in a duel over a woman.

Amazed at herself, Cassandra called a halt to such speculations. Her imagination must be overheated by fever, she decided. Better to wonder what his education had been instead of what female liaisons he might have had before coming here to the plains. But she'd wonder later—when she wasn't so sleepy.

"Droppin' off agin," said Nicodemus Pelt. "Still, talkin's a good sign. I seen women come through Indian attacks who never spoke agin."

As they traveled steadily southwest, she heard them talking of the men they would meet, and she became afraid. What would happen to her if the other mustangers refused to let her travel with them? Left behind, she would wander a few days, then die for lack of food and water. Even if they gave her supplies and a horse, she doubted that she could find her way to a settlement. Or what if they let her stay because they wanted a woman for—for—? Cassandra felt like crying. She couldn't possibly allow something like that to happen. She had seen such poor souls on the streets of Boston, and her mother had explained their fate in a few blunt words. Cassandra thought she'd rather die than be reduced to such a life.

If only there were some service she could perform until she found someone to take or send her back home to Massachusetts. What did mustangers *do*? she wondered desperately. What could she do that they might find useful?

That evening, still weak and light-headed but determined to prove that she wouldn't be a burden, Cassandra sat at the campfire, ate stew from their community pot, and drank coffee with them, although she had to share Alexander Harte's cup. The sharing sent a strange shiver up her spine, and she politely turned the horn vessel and drank from the opposite side. He, on the other hand, didn't seem to notice, for he took the cup back and drank where her lips had been. It would have seemed an intimate thing had he done it on purpose.

Lest they think that she was going to be a drain on their supplies, she ate sparingly, and when the meal was over, she said, "I know how to cook over a campfire and execute other outdoor duties." She hoped they wouldn't want any immediate demonstrations, for she had pretty well exhausted her small reserve of energy.

"Maybe later," said Alex. "You're looking a bit peaked for camp chores just yet."

Cassandra breathed an unheard sigh of gratitude for his consideration and for his use of the word *later*, which meant, she hoped, that he had no plans to abandon her.

"How old are you, missy?" asked Nicodemus abruptly.

"Seventeen," she replied.

"Thought so."

He gave Harte a telling look, which returned Cassandra to a state of uneasiness. Was seventeen too young? Too old?

"You said you was out here with your pa, but you didn't say what business he had in Comanche country. Was he one a them preachers tryin' to bring the poor heathen Indians to Jesus?" Nicodemus asked. "Or maybe he was sellin' 'em whiskey an' guns so's they kin kill off more whites."

"My father was a scholar, Mr. Pelt," she replied, confused by his sarcasm. "He studied Indian languages."

Both men looked confounded at this explanation.

"Papa held a professorship at Harvard College," Cassandra added. "In—in languages. Latin and Greek—and Hebrew. Actually, he had a theory that Indian languages were descended from Hebrew." An untenable theory, in Cassandra's opinion. She would have hesitated to mention it had she not judged her companions unlikely to hold any informed opinion on the relation of ancient Hebrew to contemporary Indian tongues. "He theorized that the Indians were one of the lost tribes of Israel." Cassandra herself wasn't convinced that the Indian languages were related to each other, much less Hebrew. "He was compiling dictionaries," she finished lamely.

"The tracks showed that you rode in with the Indians," said Alex. "Were you and your father captives?"

"No," she replied. "They had extended us hospitality. I don't understand why they killed him."

"I don't understand why they didn't kill *you*," muttered Nicodemus, "or carry you off. Generally speakin', they kill the men an' carry off the women an' children."

"I tried to save Papa," whispered Cassandra. "One of the Indians was going to scalp him, and I—I attacked the warrior."

"With what?" asked Harte, visibly astounded at the idea of a young girl attacking a Comanche.

"With the Kiowa's Bowie knife. He was already dead," she hastened to add, "so he didn't need it. I slashed the Comanche's face," she mumbled, "but then he knocked me down, and, well—you saw the rest."

"Scarred by a woman," muttered Nicodemus. "That explains why he passed up a good blond scalp an' left you to the buzzards. No way he'd figger anyone to come along an' hep you." Nicodemus scratched his heavy, gray-streaked beard. "What it don't explain is why a Comanche would break his own rules of hospitality an' kill your pa."

"They wanted his paper, and he wouldn't hand it over—neither his notes nor his blank sheets. The research was his life's work," said Cassandra earnestly. "He tried to explain to them how important it was. Why, Papa valued his notes as much as the Comanches value their horses, and I'm sure the Comanche wouldn't have wanted to give away his horse, not if it was his only one."

"Nope," Nicodemus agreed. "If he had two, he might give away one, figgerin' he could soon steal or catch another, but he sure wouldn't put hisself afoot."

"Well, there," said Cassandra.

"But he wouldn't see no wad a paper as bein' anythin' near as valuable as a horse."

"But that's just the point; the paper was important to Papa, while the Indian didn't have any use for it."

"The Comanches value paper more than you might think." Alex rose from the fire and stretched.

Cassandra watched the muscles ripple along his arms and across his chest and shoulders. Even through his shirt, she could see them flex. Hurriedly she lowered her eyes, sure that, in staring, she had indulged in unmaidenly conduct.

"They like paper to stuff their shields," he added, seemingly unaware of her interested, if embarrassed, scrutiny. "When they raid a settlement, they're usually looking for livestock, and they'll carry off women and children, but they also fancy books."

"They killed my father over—over stuffing for a shield!" Cassandra's voice broke at the irony of it.

23

"A good shield, well made and well handled, will deflect a bullet or an arrow," said Alex.

"That's a fact, missy," Nicodemus agreed. "Didn't your pa defend hisself?"

"He didn't carry weapons," Cassandra mumbled, knowing that her father's pacifism would sound ludicrous to these men, who bristled with rifles, pistols, and knives. "He didn't believe in violence."

"Didn't believe in violence!" Alex exclaimed. "What the devil was he doing out here then? And why would he bring along a young girl if he had no way and no intention of defending her?"

"He thought—he thought it would be an instructive experience for me," she whispered. Were they angry with *her*? Nicodemus was muttering to himself, and Alex Harte's features had tightened into grim lines. "My mother died last year, and I had no one else, you see, no close family, only a few cousins, so Papa came home for a bit and then took me back with him."

"If he had a position at Harvard College, he should have stuck with that," snapped Alex.

Cassandra could only agree, although she said nothing. It would hardly be proper to criticize Benjamin Whitney, so newly dead, no matter how feckless his conduct now looked. Initially, she herself had thought that the excursion would be a wonderful adventure for a Cambridge schoolgirl to whom a weekend at her cousin's house in Plymouth was a treat.

Only when they actually left civilization behind and found, with the help of their Kiowa guide, their first band of Comanches did Cassandra begin to doubt the wisdom of the project. In subsequent months, nothing happened to convince her that the Comanches were basically a friendly people as her father insisted. Cassandra didn't like them, and even when she learned enough of their tongue for rudimentary conversation, she discovered that she had nothing in common with Indian girls her age. They in turn had no interest in her beyond tugging curiously at her fair hair, which always made her think that they were imagining how it would look on a scalp pole. In short, she had been afraid of them, although she had concealed her fear, knowing their contempt for cowardice.

"Well, you got guts," said Nicodemus, interrupting her thoughts. "Hard to imagine one lil white gal at-tackin' a warrior. Still, if you hadn't done that, they wouldn't a used the lance on you. Likely you'd be someone's squaw by now, or maybe a slave."

"Miss Cassandra's looking pale, Nicodemus," Alex Harte interrupted quickly. "I think she needs to get some sleep."

Cassandra *felt* pale, and the thought of being some-one's squaw pursued her into dreams, where she met again that terrible, squat warrior who had plunged a borrowed lance into her shoulder. The dream was un-bearable, a terrifying ordeal which ended suddenly when a deep, kind voice spoke her name and her Co-manche enemy faded into mist and silence.

"Wake up, child." The voice freed her, and she opened her eyes to a moonlit clearing where Alex knelt at her side.

Still terrified, Cassandra sat up and locked her arms desperately around his waist, burrowing her head into his shoulder as the fading shudders wracked her body.

"It was just a bad dream," he murmured, his own arms encircling her in a loose embrace. He didn't ask what she had dreamed or tell her not to be silly. He just held her until the trembling subsided, then asked casually, as if she were a child who had skinned an elbow, "Better now?"

She nodded, terribly embarrassed. One did not go about hurling oneself at strange men, no matter how avuncular their attitudes. In fact, Mr. Harte was not *all* that much older than she, she guessed resentfully, although he obviously thought of her as a child. She'd told him she was seventeen! "How old are *you*?" she asked impulsively, then wished she hadn't. He'd wonder why she wanted to know.

He did look surprised but answered readily, "Twenty-nine."

Well, she thought, he was only twelve years older, although why she should care—well, of course, she cared! He was so self-sufficient. How long did it take to develop that kind of confidence and expertise? If someone abandoned him in the middle of nowhere, he'd survive. He had come out here of his own free will, although she had no idea why. "What does a mustanger do?" she asked.

Having taken his comforting arms away, Alex Harte sat back, cross-legged, and replied patiently, "Catches wild horses, gentles them a bit, and sells them. Nico and I—we've just come back from selling a herd."

"I could help with that," said Cassandra. "I'm a fine horsewoman. Why, I can even ride astride—if you'll lend me a horse," she added. "I suppose the Indians took ours."

"They did," Alex confirmed. "However, there aren't many girl mustangers. None, I'd wager." He looked amused.

"Well, I can cook and wash and do camp chores. I'm getting stronger every day, and I'm a hard worker."

"Cassandra—"

He was going to say she couldn't stay with them. "Could you at least teach me to shoot?" she begged. They were right in saying that her father should not have come to a violent country with no means of defending himself or her. "I need to know how to protect myself."

Alex smiled tolerantly. "Do you have a gun?" he asked.

"No, but maybe I could earn a gun working for you." Which would keep him from leaving her on her own, at least for a while. "If I could earn a gun and a horse

and maybe some supplies, before you—before you—"
She couldn't even voice the terrible prospect of being
left alone again.

"Cassandra," said Alex gently, "we're not going to
abandon you."

"You're not?" Two small tears of relief slid onto her
cheeks, but she prayed he wouldn't notice. He wasn't
the kind of man to put up with a teary, weak-kneed
female.

"I can't guarantee your safety out here, anymore
than I can guarantee my own or that of my men, but
I'm not going to desert you, nor would Nicodemus,
for all he may come across as a reluctant protector.
Now you go back to sleep and stop worrying."

"Yes, sir," she replied obediently.

"And you can call me Alex. *Sir* seems a little formal
under present circumstances." Chuckling, he rose and
returned to his bedroll.

What a kind man, she thought. How could she have
taken him for a victimizer of women or someone who
had come to the frontier to escape debts or scandal?

Chapter Two

Cassandra had been dozing. When she awoke, the familiar sounds of the prairie had given way to an oppressive silence. She could hear nothing but the hushed plop of the horses' hooves and the brushing of the travois through the grass. No insects, no birds. No relentless pressure of wind through the grass. She peered out from beneath her canopy and saw the sky; once blue and cloudless, it was now an eerie yellow that stretched out behind her until it blended into the motionless grass.

She shifted so that she could brace herself on her good right arm and twist to look beyond the horse. The scene ahead was terrifying, for the sky boiled black and gray at the far horizon. Rolling clouds bore down upon them, still distant but moving fast and throwing giant shadows across the landscape. The silence broke with a muted roar of distant thunder, and just as suddenly there was wind, howling, tearing at her canopy, and flattening the grass around her.

Everything seemed to happen at once. She heard the men shouting to one another, their voices snapped away on the wind so that she could not understand the words. Nicodemus turned the pack train away from their line of march and whipped the animals into a run toward the east. Ahead a monster bolt of lightning cut the black clouds, and into the thin line of daylight between cloud and prairie, twisted black funnels snaked toward the earth as if to grasp and snap it up into the tempest.

Alex, rather than racing after Nicodemus, grasped the bridle of her horse and dragged it headlong into the wall of encroaching darkness. To escape being pitched into the grass, Cassandra had to throw herself back onto the blanket that was suspended between the travois poles. He must be mad to run the horses into the heart of such a storm. The only landmark ahead was a small mound. Surely he didn't plan to ride up where the lightning could find them and the rain and wind catch them unprotected?

Minutes later, accompanied by a roar that sounded as if the very earth were being hurled from its pinnings, Alex dragged her from the travois, pulled the horses down onto their sides, and covered her body with his. She saw, before her vision was blotted out by driving rain, that they were sheltering in the lea of the little hill. With that ominous roar bearing down on them, Cassandra thought death imminent and clung to Alex with a strength born of terror. The weight of his body was crushing, but she would no more have released her hold on him than she would have climbed that hill to let the storm sweep her away.

After a time the noise receded, and she could feel the drumming that shuddered through Alex's body, beat against the ground, and pummeled the horses, who neighed in terror. She put her mouth to Alex's ear and asked, although afraid to hear his answer, "What's happened? Are we going to die?"

"Tornado," he replied, shifting slightly so that his lips touched her ear.

She trembled as she felt the warmth of his breath, intimate and reassuring when all around her the world had turned into cold, threatening chaos.

"Lie still," he ordered. "We have to wait it out." Then he took his mouth away and rested his cheek against her forehead, one large hand cupped protectively over the other side of her face.

He hadn't answered the second part of her question, which meant that he did think they'd die. What she felt now was the last thing she would ever know on this earth—the touch of Alexander Harte's cheek against her temple, the rough-textured, gentle-handed protection of his palm and fingers against the side of her face, and the heavy weight of his body sheltering hers. He'd already saved her life once, but not at the risk of his own. Now he was trying again, taking all the punishment of the storm upon himself. She realized that he could have escaped with Nicodemus, but he had stayed.

She found both his protection and his physical closeness overwhelming. Cassandra had never been kissed by a man, nor had she entertained suitors. Her mother, having herself remained single until the age of thirty-five, had discouraged the young scholars who visited the house and looked at Cassandra with longing, and certainly Cassandra had not felt deprived. Their conversation was interesting, but otherwise she had been uninterested.

Now, however, with a man's lips brushing her temple, she thought that she would like very much to be kissed by Alexander Harte, who was no pale young classicist drinking tea in her mother's parlor while he discussed Plato and Aristotle, no frock-coated Congregationalist pastor come to call on a Sunday afternoon. If she were ever to be kissed, this would be her last chance, and a man whom she found astonishingly attractive now held her in his arms.

Deciding that, with death so close, some liberty might be taken with the proprieties, she stretched up to reach his ear and asked, above the drumming of the storm around them, "Alexander, would you please kiss me?"

She felt him stiffen, and she could hear the astonishment in his voice as he pulled away. "What was that?" he demanded. At the same time something cold and hard bounced off her now unprotected forehead. She thought he then refused, but she had just taken a second knock on the forehead, and her own gasp might have obscured his reply.

As abruptly as the storm arrived, it moved on to the north, and Alex pulled away from her. Cassandra, dazed, sat up and put her right hand to her temple, where she found a sizable lump. "What happened?" she asked, wondering for a confused moment if Alex, shocked at her request, had hit her. Surely not.

"Hail," he replied succinctly.

All around them were drifts of the ice pellets, and the horses were struggling to their feet, fighting for purchase on the slippery, shifting hailstones. Alex too rose, but stiffly, and Cassandra realized that if she was suffering from the impact of one or two ice balls, he must be black and blue all over the back of his body, for he had been completely exposed.

"Is your shoulder all right?" he asked, wincing as he bent forward to help her up.

"It must be," she replied. "I haven't thought of it since I first saw the black clouds." How humiliating! Had she really asked him to kiss her? And, worse, had he really refused?

"The travois is ripped to pieces," he muttered, "and I need to find out how Nicodemus fared. I reckon you'll have to stay here while I—"

"I'll ride with you," she interrupted, terrified at the prospect of being left behind while he went searching for his partner. "Please!"

"Well then, we'll have to ride double," he responded with slow reluctance. "You aren't in any condition—"

"There are two horses," she interrupted again, unable to face the thought of sharing a saddle with him. Not after his rejection. "I'll ride one of them."

* * *

Alex glanced sideways at the girl, who sat bolt upright in her saddle, cheeks as pale and translucent as the hailstones they'd left behind. It would be a miracle if she didn't faint and tumble off, doing herself further injury, but the look on her face told him that she wanted no help from him. Why the devil had she asked him to kiss her? He would bet his last ounce of black powder she didn't go around kissing strange men, probably hadn't kissed any men at all, so why start with him?

If he'd held his peace a few minutes longer till the storm passed on, they could both have pretended she never spoke, but his conscience had triggered that rejection, mainly because he'd been ashamed of wanting to do just what she'd asked. In fact, he'd wanted more than kissing, more than that child probably knew anything about. She might be slender; she might have looked at first glance like a boy, but today with her body lying under his, she'd felt like a woman, soft in all the right places and damned tempting.

Well, he'd have to stop thinking that way since he'd be responsible for protecting her when they got back to camp, if the camp still existed. The storm could have caught his other three men as well. In fact, he had begun to wonder where Nicodemus was. They should have met up before now.

Alex glanced at her again. Nico had it right. She was no child. He just hadn't wanted to see it. Cassandra was a beautiful young woman, hair like corn silk, skin turning gold in the sun, and eyes—Lord, he'd never seen eyes so blue or so trusting. Before today she'd looked at him as if he were the only man left on earth. Of course, in her vicinity there weren't but two, and Nicodemus hadn't been all that friendly.

Alex sighed. She'd soon meet three more men, and what would she make of them and they of her? Pinto would be the worst problem—just her age and thought he was cock of the walk. Alex would have sent him away months ago, but the boy had a knack with horses. Pinto seemed to know what a horse was going to do before the horse did. And talk—the boy had been known to talk a wild mustang into cooperation. It was uncanny.

But on the other hand, Pinto could be obnoxious and, with a female involved, relentless. He wouldn't see Cassandra as a child to be protected; he'd see her as fair game, so there'd be trouble unless Alex could cut it off at the outset. Generally speaking, he kept the boy in line with hard words, although at times he'd been tempted to use his fists.

"Cassandra, are you all right?" he asked sharply.

"Of course," she replied, blinking.

The girl had swayed in her saddle, and a gray pallor tinged her face. Where the hell was Nicodemus? He should be in sight by now. Anxiously, Alex glanced again at Cassandra, but she seemed to have got herself in hand.

Another of his riders would be taken with her, but Aureliano wouldn't make a nuisance of himself. Chances were that Aureliano, a handsome, personable young fellow, would fall hopelessly in love and treat Cassandra with conspicuous Latin gallantry. How would she respond to that? Probably she'd switch her affections at the first sweep of the boy's fine Mexican sombrero. Alex experienced a surprising burst of ill will at the thought, then reminded himself that Aureliano at twenty was a suitable age for a girl seventeen, whereas a man of twenty-nine—disgusted, he dropped that line of thought. *He* wasn't looking to turn suitor, certainly not of a young Yankee girl who'd probably asked for a kiss out of pure fright.

The last of Alex's riders was Bone. None of them would find out what Bone thought of her; he spoke so rarely as to be almost mute.

"There's Mr. Pelt," said Cassandra.

33

The mountain man was riding toward them, trailed by the pack horses. It looked as if none had been lost, which was a relief, the one good thing that had happened today, beyond the fact that he and Cassandra had survived.

Nicodemus pulled even and dismounted. "Good afternoon, Mr. Pelt," Cassandra said and swayed in her saddle. Slanting Alex a curious glance, Nicodemus hastened to lift her off. "You'd best see to Mr. Harte," she murmured in a shaky voice. "I fear he has sustained bruises during the storm."

She was already sagging in the giant's arms, so he picked her up and asked, "How come you let her ride?"

"The blanket we had on the travois was ripped to pieces," Alex replied as he too dismounted.

Nicodemus peeled back her shirt to examine the wound while Alex quickly turned away from the exposed white skin of her shoulder and breast. He busied himself locating an undamaged blanket in one of the packs while Nicodemus insisted that Cassandra take a dose of the bitter medicine. She dozed through the construction of a new travois, and by the time they were ready to resume travel, she was asleep.

"You figure we'll make it to the base camp tonight?" asked Alex when they were under way.

"Doubt it," Nicodemus replied. "We lost two-three hours skirtin' that storm."

"You may have skirted it. I sure as hell didn't," said Alex ruefully. "I've got more bruises on my back than a doctor has dead patients."

"Hail, eh? That how she got the lump on her forehead?"

"What'd you think—that I hit her?"

"Well, somethin's changed with her. This mornin' I'd a guessed she was half in love with you."

"Nonsense," snapped Alex.

"This afternoon," Nicodemus persisted, "she didn't look at you once, much less speak."

Alex gritted his teeth. He didn't appreciate ending up on the wrong end of everyone's opinion when all he'd been guilty of was practicing gentlemanly restraint. Maybe next time she asked him for a kiss, he'd give her one and cure her of asking. Likely though, she was already cured.

Cassandra couldn't meet his eyes. Every time he spoke, she anticipated a lecture on girls who acted provocatively with grown men. Didn't he realize she'd thought they were going to die? Otherwise, she'd never have—but that didn't excuse her. There *was* no excuse for her conduct.

Now they'd insist that she leave. They'd think her immoral, a source of potential trouble in their camp. Cassandra blinked back tears. If only she could tell them that she wasn't a bad girl. Truly, she'd never— but she couldn't say anything. She was too humiliated—and frightened.

Alex stared at the rippling sheet of pale gold spilling over her shoulders. Cassandra had released her hair to dry by the fire once they made camp for the night. She sat wearily in the circle of light, head bowed, cloaked in that golden veil from which he could not take his eyes. When at last she stirred, Alex turned away quickly.

"Mr. Pelt, do you have a comb I could borrow?" she asked hesitantly.

"Nope," Nicodemus replied.

Cassandra glanced at Alex, then looked away, and he knew she wouldn't ask him. He sighed and went to his saddlebags. "Here," he said, tossing a comb into her lap.

She bobbed her head in thanks and began to draw the teeth slowly through the long silver-gold strands. Soon she encountered difficulties. In unbraiding her hair, she hadn't stopped to think that she wouldn't be able to redo it with only one hand. Although she was close to tears, he let her flounder a few more minutes, hoping that Nicodemus would offer assistance; then he stalked over and took the comb.

Alex ignored her mortification and began to comb out the tangles, marveling at the silken texture of the strands sliding across his fingers. "You want it braided again?" he asked. The child was trembling under his hands like a bird trapped in a snare. What the hell did she think he was going to do once he'd finished the braid? Tear off her clothes?

And why couldn't Nicodemus have taken care of her? Alex wondered, disgusted with himself because of the tightening in his loins. She didn't seem to have any such effect on the mountain man. Then again, maybe he should be grateful that Nicodemus was tending the wound. God knows what would happen if Alex had to pull away her shirt and—he cut off those uneasy thoughts. It had been too long since he'd had a woman; that was the problem. And now he'd managed to get himself obligated to offer the girl protection while he had to stand off from her himself. *Oh hell!*

When Cassandra opened her eyes, she had to squint into the noon light to make out her surroundings, a pleasant creek shaded by spreading oaks, bordered by lush grass and wildflowers, the sounds of running water and bird song in the background—and tepees. Terrified, she stared at the three tepees lined up under the trees and began to fumble desperately with the straps that held her to the travois.

"Nothing to be afraid of." Alex appeared above her and bent to release the bindings, but Cassandra's eyes darted about the encampment, looking for Comanches.

Nicodemus led a pack horse across her field of vision and began to release the packs. How could they be so cruel? Did they think she'd want to camp with Indians after—

"What's the matter with you, girl?" Nicodemus asked. "You're as white as white water in a mountain stream." Then he noticed the direction of her horrified gaze. "No Comanches around here. Just these tepees we traded for."

Cassandra swallowed hard.

"The Comanches, they know how to live out here. We're just follerin' along like sensible folk. Mustangers ain't got time fer buildin' log cabins when we can cart a tepee along without no trouble when it's time to move."

Alex offered his hand to pull her up, and Cassandra's heartbeat fell back into a normal rhythm. Still, she couldn't look at the tepees and turned instead toward the creek where she could hear a voice back among the trees.

"That'll be Pinto," said Nicodemus. "No Indian blood in that rascal."

Shortly thereafter, a slender fellow with straggling yellow hair led a skittery mustang into the camp. He had the horse's head pulled down so that he could whisper into its ear. Then he spotted the newcomers and let out a triumphant whoop. The horse stopped short and pulled back against the hackamore, its eyes rolling.

"This here's Pinto," said Nicodemus, "so-called because we 'spect his mama was a horse. Sure he ain't good for much but talkin' to mustangs."

When Pinto tossed an obscene remark in Nicodemus' direction, Alex snapped, "Watch your mouth!"

"What for?" asked Pinto.

"This is Miss Cassandra Whitney, who's not used to—"

"A girl?" Pinto threw the lead rope to Nicodemus and headed for Cassandra, his sullen glare disappearing at the news of her sex. "They had girls there, an' you wouldn't let me go along?"

The nervous horse reared, and Nicodemus, shouting at Pinto, hauled the animal down with sheer physical power.

"Nice to meet you, girlie." Pinto grinned at her, exposing gaps in his teeth.

Nicodemus, having subdued the horse, slapped the rope back into Pinto's hand.

"Where are Bone and Aureliano?" Alex asked.

"Bone's off trackin'. Mendoza's staked out at a waterin' hole. You sure have fine hair, pretty lady. Hush now, horse; you an' me are old friends, we are."

The horse quieted, and Cassandra tried to sift the boy's comments one from the other, not sure if he had been commenting upon her hair or the horse's.

In the meantime Pinto had turned to Alex and asked eagerly, "What'd ya bring me? Did ya bring me a pistol?"

"I did," said Alex shortly.

"Nice horse, beautiful horse," Pinto crooned. "Did ya bring me a hat?"

Cassandra found his boyish eagerness rather endearing. Too bad his teeth were in such a deplorable state.

"I did," snapped Alex.

"A fine hat, better'n Aureliano's?"

"They didn't have fancy sombreros. I brought you a regular hat."

Cassandra wasn't sure why Alex treated the boy with such surly impatience.

"I don't want no regular hat. Easy, horse. How kin I shine up to a pretty girl with some regular ole hat?"

"You don't want it?" Alex had fished out the hat, a broad-brimmed, high-crowned affair such as Cassandra had seen in various states of disrepair on the shaggy heads of men all along the frontier. He punched it carelessly into shape and thrust it toward Pinto.

"Hell, it's all beat up," complained Pinto, patting the neck of the animal, which had begun to dance restlessly again. When his pats failed, he pulled the horse's head around and blew into its nostrils.

Cassandra stared as the horse quieted and nuzzled Pinto. Were they kissing one another?

"You don't want it. Fine. Here, Cassandra." Alex clapped the hat on her head.

She reached up uncertainly to touch her new acquisition, mumbling her thanks. Although unbecoming, it would shade her face from the sun.

"I din' say I wouldn't take it." Pinto glared at Alex. "Well, damn," muttered the boy, "I'll just have to git Aureliano into a poker game an' win his hat."

"Aureliano's too smart to git in a poker game with you, boy," said Nicodemus. "Now hep me with these here packs."

Nicodemus tossed one to Pinto, who had tied the horse to a tree after a few more intimate whisperings.

"Did you bring me a good Colt pistol like yours, Cap'n?"

"Already said I did," Alex replied, "but you better clean this one. Otherwise, you can't expect it to last any longer than your last. Now get these packs put away."

"I wanna see my gun." He had dropped the pack and was edging again toward Cassandra. She could see his eyes change when he discovered that she was taller than he. "How old are you?" he asked suspiciously.

"Seventeen," said Cassandra.

"Me too." He gave her a grin that made her uneasy. "I don't even half care you're so stupid tall, but then I ain't seen no girls in seems like forever."

Cassandra flushed resentfully, having always been self-conscious about her height.

"How about a kiss? I ain't had no kisses lately."

Horrified, she shot a quick glance at Alex, who was watching closely. Wasn't he going to tell this obnoxious youth to leave her alone? Did he think that because she'd asked him for a kiss, she'd welcome one from—from—? Overcome with indignation, she snarled, "Get away from me."

Pinto blinked. "Listen, girlie, Cap'n Harte an' Nicodemus had their turn. Why else'd they bring you back here if it ain't fer the rest of us to share?"

Horrified, Cassandra turned toward Alex Harte. Was that why he had saved her?

"Back off, Pinto," snapped Alex.

"What'd ya mean? It's my turn, ain't it?"

"We brought her along because the Comanches left her for dead and there wasn't anything else to do."

Pinto shot a sulky look from one to the other, then untied the horse and tramped away. Cassandra dipped her head. Alex had sounded as if he neither liked her nor wanted her around. Feeling lonely and frightened, she wished she were home in Massachusetts.

Cassandra sat quietly by the fire after dinner, listening to the men talk. She had met the last two members of the mustanging party, Aureliano Mendoza, a handsome young man who flashed her such a melting smile and made her such an elaborate bow that she had almost giggled, and Bone, who was thin, white-haired, leather-skinned, and silent.

About four of the men she had gathered information—some told to her, some picked up from their conversation. Aureliano's father had fought beside Alex Harte at San Jacinto, the battle in which Texas won its freedom from Mexico. Pinto, whom Alex had found in a saloon, belonged to a hunting and farming clan that had come from Tennessee in covered wagons, crossing the Sabine into Texas. Nicodemus Pelt was a mountain man who had trapped all over the

West and walked into Texas after his third wife died
and the beaver got scarce wherever he had been before. Alex found him at a trading post. Alex himself
had family in east Texas, a sister and brother-in-law
who had come from Louisiana to settle in the Stephen
F. Austin colony in the 1820s, although Alex had
evidently emigrated at least ten years later. About
Bone, however, no one seemed to know anything. He
had ridden into their camp when they were already
rounding up wild horses, proved to be a tracker
of great expertise, and stayed on. Had she dared,
she'd have questioned him, for he piqued her curiosity, but Bone carried with him an invisible shield
of reticence.

"We got a buyer up north come August if we can
get together a hundred or more horses," Alex was saying.

"We already have fifty," said Aureliano, "and Pinto
has maybe half gentled."

Alex shot Pinto a black look, and the boy muttered,
"Hey, it's easier to catch 'em than gentle 'em, Cap'n."

Why did Pinto call Alex captain? Cassandra wondered.

"Bone has found a herd of young male horses," Aureliano continued. "Now we have the mares back, we
can bring that herd in with no problem, eh?"

Alex nodded. He had unwrapped the parts for two
rifles and begun putting one together.

"What kind of gun's that?" asked Pinto eagerly.

"This one's a six-shot carbine made by Colt."

"Damn, you mean it's one a them revolving ones
like the pistols?"

"The other's an eight-shot rifle. Ring lever mechanism."

"You ain't gonna shoot a buffalo with either one a
them," said Nicodemus.

"That's right." Alex tested the cylinder. "But for a
man on horseback shooting at Indians, they do just

41

fine. Army used them in Florida against the Seminoles."

"Hey, lemme buy one off ya," said Pinto.

"No." Alex began to assemble the eight-shot
weapon. "We heard some news up at the trading post.
They're saying Van Zandt and Pinkney Henderson
signed an annexation treaty in Washington City in
April."

"You don't need two a them rifles," Pinto interrupted.

"The treaty will make Texas a United States territory," Alex continued, ignoring Pinto.

"I'll give you twenty dollars."

"No."

"Why not? You want more?"

"Cassandra's going to learn to shoot with the other.
The recoil won't be so likely to knock her over as, for
instance, Nicodemus' Hawken would."

Cassandra looked up in surprise. He'd been paying
attention when she asked to be taught to shoot. He
even planned to lend her a rifle.

"Nico's Hawken would knock over a buffalo if the
buffalo fired it," observed Aureliano, grinning.

"Girls can't shoot," said Pinto contemptuously.
"Lemme have the rifle."

Cassandra found herself disliking Pinto more every
time he opened his mouth.

"You're no shakes with a gun yourself, Pinto, and
only time will tell about her," Alex drawled as he
continued to work on the eight-shot Colt. "Course, the
problem with the treaty is—" he held the rifle up to
inspect it "—we don't know whether the U.S. Senate
will ratify it."

"They won't," said Cassandra. "Henry Clay will
never let Texas into the union."

Only Pinto wasn't gaping at her, but then she
doubted that he was interested in anything except the
rifle.

"If I was rich like you," he said to Alex with a sly, resentful glance, "I guess I could afford to refuse good money for a rifle I didn't even need."

If Alex was rich, why was he out here mustanging? Cassandra wondered.

"No matter what Henry Clay thinks, President Tyler's worried we'll hook up with England and build ourselves an empire in the West," said Alex, glancing curiously toward Cassandra as he spoke.

"I'll give you the money and my share of the sugar," Pinto offered.

"So you could do what? Steal someone else's share?" grunted Nicodemus. "Why don't you just leave it, boy? Alex ain't gonna sell you the rifle. Lemme have a look at that eight-shotter, Alex."

"All right. You can have my cut of the next herd," said Pinto.

"Forget it. I'm not going to trade for the gun," said Alex, passing it to Nicodemus.

"Well, why didn't you bring me one back?"

"You asked for a revolver; that's what you got."

"Well, I'd a asked for a rifle too if I'd a known about 'em," said Pinto, scowling.

Because the tension made her uneasy, Cassandra tried to move the conversation back to politics by saying, "I doubt that the Senate will ratify. The anti-slavery forces are too strong, and they'll never accept another slave state." She was uneasily aware that Pinto, having lost out on the rifle, had transferred his attention to her. "And the United States has a treaty with Mexico. That's one of the reasons that annexation was defeated in '36."

"In '36?" Alex grinned. "In '36 you were what? Nine years old?"

"I could read," said Cassandra indignantly, "and I've always been interested in national politics."

"Well, I'll tell you," said Alex, "if the Senate defeats annexation, they'll be mighty shortsighted."

"I don't see that," said Cassandra.

"They'll be cutting the country off from the Pacific and setting up a rival power."

"Texas?" Cassandra grinned. "There's nobody here but Indians. There's—stop that!" She turned and glared at Pinto.

Alex was on his feet instantly. "Pinto, I warned you."

"Hey, what'd I do? She smells nice. I just wanted to have a sniff."

"And you are malodorous," snapped Cassandra. "Stay away from me."

Pinto looked confused, probably by her vocabulary, she decided. Alex gave them each a long look and settled back into his place across the fire.

Nicodemus said, "Maybe she don't need nobody to teach her to shoot, Alex. She's got a tongue like a strikin' rattler, I swear."

Alex rose, stretched, again making her uncomfortably conscious of his body, and said, "Time we all turned in."

"Where's the girl gonna sleep?" asked Pinto. "I got plenty a room by my bedroll."

Alex gave him a long, hard look. "She sleeps by me."

Nervously Cassandra glanced sideways at him.

"That mean she's your woman? I thought we was supposed to share."

"That means she's her own woman, and she sleeps by me so she doesn't have to worry about you."

"Yeah, sure." Pinto sneered. "Anythin' you say, Cap'n."

Cassandra could hear Nicodemus muttering the word *trouble* and knew he was talking about her. Alex was rigid with anger, and even cheerful Aureliano looked uneasy. Cassandra feared that they would all end up hating her, and yet these men were her only hope of survival.

Then, without saying a word, the man they called Bone picked up her bedroll and carried it across the campsite to drop it beside another, which she took to be Alex's. He nodded to her, still silent, went to his own blankets, and the tension diffused; the other men were stretched out and sleeping within minutes. Alex assigned Pinto to night herd, rewrapped his new guns, and lay down beside Cassandra without even saying good night.

She sighed and thought of the soft feather beds in her mother's house. The ground beneath her was hard and would grow cold by morning. Tomorrow, ignoring the pain of her healing wound, she would have to make herself useful. August, Alex had said. They had a buyer up north in August. That was two or three months from now. No doubt she would be taken along and turned over to someone else who'd rather not accept responsibility for an unattached woman, and on from there until, if she were lucky, she managed to get to a railroad or coach line and make her way home.

If she lived to see Massachusetts again, what would she do when she got there? Cassandra squeezed her eyes shut. No use to think that far ahead. First, she had three months to get through, during which she must somehow avoid causing dissension among these rough men. She sighed and shifted her position again.

"Cassandra, why are you still awake?"

She went still.

"Are you in pain? You need one of Nico's potions?"

"No, thank you," she replied in a small voice, seeing herself once more as a source of irritation to him. Now her physical discomfort had kept him from much-needed sleep.

"If you're worrying about Pinto, relax. I'm not going to let him bother you."

"It's just that I hate to—to cause you so much trouble," she said in a faint voice.

Alex laughed softly. "I'm used to trouble." He was silent for a time, then said, "You'd best get to sleep.

We rise early, and you can help Bone with breakfast tomorrow."

He had thought of something for her to do. Comforted, she smiled in the darkness and turned on her side toward him. "Thank you," she whispered.

"Don't thank me. You couldn't be a worse cook than Bone."

Cassandra wished she could reach out and tuck her hand into his, but that would be almost as improper as asking him to kiss her. Thank God, her unseemly boldness had never been mentioned again between them. "Good night, Alex," she whispered.

"M-m-m." She could tell that he was almost asleep. Determined to do the same, she closed her eyes. Tomorrow she had duties to perform, and if she did well, perhaps she could take over for Bone, and Nicodemus might see her as an asset to the camp instead of *trouble*, and Alex might continue to be kind, as he had been just now.

Chapter Three

"Bone—he's lustin' after Cassie," Pinto announced. There was an air of challenge and danger about him as if he craved confrontation—although not with Bone, who had eaten and left for night herd. "He touched her, Bone did. Maybe you better talk to him about that, Cap'n."

Alex gave him a glance of contempt.

"Bone don't let no one touch him," the boy persisted, "an' he don't touch no one. Reckon that means he's decided to go after her, don't you think, Cap'n? Me, I figger she's leadin' 'im on. Cain't blame poor ole Bone if he follers."

Cassandra, furious, straightened from cleaning pots and started to protest, but Alex shook his head.

"I think you oughter have a talk with her, Cap'n."

"You're right," said Alex. "Bone doesn't like anyone close, so if he touched her, he must have had a reason."

"Like I tole you, he's got his eye on her."

"Bone gave me a knife," Cassandra revealed angrily.

Alex frowned. "Why would Bone be giving you a knife, Cassandra?"

"Courtin' present," said Pinto, grinning defiantly.

"He gave it to me for protection because Pinto grabbed me," snapped Cassandra. Pinto had pursued her relentlessly when the others were away from camp, watching her, creeping up on her. Finally that afternoon he had acted. Although she hadn't planned to tattle because Bone had appeared like a silent ghost

47

and frightened the boy away, Pinto deserved whatever he got; he generated his own problems.

"Grabbed you?" Alex turned to the boy.

"Hey, I like girls as much as Bone." Pinto, still grinning, stood his ground.

Without warning, Alex backhanded him. The camp crackled with tension as Pinto's fingers moved automatically toward his gun, but Alex was ahead of him. Cassandra hadn't even seen the movement of Alex's hand; it was that fast.

"Sure you want to try it?" he asked the boy coldly.

With the Colt revolver pointed at him, Pinto inched his hand away from his own gun. He was sent, chastened for the moment, to take Bone's place, and that night Cassandra became a student in a new subject.

Bone taught her how to draw a knife, how to hold it, and how to defend herself. The lesson was conducted silently while the others looked on. After that, Cassandra carried the knife in a sheath at her waist, and Pinto's harassment had to be pursued from a distance.

How had Pinto dared to slander Bone? she wondered. The mute tracker had a formidable reputation. The others said that he could find water where none had been found before, track a man or an animal over bare rock, ride a horse into the ground without tiring, go for days without food or drink, kill and scalp an enemy without blinking. Cassandra found the last hard to believe, for Bone treated her with silent consideration, and she returned the courtesy, always thanking him for his help.

The next night another phase of her education began as Alex handed her the lever-action Colt rifle. Before she was allowed to fire the weapon, he taught her to load it. She learned how to set it at half cock, to pour powder into the chambers of the cylinder, to insert the lead ball and seal each chamber with bear grease, then how to fit the percussion caps onto the nipples.

Alex made her load weapons every night—her rifle, his Colt pistol, Nicodemus' Hawken, even Bone's flint-lock cavalry pistols. Alex said that in an Indian fight she would have to load for everyone. Shuddering at the thought of an attack whose outcome might depend on her ability, she concentrated and she learned.

One evening as the setting sun splashed rivers of red and purple across the western horizon, Cassandra was performing the last maneuver in loading her own rifle. When she put the soft copper percussion cap on the nipple, it fell off. She pinched it gently, fitted it over the nipple again, and it fell off. Muttering, she nipped it between her teeth. Then, of course, it wouldn't go on at all. Now what? She gave it a tap. No luck. Exasperated, she tapped it hard. The shot echoed across the camp, causing her somnolent companions to jerk into full alert. Pinto, to whom the mis-fired bullet had come closest, went straight from a sitting position to an impressive leap in the air.

"Warned you about handling those percussion caps gently," Alex drawled. "Why, you nearly gutted Pinto."

Bone smiled—the only smile Cassandra had ever seen on his face.

Another time Cassandra, in one of her loading sessions, hung a bullet up in the barrel of Nicodemus' Hawken.

"You cain't shoot it out," snapped Nicodemus. "You'll rern my gun."

"You gonna show her how to take the Hawken apart," asked Alex with lazy patience, "or do I?"

"You," snapped Nicodemus. So she learned how to disassemble the Hawken, just as she had previously learned to take apart her own rifle for cleaning. The barrel, once released, had to be plunged into hot soapy water, which was drawn up inside by the suction of the cleaning rod.

"Soap?" she had cried ecstatically when Alex explained the process. "Can I have a bath?" Cassandra hadn't seen soap in months and couldn't believe he intended to reserve the precious bar for rifle cleaning.

"You'd rather have a bath than a reliable weapon? When you need meat or protection from unfriendly Indians, a clean body won't help," he retorted.

Pinto, always looking to stir up trouble, offered her soap if he could join her at the creek. The very thought made Cassandra cringe, and she dropped her request. All night she dreamed of Comanches with Pinto's face.

By the time she had learned to load and clean the rifle, her wound was well healed if still painful. Then Alex began to teach her to shoot. She anticipated those lessons all day, torn between eagerness and dread because she knew that he would be touching her. Her sensitivity to the fact that he usually avoided contact made her doubly aware of him. She yearned for his proximity and was, at the same time, deathly afraid that he would sense her yearning, that she would betray herself when he stood behind to instruct her, when he adjusted the position of her hands and arms, the one time he had rubbed her shoulder after she winced at the recoil of the rifle.

She worried that the others would notice and laugh at her infatuation. Certainly if Pinto realized how Alex Harte affected her, he would announce her humiliation to the camp, for it was obvious that Alex did not return her interest. He was courteous and kind but completely impersonal. While Pinto grasped every opportunity to display himself, shirtless and posturing, Alex washed and changed his clothes privately. She saw his body only in tantalizing glimpses, which stirred her blood, while the cocky Pinto would have moved her to laughter had he not made her so uneasy.

She became a fair shot. Probably she would have been better, she decided, had she not been paying more attention to Alex than she was to aiming and firing at targets. Alex said if she had any trouble with

Pinto to shoot him. To Pinto he said, "If I get back some evening to find you've been bothering her again, *I'll* shoot you." Pinto had laughed as if he didn't believe it, and Cassandra decided that he had some uncontrollable desire to see how far he could push people, how much trouble he could make before someone stopped him. He craved danger, perhaps death. Still, understanding didn't make her like or trust him.

Because she wanted to join the others mustanging, she exercised her left arm and shoulder, ignoring the pain. Before she should have, she rode in the afternoons, gritting her teeth as she saddled, swung astride, and kneed her horse into motion. Also she listened and stored away their talk about horses and about the methods of catching and gentling them.

The year before, in 1843, the mustangers had built a brush and post oak corral near a water hole in the Cross Timbers and driven hundreds of horses into it. This year before Cassandra joined them, they had concentrated on horses thin from a hard winter and mares slowed because they were heavy with foal or weak from nursing. Such easy prey made up the spring herd. During the first weeks of her stay in the camp, they had used the pack mares to capture and tame young male horses driven from the wild herd by stallions. Cassandra thought she could participate in such methods.

However, they talked of others she would never master. For instance, only Nicodemus was good enough to take a horse by creasing, which meant stunning the poor creature for a minute or two by putting a shot through the muscular part of his neck. Although Nicodemus admitted to having done this, he considered it a waste of powder and horseflesh, for the shot usually missed or the horse died.

The men also discussed taming strategies. They turned the creatures from completely wild to half wild by roping them to gentle mares and by riding them into submission in sandy creek beds where a fall would do the rider less harm or in deep water where the bucking did not cause aching bones. They also choked their captives, pulled them to the ground, and blew in their nostrils; this was Nicodemus' favorite method. Because of his size he could haul down a horse with less trouble than the others.

Alex argued for the efficacy of pulling the wild hairs from around the animal's eyes, a Comanche trick. Bone didn't argue; he did it with the bone tweezers he used on his own face. Pinto said the fact that Bone used tweezers rather than a razor meant he was Indian, but this was speculation and undoubtedly malicious on Pinto's part. Light and wiry, Pinto talked the mustangs into submission. Cassandra didn't think she'd ever be a successful horse tamer, but she longed to try her hand at catching them. So she gritted her teeth and rode, as week by week the weather warmed, and they moved south hunting their quarry.

It was a hard life and dangerous, always on the move, always on the lookout for Indians. It amazed her that she had managed to fit into this man's world at all. Until the last year, her time had been spent in the company of women and girls, her mother's students and the mistresses in the school. Her father's life, when he lived at home, had intersected with theirs only peripherally. The men from his world appeared on the odd weekend, then disappeared along with the best china teacups that were brought out to entertain them. When she was very little, Cassandra had thought the men must spend the weekdays in china cabinets with the cups and saucers.

And all these people—the scholars who came to tea, the ministers who appeared on Sunday afternoon, the schoolmistresses and female students who peopled the weekdays—all lived lives of the mind, whereas here on the plains her companions, day after day, were men who lived physically, adventurers who faced the dangers of their existence unafraid. But Cassandra was afraid. In Cambridge nothing had threatened her but the occasional storm that shook the upper floors of her mother's frame house. The only adventures were intellectual. She remembered when her father first advanced his theory that the Indians were descendants of the lost tribes of Israel. Teacups had rattled in their saucers that day. Heated argument followed, frightening to an eight-year-old Cassandra.

How she wished that an academic tempest or even a New England storm were all she had to dread today. Every horse that approached the camp carried, in her mind, a Comanche bent on murder. These phantom warriors pursued her in dreams, from which she awoke sweating, listening frantically for the slow sound of Alex's breathing, searching the darkness for his darker outline on the ground beside her.

He, she gathered, was the greatest adventurer of them all. His father had been in Andrew Jackson's army challenging the British at New Orleans in 1815, a Tennessean who liked the city and sent for his family when the fighting ended. Alex was born there, and his father became a successful merchant and cotton factor, but when Alex was seventeen, his father died, and Alex came west to Texas to join his older sister and her husband.

Cassandra noted with pleasure the similarities in their lives. She too had come west at seventeen after the death of a parent. Wistfully she mused on their parallel paths and wondered if he had noticed, wondered if he found the coincidence significant. Surely, it was. Of course, there were distressing parallels; both of them had faced great danger—Cassandra without seeking it, Alex eagerly. He had evidently got off the boat from New Orleans in 1832 and thrown himself immediately into a rebellion against Mexico, for which he had been soundly chastised by his wealthy brother-in-law, who wanted no trouble with the government from which he had received his land grant. Alex's fondest memories of the incident were the balls organized by the impresario Stephen F. Austin to placate some Mexican colonel who had come across the Rio Grande to put down the rebels. Cassandra was speechless with jealousy at Alex's reminiscences of the senoritas he had danced with.

He had also fought in the rebellion four years later that made Texas an independent republic and had been lucky to escape with his life from the massacre at Goliad, his escape arranged by the wife of a Mexican officer. Cassandra shuddered to think of how close he had come to death, and she chastised herself for her foolish jealousy of the woman who had saved him. She was jealous of women she didn't even know on behalf of a man who treated her as if she were ten instead of seventeen.

Why couldn't she have developed a fondness for Aureliano, who seemed to have one for her? He told her long, nostalgic tales of his mother and sisters, his gallant father, who had fought with Alex, and his brothers. Aureliano treated her with great courtliness, and even when he sighed for the beauty of the dark-eyed senoritas he had left behind, he hastened to add that his heart was equally aflame for blue eyes and fair, flaxen hair.

Cassandra giggled. Fair, flaxen hair? Aureliano hadn't been able to say it in English and had enlisted an exasperated Alex to translate. At first, she had hoped Alex might be jealous of Aureliano's light-hearted courtship; then, chastened, she decided that his exasperation showed that he thought both of them silly children.

Even gruff Nicodemus talked to her more than Alex did. In fact, one night when she asked if he had ever been married, he replied that he had had two Indian wives and one white, but that he'd marry no more. Although she was shocked to hear that he had twice married Indian women, she asked why he ruled out further domesticity.

"Domesticity?" Nicodemus snorted.

"Well, even a tepee is a domestic base of sorts," Cassandra stammered.

"How about a barricade of dead horses and logs?" asked the mountain man bitterly. "My last wife, the white one, died shootin' at Arapahoes, Cheyenne, and Sioux from behind a dead horse—her an' me an' a bunch of Shoshone and mountain men headed by an ugly ole fella name of Henry Frack. He died covered with blood, propped up agin a stump, an' she looked prettier'n him, but she was still dead, shot full of arrows with her rifle in hand."

"Oh, Nicodemus, I'm so sorry."

"Well, no need to be sorry," he muttered. "Alice an' me had three good years. She learned trappin' from her pa an' kep at it when he died. We worked the lines together, an' we was mighty happy. Prob'ly jus' as well she died. At least she didn't have to bury no young uns," he muttered. "Losin' babies is hard on a woman. On a man too."

He looked so morose, Cassandra's heart ached for him.

"I lost babies. Half-breeds. An' three wives now, so I ain't marryin' no more."

She couldn't disagree. After such a life, who would want to marry and risk more heartache? Still, Nicodemus had told her about it. Any information she picked up about Alex came from others. He cared nothing for her, she admitted sadly. She was pining in vain, like a silly schoolgirl after a hero in a book. Maybe he was right to treat her like a child.

Alex watched her dreaming by the fire, the light reflecting gold off her skin and the long braid that fell over her shoulder and across the buckskin covering her breast. He hated to go near her for fear of catching

55

her sweet scent, although he knew she had neither perfume nor flowery soap to tease his senses. She was lucky to find clean water in which to bathe away the sweat and dirt of the rough life they lived. And she lived it so well. They were all her followers: Pinto, who lusted after her, even knowing his pursuit tempted Alex to violence; Aureliano, enmeshed in the snares of romantic infatuation; Nicodemus, who showed her grudging respect as he watched her mastering skills that her civilized childhood had never prepared her for; Bone, who had developed a strange, silent feeling of guardianship; and Alex himself, who was coming to want her as much as Pinto did, but with the difference that his conscience made in how he acted on that desire.

Her presence beside him at night was driving him to distraction, and he had begun to calculate desperately how and when he could find someone else to take responsibility for her. They were moving south and capturing horses more rapidly than he had expected. Perhaps he could take a herd to market in July and use the opportunity to send Cassandra home. After the July sale they could gather another herd to sell up north in August. But where could he leave her this far south? And if he couldn't find a place, how was he to keep his hands off her if she stayed in camp another month or more, looking at him with those longing eyes?

"You know what I want to do to you?" Pinto whispered.

Cassandra glanced up at him anxiously.

"You'd like it," he assured her. "You'd like it a lot."

She shivered, wishing Alex would notice and intervene. If she complained, Nicodemus would glare at her—as if Pinto's nasty, frightening whispers were her fault.

* * *

"Ever'one who's lived down in that southeast cotton country has the fevers," said Nicodemus. "Alex don't git took bad, jus' a day or so, an' he's back in the saddle."

She had awakened that morning to find Alex muttering in his sleep. She could feel the heat coming off him, see the sweat beading on his skin, and had roused Nicodemus immediately.

"So you jus' do what I tell you, an' he'll be fine."

"But I've never—"

"Nuthin' to it. Keep yer bowl fulla cold water from the crick, dip yer rag, an' wipe him off."

"But couldn't you—"

"We got horses to catch, so you jus' keep wipin' him off. All over."

"All over?" echoed Cassandra, horrified.

"Well, as all over as you kin." Nicodemus thrust the bowl and rag into her hand and departed.

Frightened, Cassandra knelt beside her patient. What if Alex died? She dipped the rag into the water and patted it onto his face. His eyelids flickered, and she snatched her hand away. Alex kept his distance from her. He wasn't going to like this. He'd probably open his eyes and shout at her for touching him.

Then he began to toss restlessly on his blanket, and she dipped the cloth again and stroked the cool water across his forehead. His restlessness subsided. All over, Nicodemus had said. Swallowing, she ran the cloth over the corded neck and onto the part of his chest exposed by his shirt. Then she went back to his face. Was she supposed to take his shirt off? She eyed it uncertainly as she bathed his cheeks. He turned his face against her hand. Maybe he wouldn't yell at her; the cool water seemed to sooth him.

Hesitantly, she unlaced his shirt, then caught her breath, staring. He mumbled again, and she hurriedly applied the wet rag, stroking it over the heavy shoulder and chest muscles, then daringly onto the ridged

57

Elizabeth Chadwick

abdomen. Her hand was trembling, but he was quiet under her touch.

Lord, but he was beautiful. She wanted to go on touching him forever. And she could. Well, not forever, but for today. As long as she kept him cool and comfortable, she could look and touch all she wanted. Enthralled, she did, studying and stroking every exposed line of him—nothing below the waist, of course. No matter what Nicodemus said, she wasn't taking off any man's pants. She almost giggled to think of how horrified her mother would have been to see Cassandra stroking a man's body. She ran the cloth again over his abdomen and could have sworn the muscles tensed. Fascinated, she repeated the motion.

"Come here."

Cassandra's eyes flew to his face.

"Come here, sweetheart," he mumbled, his hand closing with hot strength over her wrist and pulling her closer. The bowl spilled. The rag dropped from her fingers as he drew her down onto his chest and immobilized her with one relentless forearm while he cupped her head with the other hand and forced her mouth to his.

Before she could panic, she discovered that his kiss was soft and beguiling. The hot, persuasive touch of his mouth sent a flood of delight through her. She had never felt anything so sweet. Relaxing against him, trembling, she slid her arms around his neck.

Alex's arms tightened; his hands stroked, sending shocks of excitement along her nerves. Then he slid his hands between their bodies and onto her thighs, fingers gently prying them apart. She moaned in soft acquiescence and snuggled her hips against him.

"Ah God, I knew you'd be like this," he muttered, and holding her firmly, rolled so that he lay between her legs, his mouth once more on hers.

The burning pressure of his body and the seduction of his mouth sent a wave of dizzy rapture over her.

"Sweet," he mumbled against her lips. "Sweet girl, I want you so much." Then he stopped whispering to her, stopped moving.

He still lay over her but with a difference; his body was quiet, his mouth no longer fitted to hers. Alex was asleep! The most exciting, shocking moment of her life, and he had fallen asleep! She struggled out from under him. When she rolled him onto his back, his eyelids lay closed, long black lashes against his cheeks. She snatched up the forgotten bowl and went to the creek for more water.

That night Nicodemus told her that she'd done a fine job, that her patient was much improved. Pinto whispered to her, "I seen you two. Fell asleep, din' he? I wouldn't."

Cassandra tried to get away, but his hand tightened.

"You'd like me better. Some of these times when he's off lookin' for horses, you an' me, we'll git together."

She pulled free and ran.

Pushing the sombrero back so that it hung from his neck on its thongs, Aureliano leaned forward to drink at the water hole. Then he straightened and wiped the water and sweat from his face. "I am not mistaken," he lamented. "My broken heart tells me that it is true."

Alex laughed and replied, "I've seen your heart broken before, Aureliano; it always heals up as soon as the next pretty face comes along."

"Ah, but to lose the flower of my life to a man of many years such as yourself." He gave Alex an ingenuous grin.

"You haven't lost the flower of your life," Alex retorted dryly.

"No?" Aureliano sobered. "I see how she looks at you, amigo. The little one is in love."

"Nonsense," snapped Alex. "If she's in love, it's with

59

the idea of half a plantation on the Brazos."

Aureliano looked surprised for a moment, then shrugged. "What woman is not attracted by the comfort and security a man can offer her? That is as it should be."

The boy's answer irritated Alex, but he had no time to dwell on it because a bloodcurdling shout intervened. Both men faded into the shrubbery in anticipation of the mustangs Nicodemus and Bone would be driving their way.

On the way back to camp, Alex considered what Aureliano had said. Then, disgusted, he remembered his own erotic dreams. They were so real he expected to wake up with Cassandra in his arms, so real that it was almost as if he'd made love to her—almost made love to her. He always woke up too soon. And it was driving him crazy.

He reckoned they were three to five days north of San Antonio with a good herd assembled. Now might be the time to broach the idea of an interim sale. With any luck, he could find someone to leave Cassandra with before the situation in camp deteriorated further. The only problem he could see was that two years back the Mexicans had captured all the American men and taken them away. There might be no English-speaking families left in San Antonio.

On the other hand, she'd said she was quick enough with languages to have picked up Comanche in a short time. No reason she couldn't learn a civilized tongue like Spanish in even less. And if she never learned a word, she'd be better off in the care of some kindly senora than she was here.

As soon as he made the suggestion, Cassandra understood. Alex wasn't worried about ending up with too many horses in August. He was opposed to having her around so long. She daydreamed of being in his

60

arms once more, and he didn't even remember it. At the time, he'd probably thought he was kissing some senorita.

"I'm in favor," said Pinto enthusiastically, "an' it's my turn to go. Who-ee. Thinka all them purty *Mexicanas*."

Cassandra gave him a bitter look. If he hadn't pursued her and made so much trouble, Alex might not be so anxious to get rid of her.

"Maybe next time," said Alex to Pinto.

"Next time?" The boy bristled. "It's my turn."

"Cassandra's going, not you."

There was the confirmation. Her heart sank. She didn't want to go home so soon. There wasn't anything to go home to. An empty house, a few sanctimonious cousins, some money, quite a bit actually, but who was to say she'd ever make it back to claim the inheritance?

"All right, me an' Cassie'll go. Good as she's gittin' with horses, us two can handle the herd all by our own selves."

Cassandra's eyes jumped anxiously to Alex. Surely he wouldn't send her off with Pinto.

"Not likely anyone in camp would want to leave the horse-trading and money handling to you, Pinto," said Alex.

"All right, you can sell the horses while me an' Cassie are havin' a high ole time in San Antone."

Drearily Cassandra wondered what San Antonio was like. Did it have shops? A railroad? A stagecoach line?

"I'm taking Aureliano to translate," said Alex.

Cassandra looked up sharply. Translate? They didn't speak English in San Antonio? Her anxiety escalated.

"So the Mex'll go too," snapped Pinto. "I don't care, just so long as I git to."

"Four's too many," said Alex.

"I could stay here," Cassandra offered eagerly. "I could help catch more horses for the northern trade."

"Oh well, if she' gonna stay, you an' Aureliano can go, Cap'n, an' I'll stay an' look after Miss Cassie."

Pinto's grin signaled another troublemaking campaign. Whatever his motives, she didn't want to be left with Pinto, and her eyes darted unhappily from one face to the other.

"I'm for sellin' what we got gathered up," said Nicodemus slowly, "but I'll do the tradin'—me an' Aureliano an' Pinto, since he seems so set on goin'."

Alex frowned. "Cassandra—"

"Cassandra don't need to be left where she cain't speak to no one an' like as not cain't git word to her kinfolks. We leave her up north with traders, they'll be a wagon headin' fer the settlements. Down in San Antone where's she gonna go? Mexico City? Laredo? No sense in that."

Nicodemus prevailed, and she had another month, maybe two. Who knew what would happen in the meantime? She slanted a glance at Alex, who looked furious. She hadn't realized how much he disliked her.

Chapter Four

The first day, Alex staked Bone out at a water hole and, taking Cassandra with him, showed her how to drive the mustangs toward the trap. It was exhausting work, and her shoulder ached abominably at day's end, but she had begun to find it exhilarating. The second day when she was tearing along, flapping her hat at a small bunch of mustangs, she felt like whooping from sheer exuberance; she laughed aloud, earning an odd look from Alex when he heard her.

On the third day all her newfound confidence dissipated. Traveling toward the Pedernales River, they began to hear noises, muted by distance yet ominous. Cassandra watched Alex and Bone exchange frowns. They slowed the pace, sometimes stopping to listen and to peer ahead. The sounds escalated into continuous gunfire and bloodcurdling shouts, then faded. Instead of turning back, the two men urged their horses into a trot until they saw on the horizon a band of fifty Indians galloping toward the west. Panic-stricken, Cassandra wanted to flee in the opposite direction, but her companions refused.

"We have to go south," said Alex. "Damn, I hope those Indians didn't catch Nico and the boys."

"Buzzards," warned Bone. "Better see what's dead." Cassandra's eyes swiveled toward him in astonishment. He had spoken, his voice a rusty whisper.

Alex nodded. "You want to stay behind, Cassandra? You can wait here while we investigate."

"What if there are more Comanches?" she asked, looking toward the river and the buzzards. The whole scene on that wooded knoll came back to her in vivid detail—the lance with the scalp lock waving above her, the vultures circling. She shuddered, thinking that she couldn't—she just couldn't ride into what might be a Comanche ambush. "Maybe we could go east, then south," she said in a quavering voice. "We'll be taking a terrible chance if—"

"I took that chance when I came after you," said Alex. "You want to ride away when Nicodemus and the others might need help?"

Cassandra went with them because she was afraid to be left behind, but even in the bright sunshine and hot, still air, she felt cold with fright. To her their cautious advance seemed like a funeral procession—their own.

"Hold up," shouted a voice as they approached the trees near the river. Cassandra's hands, icy with cold sweat, tightened automatically on the reins. It took several minutes before the actual situation penetrated: the man rising out of the grass with a rifle pointed at them had spoken in English, although his face had been burned bronze by the pitiless Texas sun.

Alex sat his horse calmly, making no move to draw a weapon. "We heard the commotion and saw some Comanches."

"They see you?" asked the man with the rifle.

"Don't think so," Alex replied. "If they'd seen our horses—" he gestured toward their small herd "—likely they'd have stopped to try a bit of thievery."

"Alex Harte, is that you?" Another man slid into view.

Alex squinted at him. "Well, I'll be damned. It's been a few years, Jack."

"Just about two," the man replied. "What are you doin' out here? Thought you'd be back home gittin' rich."

"Your fault as much as anyone's I'm not," said Alex, dismounting easily and shaking hands. "My brother-in-law and I had a real falling out about my taking off with you to chase General Woll back into Mexico. Jean Philippe had cotton to ship, and I was supposed to take it down river."

"Well, he never was much of a patriot, your brother-in-law," said Hays dryly, "but that still don't explain what you're doin' out here in Comanche country."

"Mustanging." Alex turned to his companions. "Cassie, this is Captain John C. Hays of the Texas Rangers. You are still rangering, aren't you, Jack?" The man nodded, staring hard at Cassandra. "Jack, this is Miss Cassandra Whitney of Massachusetts, and beyond her is my partner Bone."

"Ma'am." The ranger tipped his hat to Cassandra and nodded to Bone, who had not dismounted.

"Guess I don't have to ask what you're doing here Jack. I saw the Comanches hightailing it west."

"Yup. We was lookin' for 'em, an' we found some. 'Bout eighty."

"Eighty?" Alex came to lift Cassandra from the saddle.

On an ordinary workday he no longer showed her such gentlemanly concern, which would, after all, have been silly. She was quite capable of dismounting on her own, and they were all equally tired at day's end. She wondered if she was expected to curtsey to the ranger captain. If so, it would be a ludicrous exercise since she was wearing buckskin trousers that had belonged to Aureliano.

"Well, you sure must have killed quite a few, Jack."

"Thirty, thirty-five. Comanches always take their dead with them, so it's hard to tell how many you downed." He gestured toward the river. "Come on back to camp."

"Thirty-five out of eighty. That's good shooting."

"Government give us five-shot Colts left over from

65

the Texas Navy." Hays laughed humorlessly. "Them Comanches are probably still wonderin' what hit 'em. They had to realize there was only fourteen of us when they attacked, which is just what they like—all the odds in their favor—but with five shots each before we had to reload, it must have seemed to them like they was fightin' a hundred men instead of fourteen. 'Member Sam Walker? He's with us."

"Is he now?" exclaimed Alex, obviously pleased.

"Got a lance wound, him an' one other. We was pretty lucky considerin' how bad they outnumbered us. Likely we'd all been scalped if it wasn't for them pistols." They broke through the trees into a camp. "The revolvin' firearm is goin' to turn the tide on the frontier," said Hays solemnly. "That is if some fool trader don't start sellin' 'em to the redskins." He introduced Cassandra, Alex, and Bone to his men, all of whom eyed Cassandra curiously. Until Alex explained her situation, they obviously had no idea what to make of a woman in a mustanging band.

"Well ma'am," said a slender young man with blue eyes and hair shaded toward red, "it's reassuring to meet someone who lived through a lance wound." This was Samuel Walker, who had such a wound himself. He seemed too mild-mannered to be an Indian fighter, but the longer she listened to the reminiscences around the campfire, the more she realized how wrong she had been about that young man.

He had not only answered President Houston's call for volunteers two years earlier when a Mexican general crossed the border and captured San Antonio, but had gone on to attack Laredo, he and three hundred other men who were disobeying orders to disband. He and his fellows had been captured by Mexicans, and many never lived to see their country again; Walker had escaped.

"How is it you're so smart, Alex?" he asked good-naturedly. "You weren't in San Antonio when Woll

66

shipped all the Americans off to prison, an' you had the good sense to go on home instead of getting caught with us at Laredo."

"Not so smart as you might think," said Alex, grinning. "You went off to fight with the Mexicans, and I went off to fight with my brother-in-law. Turned out bad for both of us."

Cassandra wondered about Alex and his brother-in-law. He said so little about his family, but she now knew that they had quarreled over Alex's first military adventure when he was seventeen, and this conversation proved that their last quarrel ten years later had been of the same nature.

Her speculations were cut short when Alex asked, "Are you sleepy, Cassandra?" She shook her head emphatically, not wanting to be sent away like a child at bedtime. "Show Sam your rifle," he suggested, and Cassandra went to get it.

"A rifle's something to keep by you, little lady," said Sam Walker. "This country is swarming with Comanches."

She wouldn't have said it was swarming, but the two parties she'd seen were plenty enough for her. She handed the rifle to Walker, who handled it awkwardly, being heavily bandaged because of his lance wound. He looked the weapon over and laughed aloud, much to Cassandra's surprise.

"Why, I haven't seen one of these eight-shot Colts since I was sloggin' through the Everglades, fightin' Seminoles with General Harney. Where'd you get it, miss?"

"From Alex," Cassandra replied. "Where are the Everglades?"

"That's a big swamp in Florida full of redskins, alligators, and snakes," said Walker. "I don't recommend it unless you're real hard up for an Indian fight."

The other men laughed. Cassandra shivered and glanced sideways at the ranger. Those blue-gray eyes of his didn't look so mild now, and she remembered that Aureliano had talked of the men who died at the Alamo—Travis, Bowie, and Crockett, men with blue-gray killer's eyes. He said the Mexicans called them *diablos Tejanos*, Texas devils, and that the women and children who had survived the slaughter there said the bodies of Mexican soldiers were piled in stacks around the Texans, all of whom fought to the death.

These men, by learning to live in such a country, had become something never seen by the civilized society in which she had been raised. She felt more and more alien, although the rangers treated her with great courtesy. She almost wished that she had let Alex leave her in San Antonio, but then, she reminded herself, San Antonio did not sound like a civilized place, not if it was always in danger of attack by Indians and vengeful armies from Mexico.

"Time we turned in." Cassandra looked up, taken by surprise. Alex leaned over and put a hand under her elbow. His smile was slow and reassuring, and she followed him to their blankets willingly. She had had enough of fear for one day, but she had one more surprise coming before she could escape into sleep. Alex tied a rawhide thong loosely around her wrist and asked her to tie the other end to his.

"Why?" she asked, confused and alarmed.

"I'm dead tired," he said quietly, "and this is dangerous country. Comanches have been known to slip into a camp and abduct a woman without waking a soul."

Cassandra stared at him with horror.

"This way no one can bother you without me knowing."

Hands trembling, Cassandra tied the knot that linked them together.

"Actually," said Alex, grinning, "it's a Comanche trick. A warrior will have a rawhide thong running from his tepee or mattress to his wife's. If he wants her, he just gives it a tug."

Cassandra turned bright red as Alex, chuckling, stretched out on his bedroll.

"Pretty stars tonight," he remarked casually.

She frowned at him, but when he had gone to sleep, she was still thinking about what he had said—not about the danger of Comanches, but of a tug on the thong about her wrist, a tug meant to summon her to Alex's bed. She knew he had been teasing, but the thought sent a flush over her body, reminding her of how it had felt to be with him. When she finally dropped into sleep, she dreamed of lying in Alex's arms, his hard body stretched against hers. The dream woke her up, and she remained wide-eyed until the first streaks of rose light bloomed on the eastern horizon.

The rangers bought the horses that Alex, Bone, and Cassandra had caught in the last few days. "We'll break 'em ourselves," said Captain Hays. "Lost some of ours to the Indians." He gave Alex a claim on the treasury of the republic in exchange and advised him to redeem it quickly, just in case Texas joined the United States and nobody wanted to pay the republic's considerable debts.

"Heard anything about annexation?" Alex asked.

"Nope," said Hays, "but there's gonna be two elections hangin' on it. If the U.S. Senate doesn't pass the treaty, the question of takin' in Texas will be thrown into the presidential election. Of course, the Whigs will be against it, but Jackson still controls the Democrats."

"President Jackson himself opposed annexation when it first came up," said Cassandra, causing all the men to stare at her. "Well, he did. And the United States still has the same treaty with Mexico. It can't legally take Texas in."

"Jackson may have put off annexation, miss," said

Captain Hays, "but he wants Texas in the union, an' he'll push through a Democratic candidate of his own beliefs."

"Who's running to replace Houston here in Texas?" asked Alex. "I've been out of touch."

"Burleson for the war party," said Hays, "an' Houston's man, Anson Jones, for annexation. You votin' for Burleson? I recollect you fought in Lamar's Apache campaigns in '39, an' Burleson's a Lamar man; he wants a Texas empire."

"Lamar's a dreamer," said Alex. "Texas doesn't have the kind of money it takes to pursue an empire. Texas doesn't have *any* money. I'll be lucky to get this scrip redeemed even if we stay a republic." He waved the payment voucher he had received for the horses.

"You can always take it in land," said Hays.

"Oh? How'm I gonna divide a land voucher up between five men? No, I'm votin' for Houston's man— if I'm anywhere I can vote."

"Alex is a planter. Have you forgotten that, Jack?" asked Sam Walker, grinning. "All them rich planters want annexation 'cause it'll be good for trade. He just fights Indians and Mexicans for fun."

"Alex isn't a planter anymore," said Alex, grinning back, "but I fought with Sam Houston at San Jacinto, and I'll stand by him now. Texas belongs with the union."

A planter? Cassandra wanted to ask what that meant but knew better than to question him. It obviously had to do with his family, whom he never willingly discussed. She had thought the brother-in-law owned the plantation, not Alex. Every other thing she had ever learned about Alex had to do with fighting. Mr. Walker must be right. Alex went to war for the fun of it. She looked at him wistfully—so tall, browned, and handsome, so unafraid in this wild land. How long would he stay alive if he threw himself into every dangerous situation that came his way? Cassandra shivered. She had to overcome this infatuation with a man who lived so dangerously and espoused a life-style in which a gently bred, well-educated New England girl could hardly be considered an asset. Every time she said anything intelligent, he looked at her as if she were talking in tongues.

Cassandra lay on the soft sand of the creek bed, the water rippling over her as cool and sweet as an angel's breath. Sighing, she turned her face from side to side. Tendrils of wet hair clung to her cheeks and shoulders like beneficent fingers. On the rock beside her lay a precious sliver of Alex's soap, but she didn't want to move. If she stayed here long enough, the water would soak into her, reviving her sun-dried body and washing away all the dirt and sweat of the last days—amazing days.

As difficult as they had been, she wouldn't have missed them. The mustangers, reunited after Nicodemus' successful trip to San Antonio, had come upon a large herd of horses led by stallions who had no intention of allowing themselves or their mares to be caught, fast horses in top condition, well fed on lush spring and summer grass. After various abortive strategies, Alex had decreed that the men ride the herd into exhaustion, and that's what they had done.

Cassandra had been astounded to learn that a wild horse herd, if pursued, would stay within its own territory, running in circles. Knowing that, Alex had sent his riders out in teams on fresh horses to keep the herd moving. For three days and nights they had done this, allowing the mustangs no rest and no time to graze or drink. They had literally driven the herd to its knees. The first day the drive had been exhilarating, the second less so; by the third every bone and muscle in Cassandra's body ached. Alex, taking pity on her, offered the soap and an hour in the creek by herself.

She smiled up at the branches as they shifted lazily

in the breeze. The color of the sky deepened before her eyes, for the sun was slipping down into its western cradle. Soon she would have to forsake this luxury, dress, and return to camp, to work, and then to a hard bed. Reluctantly, she sat up and scooted deeper into the water to wash her hair. It felt so good to be alone. Among the many difficulties of her present life, the lack of privacy was starting to bulk large in her mind. Someone was always around, especially Pinto, who could spoil any pleasure and disturb any rest.

Just yesterday he had caught her alone and, eying her insolently, said, "Seventeen's all right. I had me a girl once was twelve. She din like it much at first, but she changed her mind."

Horrified, Cassandra had fled. He'd attacked a twelve-year-old child? She couldn't get it off her mind, and consequently she had been hesitant to take Alex up on his offer of a bath. Only after he made it very plain that no one would disturb her in the creek had she seized the opportunity. This might be her last moment of privacy before they left her somewhere up north where Alex would disappear from her life.

She shook off that gloomy thought. She had a few more minutes of glorious solitude and comfort, and she didn't want to waste them fretting. Sooner or later she would have to say good-bye to Alex, and feeling sorrowful would not delay their parting. She gave her hair one last underwater swish, swept the sliver of soap from the rock, and lathered every inch of her body. She had come into the stream feeling that dirt was embedded in her very pores. After a vigorous scrubbing, she splashed away the soap and reluctantly waded toward shore.

The temptation to lie down again in the water was great, but she resisted. If she stayed too long, someone might come looking for her, and she did not want to be caught naked. The glade was shadowed in dusk as she reached for her poor tattered trousers. Then she froze, for she saw yellow eyes gleaming across the clearing. Cat's eyes. She squinted at the large shadow that went with the eyes. Oh, God. She had no idea what to do. If she called out for help, the creature might spring. Her rifle was propped against a tree beside her, but she had the sinking conviction that she'd never be able get her hands on it in time to fire. Paralyzed with fear, she stared into those yellow eyes, hardly breathing, sure that if she moved the cat would attack.

"Cassandra!"

Alex's voice sounded from the woods, but she dared not answer.

"Cassandra!" The second call was more irritable than the first. "I didn't say you could stay in there forever."

She could see the animal tense, and she glanced sideways at the gun. Could she get it?

"Answer me, damn it!"

Alex was to her left, coming from the camp, the cat across from her. If he stepped into the clearing, unaware of the creature, it might spring at him.

"I know I promised you'd have the place to yourself."

He sounded closer still and worried. He wouldn't wait much longer, even at the risk of interrupting her bath. She glanced again at the rifle, afraid she'd never be able to hit the cat—even if she got the gun in time.

"All right, Cassandra, you damn well better be dressed." He stepped into the clearing and stopped short, staring at her.

Dimly she realized that his shock was the result of confronting, without warning, a totally naked girl. He hadn't seen the cat. "Alex," she said in a singsong voice, "there's a big cat across the clearing on your left."

But the drone didn't fool the cat. As it sprang, Cassandra snatched up her rifle. Before she could shoot,

Alex's gun barked, and the creature hung an instant in midair at the apex of its leap, shuddering a second time before it fell to earth, two feet short of Cassandra. She had brought her rifle up and put a ball into its head.

Alex approached the panther cautiously, ready to shoot again if it showed signs of life, but Cassandra was past practical considerations. She backed up and fell against the rock, shaking like a woman in the throes of fever. Satisfied that the cat was dead, Alex turned and saw how badly frightened she was. One long step put him in front of her, and he took her into a rough embrace. "It's all over," he murmured against her hair.

"Alex!" Nicodemus' voice intruded abruptly.

"It's all right, Nico," Alex called back. "We killed a panther. Just go on back to camp. I'll bring Cassandra along shortly." His arms had tightened. "Do you know what a good shot you just made?" he asked her.

She put her arms around his waist and buried her face against his shoulder. She didn't care about good shots.

"That's all right," he soothed. "Just hang on till you stop shaking. You've got a right to be scared." With one arm around her waist, he used the other hand to smooth the wet hair back from her face. "But you don't have anything to be scared about anymore," he assured her. "I've got you." He slipped his hand under the weight of hair and rubbed the back of her neck comfortingly. "Maybe you ought to get some clothes on now," he suggested.

For the first time something other than fear penetrated Cassandra's consciousness. She realized that she was standing in Alex Harte's arms without a stitch of clothing on her body. It was the last straw. She began to cry.

"Cassie, come on now," he murmured. "There's nothing to cry about. My God, sweetheart, here you faced down a panther, you warned me—otherwise he might have got us both—and then you finished him off with a damned near perfect shot. So why are you crying?"

"I don't—I don't have any clothes on," she hiccuped.

"Yeah, well—" He looked down at the same time she looked up. It was as if a flash ignited between them. Alex took her mouth in a kiss so hungry that it stunned them both, and she melted against him helplessly, flooded with desire. His passion so long suppressed, Alex responded by covering her soft, bare bottom with one large hand and rolling her against the quick swell of his desire. Another wave of heat suffused Cassandra, and her legs gave way. He had to tighten his hold to keep her upright.

"Honey, Cassie, are you all right?" he asked anxiously. Lord, what had he done? This girl didn't know anything about men, and he'd treated her like some New Orleans tart. Cursing himself for a fool and a lecher, he bent and swept up her clothes, which, with difficulty, he managed to put on the trembling girl. Then he sat her down on the rock and, squatting on his heels in front of her, said, "Cassie, I'm sorry. That was unforgivable of me, and I promise you it won't happen again."

Her eyes were wide with what seemed to be a sort of dazed surprise, her lips softly parted in invitation, but she said nothing. Alex could have groaned. Her collapse in his arms had put a quick rein on his passion, but looking at her sweet, young face set him on fire all over again. He stood up quickly and turned away from her. "What I did," he muttered, "well, no gentleman takes advantage of a lady, especially when she's just been scared half to death. I hope you'll see fit to forgive me, Cassandra. And as I said, it won't happen again." When he turned back, tears were slipping, one by one, down her cheeks.

Elizabeth Chadwick

"We'd better get back to camp now," he added gruffly. "Nico and the rest will be worried." He paused for a response, but there was none. "Cassie, can you walk?" She didn't move. Reluctantly he asked, "Shall I carry you?"

Cassandra didn't think she could stand that, so she forced herself to rise and, head bowed, started across the clearing, blinking hard to stem her tears. His kiss—she could hardly take in how overwhelming it had been. She had thought she belonged to him, that he had claimed her, and she had acquiesced—gladly. How then could he say that it would never happen again? How could he apologize for something so earth-shaking—unless, of course, it hadn't been earth-shaking at all for him. That must be it. While she had fallen in love, he had just embarrassed himself by kissing a silly girl.

After the kiss, Alex treated her with distant courtesy. Nicodemus skinned the panther, thinking she'd like to take the pelt back to Massachusetts, but to Cassandra it was a trophy reminiscent of humiliation. No wonder Alex wanted nothing to do with her. First, she had asked him for a kiss, and he had refused. Then when she threw herself at him, naked, he had kissed her all right but regretted it almost before his mouth had left hers.

Ashamed of the encounter, she strove to regain his good opinion. No one worked harder than she. She rode longer hours than anyone else, took every assignment, and volunteered for others, even attempted to help with taming once the mustangs were caught, but when she took a bad fall, Alex forbade her to ride wild horses any longer. It was one of the few things he said to her in several weeks.

The further Alex distanced himself, the closer Pinto came, adding to her dismay, for she no longer felt protected. Alex probably thought she'd welcome Pinto's advances as she had his. One day when she came back to change mounts, she was alarmed to find herself alone in the camp with Pinto, something she usually managed to avoid.

"Well, it's about time you come to see me, Cassie," said Pinto. "I knew you'd show up sooner or later once you realized the cap'n didn't have no interest in you. I got more to offer'n him anyways. You wanna see?"

"I'm just here for a fresh horse," she snapped, not sure what he meant. "Would you please get me one?" She usually got her own, but she wanted to send him away.

"Shore, honey, I got just what you wanna see."

His smile was especially unpleasant, and to her horror, his hands went to the buttons of his pants. Cassandra backed away.

"Don't run off. I seen how you like looking at me."

"I do not!"

"Sure you do, an' I got better'n you seen yet." He released the last button and pulled open his trousers. "How about that?" he asked, grinning.

Suddenly Cassandra was no longer embarrassed; she was incensed. "You're disgusting. *That's* disgusting."

"Why? Ain't you never seen one? Well, take a good look, honey, 'cause I—"

She snapped her rifle up and directed it at the limp, ugly thing of which he was so proud. "I guess if I can hit a moving panther in the head, I can certainly shoot off that—that—whatever you call it."

Pinto turned dead white and backed up with his hands over his recently displayed privates. "You wouldn't!"

Cassandra pulled back the hammer, and Pinto fled. After him she shouted, "Disgusting, obnoxious, dreadful, evil . . ."

Nicodemus appeared and looked at her questioningly.

Her rifle still clutched protectively, Cassandra said, "I've come for a horse," and she stumbled off to get one.

"Pinto," said Alex, an ominously quiet tone to his voice, "I don't know exactly what happened this afternoon, but if you ever so much as speak to Cassandra again, you're out of the group. I won't even pay you your last cut."

"You can't do that."

"I can and will. In fact, I may just shoot you right now."

"What'd she say about me?" He gave Cassandra a murderous glare. "I ain't done nothin'. She's lyin'. Ever'one knows women are liars."

"Everyone knows you're a liar, and she didn't say anything. Nico did."

"You can't afford to lose me," said the boy smugly.

"Everyone is expendable, Pinto, and you're more trouble than you're worth. Fact is, Cassandra does more work than you do, and she's damn good at it. Besides that, she's not obnoxious, and she can cook."

"And you got your eye on her," sneered Pinto. "You're pro'bly sleepin' with her."

Alex, his face as cold as death, drew his gun.

"You're not gonna shoot me," said Pinto with cocky bravado. "You ain't the kind to shoot someone who ain't done nothin', an' I ain't."

"Oh, but you have," Alex retorted, and he slashed the barrel of the gun across Pinto's forehead, knocking him down. "Now remember what I said. Next time I'll shoot you, and then if you're still alive, I'll throw you out of camp to fend for yourself."

Alex was livid. Did he know what had happened that afternoon? Cassandra wondered uneasily. What if he asked? She could never talk about it. And why was he defending her when he had treated her like a pariah for days?

Sullenly Pinto picked himself up off the ground, a

bleeding gash across his forehead, and stumbled off toward the herd, but the glance he threw over his shoulder at Alex was malevolent, and Cassandra shivered to see it.

"He means to get even with you," she warned, her voice shaking. She didn't think she could stand it if any harm came to Alex through her, and she meant to keep a close eye on Pinto. She would watch Alex's back, as the men said.

"Well, he may have that in mind," said Alex dryly, "but he'll have to hurry. You and I are heading north."

Cassandra's face went white. She hadn't thought it would be so soon. "You mean to leave me with someone at trail's end?" she asked unhappily.

"Of course. You can't stay with us forever."

"Why are you doing this? You must think I encouraged him."

"This is no life for a girl," said Alex evasively.

So she was right; he did think she had encouraged Pinto; otherwise he would have answered her accusation.

"You need to get back to your people."

"What people?" she asked bitterly.

"You said you had cousins."

"They care nothing for me."

Alex gave her a long look which she took to mean that no one here cared for her either. What was she to do? She didn't *want* to leave. If she could only stay, maybe Alex—but why was she thinking that way? He'd made it abundantly clear that he wanted to send her home as soon as possible.

Even if he were interested in her, what future would there be for them? Mustangers didn't marry and take their wives on the hunt. And if they did, would she want that sort of life? Always in danger of capture by Comanches, or attack by wild animals, not to mention the grueling work and grim living conditions. She'd be a fool to consider staying if anyone wanted her to, which no one did. Cassandra blinked back tears and went to her bedroll.

The next day Bone located a new herd, and Cassandra wondered if she had gained another reprieve. Surely they wouldn't pass up such an opportunity. The general movement of the mustangs was north, just where Alex wanted to go. He'd have to take at least another week to gather up this herd to add to the one they already had.

However, Alex had other ideas. "Bone, you and I and Cassandra will be leaving for the Trinity tomorrow."

Bone refused, as did the others, although Alex argued that it wouldn't be proper for her to travel alone with him.

"If you're in such an all-fired hurry to get the girl up north," said Nicodemus, "you'll have to do it your own self—proper or no."

"You want to miss the northern buyer?" Alex snapped.

"Nope, an' I don't want to miss this herd neither. Stay or go as you please, Alex. We're stayin'."

Alex turned angrily to Cassandra. "We'll leave tomorrow morning," he said brusquely.

Cassandra stopped feeling sad about her imminent departure and glared. Did he think she was going to throw herself at him as soon as they were alone? Well, he was wrong. She might be stupidly in love, but she had more pride than to plead for his affection.

On the other hand, it would serve him right if she subjected him to a little discreet flirting. But what did she know about flirtation? Nothing. She sighed and headed for her blankets, tempted to give him a good kick as soon as he got to sleep. Of course, he'd know who had done it.

Discouraged, she admitted that she was unlikely to think of any way to get even with Alex Harte, and getting even wasn't what she really wanted. She wanted to be loved. She wanted him to be a New England gentleman who could make her an honorable proposal of marriage. Of course, if he were a New England gentleman, she probably wouldn't be in love with him. And no one married a mustanger.

It was hopeless, and she was a silly goose, an epithet she had never thought to apply to herself. Restlessly she turned away from Alex, who lay only a few feet from her. At least she didn't have to look at him. Then she turned back, remembering that there wouldn't be many more nights when she *could* look at him.

Chapter Five

"We take horses and woman," said the Indian. He and his companions had appeared on the second day of the drive north while Alex and Cassandra were eating their noon meal.

"No, you won't," said Alex, snapping his rifle up to point directly at the Comanche spokesman.

The leader sneered. "We put three arrows in heart before you pull trigger on smoke stick."

"Wrong again. I've got six bullets in this rifle," Alex countered. "You get number one. That leaves five for your friends."

The Indian frowned. "White man speak with tongue of snake. No gun hold six bullets."

"Reckon you haven't heard what happened to the eighty or so Comanches down near San Antone who thought they could take on fourteen rangers." He used hand motions to be sure they understood the numbers. "Thirty-five dead Indians, no dead whites. The rangers had guns like this one." He nodded toward his weapon, and Cassandra listened carefully to the grunted conversation that followed between the three Indians. They thought Alex might be lying but weren't sure enough to ignore his threat. "My woman's got an eight-shot rifle," Alex added for good measure, "and can put a bullet between the eyes of a panther in mid-air."

Cassandra's heart leaped when he referred to her as "his woman." Determined to justify his faith in her, she aimed carefully at the warrior on the leader's left.

"Maybe you'd like to trade for the woman's panther skin," Alex suggested with a sneer.

Cassandra could see that he had won his bluff. The Comanches were backing away. She and Alex, silent, rifles in hand, watched them mount and ride off. Then Cassandra let out a long, shuddering breath. "I hate them," she said vehemently and began to tremble.

"You sure put up a good front," he remarked, watching her struggle with tears. "But we weren't in that much danger." When her tears overflowed, he sighed and pulled Cassandra into his arms. "I guess I should be happy you stand up so well under pressure," he muttered, "but I sure don't understand why you go to pieces when everything's all right again."

So glad to be alive and in Alex's arms rather than in the hands of the Indians, Cassandra pressed against him and raised her face blindly for his kiss. He had told them she was his woman, and she wanted to be. She wanted him to love her.

"Cassandra," he muttered in protest and then succumbed to her need and his own response to it. He deepened the kiss, and when she, with a girl's innocent passion, failed to open to the pressure of his mouth, he tugged at her lower lip with his teeth. As she gasped in surprise, he plunged his tongue into the tempting interior of her mouth. The wet friction sent a wave of heat over her; he felt her skin warm under his hands. Then the urgent pressure of her hips made him realize how close he was to taking her and how much in danger she was of allowing it. If he did, she wouldn't thank him. Chances were that she didn't even know what her body seemed to be asking. Alex lifted his head and drew a deep, harsh breath as he set her away from him.

"We need to get moving and drive this herd as far as we can push them while the light holds." Cassandra stared at him with incomprehension. He reckoned the girl was still in a sensual daze and cursed himself for letting this happen. "Pack up and mount," he ordered. "Those Indians might have twenty friends over the next hill."

They rode out moments later and continued riding long after dark with only moonglow to light the way. As the weary hours passed, he kept a careful eye on her and found no cause for complaint. She was a brave girl as well as beautiful, intelligent, and more hardworking than any woman he'd ever known. She encompassed everything a man could want in a wife if he happened to be in the market for one. Unfortunately, Alex wasn't. He had no place in his life for a woman. However, he knew that he could seduce her, and he wanted to. He wanted to plunge himself into her; he ached for it, but if he did, what then? Marry her and send her home to his sister? Eloise wouldn't welcome her, and Cassandra would do him no good if she were living a life of luxury on the Brazos while he pursued his own ends out here.

Then he frowned, an unpleasant suspicion creeping into his mind. Was that what she wanted? To marry into wealth and luxury the way his sister had? He didn't doubt that Cassandra had never been with a man. Every liberty he allowed himself took her by surprise. Nor did he believe she could fake either her startled reactions or the heated responses, but she might be encouraging intimacies in the hope of trapping him into a proposal.

Shaking his head, Alex groaned softly. God, how he wanted her, but he'd damned well better keep his hands off. Seducing a virgin would lie heavy on his conscience. He'd been brought up to be a gentleman, not just in name but in fact, and Cassandra, unfortunately, was off limits unless he planned to offer marriage, which he didn't.

* * *

When the moon set after midnight, he called a halt, half convinced that weariness would have cooled their passions. They ate cold food from the saddlebags; then Alex dropped her bedroll on one side of the fire, his on the other. He had not placed their blankets side by side since they left the main camp and set out north on their own.

"No," she said, her teeth beginning to chatter. "You were the one who said Comanches could steal a horse or a woman without anyone being the wiser." She picked up her roll and plunked it down beside his. "I'm not sleeping off by myself with those Indians roaming around."

"Cassandra—"

"And I don't care what you say." Her lower lip was thrust out stubbornly, and Alex found himself staring at it with hunger as she continued. "I realize you're doing the gentlemanly thing, Alex, observing the proprieties and all that, but this isn't a civilized situation and—"

"You're damned right it isn't," he muttered angrily. How much control did the girl think he had? She was playing with fire. "What is it you want, Cassandra?" he asked harshly. His tone caused her eyelids to flicker uncertainly and her mouth to close. She took a half step back. "Changed your mind? I thought you wanted to sleep with me."

"N-not *with* you," she stammered.

He had an iron grip on her wrist and was drawing her reluctant body toward the bedrolls.

"I d-didn't mean—"

"Then what did you mean?" Motivated by an angry desire to teach her a lesson as well as an even more impelling desire to taste, at least briefly, the temptation she offered, he put his hands on her waist and pulled her down.

"Alex?" Her voice faltered and then faded out under the pressure of his mouth.

Elizabeth Chadwick

"Women should make up their minds," he muttered, rolling on top of her so that she couldn't have moved if she wanted to. Against the inside of her thigh she felt a hard, pulsing pressure. She knew it must be that pathetic, wrinkled little thing Pinto had exhibited, but Alex's was obviously neither pathetic nor little, and again her body was suffused with heat and fear. Was he going to take her? Did she want him to? she wondered, close to panic. She did want him, but she was afraid.

Probably she wouldn't even like it. The girls at school, those who claimed to be knowledgeable, said that it was something only men liked. But his fingers were at her breast, rubbing the tip until she twisted beneath him in an aching rictus of desire. With a mind of its own, her body pressed against that hard intrusion between her thighs.

Alex groaned her name and reached for the knotted belt of her trousers. Then suddenly his fingers were at the junction of her thighs, and before she could protest—and she did want to protest—he had touched her most private part in such a way as to cause an explosion of sharp pleasure within. Although tremors of sensation continued to radiate through her body, she herself went still, too stunned to protest or respond further.

Alex realized that he had carried her far beyond her experience or imagination. He rolled away and lay on his back, staring into the darkness as he attempted to control his frustration. Taking deep, slow breaths, his mind reeling with confusion, he thanked God that he had managed to stop, even as he resented having been put into a position where he had to. In just about two minutes, when her mind would take over from her body, she was going to blame him, although he was the one who had been trying to avoid this. "Damn it, Cassandra," he burst out resentfully, "you've got to keep your distance. I'm no saint—not by a long shot—

86

and you aren't helping this situation at all."

"But I didn't—"

"Didn't mean for things to go this far? You're lucky they didn't go further. What the hell are you up to? I know you're scared of Indians, but losing your virginity won't make you any less scared."

"I didn't want to lose my virginity," she replied in a frightened, wavering voice. "I just wanted—"

"—to see how far you could push me?" he suggested harshly. "In case you don't know it, you weren't in any condition to stop things if I'd had a mind to go on."

"You think I was teasing you?" she asked, her voice trembling with hurt.

"Well, I don't think you were overcome by Christian love," he replied dryly. "I reckon, to give you the benefit of the doubt, that you're young and curious, but I don't want to be the object of your curiosity." Alex realized that his conduct wasn't very chivalrous, but cruelty would be more successful in putting a stop to this than kindness.

"Young and curious!" she exclaimed. "I may be young, but I'm not—not *curious*!" The word held a world of disdain. "And I may have been afraid, but—but I'm in love with you; I'm—"

"Be quiet!" he snapped angrily. "You're not in love. You haven't known me long enough to be in love. If there's any love involved here, it's love of the easy life. You and my sister are two of a kind, and let me tell you, it won't work out for you any more than it did for her."

"I don't know what you're talking about," stammered Cassandra.

"You don't know I own half a plantation on the Brazos?" he demanded sarcastically.

"I thought your brother-in-law was the landowner."

"Oh, he was." Alex's voice grated with irony. "That's exactly what my sister saw in him. He owned

87

Elizabeth Chadwick

a big plantation and a lot of slaves, and Eloise saw herself living the gracious life, waited on hand and foot—"

"Slaves?"

"Of course. As you pointed out, we weren't taken into the union because Texas is slave country. So is Louisiana."

"But I thought—"

"They're the ones who produce all that gracious living my sister coveted. Being a cotton factor's daughter wasn't good enough for her, any more than being some eccentric professor's daughter was good enough for you, evidently. Well, it didn't work out too well for my sister. She married Jean Philippe, and he gambled away the plantation in Louisiana. Eloise ended up on the Texas frontier trying to build herself the good life all over again while Jean Philippe continued his old ways. And if you think you can marry me and head for the Brazos—"

"She got exactly what she deserved," snapped Cassandra.

"What?" Alex paused in confusion.

"Didn't you say she disdained your father's hard-earned success for a life made easy by the sweat of poor enslaved Negroes, kidnapped from their native—"

"Are you an abolitionist?" Alex demanded.

"I certainly am." For just a moment she hesitated. Alex owned slaves? That meant she was in love with a slave owner. Still, love or no love, she had to have the courage of her convictions, and she abhorred slavery. "I *am* an abolitionist, and I certainly have no desire to profit from the bondage of others."

"I'll be damned," Alex muttered. Here was an unexpected twist. The sound of her voice left no doubt that she found slavery and slave owners repellant. He'd made a fool of himself with his accusations. Still, she'd said she loved him. What was he to think?

"You owe me an apology," said Cassandra. "I haven't the slightest interest in your money or your land or—"

"Then what the hell do you want from me?"

Remembering that she had declared her love, she was overcome with humiliation. What could she say?

"I'm going out to ride night herd," Alex muttered. "Those Comanches could be waiting for a chance to run off the horses."

Cassandra wanted to protest his departure. She was afraid to be left alone, and she didn't want him to leave angry. But pride kept her from pursuing the matter. "Wake me when it's my watch," she murmured instead.

Alex had no intention of doing that. He'd worked her hard the last few days and intended to do the same tomorrow. She needed the sleep. As for himself, exhaustion might serve to dull his desire, although it hadn't yet. A man didn't come that close to satisfaction without paying a price when he had to forgo release.

Besides, he needed the night to think over what had happened. Love, she'd said. He didn't believe it. What did a girl that young know about love? She was just clinging to him because she was afraid—of the Indian threat and of being left with strangers when they reached their destination. He didn't blame her, but that didn't mean he'd marry her, any more than he'd take advantage of her and then not offer marriage.

He knew he'd caused the girl humiliation, but maybe now she'd forget this calf love and leave him alone, damn her. He'd done well to avoid matrimony, he assured himself. Women wanted a man's freedom, which was more than Alex was willing to give. He'd had enough of recrimination from Eloise when he tried to live life according to his own convictions and desires instead of devoting himself to her precious plantation. Not that Alex's reluctantly expended time and effort had done her much good; Jean Philippe could always gamble away as much as Alex could produce.

As soon as he rode off, Cassandra's conscience attacked. After all, she had allowed something highly improper to occur. And then Alex had accused her of inviting his advances—could that be true?—and of wanting to marry him, a matter on which she wasn't clear herself. Much as she loved him, she couldn't possibly want to marry a slave owner. Sadly disappointed in herself and him, she drifted off to sleep, having set herself to awaken in four hours for her turn on night watch.

The very idea of being by herself out there in the dark terrified Cassandra, but she wouldn't let Alex know that. He had as much right to sleep as she, and she had already earned his disdain. At least, when he left her, he would remember something laudable— that she did her share. With that thought, she rode out to relieve him.

When she reined her mount in beside his, Alex felt remorse for his earlier tirade. He, being the elder, had no business blaming her. He thought of sending her back to camp, but to do so would be to make light of the courage she had shown in coming to take her turn.

"If you see anything amiss, fire one shot," he ordered. Then he turned his horse away with the gold of her hair a remembered glory in his mind. How many days to the rendezvous? he wondered. He both desired and dreaded a fast journey. The adventure he had sought in coming out here seemed less compelling now that Cassandra would no longer be a part of it.

For three days they drove the horses hard in the stifling August heat, riding from sunup to sundown, trading watches after dark. On the third night Alex returned to camp toward morning almost convinced that the night watches were a waste of sleeping time. He rested a moment on one knee, studying Cassandra's face and wondering how he could once have mistaken her for a boy. Her bone structure was too delicate. She would be as beautiful in old age, if she lived to see it, as she was in youth. And that golden hair. He laid a hand on her shoulder to shake her gently, then paused to savor the fragility of the bones under her shirt. She was so slender for a tall girl. He ran his fingertips lightly down her arm until he touched her hand, and she sighed, still asleep, and entwined her fingers with his.

He hated to disturb her, and why should he? The horses were quiet tonight, as exhausted as their keepers. The absence of moonlight made it unlikely that the Comanches, if they were anywhere in the area, would strike. They believed that a man killed on a moonless night could wander in the dark forever, unable to find the afterlife.

Just once Alex wanted to sleep with Cassandra in his arms. And what could it h   for a few hours? He'd awaken first, and she'd neve   ow. With a sigh of pleasure, he stretched out and drew her body into the curve of his. They fit together like puzzle pieces—cut to match, he thought just before sleep overcame him.

Cassandra awoke at first light, blinking in sleepy confusion with the unformed thought that something was amiss. The fire had died, but she was cozily warm. That brought her eyes wide open as she looked at the source. She lay curled in Alex's arms, and he was fast asleep.

He had a beautiful mouth, she thought wistfully, a tempting mouth for all that his unshaven face looked rough and somewhat threatening. And his body, so hard against hers, felt wonderful. She luxuriated in the feeling until she realized what was wrong. Horses.

No one was watching the horses. Why hadn't he wakened her? Lord, had the herd run off—leaving them afoot? She swallowed hard and succeeded in controlling her panic but not before Alex stirred.

"What is it?" he asked.

"The horses. No one's—" She felt the tension leave his body.

"They're all right," he muttered. As he began to disentangle himself, his hand brushed against her breast, and they both went still.

Cassandra, looking straight into his eyes, saw them gleam, felt his hand move to the laces of her buckskin shirt. She closed her eyes as he tugged it open, and because her eyes were closed, the first hint she had of what he planned to do was the warmth of his breath on her breast just before his mouth touched her. A long shudder ran through her body when she felt the suckling pull of his lips. He continued until she whimpered with passion. Then he thrust his thigh between hers and pressed. She pressed back as the ache that was its own pleasure spread over her body.

When Alex took his mouth from her breast, she made a mute sound of protest. "God, Cassie," he muttered, thinking himself a fool for hesitating, "do you really understand what's about to happen?"

The mindless, feverish yearning that had overtaken her began to recede, but her body wished him silent.

"I want you," he muttered, "but you're so young." He sounded more sad than passionate. "And I don't make a habit of seducing young girls."

There it was again. He thought of her as a child. Cassandra sighed. "I understand," she replied sadly.

"Do you really? Do you have any idea what was about to happen?"

"Of course I do," she replied resentfully and sat up. "Do I have to put it into words?"

She sat cross-legged, elbows planted on her knees, and dropped her face into her hands, evidently forgetful that she was bare from the waist up. Alex stared at the pretty, pointed breasts swinging forward from her slender frame. Lord, she was a beauty, and he was throwing it all away.

"Fornication," she muttered.

Alex snapped his eyes from her breasts to the hands that covered her face. "Cassie," he protested.

"You'd never believe I had a good Christian upbringing, but I did. Even out here, I always say my prayers, and yet I was just as eager to—to fornicate as—"

"Cassie, fornicate's not a very romantic word," he interrupted dryly.

"Well, since you don't love me and you can hardly wait to dump me at some frontier trading post, it's not a very romantic situation, is it? I'm really—" She gulped back tears "—really fortunate that you don't want me very *much.*"

Alex was so taken aback that he hardly noticed when she began to cry. Didn't want her? She couldn't have been more wrong. He'd never wanted a woman so badly. And she thought he could hardly wait to get rid of her? That wasn't true. The prospect of never seeing her again ate at him worse than his frustrated desire to make love to her. He hadn't wanted to *fornicate* with her—although God knows he'd done some of that in his time. Fornicate? She was wrong. He'd wanted to make *love* to her.

He looked up and realized that she was weeping into clenched fingers. "Now Cassie," he murmured, gathering her into his arms. That maneuver brought her elbows instead of her breasts into contact with him. "Cassie, you've got it all wrong," he assured her, shifting awkwardly.

"What have I got wrong?" she sniffed.

"Well, for one thing, I want to make love—not—fornicate. I want it every bit as much as you do."

"I don't want to anymore."

93

"You will again," he assured her.

"But you *do* want to leave me at that trading post."

"No, I don't."

"You don't?" She stopped, confused. "Well, you don't love me, so what does any of the rest matter?"

Alex sighed and admitted to himself, as well as to her, "I do love you."

"You do?"

"Yes, but it's nothing to celebrate about." He leaned his chin wearily on the top of her head. "Sweetheart, you're too young for me—"

"I am not."

"—and I'm hardly situated for taking myself a wife."

The word *wife* silenced Cassandra because she knew that, much as she loved him, he was an adventurer and, as such, no good for her. She should never have come west. When her father proposed it, she should have said no. Instead, she would now, if Alex asked, consider staying, and with a man who might well get them both killed before the year was out.

"Still, we'll have to get married," he continued, "because I'm not going to give you up." He paused and added, "Nor am I going to take your innocence and then desert you."

Well, it was hardly the proposal girls dreamed of. The lover, hand on heart, was supposed to kneel romantically to declare his devotion and honorable intentions. Alex hadn't even asked for her consent.

"We'll have to hope we find a preacher up north."

There were a million things against their marrying, she reminded herself without much conviction, for her heart was beating with runaway excitement.

"I guess we can have the honeymoon on the way back."

The honeymoon? Cassandra shivered at the thought, remembering the touch of his hands and mouth on her body. Could she pass up the chance to marry him when the alternative was a safe, passionless life in Cambridge?

"That suit you?" He gave her a slow, warm smile that melted her bones, and she nodded helplessly just before his lips closed, hot and compelling, over hers.

"Reckon we're engaged," he added as he pulled away, "and we've also got a herd to move out."

Cassandra's eyes followed him wistfully as he rose to stir up the fire for morning coffee.

Chapter Six

"A preacher?" Odell Webber, who owned the trading post, looked astounded. "No sir, we ain't got one. Fact is, I don't think there's ever been a preacher this far west, not in my time anyways. Who would he preach to?"

Cassandra glanced at Alex from the corner of her eye. Had he proposed because he'd known they couldn't marry?

"No need to look so downhearted, missy," said Odell, a gray-haired, long-shanked fellow with peculiar stains on his beard. He and Alex were seated on kegs with their backs against the counter. Cassandra wandered restlessly around the small, crowded log room looking at the meager supply of merchandise. "It don't take a preacher to git married." Odell spat toward a bug that was creeping across the dirt floor. The bug continued imperturbably on its way. "Got a possum in the pouch, lil lady?"

"No," Cassandra answered through gritted teeth, after puzzling over the question. Alex suppressed a chuckle.

"Well, don't make me no never mind, but if ya want ter git married, whyn't ya jist go ahead an' do her. Here in Texas we call hit agreeable marriage. If there ain't no preacher ner county clerk handy, ya jist agrees to marry, an' ya are." He spat at the bug again. "Course, there be laws. After some time passes, not

sure how much, ya gotta go an' do hit up formal like—
if ya live long enough."

"He's right," Alex agreed. "The republic has made
provisions for people who don't have a preacher
handy."

"Shore," said the enthusiastic Odell Webber. "Hendricks oughter be back by nightfall an' happy to see
them horses. He kin stand up fer ya, Alex, an' mah
woman here—I call her Bluebonnet—" he pointed to
the squat Indian woman who had yet to say a word
"—Bluebonnet kin stand up fer you, missy."

Cassandra tried to smile at Bluebonnet, who, although short, was amazingly muscular. The name
seemed an unlikely choice on Mr. Webber's part. Bluebonnet was the least flowery person Cassandra had
ever seen.

"An' I'll give the bride away," said Webber, "not
but what I hate to be givin' away such a tasty morsel
as you, missy. Wouldn't think of hit, ceppin' I got me
a fine wife of my own." He beamed fondly into the
wide, expressionless face of Bluebonnet. She continued to scrape the flesh from a buffalo hide.

"We kin have a ceremony an' a shivaree an' ever-
thin'."

Could this plan really be legal? Cassandra searched
her mind for precedents and recalled that in the Middle Ages people married without benefit of clergy. The
plighting of a troth had been considered binding. Still,
she thought, sighing, she'd rather have had something
conventional. "Does—does anyone know the words to
the marriage ceremony?" She certainly didn't, never
having been to a wedding.

"Words don't matter," said Odell Webber. "Me an'
Bluebonnet didn't say nothin'."

Cassandra wondered if Bluebonnet *ever* said anything.

"I got a fine shed out back you folks kin have fer the

weddin' night. Jist have ta move a few hides out of hit."

"I know the vows," said Alex gravely, "if this is what you want to do, Cassandra."

Did she? She could back out now and maybe travel east with the missing horse trader, Mr. Hendricks. Was Alex hoping she would? But she didn't want to back out, even if it meant spending her wedding night in a hide shed.

Cassandra was married six hours later wearing the same buckskins she'd acquired in May, Aureliano's hand-me-downs. She had hoped Mr. Webber might have a dress available among his supplies, but he didn't. "Who'd I sell a dress to?" he asked. "You kin wear one a Bluebonnet's. She's got two."

Cassandra had had to conceal her superstitious horror; she didn't want to marry in the dress of a Comanche squaw. She didn't want to do anything in a Comanche's clothing.

The only beautiful thing about the ceremony was repeating the vows after Alex. At that moment, looking into his eyes, she felt like a bride. During the wedding feast that followed, she felt like a squeamish intruder, barely able to eat the bear steak with its accompanying corn bread and yams cooked in bear grease. Webber also provided whiskey, but Cassandra didn't drink it, and she noticed with relief that Alex drank very little. Odell Webber told her repeatedly how lucky she was that he had shot the bear several days earlier.

"Been eatin' salt pork fer a month afore Mr. Bar ambled inter the clearin'. Yams jist come in too. Bluebonnet planted 'em her own self, an' likely you know Injuns ain't much on plantin'—leastways Comanches ain't. Bluebonnet's purebred Comanche, ain't ya, sweetheart?" Bluebonnet, still silent, reached a greasy hand into the pot. "Nuthin' like yams an' bar grease," said Mr. Webber, who was becoming noticeably intoxicated. "Bar grease, hit's nearly as good on corn bread as hit is on yams."

Cassandra, having tasted it for the first time, considered bear grease much more suitable for anointing bullet patches and cleaning weapons, and she heartily wished the feast would end. Mr. Hendricks was consuming even more whiskey than Mr. Webber.

"You young folks gittin' hot an' flustered?" demanded Webber coyly. "Wantin' to git on with the weddin' night, am I right?" He tossed back another tin cup of whiskey.

"Cain't say I blame ya." This was addressed to Alex. " 'Twas me, I'd be rarin' to plant my hoe in that furrow."

Cassandra felt her face turning red.

"Time to put the bride an' groom ta bed."

What did he mean? she wondered desperately. Surely he didn't—he wouldn't come into the shed with them.

"I know jist the song fer the shivaree," said Mr. Webber. "You'll like this 'un, Alex." He belched and then, staggering to his feet, caroled, " 'Will you come to the bower I have shaded for you-ou-ou? Our bed shall be roses all spangled with de-e-ew.' " Waving his whiskey bottle in one hand, he grasped Alex's arm with the other and pulled him up from the rough log table. Alex reached down to encircle Cassandra's waist and lift her up beside him.

"Wassa nex' line?" mumbled Mr. Webber.

" 'Lie,' " said Mr. Hendricks.

"Hu-u?"

" 'Lie on roses.' "

"Oh yeah. 'Under the bower on roses you'll lie,' " bellowed Mr. Webber.

" 'You'll lie,' " echoed Mr. Hendricks.

Alex tried to outdistance the two men, but they were determined to play their parts in the bedding of the bridal couple. Cassandra just wanted to disappear, especially when the next line was sung.

"'A blush on your cheek,'" chortled Mr. Webber, trying to kiss her cheek as they spilled through the door to the shed. Initially Cassandra tried to stop when the rancid odor assailed her; then she plunged on to avoid the trader's kiss.

"'And a smile in your eye,'" howled Mr. Hendricks, doubling over with laughter.

Cassandra gave him a cold look as Alex lighted the coal oil lamp.

"Good night, gentlemen," he said firmly.

"Good night?" Mr. Webber looked indignant. "Gotta put you two to bed, proper like."

Cassandra shivered in the curve of Alex's arm.

"Ah, come on, Odell," cried Mr. Hendricks. "How's she gonna git a smile in her eye—" again he was overcome with snickers "—if you an' me don' leave 'em to it?"

"Leave 'em to hit; I like that. Leave 'em to hit." Mr. Webber nodded several dozen times. "One more chorus." He insisted that they lie down on the bedrolls.

Cassandra could hear Alex's impatient hiss of breath, but they were serenaded one last time before the two men staggered out, still singing about the "blush on her cheek."

"What *was* that song?" she asked, sitting up quickly.

"Odell fought at San Jacinto too. That's what we sang going into battle."

They'd won Texas from the Mexicans singing that— that shameful song? Cassandra could hardly believe it.

"Well, we had a German playing a fife and a Nigrah with a drum and two other fellows. That was the only song all four of them knew."

Cassandra watched him as he unlaced his shirt and pulled it over his head, revealing the powerful muscles of his shoulders and arms and the dark furred chest.

She was about to be made a woman by this stranger, here in a room where the smell of carelessly cured hides was making her dizzy and nauseated.

"You having a change of heart, Cassie?" Alex asked.

She blinked back the stinging tears and shook her head.

Alex dropped down beside her on the joined bedrolls and said quietly, "We don't have to stay here, you know."

What was he suggesting? Cassandra raised her eyes to his in the mellow lamplight. Did he mean to send her away?

"This isn't exactly my idea of a good place for a wedding night," said Alex dryly. He bent forward and touched his lips to hers. "There's a nice, private grove by the river."

Cassandra bit her lip.

"I'm not offering you an annulment, Cassandra. We're married, and I mean to lie with you. I've waited too long already, but it doesn't have to be in this room."

She put her hand in his and rose from the blankets.

"Stop," she begged. Just seconds ago her body had been trembling with eagerness. Now she was desperate to get away. "Please, Alex." He was *hurting* her.

"It'll be all right," he murmured.

Cassandra tried to escape, but she was pinned under his weight. He must be doing something wrong, she thought, panic-stricken. Otherwise she wouldn't feel as if she were being torn apart by his relentless intrusion. And then she *did* feel herself tear. In the darkness tears burned her eyes. She could hear the bubbling flow of the creek beside which they had thrown their blankets, the mysterious night noises of forest and prairie, and superimposed on these quiet sounds, the harsh, accelerating rasp of his breathing as he drove into her body. Sniffing back tears, Cassandra bit hard

Elizabeth Chadwick

on her lower lip so that she would not cry out again. She had, after all, thought she wanted this. She *had* wanted it, not knowing how much it was going to hurt.

At last he was done. She heard the soft groan as his body shuddered against hers; then he rested for a moment, his lips at her damp hairline. Finally, sighing, he heaved himself away and lay on his back, one forearm resting across his eyes. "It won't hurt so much next time," he promised quietly.

Cassandra wanted to believe him, but she could feel the hot trickle of blood and wondered how badly she had been injured. Should she tell him she was bleeding? He evidently expected to do this all over again; he had, after all, spoken of *next time*. Would he wait until she had healed? Lord, she hoped so. Then, at least, she'd have the interval to resurrect her courage.

Alex wanted to take her in his arms; in truth, he wanted to make love to her again, but he realized that it had been a disaster for her. Maybe if she hadn't panicked when she felt him at the barrier, it would have gone better. He'd had a few virgins when he was younger and never left them in tears. In fact, he was accustomed to giving pleasure, not pain. What an irony that the one woman he did love was the one he had frightened half to death.

But then Cassandra wasn't a woman, and he had only himself to blame. He'd taken a child bride and hoped to elicit a woman's passion from her. Still, it was hard to believe that she could be so eager one minute, then struggling to escape the next. Sighing, he turned onto his side in preparation for sleep. Tomorrow they would leave early for the long ride back. During those days together, perhaps they could work things out.

Cassandra waited until she was sure Alex slept before making her way through the darkness to the creek. She had to clean herself up and hoped the cold water would stop the warm ooze of blood that frightened her so badly as it continued to dampen her thighs.

With no horses to herd, the return trip went much faster. Every evening he asked her, increasingly worried, if she still bled. Embarrassed, she nodded without meeting his eyes. Every night she slept in his arms, unthreatened by any further sexual overtures. His kindness deepened her love, but still she found the other intimacies of marriage embarrassing. Where once Alex never undressed in front of her, now he stripped off his clothes to bathe at the end of the day's ride. When she hung back, he insisted that she do the same, and he studied her with open approval.

Increasing curiosity made Cassandra peek at him. The first night on the trail his casually displayed body frightened her and brought back memories of the pain she had suffered when he pressed against and into her. The second night the fear was leavened with admiration. She found his body intriguing and would have liked to stare openly—without his knowing, of course. She began to feel again the physical tide of her attraction for him.

His face and hands were brown, his upper torso and arms lighter but nowhere near as pale as the white of his legs and lower body. She was also fascinated with the patterns of hair that spread across his chest, tapered to a whorl at his navel, then spread out again around his manhood. Cassandra closed her eyes on that observation, but in a few minutes she was watching him again, surreptitiously, noting the light furring on his arms and legs, the flexing muscles of his buttocks as he walked away from her.

Much as she loved him, his sheer power was intimidating. He had made her ache for him before their marriage, and now she felt occasional twinges of those longings again, but mixed with fear. As for Alex, there was no ambivalence about what he wanted. He was waiting for her to heal, and she hadn't, not quite.

How often did married people ordinarily do what he had done to her? she wondered uneasily. Soon they would be back at the camp with the other mustangers. Surely he wouldn't—not with other people sleeping around them. Her face turned crimson at the thought. Why hadn't she anticipated these problems before she fell in love?

Much as she dreaded the prospect of having that first disastrous experience repeated, she still felt dizzy with happiness at his slightest attention, and he was, for all his impatience to repossess her body, very kind. As they rode, he asked about her childhood and listened with interest to descriptions of life at her mother's school among the proper girls of good New England families and to tales of mischief among the boarding students. She imitated for him the dialect and conversation of the Irish maids and, blooming under his attention, went on to mimic the stuffy ministers and solemn scholars who called on weekends because of her father's eminence and her mother's severe beauty and impeccable Puritan lineage.

Cassandra had never thought of herself as an amusing person or considered her girlhood a subject of much interest, but she delighted in eliciting Alex's laughter and joined him in it with a gaiety she had never felt before. For hours at a time she forgot that sooner or later she was going to have to make her body available and endure more pain in order to provide her husband with pleasure. Of course, she realized that she had given him pleasure, but that favor had not been returned. Then she reminded herself sternly that her more worldly friends had warned that the marriage bed was a man's arena. Unfortunately, they hadn't mentioned that the woman played Christian to her husband's lion.

Alex occasionally told her tales of his own boyhood in New Orleans and more often of his military adventures in Texas. He must have volunteered for every armed encounter since he arrived in 1832, which was surely more than patriotism demanded of a man. Now that he was married, no doubt he would be slower to put his life in danger. She didn't think she could stand it if he were killed. She glanced sideways at him, realizing suddenly that he hadn't offered to give up mustanging. Instead he was taking her back to a perilous occupation, exposing both of them to danger, although he owned part of a plantation east of here. That he never suggested they return to civilization was perhaps her own fault. The one thing on which they disagreed consistently was slavery. Cassandra called it a moral outrage; Alex countered that it was an institution without which the cotton economy could not flourish.

"Cotton planters can hire hands just like other farmers," Cassandra insisted.

"Oh yes," said Alex, "that works out wonderfully. A man in Louisiana tried it. When picking time came around, his hired workers went out on strike, demanding twice the wage. He couldn't pay it and lost his whole crop, plus what he'd put into growing it. Hired labor ruined him."

"Slavery is still immoral," Cassandra persisted, "and that's why the United States Senate turned down the annexation treaty." They had received the news of the Senate's rejection during their stay at Webber's. "Samuel Adams said the Texas Revolution was fought solely to reestablish slavery where Mexico had abolished it."

"Mexico may have laws against slavery, but the government never made any trouble about it," Alex said. "The Mexicans wanted to attract rich settlers and benefit from the prosperity cotton brought with it."

"Well, the Republic of Texas will never become part

of the Union," predicted Cassandra, "not while it's dedicated to the spread of slavery."

"What spread?" snapped Alex. "Slavery's gone as far as it can go. There's not enough rainfall to grow cotton any further west, and we don't allow slave trading, so there'll be no *spread* for the self-righteous, holier-than-thou abolitionists to complain about."

The argument ended with the two of them glaring at one another and a long, uneasy silence. Then Alex relented and changed the subject. "What kinds of things did you study at this school of your mother's?"

Relieved at the dissipation of his anger, Cassandra replied, "Latin, Greek, rhetoric—"

"What about cooking and piano playing? I thought girls' schools taught all those womanly arts."

Cassandra glanced at him warily. Did he think her unfeminine? Probably his sister played and sang, embroidered beautifully, and danced with the grace of Terpsichore. "I can play the piano," she said, trying to smile and seem lighthearted, "in case you plan to take me where there is one."

His face closed. Alex never told her about life on the plantation. Did he still think she had married him because she wanted to establish herself as a lady of the manor?

"We'll camp here," he said brusquely. It was the third night out, and the grove he had chosen with its spring and tree-shaded clearing was familiar. Her memory of the trip north told her that tomorrow they'd rejoin the mustangers.

They made camp, put a pot of beans on to simmer over the fire, and then Alex stripped off his shirt beside the spring. The pool was not deep enough for a bath, so Cassandra took a rag from her pack and dipped it to wipe the dust from her face. Then she unlaced her shirt and patted cool water over her neck and chest.

"Are you still bleeding?" Alex asked.

She froze, her hand holding the damp cloth at the

back of her neck. Cassandra was tempted to lie, although she knew how worried he'd been about her. Tomorrow they'd be back with the others. Given the lack of privacy, he wouldn't bother her there, so if he thought for one more night that she couldn't—but the bleeding *had* stopped that morning, she reminded herself, and she had *wanted* to marry him. No one forced her. Therefore, her fear was no excuse to deny him his proper rights as a husband. Then she remembered their wedding. Were they truly married? she asked herself. If she didn't please him, he could leave her; she had no legal claim on him. And if she tried to back out on her wifely duties, he would certainly leave her. Besides that, she *wanted* to please him. She loved him!

"Cassandra?"

"I've stopped," she said.

"You're terrified, aren't you?" he asked gently. "Poor Cassie." He enfolded her in his arms. "I'm sorry it was so bad the first time. Sometimes, I reckon, that can't be helped, but it will get better." He'd make sure of it. He had pleased a lot of ladies in his day; he'd damn well manage to please his own wife as well.

However, all his good intentions weren't enough. Cassandra was as tense as a drawn bow. At least, the first time she'd been ardent up to a point, the point where he'd started to hurt her. Lord, he'd never heard of a woman bleeding for three days over the loss of her virginity! You'd think he'd raped her, whereas he'd done all he could to treat her gently and prepare her, and had succeeded so well that she was quivering under his touch when he came to her.

Now she was so frightened that he couldn't arouse her at all, while he, after all the foreplay, got beyond the point where he could have stopped if he'd wanted to. He took her, but she was submissive, not ardent.

Afterward, he asked sympathetically, "Are you all right, Cassandra?"

She bobbed her head but avoided his eyes. Alex sup-

Elizabeth Chadwick

posed she must be. She might have experienced some
discomfort once he was inside her, but at least she
wasn't bleeding again. On the other hand, she wasn't
ecstatic. He felt like cursing, but that would hardly
reassure the frightened girl lying in his arms, fighting
back tears. Hell! Was this some sort of payback for a
misspent youth? "Reckon the beans are ready," he
muttered.

Cassandra put her clothes on and went to dish up
the meal. She knew she'd disappointed him but didn't
know what she was supposed to have done. She hadn't
tried to stop him—or cried. She hadn't even bled this
time. What did he want? He, at least, seemed to have
enjoyed it. Blinking away confused tears, she turned
to hand him his plate.

Alex's return with Cassandra elicited a mixed reception. "Married?" Nicodemus exploded. "You oughter be ashamed a yerself, Alex. Yer gonna git her
killed."

Alex's expression when he heard this accusation became almost as black as the mountain man's, and
Cassandra wished that Nicodemus had kept his opinions to himself. If Alex were made to feel guilty, he
might send her away.

Aureliano, however, beamed at them, wishing them
great happiness and many children. Children? That
would be a mistake as long as they were out here
mustanging, thought Cassandra anxiously. No, she
mustn't—

"But Nico's right about the danger," Aureliano continued. "You must send her to Devil's Wood, eh?"

At the mention of his sister's home, Alex's mouth
tightened grimly. "Cassandra stays here," he snapped.

She went limp with relief. She didn't want to be
shipped off to some dreadful place where hapless Negroes labored in chains and were cruelly treated, per-

haps even whipped. She had read the abolitionist
pamphlets about the horrors of slavery.

"Who married you?" asked Pinto suspiciously.

Cassandra's heart began to race. Alex might take
their *agreeable* marriage for granted, but she found it
a source of embarrassment and insecurity. She didn't
want these men to know that the bond was casual
rather than legal.

"We're married," Alex replied coldly. "What business is it of yours how we managed it?"

"It's my business 'cause it ain't fair," said Pinto.
"Ain't fair, you havin' a woman all to yourself. This
is supposed to be a share-an'-share-alike company."

"Shut up," snapped Alex. Sullenly Pinto did.

Then, when Cassandra was on the verge of tears over
the inhospitable reaction her return had provoked,
Bone thrust a bedraggled bunch of wildflowers into
her hand. "Bride's supposed to have flowers," he muttered in his rusty voice.

The tears did spring to Cassandra's eyes, and she
stretched up on tiptoes to kiss the tracker's cheek.
Bone's weathered face flushed, and Alex muttered,
"Glad someone thought to treat her kindly." He shot
a cold glance at the other three. "Poor girl didn't even
have flowers on her wedding day. I didn't think of it,"
he admitted.

Cassandra gave him a misty-eyed smile and said, "I
had Bluebonnet. Have you forgotten?"

Alex chuckled, and Cassandra, with the drooping
little bouquet in her hand and her husband's smile
warming her, thought she had never been happier.

"Ain't ya gonna kiss me?" Pinto asked.

"No," said Cassandra before Alex could take offense,
and she slipped into the protective circle of his arm.
No one was going to send *her* home! she promised
herself.

Chapter Seven

"We can't. Not here," Cassandra whispered one cool September night when Alex touched her breast under the blankets.

She heard his teeth click together in exasperation, but the caressing fingers withdrew. Instead of pulling her into his arms, as he did some nights, he turned away and fell quickly into sleep, leaving Cassandra torn with guilt and resentment. She loved to sleep curled in his arms—as long as she managed to roll away by morning when the others might see. What was she supposed to have said? she asked his back. Why did discretion have to be *her* responsibility?

Am I using discretion as an excuse to evade him? she asked herself. She slept badly that night, and they were both short-tempered in the morning.

Pinto, Aureliano, and Bone, under Nicodemus' leadership, had gathered and gentled a number of mustangs while Alex and Cassandra were away. Upon their return, it was agreed that the group would drift south, capturing as many additional horses as they could to sell in San Antonio. Because the mustangs they came upon were well fed and hard to catch, the group again resorted to running them in circles.

Alex and Cassandra took a shift together in early October when the herd had been moving for two days. As soon as the horses slowed, the riders had only to approach and they were off again, nervous of the slightest intrusion into their territory. Alex had just done this, then nodded his head toward an island of trees nearby. Obediently Cassandra followed him to the stream that meandered through. She was thirsty and glad of the brief respite.

"About time we're alone," he said quietly.

She glanced at him in surprise. "But—but the herd—"

"They'll run awhile on their own," he replied, "but I'm not going to last much longer. This has got to be the damnedest honeymoon a man ever had."

Cassandra's cheeks turned pink.

"Just to speed things up, why don't you take off your clothes while I take care of mine," he suggested.

Reluctantly she removed her moccasins. Then she pulled the tails of a white shirt from a black pair of pants given her by Aureliano as a wedding present. Each had been part of his going-to-town wardrobe, and she appreciated his generosity. No clothes belonging to any of the others would have fit her, except perhaps Pinto's, but the thought of wearing anything of his made Cassandra shiver with distaste.

Aureliano's shirt was full through the body and the sleeves and fit her well enough. The pants she considered embarrassingly tight, but her buckskins were tattered and wouldn't last the trip if she wore them daily. Glancing nervously at her husband, she wiggled out of the trousers. They were too snug to accommodate her ragged underwear, the last remnants of her Cambridge wardrobe, so she was bare once she removed the pants.

"Now, come over here." said Alex softly. He'd thrown a saddle blanket on the yellowing grass. When once he had her beside him, he smoothed a large palm over her shining hair and murmured, "I wish we had the time to unbraid it. I'd like to make love with your hair falling all around us." He cupped his hand over the back of her neck and drew her body against his while he ran the other hand slowly from her shoulder,

111

down her side, fingertips brushing her right breast; then over the curve of her waist, long fingers stroking her stomach; and on until he flattened the palm against the tender curve of her bottom. Cassandra shuddered as futile passion flared in her thighs.

Alex's mouth came down, soft and encompassing, slowly—as if they had all the time in the world. In seconds they lay stretched against each other. "We fit," he murmured, rubbing his hand in circles where her waist curved into her buttocks. He slid one finger into the cleft and stroked.

Cassandra felt hot and dazed. His lovemaking seemed different, slower and more provocative—even though time was not something they could afford to waste. Out there beyond the trees, those wild horses, with memories only as long as the next clump of grass, would be slowing, maybe pausing to rest and graze and, in doing so, negating two days of hard riding. "Alex?"

"Hm-m-m?" He traced the convolutions of her ear with his tongue, and she shivered.

"The h-horses," she stammered.

"They'll be there when we get back," he murmured and slid his fingers delicately between her legs.

Cassandra groaned, the horses quickly forgotten as he stroked her and built an unbearable ache, a clutching desire for something she had never had. When his finger slid inside her, she cried out, and her fingernails dug into the muscles of his upper arms.

"Now," he murmured, his voice warm with satisfaction. Then he took his fingers away and slipped between her legs, entering her quickly and rocking up easily into her body as he held her hips in position to receive him.

For a moment Cassandra stayed with him, but then the aching excitement seeped away, leaving her close to tears. Alex, she knew, was now too caught up in his own flight to realize, and even if he did—well, what could she say to him? Maybe what she'd had was all there was for women; the loving this time had been both better and worse. He'd brought her more pleasure but great frustration as well. Minutes later, his breathing slowed, and she edged away. "There's someone coming," she whispered.

Alex opened his eyes, and his glance sharpened as he listened. "Damn," he muttered and rose to his feet in one lithe motion, reaching down to pull her up after him. He swept up her clothes and handed them to her before she'd hardly caught her balance, and they both dressed hastily, for they could now hear the sound of hoofbeats.

"What the hell happened?" Nicodemus demanded as he pulled his horse up beside the stream.

"We just stopped for a drink," said Alex calmly.

"The hell you did. Them horses is out there eatin' their heads off."

"*Buenos días,*" Aureliano called as he too pulled up.

Cassandra wondered how many others would arrive before she managed to get her shirttail tucked in.

"Two days we run them horses, an' you two let 'em come to a dead halt so's you can dally in the grass."

"Ah, Nico," said Aureliano reprovingly, "they are newlyweds."

"That's right; they're married. They got the rest a their lives fer sportin', but here an' now, winter's comin' on. We gotta catch horses while—"

"Winter?" Alex laughed. "It's only October yet. We've got a month or two before—"

"Before I decide I ain't gonna have my hard work thrown away by a man who can't keep his pants on. I tole ya—"

"All right, Nico," Alex interrupted. "Leave it. It won't happen again."

They rode out to restart the herd, Alex and Cassandra staying past their shift to help, and on the third day they were able to take twenty horses, not all of which could be tamed enough to join the herd that would be taken to market. That was always the way of it, thought Cassandra wearily as she dropped onto her blankets after another long day.

"Where do you think the slavers came from?" Alex demanded. "The North, that's where, and half the time they bought the Nigrahs off African kings who got rich selling their own people or their next-door neighbors."

"Even if that's so," said Cassandra haughtily, "it doesn't excuse profiting from the sweat of another's bondage. If there weren't a market for slaves—and Southerners provide the market—"

"By God, Cassandra, you are the most irritating woman," snapped Alex. "I ought to dump you at the first trading post we come to."

Cassandra, who worried constantly that he would do just that, burst into tears, cutting off his harangue.

"Sweetheart," he mumbled, taken aback by her tears, "there's no reason to cry. It's just an argument." She continued to weep. "This isn't about slavery, is it?"

She didn't answer yes or no, for she was unwilling to admit her fear that he wouldn't, in the end, honor their irregular marriage.

"Cassandra, I want to know why you're crying."

She shook her head, trying to stem the flood of frightened tears.

"Is it because I said I ought to leave you at some trading post? You know I didn't mean that."

"No?" she asked, overcome with the bitterness of her position. "Why wouldn't you? We're not really married. If I say something you don't like, you're perfectly free to—"

"Cassandra, I love you. I wouldn't do that."

* * *

Under the rough blankets, Cassandra shivered. It was November and cold winds had begun to blow down across the plains from the north. "Are you cold?" Alex murmured.

"Yes." She was cold and dejected as a result of their argument earlier in the evening.

"Come here and cuddle," he offered, drawing her closer. She went willingly, and Alex fumbled with the thong that fastened her trousers, then slipped them over her hips.

"What are you—"

"Sh-sh-sh," he whispered.

She could hear the amusement underlying his voice as he ducked under the blankets to divest her of the buckskins.

Good grief, she thought, her depression fleeing as goose bumps rose on her bare skin. "Alex, we can't—"

"We're not going to do much," he whispered into her ear. "Just stay still and be quiet."

Stay still? A few more wiggles and Alex was naked against her, naked and aroused. Cassandra's face burned in the darkness. Was he doing this to embarrass her because she'd argued with him?

"No one's going to notice a thing," he whispered as he slipped his manhood between her thighs and then pressed upwards before beginning just the slightest rocking. A quivering started up inside her, and it felt wonderful. She wanted the feeling to grow and grow until her whole body dissolved, and yet she also wanted it to stay the same, exactly the same because it was so delicious.

"You're getting warm and wet," he murmured.

She trembled, wanting to turn on her back and yet afraid because if she did, that would be the end of it for her. And besides, the others might know what was happening.

He lifted her thigh onto his. The tiny motion became a little longer, touching more of her, more delicious, and she contracted around him as he slid into her. However, for her, that was the end. She could have cried, but she held back the tears because she loved him so.

"Are they Comanches?" asked Cassandra, terrified.

Alex, who had dismounted when they got to the top of the hill, stared at the approaching party. "Not likely," he replied. "You ever seen a Comanche dressed in black?"

"It's a priest," cried Aureliano. "We must go to meet him. I can make my confession."

"Wha'da *you* got to confess?" asked Pinto. "None of us been able to do nuthin' 'cept Alex, who *says* he's married."

Because Cassandra looked distraught, Alex didn't snap at Pinto. Instead he stared thoughtfully at the priest. "Aureliano's right," he said. "We'd best go meet them."

"Pro'bly they're horse thieves," muttered Nicodemus.

Far from being thieves, the men bought ten horses. Three of the four were traders from Mexico who had come up to deal with the Indians. The fourth was, as Aureliano surmised, a priest. He had come to convert the Comanches, evidently against all advice, for the Spaniards had given up on that tribe as prospects for Christianity years ago, and their efforts to establish missions in Texas had always met with partial or complete failure—or so Alex murmured to Cassandra while Aureliano was talking to the priest. Cassandra wondered how long the man of God would survive if he actually found any Comanches. They'd probably take his Bible to stuff their shields and then scalp him.

After the horse trading was concluded and Aureliano had taken the priest aside to make his confession, Alex held a strained conversation with Father Annunziata, occasionally using Aureliano as a translator.

Whatever they were saying, it evidently delighted Aureliano but not the priest.

"He asks if you are Catholic," Aureliano said to Alex.

"Tell him I'm not," snapped Alex, becoming more irritated as the conversation progressed, "an' he damn well better do what I ask, regardless."

"Amigo," protested Aureliano, "I cannot threaten a priest."

"Well, I can," said Alex and pulled the man further aside for an intense conversation, after which he beckoned Cassandra over and announced, "We're getting married."

"Thought you already was," sneered Pinto.

"We are—according to Texas law—at least, for six months until we can find a county clerk."

Six months? That was the first Cassandra had heard about six months. She counted on her fingers. February. Would there be a county clerk in San Antonio?

"But it wasn't a religious ceremony, so Father Annunziata here will take care of that. All right, sweetheart?"

He looked so pleased with himself. She hadn't known he'd been worrying about her complaint that they weren't truly married.

"And one of the traders has a dress you can borrow."

She looked over at the brown-faced, beaming Mexican who, indeed, had pulled out a two-piece garment, bright with embroidery.

"I remember how you wanted a dress and Webber didn't have one except for Bluebonnet's," said Alex.

Cassandra wondered if the Mexican's dress had been on any Indians. Probably not, but that was, no doubt, what it was intended as—a trade item for some squaw. Her wedding dress was to have been paid for in horses or skins and worn by someone like Bluebonnet. Cassandra sighed and managed a smile for her husband. She appreciated the thought and so would accept the wedding, although the ceremony was in Latin. Her mother would be horrified to see a daughter of hers married in a papist rite.

"There," said Alex when it was over. "You've got the church part. Now all we have to do is find a county clerk." Then he frowned. "By God, we've got another problem."

Cassandra looked at him anxiously. It was bad enough being married in the wrong religion. Could this be considered a marriage blessed by the church when she didn't belong to Father Annunziata's church and he had, in fact, been threatened into performing the ceremony?

"You're only seventeen."

"I'll be eighteen in January," she said defensively.

"I think women have to be eighteen to marry without parental consent."

"I don't have any parents."

Alex scratched his head. "Well, whatever the law, I reckon we need to find that clerk and get it legalized."

Cassandra agreed, of course, but she was surprised at his sudden sense of urgency. He'd been perfectly happy with their *agreeable* marriage for three months now.

The Mexican traders pulled out bottles of hard spirits and passed them around in celebration of the wedding. At least *they* considered it legal, she thought wistfully, although it made her very nervous to see all the men drinking. Strong drink had never been served in her parents' home. She didn't know quite what to expect, and the worst of it was that Alex had joined in. Would they all get drunk and start singing scandalous songs as Mr. Webber and the horse trader had done after Cassandra's first wedding?

"Cassie," Alex said later in November, "do you have something to tell me?"

She couldn't think of anything special. Was he referring to her insistence yesterday that the bacon had spoiled. The stuff smelled bad enough to make your stomach heave. All the others, including Alex, had refused to throw it out, so if they got sick, it was on their own heads, she thought irritably. "I can't think of anything."

"Look at me," he commanded. "How long is it since you've had a monthly?"

Surprised and embarrassed, Cassandra mumbled, "I don't know." Just because he was her husband didn't mean she had to discuss private female things with him.

"Are you listening to me?" he demanded.

"Of course. I said I don't know."

"I don't think you've had one since August."

Cassandra shrugged. "It's probably all the horseback riding." But he was right. She hadn't bled since her wedding night and the following three days—Cassandra glared resentfully at him. It was obviously his fault.

"Don't you usually have a flow every month?"

"I suppose so. Well, sometimes I don't."

Alex sighed. "Has it occurred to you that you might be with child?"

Cassandra's eyes went round with surprise.

"I can see that it hasn't," said Alex dryly.

"But I don't want to," she cried. "You must be wrong."

"I doubt it. Why don't you want to?"

"Because you'll send me away." Her eyes filled with tears. "Because I'm not sure we're really married."

"I think we'd better get down and talk about this," he said gently.

"Nicodemus will be mad if we do. Don't you remember the last time?"

"The hell with Nicodemus!" he snapped. "Anyway, it's for a different reason." His eyes twinkled.

Cassandra didn't smile back. She couldn't be pregnant!

"Sweetheart, it's not a disaster. Wouldn't you like to have a baby of your own?"

"Where?" she demanded. "Where would I be when I had this baby? More important, where would you be?"

"All right, let's approach this sensibly. First, we *are* married. We'll take care of the legalities when we can. As for your staying out here, you have to admit, Cassie, that this isn't a very good place for a woman to be carrying a child. The riding, for one thing, is dangerous."

"If I'm really with child and I'd been going to lose it, I'd have done so," she muttered, beginning to believe that she might actually be pregnant and terrified of being separated from him. "If *I* have to leave, what about you?"

"I've promised to stay with the group till spring, but I should get back before the baby's born."

"And where will I be?" she demanded, tears flooding from under her lids.

"With my sister, I guess," he answered reluctantly.

"No! I won't live where there are slaves. I'll stay right here. Why do you want me to go away?"

"Cassie," said Alex patiently, "I don't want that. Even though our situation drives me crazy, I'll miss you."

"No, you won't, because I'm going to stay. I'm fine. Heavens, I didn't even know there was anything wrong—well, not wrong—but I didn't know. You can't send me away. Christmas is coming. Our first Christmas."

Her desire to stay was madness. Alex knew it, and yet he had the sinking feeling that she, not he, was going to prevail. He hated the idea of sending her to Eloise, who wouldn't welcome her. Maybe if he could keep her in camp instead of out riding in the cold wind, he'd compromise on Christmas, but after that she'd have to go. He'd take her to San Antonio with

120

the herd. From there he ought to be able to hire someone to see her to the Brazos. "Hush, now," he murmured, putting his arms around her. "There's nothing to cry about."

In December the weather turned colder. Nor were they finding many horses. When they had gone a week without adding an animal to the herd, it was agreed that the mustangs they had would be driven to San Antonio. Then, weather permitting, they would move north.

"Bound to be some in the cedar brakes," said Nicodemus. "If they sense a bad winter comin', they look fer shelter an' tree bark to eat when the grass gives out."

Alex agreed, glancing unhappily at his wife. He too sensed a bad winter coming and knew he should send Cassandra back to his sister. If he'd had his way, they'd have given up for the winter, but the others wanted to continue, and Alex had made a pact with them before he ever met Cassandra.

"Three of us will take the horses to San Antonio," he announced. "The rest of you can break camp and head north with the tepees. We'll buy supplies and catch up."

"I ain't headin' north," said Pinto. "It's my turn to go to town."

"Look, Pinto," said Alex reasonably, "Aureliano has to go because he's the best Spanish speaker, and Cassie and I have to go too."

"How come?" asked Nicodemus. "If you're plannin' on sendin' her back—"

"That's not it," Cassandra interrupted. "We're looking for a county clerk to formalize our marriage."

There was a stubborn glint in her eye that Alex recognized. She wanted that license before her child was born, Alex surmised, and as her waist had thickened, he assumed that he was going to be a father, possibly

Elizabeth Chadwick

as early as May—which meant he had to send her
back East.

"You already been married twice," said Pinto.
"How many times you wanna do it?"

"What do you care?" snapped Cassandra.

"I don't, an' I'm one as is goin' to San Antone 'cause
it's my turn. I don't care who else goes. If the Mex has
to, then you can go with *me* to git your license. Does
that mean us'll be married too?" He gave her a nasty
grin.

"I ain't arguin' that you shouldn't send her to yer
sister—" said Nicodemus.

"He's not," Cassandra interrupted. "I'm not going
anywhere but to San Antonio and straight back here."

"Cassie, you know you can't stay much longer," said
Alex gently.

"—but not from San Antone," Nicodemus pressed,
"not by herself. An' you cain't rightly go with her
'cause yer the feller who started this whole mustangin'
business. Likely you kin peel off further north an' send
her from Austin. Be a lot safer—"

"What about the license?" Cassandra demanded.

Nicodemus ignored her. "Be a lot safer to send the
girl from Austin where you kin doubtless find some
English-speakin' feller, maybe even a woman to escort
her."

"Austin it is," Alex agreed, thinking that he'd have
a few more months with her.

"What about the license?" she whispered.

When they were in their blankets that night, Cassandra, having nursed her anger all day, said resentfully, "You don't *want* to marry me legally. That's why
you wouldn't go to San Antonio."

Alex chuckled and pulled her into his arms. Then
he whispered, "If I'd taken you to San Antone, I'd have
had to send you on to Devil's Wood. This way we can
stay together a couple more months, and I'll have you

122

practically all to myself while they're gone." He ran his tongue delicately over her lips, almost driving the complaints from her mind.

"Can we get a—a license—stop that, Alex!" He had nipped her earlobe, sending shivers down her neck and arm.

"In Austin? Sure, we can," he assured her.

"I'm not going anywhere from Austin," she warned.

Alex sighed. When the time came, she'd have to go. In the meantime—well, he'd make the most of it.

Alex didn't gain the privacy he'd hoped for when three of the group went south to San Antonio. The December weather turned so cold that they were forced to dig a fire pit in the biggest tepee and sleep inside with Bone. Cassandra lost track of the days as they struggled north facing a freezing wind. How could they celebrate Christmas if they didn't know what day it was? she wondered as she huddled in her saddle, wrapped in a Comanche buffalo robe that Alex had bought from the Mexican traders.

How ironic. She'd refused to wear Comanche clothing at the trading post. Now she didn't care who had worn this robe as long as they didn't want to take it back. Alex, constantly worrying about her, kept making noises about sending her to the frightening Eloise as soon as possible. Shivering, she put that problem from her mind. She'd deal with it when and if they got to Austin. Maybe by then she could talk him into going with her. Surely the mustangers would soon give up for this season. Even Bone, who seemed to notice neither weather nor any other hardship, was not riding as far afield looking for mustang tracks. Probably because there were none. If she were a horse, thought Cassandra, she'd have gone south to Mexico, not north to the cedar brakes.

One morning when they were beginning to look for the return of the others, Bone poked his beaky brown nose from the tepee flap to assess the weather, then advised Alex and Cassandra to spend the day inside. "Bad cold," he explained. "Too much for Cassie."

Cassandra hadn't the energy to protest. She'd already proved to anyone who was interested that she was a hard worker. The freezing air creeping in around the briefly opened door flap convinced her that the weather might indeed be "too much for Cassie." Nor did she argue with Bone's contention that she shouldn't be left alone.

"What about you, Bone?" asked Alex. Cassandra could see from the hot gleam in his eye what he had in mind if they were left alone in the tepee. Well, fine. As long as she got to stay under the blankets and buffalo robes, he could do what he liked.

Bone looked surprised at Alex's question. "Cold don't bother me," he replied. Within minutes he had gone.

Alex smiled at her and muttered, "Alone at last. Get under the covers."

"Shouldn't we wait till we can't hear his horse's hooves any longer?" she asked dryly.

"Hell, I've waited for days," he replied. "The cold snap hit before the others had hardly disappeared over the next rise. If we don't hurry, like as not warm weather will blow through, and Bone'll be back to drag us out."

"I can't imagine why," said Cassandra, scuttling under the blankets. "There's not a wild mustang within a hundred miles." If he were truly in a hurry, she thought, he wouldn't take so much time beforehand. As a result, she wouldn't feel so much frustration at the end.

"Keeping you here is pure selfishness on my part," he muttered, "but I'm glad I've got you."

Pleased and touched, she wiggled obligingly out of her buckskins. She hoped the others would remember to purchase clothing for her in San Antonio. Alex, now naked as well, had begun to stroke the edges of her breasts, which were somewhat swollen and more sensitive than they had ever been.

The last time, Nicodemus had forgotten to bring any clothes for her. She moved restlessly as Alex stroked nearer and nearer but never touched her nipples, which tingled in anticipation. Staring into the dark, smokey upper reaches of their tepee, she worried because she was fast reaching a wardrobe crisis. She could no longer wear Aureliano's clothes, and the loose buckskins were becoming tight and, worse, embarrassingly tattered.

He touched the hard tip of her breast at last, and she could no longer ignore what he was doing to her; her whole body jerked. Before she could think about how much she had wanted that touch, his mouth closed over her nipple, and the suckling pull of his lips sent a hot tide of hunger through her. This was going to be bad, she thought grimly. He had obviously been teasing when he spoke of having to hurry. He was definitely taking his time. Before he finished, she expected she might be on the verge of tears, yearning for that mysterious culmination that never seemed to come.

He moved his mouth to the other breast while he brushed his thumb over the tip of the first. She was burning and knew that soon his hand would move to her stomach, then her thighs, rousing her inner fire to an unbearable pitch. She waited, trying to think of something else so that she would not be so disappointed in the end, but he continued to toy with her breasts until she yearned to tell him what to do next—even if it made her miserable. At least for a few minutes she'd have that pleasurable pain of which she never got enough. But of course, she'd never say anything. She'd be a fool to invite the ending she expected. He was rubbing his tongue against her breasts and it was so rough and exciting she thought she'd scream if he didn't touch her else-where. To her horror, she gasped, "Alex," a clear note of pleading in her voice.

"Hm-m-m?" He transferred his tongue to the other breast.

Cassandra arched helplessly. She *wanted* to be touched. His hand was still on one breast, unmoving, but his lips suddenly drew sharply on the other, send-ing a shaft of longing into her body. She turned her hips yearningly toward him, but he didn't shift so that she could press against him. Cassandra had never felt frustration so sharp. What was he *doing*? she won-dered desperately. This seemed deliberate torture on his part. The deep suckling came again, and without thought, she gasped, "Touch me."

He went still. "Where?" he asked, his voice husky.

"Oh, please." She'd welcome him if only—

"Show me." He took the hand from her breast and covered her clenched fist with it. "Put my hand where you want to be touched." He straightened her curled fingers, and trembling, flushed with embarrassment, she guided his hand down her body.

"Ah, here," said Alex softly as his fingers slid into the silky, golden curls.

Cassandra shuddered as he began to stroke her. She was no longer thinking, only anticipating mindlessly as the tightening ache quivered and strengthened in-side her and her inner heat turned liquid. His palm was against her, and she arched her body, seeking, seeking in the tightening spiral of her desire, the re-lease that came to her, finally, in star showers of color exploding in her body, flashes of flame and ice along her skin. Then as she coasted down the farther side of her release, pulses easing so that she became aware of the hard, slow beat of her heart, Alex slid into her. She wrapped her arms around him and held him in close, grateful embrace as he followed her over the top.

When later they lay curled together under the robes, he bent to press a kiss on her mouth and smiled with warm pleasure. "We're getting there, sweetheart," he murmured.

Still dazed with surprised pleasure, Cassandra wondered where else there was to go.

His arms tightened, and he pulled her over on top of him. "Do you know how much I love you?" he asked.

If it was half as much as she loved him, she thought dreamily, the two of them together encompassed all the love in the world.

"Merry Christmas, sweetheart."

Cassandra peeked from beneath the edge of her buffalo robe at the cloud his warm breath made in the cold air. She hadn't known it was Christmas, but even without presents and plum pudding, it was the happiest Christmas she had ever known.

Chapter Eight

Again they'd returned without clothes for her. She couldn't believe it.

"What do I know about gittin' women's clothes?" Nicodemus muttered.

"I don't wear women's clothes," she retorted.

"Well, yer not gonna be here that much longer."

That's what you think, she said, but silently. She would refuse to go to Austin unless Alex agreed to continue on with her. She didn't care what any of them wanted. She wasn't leaving Alex, for whom her love grew every day.

"Like as not you kin git somethin' in town," Nicodemus added.

Cassandra shot him a vengeful glance. When her buckskins fell apart under her buffalo robe, she'd requisition Nicodemus's clothes. All too soon she'd be big enough to wear them.

The prairie fire seemed to have sprung up out of nowhere. Behind them the horizon was a wall of flames, the sky blackened with smoke. She had only looked once, but it burned in her mind's eye, that fire, hungry and terrifying. She could hear the roar of it, and underneath her horse's hooves the yellow winter grass, luring the avid flames on, waited to be consumed.

She kicked her horse again, although she knew the poor creature had no last burst of speed in reserve. As

terrified as she, her mare was running full out. All
their mounts were running full out, Alex ahead and
to her left, Nicodemus beyond him and further ahead,
the others to her right, fleeing for their lives. She didn't
want to look back. If the fire was gaining, she didn't
want to know.

Then, from the corner of her eye, she saw it happen.
Alex's gelding went down, pitching him into the grass.
Without thinking, she sawed on the left rein, dragging
the reluctant mare's head in his direction. Alex rose;
his horse didn't. Oh God! She had to get to him. The
fire no longer filled her mind. Only Alex. She pulled
harder on the rein, judging the distance, veering left.

She had seen the Comanches pick up a man afoot
while riding full speed. Would Alex know what to do
when she reached her hand to him? He was waving
her ahead, willing to give up his chance at life to save
her. She continued left. Could he mount behind her?
Or would they both end up in the grass? It didn't
matter. She wasn't willing to leave him behind. She
began to pull back on the reins, but could sense no
slowing in the mare's speed. Heading to his left, she
leaned out, her hand outstretched to him, and then he
was behind her, shouting into her ear, "Jesus, Cass, a
Comanche couldn't have done that better."

They'd done it! her mind echoed, dazed and triumphant. But the mare, double-burdened, had slowed.
Oh God! Were they going to die anyway? Alex had
taken the reins, one arm tight around her waist. He
was pulling the horse further left instead of straight
away from the fire. The others had far outdistanced
them, possibly unaware of what had happened. Alex
was heading for the trees. Why? She could feel the
heat at her back, and trees would burn.

"Pray there's water," he shouted into her ear above
the roar of the pursuing flames.

Water? She prayed, not knowing exactly why. Then
they were among the few poor trees, Alex yanking the

mare's head sharply so that they all three spilled into the shallow creek. He pushed her roughly into the water, soaking her and himself in the icy liquid while above them the tree branches exploded into flame. Alex pushed her head under. When she came up sputtering, the fire had leapt across the creek and burned on ahead of them. The trees, spindly torches, encircled them in a residue of flame. Alex pulled her against his chest and kissed her as if they'd never kissed before.

"My God, Cassie," he muttered, "I can't believe how brave you are. You could have died trying that trick. If the creek hadn't been full, we would both have—"

"I wasn't brave," she interrupted humbly. "I was terrified."

"Sweetheart, that's what courage is, doing something that scares you to death."

She shook her head. *That's what love is*, she thought.

But later, when the others had come back over the blackened prairie, she thought, *Maybe I am brave. I saved Alex and tried to save Papa. It must be love that gives you courage.* Then she wondered whether being hauled off a horse into a creek was bad for her baby. Evidently not. Nothing happened.

"Stay in bed," Alex murmured into her ear one January morning. "It's too cold for you today."

Good! she thought sleepily as she snuggled back into her warm nest of blankets. If it was that cold, maybe they'd all give up mustanging. Then she and Alex could return to civilization, preferably not the sector inhabited by his sister Eloise and her husband—what was his name?

"Aureliano's going to stay with you. He's got work to do around camp."

Cassandra mumbled a protest. She wanted Alex to stay.

"It looks like snow, so we'll probably be back early."

Later she heard noise outside the tepee and went to

peek out. Aureliano waved to her from the campfire where he was doing something or other; she didn't know what and was too drowsy to ask. Lately she had been so tired. She stared off to the east where gray-white clouds draped in heavy pouches of mist over the hills. A touch of wintery light made them glow like cold fire. Snow was coming, just as Alex had predicted. She shivered and let the skin door drop into place, glad to go back to her warm bed.

Still later she thought she heard a shout and stirred restlessly. Had Alex and the others returned so early? She brushed rumpled blonde hair back from her face and glanced around the dim interior of the tent. Maybe it was afternoon, and she had slept all day. Or maybe the sound had been in a dream. She rubbed her eyes. There. She heard something again. Muffled, but definitely a sound.

Poor Aureliano, still working while she lazed in bed. She thrust back the covers, strapped her knife around her waist, and pulled on her winter moccasins so she could go out. She'd had no breakfast and was hungry, she realized as she padded to the door to ask Aureliano what time it was.

She raised the flap and froze, terrified at the sight of buckskin-clad men, hair braided, Indian weapons in their hands, poking about the camp. The crumpled heap on the far side of the fire, red blood pooling out around him, must be Aureliano. She threw herself back into the tepee, grasping her rifle, hoping they hadn't seen her. She would cut her way out the back, she thought, panic-stricken. The knife. Where was—

A brave sprang through the door and, before she could raise the rifle, knocked it from her hands. Cassandra jumped aside, whipping her knife from its sheath and slashing at him, memories of the squat warrior who had killed her father flashing in her mind. Then she threw herself toward the flap, never thinking that there were others outside, wanting only to get away from the one who threatened her in this confined space. She had to get away. Had to find Alex.

She stumbled through the door with the Indian yelling behind her. Outside they awaited her with raised weapons. Sobbing, Cassandra looked wildly for an avenue of escape. Instead, something cracked down onto the side of her head, and she fell—down into long darkness, Alex's name echoing into the endless tunnel where gray faded into black and red pain eased into colorless silence.

Book II
The
Comanches

January 1845 to
August 1845

Chapter Nine

Oh God, he thought, *I should have sent her home*. All around them lay the wreckage of the camp, at his feet the bloodstained body of Aureliano. At least Cassie was alive; he had to believe that. "We'll start after them as soon as we've buried him."

"Not me," said Pinto. "I ain't goin'."

Alex turned contemptuous eyes on the boy. "They took the horses too. You don't go, you don't get your share."

"I din sign on for Comanche fightin'," said Pinto, "an' I ain't losin' my scalp to git back yer woman."

Alex shrugged. He didn't need Pinto.

"I won't be goin' neither," said Nicodemus.

At that refusal Alex went cold with shock. He'd counted on Nicodemus. "You helped save her life, Nico. You can't just—"

"Her life as a white woman's over," said Nicodemus. "If she's still alive, an' that's no sure thing, she's been raped. 'Sides that, they're long gone, ridin' hard, splittin' up so's we won't know what trail to foller."

"Bone can—"

"But say we do catch up with them," Nicodemus continued with relentless determination. "She'll be someone's squaw by then if she ain't dead. An' after all that, if we live through gittin' her back, you ain't gonna want her."

"The hell I won't," Alex exclaimed.

"Right now you think you will 'cause you're et up

135

with guilt, knowin' you shoulda sent her home. But if you git her back, you're gonna feel sick ever' time you look at her. You'll break her heart, you an' ever'one else who hears what happened. I seen how folks treat women what's been got back. They're better off dead or left where they be."

Bitterly Alex turned his back on Nicodemus. He knew that the odds of rescuing Cassandra were long, but he had to try, and Nico was wrong about the rest. No matter what happened, Alex would want her. Dear God! How could he let them take her? She was terrified of Comanches.

"We'll find her," said Bone. "Tomorrow we'll go."

Alex turned to him with relief. Bone was the best tracker of them all. "Tonight," Alex insisted.

"Sun's setting. We go off on a false trail, we'll never find her. Bury Aureliano tonight, start tomorrow."

Alex looked down at the body of his friend's son and prayed that Cassie hadn't suffered the same fate.

Cassandra awoke to the jolting gait of a fast horse. *Shouldn't be riding like this,* she thought fuzzily. *Bad for the baby.* Her cheek was pressed against his back, yet Alex was always warning her not to ride hard. Then she realized that her hands were tied around his waist. Through the blinding pain behind her eyes, she tried to make some sense of the situation. Oh God! This wasn't Alex—not his saddle, not his smell, not his back.

Aureliano was dead, and she—*Don't panic!* she told herself. Alex hadn't been there when it happened. That meant he was alive. He would come after her. She felt faint and nauseated with pain and fright. *Mustn't panic. Mustn't throw up!* If she threw up, the Indian—well, it didn't bear thinking on, what he'd do if she threw up on him. Cassandra felt like giggling hysterically. She opened her eyes a little, and the light sent another wave of pain crashing through her head. As she went under, she heard the Indian shouting. In Comanche. Confirming her worst fears.

When she next regained consciousness, they were still riding. How long? she wondered. If they didn't stop soon, she'd lose the baby. Was this a punishment because she'd refused when Alex wanted her to leave. She opened her eyes just a slit, remembering how much the light had hurt before, but now the sun had set. Might as well sleep. She'd need all the strength she could muster—to keep herself and her child alive until Alex found them.

The change in gait and light woke her. Sunrise. She had vague recollections of being jerked roughly from one horse and flung onto another, always tied behind a rider. And every bone and muscle ached. Head better. Body worse. They were cutting her loose. When her feet touched the ground, her legs were numb, and she stumbled into a man who had already dismounted. Dazed, she looked into his face and saw the cut, which she had given him in the tepee back at camp, and the fury, doubled in effect by the red light of the rising sun on his face. Her heart stopped as he grabbed her upper arm in a cruel grip, raising a knife in his other hand.

From behind her a voice, amused, low, and speaking in Comanche, said, "Are you going to count coup on my prisoner, nephew?" The young brave who bore the mark of her knife flushed and backed away. When he took his hand from her arm, she would have fallen, but another hand caught her braid from behind and held her upright, bringing tears to her eyes as the sharp pain wrenched her scalp.

"Turn, woman. Let's look at you."

The pain eased, and Cassandra, still wobbling, turned and looked up into the face of the horseman behind whom she'd ridden at least the last leg of this nightmare journey. He resembled Alex, she thought, confused. And he'd spoken to her in English. Had she been rescued? Then, before the impulse to launch herself into his arms could take hold, she saw the blue eyes, and her confusion doubled. Alex had dark eyes. "What is your name?" she whispered.

"In your language my name is Counts Many Coup," he replied.

The phrase meant he was a brave man or a successful killer, something like that. She shivered at the thought and rubbed her wrists where the rawhide had chafed them.

"Drink while you can," he advised, tilting his head toward the trees. Cassandra nodded and stumbled in that direction, the brave who had wanted to kill her following. There'd be no chance to escape—not here. She knelt, shivering, by a small creek. Away from the warmth of the blue-eyed warrior's body, she was freezing, her buffalo robe left behind and only her tattered buckskins to protect her against the icy January air. Bracing herself, she leaned forward to drink. He'd said *while you can*. Did he mean they weren't stopping to sleep? And surely they meant to feed her; her stomach ached with hunger.

The brave was still watching sullenly, and she had to urinate. If she didn't soon, she'd shame herself. She tried to wave him away, but when she searched out a concealing bush, he stepped after her. Grimly she turned her back and squatted behind the covering branches, telling herself that if this was the worst thing that happened to her, she'd be lucky. And Alex would be here soon. He and the others must be close behind by now. Perhaps they were just hanging back, waiting for a chance to attack.

Almost before she had her clothes in place, the brave grabbed her arm and dragged her back. She went obediently, hoping there would be something to eat. Instead she found them conducting a ceremony,

Bride Fire

smoking and offering prayers. She concentrated. Prayers to the Great Spirit and the Earth Mother. The brave pushed her down outside the circle, and she huddled there, shivering. Obviously no one was going to offer her any protection against the cold. What was Counts Many Coup doing now? He had put away his pipe and taken out a knife. Oh Lord, he wasn't going to kill her, was he?

Then the bile rose in her throat when she saw the purpose of the knife. He was scraping—oh God—it was Aureliano's scalp. He was cleaning the flesh from the back. Cassandra closed her eyes and fought off dizziness. If she fainted, they'd probably laugh. They'd hold her in contempt. She had to be brave. Aureliano was dead; he wouldn't care what they did with his hair. When she looked again, Counts Many Coup was lashing the ends of a willow twig into a circle. Cassandra shuddered as he began to sew the cleaned scalp to the willow loop using sinew thread. Cassandra had seen Comanche women making clothes with it.

They were saying among themselves that he had been brave—Aureliano. And he had been—brave and gallant and handsome. If she'd gone to east Texas, would he still be alive? Cassandra blinked away tears. How would she ever be able to stand riding behind the man who had killed him? Maybe she should ask to ride by herself. Would they let her? It was hard to think when she was so cold, hungry, and scared. And being scared wouldn't help. She had to stay alive! Just stay alive until Alex came!

If she had a horse to ride, there was a chance of escaping, but where would she go? An escape might make it harder for Alex to find her. He wouldn't know who was on the horse that took off on its own. Members of the original party had been peeling off in smaller groups at each halt. And she could freeze to death if she escaped. At least while she rode behind Counts Many Coup, his body warmth transferred to her. And her weight slowed his horse down, giving Alex a better chance of catching up.

They were rising. The blue-eyed warrior came over to her and placed his hand against her stomach. She jumped back in fear, but he only asked, "You are with child?"

The Comanches valued children. She knew that. They adopted white children into their tribe. Swallowing hard, she nodded. Maybe being pregnant would help.

"We have miles to go. If you slow us, you'll die."

Cassandra nodded. So much for special consideration of expectant mothers. Mounted now, he held a hand to her. She took it and, using his foot to brace herself, swung up behind him, obediently crossing her wrists so that he could lash them together. His warmth was a blessing no matter whom he'd killed. She closed her eyes, preparing to doze and escape the aching of her body and the pangs of hunger. She had one advantage, she thought as he kneed the horse into a gallop. She spoke Comanche, and she had no intention of letting them know it.

They'd killed an antelope and stopped to butcher it. Cassandra no longer knew how many days she'd been riding behind Counts Many Coup without food, but she was weak with hunger. "Give the woman some," he said to the youngest brave. The others scowled, but the leader was obeyed. The brave chopped off a piece of something bloody and tossed it to her. Cassandra looked at it with horror, this red thing, still warm from the animal's body.

"We are the *Tanima*," said Counts Many Coup. The others were laughing at her as they gnawed on their own pieces. "Liver eaters," the blue-eyed warrior translated for her.

She looked at the thing in her hand and felt the nausea rise in her throat. Then she looked at him, and he was watching her, narrow-eyed, while the others laughed. She raised the warm, raw thing to her mouth and bit into it, staring back at him. She had to eat. "*Tanima*," she said. She had a new word in her Comanche vocabulary. She swallowed and chewed again. It was disgusting. He nodded his approval. The others had stopped laughing.

She tried to concentrate on the conversation. There was no moon tonight, and it seemed they were actually going to stop and sleep. If she were lucky, they'd eat too. Or maybe not. They'd killed no game since the antelope. As they studied some buffalo bones, Counts Many Coup cut a piece off something from his pouch. Then he looked at her, swaying on her feet in her buckskin rags, and cut a small piece for her. "Food," he said brusquely.

She looked dumbly at the thing in her hand. What was it? Her fingers trembling, she raised it to her mouth. It *was* food. Fruity, meaty, nutty. She felt tears of gratitude rise in her eyes and blinked them away. She couldn't show weakness. It must be pemmican. She'd heard it spoken of but had never tasted any. She dropped to the ground, cross-legged, clutching her bit of nourishment. Only when the last smidgeon had gone down her throat did she remember that she hadn't thanked him. She looked up to do so, but they were talking among themselves about a message.

How could buffalo bones give them a message? Was it some sort of religious thing—like birds' entrails used as omens in ancient Rome. Did the Comanches eat birds' entrails, she wondered dizzily. Would a bird's entrails taste good? She was only a little less hungry than she'd been before, and so cold.

Concentrate! she admonished herself. Anything she could learn about them might keep her alive. Three white men, they were saying. Three white men killed. Her heart clenched in fear. But no, it couldn't be Alex.

141

Elizabeth Chadwick

Even with Aureliano dead, there were four left to come after her. And they wouldn't let themselves be caught. Nothing would stop them. They'd be here soon. As for the bones, the Comanches must be trying to tell the future. They'd just found a few old bones and were trying to read something into them. Probably some tribal custom her father hadn't mentioned.

The others were wrapping themselves in buffalo robes. No one offered her one, although she was half-frozen. She curled up under a bush, brushing loose leaves over herself from the hickory trees under which they'd camped. Counts Many Coup watched her but offered no help. As he'd said, she had to fend for herself. And she would!

They expected to reach their winter encampment soon. She gathered as much from idle remarks made as they rode, and riding was better, warmer because of the proximity of a warm body. She hoped they wouldn't stop to sleep any more. She'd awakened so cold she could hardly force her limbs into motion. Although the youngest one had threatened her with a knife to get her going, she evidently belonged to Counts Many Coup. Nicodemus had said once that she'd end up a squaw or a slave if taken by Comanches. Thank God they didn't seem to want...she shuddered. If she thought about rape, she'd lose her nerve. Counts Many Coup must have felt the shudder. She closed her eyes as soon as he glanced back. He probably thought her the laziest woman on earth, sleeping all the time. It was an escape from fear and discomfort, but today she couldn't afford it. If they were coming to the encampment, she must make plans.

Had Alex lost her trail? Little time remained if he was to rescue her before her captors joined even more Indians, making his task more difficult. Or maybe not. Maybe Alex and the others would slip up to the encampment and signal her. Then she'd sneak out at

142

night to join them. Yes. That might be better. Once this group reached the winter encampment, she'd have chores. As a slave she'd probably be set to gathering wood and buffalo chips, and then she could easily slip away when Alex came. How soon would that be? she wondered anxiously. And how was she to survive in the meantime?

Courage. That was the first thing. She could never show fear, no matter how frightened she was.

God, how she hated them! Well, that was the second thing. She couldn't show her hatred. Nicodemus admired them. He said they were brave. And sociable. They lived their lives recklessly and with great enjoyment—singing, dancing, telling tales, gambling—as well as killing their enemies. *Don't think about that!* And hospitable. Her father had said they were generous and hospitable. Much good it had done him. She didn't imagine they were generous to captives. They hadn't been so far. Well, Counts Many Coup had. A little.

But when she was a slave in their camp, how would she be treated? Would they feed her decently? Give her clothes to wear so she wouldn't freeze? She'd never survive the winter on raw liver and a square of pemmican every other day, wearing rags and sleeping in the open. She thought about the child. Hers and Alex's. How would the two of them get through another month? Much less a whole winter?

But it wouldn't be that long. At this very minute Alex might be close. She opened her eyes. Dead, yellow grass under the horse's hooves. Cold, gray sky. A winter could be a long time. No matter how brave you promised yourself you were going to be.

The tepees stretched out along the stream and among the trees. Because of the terrain, she couldn't judge how many people lived here, but it was a considerable number—no small nomadic band of one or two families. Too many for the mustangers to take on. However, in such a crowded camp, it should be easier to slip away. She shook her head, so cold and hungry it was hard to reason or make plans.

Having put on war paint and rubbed his horse with grass until its coat shone, Counts Many Coup mounted and motioned her to another horse. Did that mean she was no longer under his protection? Swallowing hard, she obeyed and allowed her hands to be tied in front of her with a rawhide thong. He led the group down into the encampment, Aureliano's scalp and two others waving from the tip of a lance. Behind him rode other warriors, displaying their trophies. Cassandra was placed between the last two, and once they had entered the camp, throngs of Indians followed, yelling, dancing, singing songs that told the exploits of tribal heroes. Emaciated dogs, noisy and vicious-looking, intermingled with the crowd, yapping at the heels of the horses and being kicked aside. Shivering with apprehension, Cassandra held her head high. *Be brave!* she told herself.

The warriors peeled off one by one, evidently as they came to their own lodges, for women and children from the throng joined them. Cassandra was afraid that at some point she would be left alone in the midst of this savage mob. However, when Counts Many Coup turned off, the two guards nudged her horse after him, then pushed her roughly from the saddle so that, hands tied and unable to stop her fall, she landed in the dust at the feet of a woman.

"I have brought you a slave, Faces A Bear," said Counts Many Coup, his eyes expressionless as he looked down at Cassandra.

The woman was short, maybe five feet tall, and stocky. She had a round face and hacked-off black hair, the part painted with a bizarre red line as if she had parted her hair with a knife. She wore a buffalo robe with geometric symbols painted on the border.

Cassandra, who was numb with cold, envied the robe.

"Do her no damage," the blue-eyed warrior instructed his wife. "She carries a child."

Before he mentioned Cassandra's pregnancy, the wide, thin-lipped face had been expressionless. Now the narrow eyes gleamed with malice, and Cassandra knew that for some reason Faces A Bear had become an enemy, although she bowed her head submissively to her husband's command.

"I go to rest and prepare for the scalp dance." Counts Many Coup then entered the tepee without a backward glance.

The wife spoke sharply, and Cassandra was yanked onto her feet by someone behind her. Faces A Bear sneered at Cassandra's ragged clothes and lack of jewelry, evidently disappointed that there was nothing of value to wrest from the new slave. "Put her to work until time for the scalp dance," said the wife, bending casually to the fire to scoop up a stick, which she then jabbed into Cassandra's side.

Cassandra gasped at the pain and the overt cruelty of the action. She might have fallen if the hands of the unseen person had not tightened. Faces A Bear turned to follow her husband into the tepee. When the stiff, weighted door flap fell behind the wife, Cassandra was still blinking tears from her eyes, her side seared and burning. *Oh God*, she thought, *this is going to be bad*. What did a scalp dance mean? Her scalp?

"Come!"

Cassandra looked down at the hands on her arms and received another shock. They were black; the person behind her, when she looked over her shoulder, was a tall Negro woman, young and striking in appearance. A midnight goddess, thought Cassandra, but what was she doing here? Had she too been captured? "Do you speak English?" Cassandra asked eagerly. The young woman neither answered nor changed her expression. "Cassandra." Cassandra

145

pulled her arm loose and pointed to herself with her tied hands.

"Black Rain," came the reply in Comanche, and Black Rain grasped Cassandra's arm again and pulled her around to the side of the tepee where a small hole had been scraped into the earth and a hide tossed into it. The black woman poured water into the hole from a bag. Then, speaking Comanche and demonstrating what she wanted done, she instructed Cassandra to stamp on the wet hide.

Already chilled to the bone, Cassandra anticipated that sloshing in that hole would freeze her feet and ruin her moccasins. She swallowed hard and bent to take them off. Then, still clutching the moccasins lest someone take them from her, she stepped into the hole and began to splash from foot to foot, fighting at each step to keep her balance in the slippery, muddy water. The black woman, who was more heavily pregnant than Cassandra, nodded and sat down nearby.

Within minutes Cassandra's calves ached, and she felt the weakness of hunger and exhaustion sweeping over her. Yet if she slowed in her tramping, the black woman looked up from her sewing and spoke sharply, forcing Cassandra to speed up. The movement at least warmed her feet.

Watch what she's doing! Cassandra told herself. The woman sewed but not with a needle. She used sinew thread, pointed at the end, and laced it through holes she had made in the hide with an awl-like tool. That looked easy enough. Cassandra thought she could make herself a garment if she had the materials, and God knows she needed clothing.

The woman left briefly, and Cassandra slowed down, keeping an eye out for her return. What would be done to her if she stopped? Would any of the people in the vicinity come to scold or abuse her? The encampment was chaotic, children giggling and chasing one another, dogs barking, women going about their chores. Only the men stood about or sat talking, and some of them were busy making weapons.

Wearily Cassandra continued her slow, awkward dance in the muddy hole and watched another procession pass through the middle of the camp, a parade of warriors, some with faces painted black, carrying scalp poles and driving horses. The crowds trailing the new party seemed to receive it with much less jubilation. There was wailing, although for all she knew it might be a victory song. She shrugged and continued to tramp on the wet hide.

When Black Rain returned, she carried a trailing strip of meat in her hand, biting off pieces as she moved. Saliva rushed to Cassandra's mouth, and her stomach cramped painfully. Gathering her courage, she spoke the woman's name in Comanche and pointed to her own mouth. The woman hesitated, then tore off an end of the long, barely cooked strip and held it out. Cassandra had to put down her moccasins to take it. As with the pemmican, she forced herself to eat in small bites and chew carefully while she continued to stamp. This time she didn't forget to say "Thank you" and was rewarded with the woman's nod.

The nod might mean that Black Rain understood English, even if she was unwilling to speak it. Why? Would she be punished? She must be a captive herself. And before that? A slave, most likely. Cassandra didn't think there were any free Negroes in Texas. Still, she and Black Rain had something in common—both captives, both English-speakers, neither Comanches. Maybe they could become allies, thought Cassandra wistfully. An ally would be such a comfort in this alien world, and Alex could rescue Black Rain as well.

Stuffing the last bit of meat into her mouth, Cassandra stepped up out of the hole when Black Rain told her to. Her next task, once her wrists were finally freed from the rawhide thong, was to pound roots into powder. She dried and cleaned her feet in the grass as best she could, put on her moccasins, then set to work again, grateful for the chance to sit.

The afternoon stretched on, Cassandra pounding and grinding until her arms ached, Black Rain mixing the resulting powder with what looked like animal organs, brains or perhaps liver. Why hadn't they eaten the liver, of which they were so fond? After all, Counts Many Coup had said they were the *Tanima*, liver eaters. And what else was Black Rain putting into her concoction? Grease of some sort and water. Cassandra tried to estimate the proportions, but couldn't because the woman kept adding a bit of this and a bit of that until she was satisfied with the results. What could the stuff be? Surely they didn't eat it.

By the time Cassandra's arms felt as if they might fall off, Black Rain had begun rubbing the mixture into a hide from which all the hair had been removed. A tanning solution, Cassandra decided, and filed the information into her memory. She too was set to working the mixture in. Well, it wasn't so bad, she decided. Just work. She'd been fed and allowed to sit down. If she could stay away from Faces A Bear and keep from being poked with any more hot sticks, she'd survive until Alex came.

But she was so tired. She glanced at the sky. Almost sunset and getting colder. Maybe there'd be more food soon. And sleep. Oh Lord, how good it would be to sleep in a tepee with a fire going. Luxury, she thought wryly, she who had once slept on feather beds with warm quilts over her.

Her wistful daydreams ended abruptly when two braves appeared, grasped her by either arm, and dragged her toward the cleared center of the encampment where a tall pole stood, scalps attached to the top. The two men lashed her to the pole and left. What did they mean to do? Torture her? Kill her? She wanted to break down and weep, which some last bit of common sense told her could only hasten her death, perhaps make it more painful.

Instead of giving way, she threw her head back against the pole, face raised to the sky, and prayed. Every prayer she knew, prayers her mother had taught her as a little girl, prayers they'd said each week in church, prayers said at table, at bedtime, at school. She whispered them all to herself until her heart slowed and her trembling ceased.

When she opened her eyes again, Counts Many Coup was staring at her thoughtfully. She tried to look brave. "I was praying," she said clearly, proud that there was no hint of tremor in her voice. "To—to the Earth Mother," she improvised. No doubt women prayed to the Earth Mother. "Who—who protects warriors and maidens yet unborn."

Several men had stopped their activities to stare at her. One spoke to Counts Many Coup, who translated what she had said. All who heard him stared at her curiously. She stared back. Since Counts Many Coup had told his wife not to harm her because she was with child, it seemed a good idea to remind them all.

Counts Many Coup turned away, and Cassandra studied the activity that had begun in the last minutes. They built a fire of dry grass beneath a cone of wood. Then a group of men, old and middle-aged, some carrying drums, filtered into the cleared area and seated themselves near Cassandra. Spectators gathered, then dancers, the women decorated with black paint, the men with red, forming lines, dancing backward and forward toward one another as the singers and drummers began a soft, slow song. The dancers stepped up their pace gradually, as did the musicians, until the noise broke over Cassandra in a roar and the dancers formed a circle around her. She held her head higher.

As the ceremony progressed, faster, noisier, the dancers left their positions from time to time and threatened her, miming her murder and scalping.

Counts Many Coup was nowhere in evidence. Were they working themselves up to kill her? A man carrying a whip with a carved, serrated blade and two lashes on the end occasionally pointed it at members of the crowd who had to get up, dance, and narrate their feats of heroism, as did the whip wielder. It seemed to be some sort of bragging contest.

How brave could they be, she questioned bitterly, when they tied women to poles and threatened them? Almost as if he could read her mind, the owner of the whip whirled and brought the lashes down on her upper arm. The sting paralyzed her shoulder, but she stared back at him defiantly and heard the murmur of the crowd swell under the sounds of singing and drumming. "Savages," she hissed under her breath, anticipating the next lash. Only anger would help her now.

But then the focus of the ceremony shifted. Warriors wearing feathered bonnets and buffalo scalps came into the clearing and seated themselves in a semicircle, a buffalo hide thrown into the opening. Cassandra let her breath out slowly, relieved that attention had moved away from her. The fire cast an eerie, flickering light across the savage faces around her, the noise of drums and singing muted, and into the opening leapt a warrior who plunged a lance into the hide and began to speak.

Recognizing the voice, she squinted into the red-lit gloom. Counts Many Coup wore no bonnet, but his lance, as she knew from the tales her father had told her, was a sign of greater bravery than any warbonnet. His chest was bare and painted in sinister black designs, as was his face. The ends of his breechclout, which fell from the fold at his waist to his knees, flew aside when he sprang into the circle, and his legs were covered with long winter moccasins and leggings that tied around his waist. There was a savage splendor about him as he began to tell of an enemy armed with a fire stick, whom he had killed with his lance. Did he mean Aureliano? she wondered. Even with a gun, Aureliano had been helpless against this man whose life was devoted to killing. And yet Counts Many Coup had been kind. Others testified to his feat, the seated warriors gave him their approbation, and he joined their circle to be followed by another claimant to the honors of bravery and death. This, she gathered, was *counting coup*. The drumming, singing, and dancing rose and fell in intensity as the warriors followed one another into the circle. Let them brag all night, she thought, as long as they ignored her. She dozed until some change in the emotional climate around her forced her to listen once more to the bloody tales being told in the leaping firelight.

The latest man to plunge his spear into the buffalo hide was not from the party in which she had traveled. The story he told filled Cassandra with dread. This warrior and his band had come upon a party of white men, three of whom were killed in a running battle. The fourth, although wounded by an arrow, had killed the war chief in hand-to-hand combat, falling at last to the club of the man who was counting coup. The warrior brandished the axlike weapon, sharpened on both ends and fastened in the middle to a handle of fourteen inches or so. His audience wailed for the fallen war chief whose bravery was extolled by the warrior. Then he praised his fallen enemy, a white man of great height—his hand measured six inches over his own head; of great power—he mimed strength and muscularity; of great bravery; a man whose soul must now wander outside the rich hunting grounds of death. Then the warrior brandished the scalp. A wave of horror dimmed Cassandra's eyes. The hair was Alex's.

The crowd screamed for revenge—a life to repay them for the life of the war chief. Cassandra understood. Hers was the only life available to them. She opened her eyes defiantly as they closed in around her.

Elizabeth Chadwick

"Cowards!" she said, indifferent to their threat.

Suddenly Counts Many Coup appeared beside her and translated. "She calls you cowards."

The fury of the crowd intensified as he looked at her, his eyes curious as to what she would say next. Cassandra felt more anger than fear. They'd killed Alex, and they would kill her; she didn't doubt it. But she wanted to leave them something to think about. She searched her mind desperately for things her father had said about their beliefs. They considered women little better than chattel, and she was the lowest of women, a slave. And they believed in ghosts.

She smiled, and the very coldness of her smile seemed to halt their advance. "The life of a female in exchange for the life of a *Tanima* war chief," she said to Counts Many Coup. "A good exchange, a proper revenge." She laughed and thought she saw an admiring humor in his eyes.

He translated, and the crowd, under the power of his voice and the contempt of her words, fell back.

"But I shall have the last and best revenge." Cassandra no longer looked at him. She stared out at the angry crowd, meeting eyes everywhere she could. "Because my ghost will haunt you." She had raised her voice. Her mother had taught elocution in the school; Cassandra could make herself heard if she chose. "My ghost will haunt you, and the ghost of my unborn child will haunt you."

He translated, and they stirred uneasily.

"The buffalo will turn aside from your arrows," she improvised, switching to Comanche. What did it matter? If she was going to die, hiding her knowledge of their tongue would gain her no advantage. "The Thunderbird will burn your lodges." She hoped that was right. Wasn't the Thunderbird a magical creature who controlled lightning and thunder, of which they were afraid? It seemed to be a successful threat. The *Tanima* no longer met her eyes.

152

"Your sons will shrivel in their mother's wombs," she shrieked, hating them. Hoping it would be true because they'd killed Alex. "I, your victim, will laugh at your misfortune from beyond the mists of death." She let her voice drop, for they were still now. "The son in my womb will curse the *Tanima*." She was finished. "So kill me," she whispered, her eyes closing in weariness.

For a time she heard nothing but the sound of the winter wind in the trees and wished they'd hurry with the killing. She was so cold. Then the blue-eyed warrior, whose voice she knew, said, "You speak our tongue?"

She opened her eyes to find the clearing empty.

"Only old women can have medicine," he pointed out, still in Comanche.

She looked at him as if she didn't understand, and he frowned. "Does some spirit speak through you?" he wondered aloud. She understood but gave no sign. "Are you a witch?" he asked in English, a hint of impatience in his voice.

"What do you mean?" If he thought some spirit spoke through her, fine.

"Well, let us see if your spirits keep you alive through the night." He turned abruptly and left.

Cassandra closed her eyes again. Freezing to death was probably easier than being hacked to pieces by a mob of savages. And if, as he said, her spirits kept her alive through the night, she'd worry about tomorrow when it came. With Alex dead, it didn't matter much. Then her mouth curved in a slight, grim smile. Weaponless, she'd held them off. He'd have been proud of her. Come to that, her parents would have been proud. An education in rhetoric and a retentive memory for her father's lectures on Indian language and customs had stood her in good stead. Too bad her luck didn't extend to a buffalo robe to see her through the night.

Chapter Ten

Cassandra awakened, numb with cold and crumpled at the foot of the scalp pole, her wrists still tied. A gray dawn touched the clearing, and around her she heard the first stirrings of the camp. *Well, I'm still alive*, she thought.

Then she remembered that Alex wasn't, and her throat ached with tears she couldn't shed. Someone might come, and she wouldn't let herself be seen crying. Pride was the only thing she seemed to have left besides life, which she couldn't imagine without Alex, without at least the hope that she'd see him again. Why continue to suffer the pain, fear, and deprivation that lay ahead when she'd never see her husband again in this world? Maybe it would be better to follow him into the next. Faces A Bear, who had been among the cruelest of the dancers, would no doubt be glad to send Cassandra on her way.

Then something happened that turned Cassandra's thoughts from death. She felt a flutter inside her, and her bowed head jerked up, as if she had heard a miraculous sound. Eyes closed in concentration, she listened to her own body, and it came again, the stirring of life. Alex's baby had moved inside her, reminding her that she did have something to live for, something left of the man she loved.

"So you are alive, Cass-an-dra." He spoke her name strangely, equal accents on each syllable as if they were separate words. "Your spirits have not deserted you."

Cassandra opened her eyes and gave Counts Many Coup a radiant smile that made him frown in puzzlement. He turned and strode away, leaving her to wonder if he planned to starve her to death, tied to this pole. They'd better watch out! she thought, remembering her threat to haunt them and grinning at her own audacity. How had she dared, with hundreds of vengeful Indians closing in around her?

Her thoughts were distracted by the sounds of wailing. The mourning period for the slain war chief had begun, and she remembered something her father had said about Comanche funerals. The relatives gave away the dead person's possessions and their own to the mourners, especially the noisiest mourners. By God, if someone would just release her from this pole, she could mourn with the best of them! She needed something to keep her warm, a blanket, a robe; anything would be welcome. Did they serve food at funerals? she wondered. The baby stirred again, and she said aloud, "Be patient, little one. If there's a feast and we get the chance, we'll attend."

"Do you speak to the air?"

Cassandra twisted her head and looked at Black Rain, who held a knife and had spoken in Comanche. Cassandra pretended not to understand, determined to refoster the idea that she did not speak or understand their tongue. Let them think last night's threats had been a supernatural event. Sullenly Black Rain translated her question into English. "I spoke to my child," Cassandra replied.

"Did your child speak back?" Black Rain asked dryly as she began to saw at the rawhide bindings.

"Of course he did," Cassandra lied blithely.

Black Rain pointed toward the tepee of Counts Many Coup and told Cassandra in Comanche that there was work to be done. Cassandra gave her a blank look and headed for the funeral. Doing Black Rain's work wouldn't provide warm clothing, and nothing had been said about breakfast.

With the Negro woman scurrying after her and giving sharp orders, Cassandra joined the crowd of mourners and began to wail. The women of the family tore their clothes. Cassandra didn't have to tear hers; they were already in tatters. The women slashed themselves with knives; Cassandra, who had no knife, used her nails to give herself a few scratches. Sidelong frowns were cast at her by the other mourners. Evidently too polite to cause a disturbance at a funeral, Black Rain went away while Cassandra wailed louder than ever, ostensibly for the war chief. In reality she hoped and believed that Alex had killed the man. With the others, Cassandra followed the corpse to its resting place. What strange burial customs they had; the body was tied to a horse, a woman riding behind to hold it in place, then curled in a fetal position for burial.

From the corner of her eye, Cassandra saw Counts Many Coup arrive, but he didn't force her to leave. She wailed louder, thinking of Alex, thinking of the miserable life ahead of her, thinking of her poor baby whom she had to protect. Her grief was convincing because it was real and this would be the only time she could express it.

Hours later—when her throat was raw with wailing, her arms covered with scratches—the bereaved family, glaring at her with sullen suspicion, gave her the blanket she craved, and she stumbled away, looking for the tepee of Counts Many Coup. Damn, she thought, these tepees all look alike. There had been no feast, and she was weak with hunger, exhaustion, and grief. Then a hand closed over her upper arm, and Counts Many Coup said in Comanche, "For whom did you grieve? You never knew Eagle Tail or his family and can have no love for The People."

Cassandra did not answer. He grunted impatiently

and repeated the question in English. Silent a minute as she sought for ambiguous phrasing, she replied at last, "All grieve for the death of a brave man."

He seemed to accept that and turned her over to his wife. Cassandra was allowed the leavings of their pot that evening but not the shelter of their tepee. She slept under a bush, huddled in her blanket and shivering, wondering how she'd ever make it through the winter. No one would be coming to rescue her now. She was on her own.

Time passed slowly for Cassandra. She got the leavings of the meals, making her little better than the skinny, ravenous dogs who swarmed over the camp. She learned to eat anything she could find—entrails, their contents squeezed out between the fingers; raw brains which she stole before they went into the tanning mixtures; roots she was supposed to pound into powder; and the camp garbage. A feast for her was a bit of half-raw turkey tossed to her by Counts Many Coup after the bird had been pitched, feathers and all, into the fire, then dragged out and stripped of its charred exterior for eating. His presence meant the difference between eating and going hungry, for Faces A Bear gave her little or nothing when Counts Many Coup and Broken Nose, a widower who ate at their campfire, were away.

Sometime during the early days of her captivity her eighteenth birthday passed, unnoticed and uncelebrated. Cassandra had little cause for celebration. She worked from dawn till dark—gathering buffalo chips and wood for the fires, stripping cottonwood bark for the horses to eat when the grass ran out, grinding everything from tobacco to meat, digging roots, trampling hides in water, scraping them, drawing them endlessly over logs and through loops, rubbing solutions into them, sewing, cooking. The tasks were endless, and she, being a slave, inherited them all. She gathered that before her arrival the terrible burden of work had fallen most heavily upon Black Rain, who was the second wife of Counts Many Coup. Faces A Bear, the first wife, worked too, but never as hard. She gave the orders and meted out the punishment, of which Cassandra took more than her share. She was poked with hot sticks, shouted at, hit, and shoved, and she was coming to hate the first wife. She wished she did have powers from the spirits; she would call a curse on Faces A Bear without a qualm.

Why did the woman hate her so much? Cassandra speculated on it as she toiled. Perhaps because she was white. Or because Counts Many Coup occasionally showed her an offhand kindness when he was in camp. Or because Little Wolf, their son, followed Cassandra around, talking to her, although, of course, she said nothing in return.

He was a valuable source of information; from him she had begun to make some sense of the convoluted family relationships in the circle of tepees of which she was a part—not that she got to sleep in a tepee. Although there were only four people in Counts Many Coup's lodge, Cassandra still slept out in the cold at night, waking half frozen each morning but afraid to attempt escape because gangs of teenaged boys ranged the surrounding areas after dark. If she were caught, they'd kill her.

But why the hatred from Faces A Bear? She sighed dejectedly. The only explanation that made sense stemmed from her attack on the young brave when she had first been captured. His fellows now called him Scarred By A Woman. He was the stepson of Talking Crow, the older sister of Faces A Bear. On Cassandra's third day in camp, his mother had tried to push Cassandra into the fire while she was cooking a strip of venison. Although Cassandra managed to throw herself to the side, the hot meat whipped around the of Talking Crow and earned Cassandra a beating so severe that Buffalo Leaper intervened.

"That one is my brother's property," Buffalo Leaper told his wife. "How will you repay him if you damage her?"

It was the first time Cassandra realized that Counts Many Coup had a brother and that the boy she had scarred was a sort of double nephew of her owner and of his wife. Brothers must have married sisters. She sighed at the complexity of it all and wondered why the men didn't seem to resent her attack on the boy while the women did.

Even the youth himself had stopped scowling at her. In fact, one day while she was gathering buffalo chips, he had suddenly appeared in her path and stared at her. Just this morning he had reached out and touched her hair, then disappeared into the trees. Did he imagine himself a suitor? She seemed to herself an unlikely object of puppy love—dirty, ragged, five months pregnant.

Of course, their women bore few babies, and many of those died. A proven ability to conceive might be a desirable trait. She gathered that Counts Many Coup had been married for years, and yet they had only one child, Little Wolf. Maybe that explained Faces A Bear's enmity; the woman might be jealous that Cassandra was with child. Buffalo Leaper and Talking Crow, married even longer, had only two children, Scarred By A Woman, who was actually the son of another marriage in Buffalo Leaper's youth, and another boy, Beaver Tail, who had yet to go on his first hunt; he still slept in his parents' tepee. Buffalo Leaper and Talking Crow hadn't had a child in twelve years or more. So it was with all the couples—there might be one child or two. Only the parents of Faces A Bear, Turkey Feather and Wolf Woman, had four living offspring, three daughters and Elk's Tooth, whom gossip named a possible successor to the dead war chief, as was Counts Many Coup. Cassandra heard all the gossip because no one thought she could understand what they were saying.

Even under the frequent abuse of the women, Cassandra gained strength, eating everything she could get her hands on and thriving on the hard work. Her worst problem was the cold. Her rags and blanket were not enough, and she knew that soon she'd fall ill if she didn't remedy the situation. The only solution she could see was gambling. Comanches, both men and women, were enthusiastic gamblers. They played dice games, betting on the combination of colors that came up when painted dice were tossed in a shallow bowl, but Cassandra ignored that game. Winning seemed to be a matter of chance, and she *had* to win. She had only her blanket to gamble with. If she lost that, she'd freeze to death.

The game that caught her interest was the hand game. A small piece of bone held by one player was switched from hand to hand with as many obscuring motions as possible, sometimes even passed to other players. Eventually the original holder of the bone extended closed fists, and the opponent guessed in which hand the bone lay, participants and nonparticipants betting their belongings on the outcome. Drumming, singing of the hand-game song, and escalating excitement accompanied the play. Cassandra's problem with the game was the song. She had to learn it and then sing it without giving away her knowledge of the language. As for guessing where the bone lay, she almost always guessed right and didn't know why the Comanches couldn't, unless it was their eyesight. Poor sight seemed to be endemic to the band. Well, that was their ill luck; Cassandra intended to win a wardrobe through the hand game, and to that end she attended every game she could, jumping up and down in excitement along with the other spectators. After several weeks, she sang along loudly, deliberately making mistakes and causing hilarity among the other women.

Cassandra followed this pattern until she had established herself as a naïve enthusiast and picked out the player who could never fool her. Then, squealing with feigned excitement, although she was actually terrified, she injected herself into the game, indicating in sign language that she wanted to bet her blanket against the woman's buckskin dress. Although Cassandra wished it were longer, the garment promised some warmth and protection from the cold winds; she could hardly wait to put it on.

Everyone laughed uproariously when Cassandra took her place opposite Falls In Water, who was the wife of Elk's Tooth, Faces A Bear's brother. The singing and drumming resumed, and Falls In Water went through an elaborate series of hand motions and changes. Everyone including Cassandra watched carefully and sang, Cassandra's singing causing Falls in Water to laugh so hard that her feints were clumsier than usual.

When finally she held out her fists, Cassandra bit her lip, looked undecided, let herself be shouted at, then won the dress. She put on a convincing show of surprised delight, all the while thinking of the leggings she had to win if she was to have protection to the knees.

Falls In Water retired to put on another dress and turn over the garment she had lost. Faces A Bear took her place across from Cassandra, who shivered with dread because Faces A Bear was a better player and would be a sore loser. Still, thought Cassandra philosophically, she had to win. Better a beating later than cold legs or the loss of her new dress. But Faces A Bear didn't want the dress, which had not yet been delivered. She pointed to the blanket in which Cassandra huddled. Cassandra pointed to her opponent's highly ornamented leggings. Faces A Bear shook her head.

For the leggings she wanted the blanket and the dress. Cassandra's heart turned cold. If she lost, tonight she'd freeze, and the woman knew it.

Cassandra was about to agree rather than lose face when the matriarch of the band chided her daughter-in-law for greed. The bet was settled on Cassandra's blanket against Faces A Bear's leggings, and with a crafty smile Faces A Bear began her hand motions. Heart in her throat, Cassandra watched every move. The drumming and singing increased in pace and volume, and Cassandra's pulse rate with them.

The sister, Talking Crow, knelt beside Faces A Bear, and they began to pass the bone—or pretend to. At one point Cassandra lost track of it. Which woman had it? Talking Crow she thought, but Faces A Bear was again shifting it from hand to hand, or pretending to. Then she held her fists out. Cassandra swallowed hard. What good would the dress do her if she lost the blanket? She looked into her opponent's eyes and saw the woman's triumphant malice, and suddenly she was sure that, as she had first thought, Faces A Bear didn't have the bone at all. She shook her head at the two closed fists, glancing quickly at the hands of the sister, Talking Crow. Had Talking Crow passed the bone to another while Cassandra was distracted by the final hand motions of Faces A Bear? The sister had one hand open on her knee, the other closed tightly in a fist.

The drums were beating wildly, echoing in Cassandra's head. "Choose, ugly one," Faces A Bear shouted and thrust her fists again at Cassandra.

In a dream Cassandra leaned over to touch the closed hand of Talking Crow. The two women's faces fell, and Cassandra knew she had won. The other players and spectators, who had been betting on the outcome, shouted to Talking Crow to open her fist. Scowling, she did, and the bone lay on her palm. Cassandra slumped onto the ground in relief. Furious,

Faces A Bear rose as if to leave, but her way out of the circle was blocked inadvertently by her sister-in-law, Falls In Water, who had returned to deliver the dress. Faces A Bear brushed against her roughly.

"Stop!" All commotion ceased at the command from Summer Cloud. Cassandra looked toward the old woman, whose face was seamed with wrinkles but whose eyes were bright and serene. She was the wife of the peace chief and medicine man Long Dancer, a woman who, past the years of childbearing, was said to have spirit power. Both Faces A Bear and Talking Crow were her daughters-in-law, or so Cassandra surmised if Buffalo Leaper and Counts Many Coup were indeed brothers. She did not understand how Counts Many Coup, with his blue eyes, could be of their blood.

"The slave, Cass-an-dra, has played well. Would you deprive her of her winnings, my daughters?" asked Summer Cloud mildly.

"A slave should not be allowed in the games," said Faces A Bear sullenly, and her sister, Talking Crow, agreed.

"You yourself chose to oppose her," Summer Cloud pointed out. "Now give over the winnings, as your sister-in-law, Falls In Water, has."

"Later," murmured Faces A Bear.

"I want to see the clothes on her now." The old woman looked Cassandra over. "She needs them. If she were of my lodge, I would be ashamed to see her dressed so poorly."

Although Cassandra looked from one to the other as if she didn't understand, she understood very well and knew that Faces A Bear had been soundly reprimanded.

"Come, women, let us dress her decently," said Summer Cloud, and suddenly Cassandra found herself stripped of her rags, among much giggling and joking, and put into the dress of Falls In Water and the leggings of Faces A Bear. As the women crowded around her, they marveled at her pale skin and fingered her golden hair. Some patted the swell of her belly and speculated on when the child would be born and whether it too would have the strange skin and hair of its mother. Although Cassandra could not talk to them, the unaccustomed warmth of the new clothing was delicious, and she laughed when they laughed, relishing what little happiness came her way.

On another day, if she were lucky, she might win a buffalo robe. She remembered nostalgically the cozy warmth of the one she had left behind. Then she remembered that Alex had given her that robe after their second wedding, the one performed by the Mexican priest and attended by the Mexican traders. Remembering, her eyes stung with tears.

Counts Many Coup returned from a successful hunt, and the camp feasted. Even Cassandra came away from the celebration with her hunger completely appeased for once. Faces A Bear welcomed her husband with a triumph that exceeded even his hunting prowess, and that evening Cassandra discovered why the retaliation for winning the leggings had been mild. Faces A Bear said to her husband, when the last half-cooked piece of meat had been eaten, "Your slave shows disdain for the warriors of The People."

Cassandra stiffened in fear and confusion.

"How so?" asked Counts Many Coup.

"Look at her hair. She wears it in the braids of a warrior."

"Maidens wear their hair in braids too," said Little Antelope, the youngest of Faces A Bear's sisters. "See, I—"

"She is no maiden," snapped Faces A Bear. "She should be severely punished for her presumption."

Cassandra shivered. Severely punished? With trembling hands she threaded the pointed end of a length of sinew through the awl hole in a pouch she was making.

"You are right, wife," said Counts Many Coup, "something must be done—"

Cassandra bit down hard on her lip. *Show no fear!* she warned herself.

"—although Cass-an-dra has the courage of a warrior, as Scarred By A Woman can tell you."

Those who were listening to the exchange howled with laughter at the boy's expense, and surprisingly he laughed as well. Caught out by her own surprise, Cassandra's eyes flew from her sewing to the face of the blue-eyed warrior.

"Still, something must be done. You are right about that, Faces A Bear," continued the husband. "We cannot have a pregnant woman looking like a warrior."

Oh God, thought Cassandra, despairing. She had seen the flash of triumph in the eyes of his wife.

"Cass-an-dra." She looked up. "Come here," he commanded in English. Obediently she rose from her place and, head high, walked to him. His knife was out. Did he mean to mutilate her? He was laughing. She felt as much sadness as fear, for she had thought Counts Many Coup as close to a friend as any she had in this camp. When he was here he saw that she ate; occasionally he praised her work. Although he made no place for her in his tepee, she had to assume that he did not see sleeping out as a hardship since he did it himself on his many forays away from their camp.

He grasped the long golden braid in which she wore her hair and, still laughing, sawed it off with his knife, taking care not to cut her. "There," said Counts Many Coup. "Now she has the hair of a woman. Are you satisfied, wife?" Cassandra glanced at Faces A Bear, who was *not* satisfied.

"My husband's wisdom is to the satisfaction of all," said the woman grudgingly.

"It is well," said Counts Many Coup, and he tossed the braid to Scarred By a Woman. "Take it in reparation, my son," he said, for among the Comanche a brother's sons were claimed as one's own.

The young brave laughed with delight and immediately began to weave Cassandra's gold hair into his own black braids. She knew that the young men begged hair from women to make their own longer, but the sight of the mixed blonde and black braids on the young man was so ludicrous that Cassandra forgot her fear and resentment and began to giggle as he finished his toilette and strutted among his peers. Counts Many Coup, laughing as well, laid his hand companionably on Cassandra's shoulder, much to her surprise. Although he provided her with what little kindness she experienced among the Comanches, he seldom touched her. Grateful for the shared moment, she smiled up at him. The only person who didn't enjoy the incident was its precipitator, Faces A Bear. Her eyes bored into Cassandra like fire into dried wood, and Cassandra's smile died.

Cassandra had nothing valuable enough to gamble against a buffalo robe, so she set about winning other things—moccasins, another dress, another blanket, an awl, a hide pouch to keep her possessions in, bags of pemmican and dried meat. She kept food for the times when Counts Many Coup was away and his wife cut back on Cassandra's meager share.

Cassandra still slept outside, and she dreaded snow. If only she had a buffalo robe. Perhaps none of the women would wager one because they *wanted* her to die. The nights got colder, and she wondered when spring would come. In time to spare her death by freezing?

Counts Many Coup proposed a raid to his fellow warriors and lay through the afternoon in front of his tepee, singing his medicine song. According to Little Wolf, his father had wolf medicine and Thunderbird medicine. The wolf medicine made him impervious to bullets. Cassandra hoped so. God knows what would happen to her if Counts Many Coup were killed. The younger warriors, among them Scarred By A Woman, gathered to his standard and danced that night. Songs of war and love were sung.

Cassandra could see that Little Antelope, the youngest sister of Faces A Bear, was deeply smitten with Scarred By A Woman, but his eyes followed Cassandra. Young couples slipped away from the dance, and Cassandra envied them their love, thinking of Alex and how much she missed him. The next morning the war party was gone, and life continued as usual in the camp.

Cassandra worked, gambled when she had the time, went to her sleeping bush each night and shivered among her growing pile of possessions. One thing she could say for the Comanches: they never stole. What she won, she kept, unless she lost it in the next game. For entertainment, she listened to the gossip, the most interesting items being the talk of who would be the next war chief. She gathered that the leading candidates were Elk's Tooth, Faces A Bear's brother, and Counts Many Coup, her husband. Buffalo Leaper was also a candidate, but more because he was the son of the peace chief, Long Dancer, than because of his own deeds. The warriors said that he fought well but was lazy and more prone to stay home by his own fire than to lead a war party.

Nothing was alleged against Elk's Tooth, but greater praise fell upon Counts Many Coup. They said he was a brave and active leader, wise in war and generous in the division of spoils. No follower of his was ever left behind to lose his scalp and thus his place in the pleasant meadows of the dead. Cassandra thought he would be chosen and wondered if his new importance would make Faces A Bear even more proud and therefore more cruel. Would Counts Many Coup's new power leave him too busy to intervene occasionally on behalf of his slave? Cassandra sighed and tried not to worry.

The other piece of gossip concerned Black Rain, now close to term. The women whispered that Faces A Bear, jealous of the second wife's pregnancy, wanted her to miscarry. How could anyone wish the death of a child? Cassandra wondered. Although Black Rain, with whom Cassandra spent hours working each day, was still cold to her and never spoke English to alleviate Cassandra's loneliness, still Cassandra could not wish her ill.

Therefore, on a fair day when the women were getting up a game of shinny, Cassandra was horrified to hear Faces A Bear insist that Black Rain play because they needed one more to make up the team. Cassandra knew that Black Rain had been showing blood and assumed that the running involved in the game would bring on the birth—too soon. Comanche babies had little enough chance of surviving; Cassandra had seen half of those born since she had been with the tribe die. Which was what Faces A Bear wanted. Impulsively Cassandra pushed into the group and said, "I'll play."

Black Rain turned to her in astonishment. "You don't know the game. You'll make a fool of yourself."

"I've watched it a million times," said Cassandra, exaggerating, but she *had* watched on fair afternoons when the women played, and she had longed to join in. It didn't look that hard. Two sticks were driven into either end of a field of a hundred yards or so. Each of the ten players on a side had a curved stick with which to send a four-inch, hair-stuffed deerskin ball to the goal. Cassandra had loved the games at her mother's school; perhaps the disadvantage of her pregnancy would be offset by her skill and height, for she was taller by eight inches than most of the women.

"Why would you do this?" Black Rain hissed.

"Because you'll lose your baby if I don't."

"You're with child as well," said Black Rain.

Cassandra shrugged. "Not as far along, and I've had no problems."

Faces A Bear spoke sharply to them. Black Rain, undecided, finally told the first wife that Cassandra wanted to play in her place. Faces A Bear scowled.

A woman on the other team said, "If she plays shinny as well as she gambles, we'll take her. You can have your sister, Talking Crow. She's old, but she's not with child." The two sisters were furious, but the other women, laughing and joking, insisted on the arrangement, and the game began.

Please God, Cassandra prayed silently, *don't let this be a mistake. Don't punish my arrogance by hurting my baby.*

At first it seemed that God was not listening because the sisters, Faces A Bear and Talking Crow, ganged up on her. It was all she could do to keep out of their way, to avoid the pushes, trips, and flying sticks. Cassandra, because of the weight of the child she carried, found that her balance was poor. However, as the game progressed, her team members began to run interference for her, and Cassandra gradually adjusted to the change in her body. Then her long legs and agility paid off, for the Comanches, even the women, spent so much time on horseback that they were somewhat clumsy afoot. There wasn't a woman on the field that Cassandra couldn't outrun. She scored repeatedly, outdistancing both the opposition and her own teammates and slicing the hide ball across her goal.

The running kept her warm, an unusual pleasure, and it gave her a sense of freedom and happiness she had almost forgotten. She laughed and ran and swung her curved stick with a contagious joy that spread to her teammates and the spectators, more and more of whom gathered as the game progressed. When it was over, breathless and exhilarated, she reeled to the side of the field and gave Black Rain an impulsive hug.

"Thank you for letting me play," she gasped, smiling. Black Rain smiled back but said nothing.

Cassandra brushed the sweat-dampened, curling hair from her forehead and took another deep breath. "It was glorious," she exclaimed, and found herself looking into eyes as blue as her own.

"You might be a woman of the Water Horse," said Counts Many Coup.

She hadn't even known he was back. In the interest aroused by the game, the return of the war party laden with scalps and horses had gone practically unnoticed. And what had he meant? The Water Horse?

Little Wolf, her admiring shadow, explained as she and Black Rain prepared the evening meal while Faces A Bear sulked in the tepee. "My father was of the Water Horse band," said the child. "That's why he's so tall. They're fast runners and so good at games that none of the other tribes will play them because so much is lost gambling."

"She doesn't understand you, Little Wolf," said Black Rain.

"Yes, she does," the boy insisted.

Gambling, thought Cassandra. If she had bet on herself and her team, she might have been able to win a robe. Now that her sweat was drying, she shivered with cold.

"When my father was a young man," said Little Wolf importantly, "there was a great meeting of The People. The camp stretched for fifteen miles. The Water Horse were there and the *Tanima*, and my father joined the *Tanima*. Then he and Buffalo Leaper became blood brothers, because my father had no brothers of his own family."

So the Water Horse were tall and fine athletes and great gamblers, thought Cassandra, and Counts Many Coup had said she might have been one of them. It must be a compliment. Maybe she could count on his protection a while longer.

"She doesn't understand you, Little Wolf," said Black Rain again.

"Oh yes, she does," the boy reiterated.

Cassandra smiled and gave him a hug that made him squirm with pleasure. He was a dear child and smarter than the others knew.

Faces A Bear and Counts Many Coup emerged from the tepee, and Cassandra wondered idly whether they had been making love. How could he stand that mean woman? she wondered. Did he know that his first wife desired the death of his unborn child? Maybe someone would mention to him that Faces A Bear had tried to force Black Rain into the shinny game. But even if he knew, would he realize how dangerous it might have been for Black Rain and her baby? Cassandra laid her hand protectively over her own child, and Faces A Bear, seeing the gesture, gave her a shove and a scolding for being slow about her duties.

When the first wife divided the food, there was nothing left for Cassandra, and she muttered bitterly, "One would think the wife of a great war chief could be more generous to his slave." Let him hear. She hoped he did. When she glanced up, his eyes were indeed on her.

After the wild exercise, Cassandra was dizzy with hunger and tortured by the smell of food, but she had to remain while the others ate because she had chores to do before the victory dance. She herself wouldn't attend; the dance would only remind her of the night when, tied to the scalp pole, she'd expected to be tortured to death, the night she'd stopped caring what happened to her because she found out that Alex was dead. Instead she'd go to her blankets where she had some dried meat. What did she care about their stupid celebrations? She didn't want to hear bloodthirsty warriors counting coup.

When finally she was free, she plodded away, thinking that she ought to make a run for it before Faces A Bear managed to kill her. In the excitement of the dance maybe she could steal some food and a horse. Maybe they wouldn't miss her till morning. She gasped in fear when Counts Many Coup clasped her arm and spoke to her.

"Why did you call me a great war chief?" he asked. "I am not the war chief. No one is until a new one is chosen."

She shivered with anxiety. Her loose tongue and quick temper had again endangered her. If she told him that she eavesdropped on the other warriors, he would know that she understood Comanche. How angry would her deception make him? "I just know," she mumbled vaguely.

"How?" he demanded. "No one can know who will be chief until it is decided by the council."

"Then maybe I'm wrong." She tried to look nonchalant.

"Women cannot have medicine," he muttered. "Not young women."

"Who says I do?" she retorted, her anxiety rising. He had asked once if she were a sorceress. What did they do to sorceresses?

"Well, we shall see if you really know," he murmured, tipping her face up and staring into her eyes. "We shall see, little white Water Horse." Then he turned and strode off to his victory dance.

His touch had been gentle, not harsh, but still he had frowned at her. Greatly disturbed, Cassandra scurried to her blankets and huddled there, nibbling on her bit of dried meat. When things got noisy, she'd leave. If Counts Many Coup thought her a sorceress and his wife hated her, flight could be no more dangerous than staying, although, Lord, she had no idea where she was or which way to go. Without the sun to guide her—and it rarely shone these winter days—she could flee in the wrong direction. And she was so tired. The game had been exhausting. She'd just close her eyes for a moment. The drums were only starting up. It would be hours before she could safely slip away.

Morning had dawned when she opened her eyes again, and then every muscle in her body ached. Well, she had saved the life of Black Rain's baby, she told herself, but had she sacrificed her own life and her child's in doing it? Wearily she rose and faced another day, which would undoubtedly be worse than yesterday because Faces A Bear hated her more today than she had yesterday. Maybe, Cassandra told herself, God had sent that heavy sleep to keep her from sure death in the attempt to escape. She'd never know.

Chapter Eleven

For the first time that Cassandra could remember, Black Rain joined the hand game. When the excitement was at its highest pitch, they faced each other. Cassandra, who had been betting wildly and winning consistently, had all her accumulated winnings in a pile in front of her. "What shall our bet be?" she demanded of Black Rain.

"Against all of it," said Black Rain, "a buffalo robe."

Cassandra drew in her breath sharply. The afternoon sky held the gray cast of snow. The temperature was cold and dropping, the air as dry and sharp in her lungs as a knife blade. Tonight of all nights, she'd need a buffalo robe. Had Counts Many Coup been in camp, she thought he'd have let her sleep in the tepee rather than leave her outside in the snow. But both he and Broken Nose were away. Faces A Bear controlled Cassandra's access to shelter.

She stared longingly at the buffalo robe. If she lost, she'd lose the extra blanket she'd won and the extra clothing. And she held the bone. She had to conceal it from her opponent by sleight of hand. Cassandra knew that she was better at guessing than concealing, and she had no idea what Black Rain's talents might be. They'd never played against one another. The singing began to die away, the drums to fade as Cassandra, who was always the first to bet, sat frozen.

"Yes," she said, glancing at the lowering sky. She had to take the chance. The buffalo robe was what she'd wanted all along. In the gambling fever, she'd lost sight of that, as well as forgetting that she could lose as well as win, but she couldn't turn coward now. She'd be despised if she did. And she wouldn't get the robe.

Cassandra displayed the little bone in her hand. She began to switch it—or pretend to while she thought of passing if off to a team member. Could she trust the women on either side? Were they quick enough? Would they want her to win? *Trust only yourself*, a voice whispered in her head. She made four passes, during none of which the bone changed hands. Then, unable to breathe, she held out her fists to Black Rain. The black woman shrugged and pointed to Cassandra's right hand. It was empty, and the precious robe changed hands.

Black Rain dropped out of the game but sat back to watch. Cassandra gambled a while longer, holding the robe out of her bets. Would Black Rain sleep cold tonight? With her baby due so soon? Maybe Counts Many Coup would call the second wife to his bed and Black Rain would be warmed in his arms. No, not likely when she was so close to term. It was said among the women that the men stayed away when their wives were with child.

"Do you have another?" asked Cassandra, catching up with Black Rain when the game had broken up.

"I have another," the woman replied, one of the few times she spoke in English.

That night it snowed, but Cassandra slept warmer than usual, all of her winnings stuffed inside the robe with her.

When Counts Many Coup was elected war chief by the council, the women whispered among themselves that Cassandra had known it would happen. He said to her, "The voices of your spirits spoke true, Cass-an-dra." Instead of scowling and accusing her of sorcery, he put both hands on her shoulders and stared into her eyes, as if searching for answers to questions he had never asked before. Then he went on to other matters, one being that his second wife should have her own tepee, as was proper for a warrior of such stature.

The initial work fell to Black Rain and Cassandra. Cassandra gathered poles and stripped off the bark. Black Rain shaved them to the proper size and pointed the butts so that they could be driven into the ground during high spring winds. Skins were prepared, and then Black Rain went to Summer Cloud, who was the expert on tepee-making. As a gift for the older woman, Black Rain brought a beautifully beaded peplum that would hang in graceful folds to mid-thigh and cover the lacing that held a skirt and blouse together.

Other women were invited to help with the sewing, but Summer Cloud supervised the crucial cutting and fitting of the skins. Black Rain and Cassandra provided the feast. It must be like a quilting bee, Cassandra thought. She had never been to a quilting bee, but she enjoyed the tepee-making party, particularly the food. She would have enjoyed it even more if she'd thought herself likely to sleep in the lodge she'd worked so hard to make and if Faces A Bear and Talking Crow hadn't been members of the party, which ended on a sour note.

As Cassandra sat helping with the final sewing, Little Wolf ran up to her and pulled out one of the ringlets into which her short hair curled on damp days. Then Calling Dove, the little daughter of Falls In Water, pulled on another curl and watched it spring back. Relaxed and happy, Cassandra laughed with the children, and both tried to climb into her lap.

"Look how her hair grows," said Faces A Bear contemptuously. "It hangs in her face like the tail of a skunk or the winter coat of Brother Coyote."

The other women giggled nervously, and Cassandra

turned to stare at her tormentor, calculating her reply carefully. Then she said in loud, clear Comanche, "The Earth Mother grows hair; not the woman. Does Faces A Bear question the ways of the Earth Mother?" A shocked hush fell among the women, and no one spoke again to Faces A Bear that day. When Summer Cloud attempted to question Cassandra about what she had said, Cassandra looked at the medicine woman with blank incomprehension. She hoped they were all thoroughly confused. It served them right—making her sleep out in the cold and comparing her hair to a skunk's tail.

The little ones were playing Grizzly Bear while Cassandra, who had been sent to watch them, sat under a tree enjoying the afternoon sunshine as she sewed. They had scraped up a pile of sand from the banks of the creek, which flowed deep and cold nearby. The sand pile was called the "sugar." Calling Dove had just been dragged by her heels around the sugar to draw a circle. The "Grizzly Bear," an older boy who would stay inside the circle, reaching out to grab and "eat" a child, had been enlisted. So had the "mother," who would protect her children by swinging them in a line away from the bear.

Cassandra grinned as the bear caught and tickled the first child, who dissolved into giggles, as did the other children. The line broke up, and the children tried to steal the bear's sugar without being caught. When the line reformed, Little Wolf took the tail position. The grizzly growled and snapped; the children, giggling and clinging to one another's waists in the line, were swung this way and that by their protective "mother."

Cassandra wondered idly what *her* mother would have thought of this game. When the baby stirred, Cassandra imagined her own child playing Grizzly Bear. She sighed and punched another awl hole in the hide she was working on. Would there ever be a safe chance for escape? Maybe white traders would come and take her away. Maybe—

The children's screams broke into her reverie, and she saw Little Wolf's head slip beneath the waters of the swollen creek. The swinging line of children had snapped him into the cold water. Cassandra, heart pounding, tossed her work aside. "Run for help," she called to Beaver Tail, the older boy who had been the Grizzly. Then she jumped into the water. The creek was running fast, and Little Wolf had not resurfaced, making her wonder if he had been washed beyond the point where he had gone in. Then she saw him snagged underwater and struggling, but the current was pulling at her. She surfaced and dragged herself back by reaching from branch to branch where the trees overhung the water. On the bank the children screamed hysterically. Then she dove under again, yanked Little Wolf loose, and kicked her way toward the surface. Her clothes were heavy with water, and the current sucked them both downstream, but men already lined the banks, reaching out to her. Why didn't they come in? she wondered. With the last of her strength and still clutching the little boy, she kicked toward the extended hands.

How could she reach out herself without losing Little Wolf to the current? Then she felt rocks under her feet and pushed desperately toward the bank, staggering into waist-deep water. Counts Many Coup shouldered the other men aside and lifted Cassandra and his son onto the bank.

"You are a brave woman," he muttered, casting a despairing glance at the still figure of his only child.

Cassandra squeezed her arms around the boy's chest, forcing water out of him, twice, three times until he began to cough and gag. "Why did no one help us?" she asked.

"When a person drowns, his soul cannot escape

through the throat, and there is no life after death for him."

"And no one would take the chance," she muttered angrily.

"You did," Counts Many Coup replied. "Did your spirits direct you?"

"My heart directed me," said Cassandra, cradling the shivering child in her arms.

It was the season the Comanches called "when babies cry for food." Game was scarce, the men always away seeking it. Grass and cottonwood twigs for the horses were running out. Cassandra, who fared worse than most, was often faint with hunger. Then they moved camp. One minute a sizable village stood by the creek; in an hour it was gone, packed up on horses and travois dragged between the tepee poles. They were moving north toward Medicine Mounds, which lay between the Pease and Red Rivers.

Cassandra had hoped initially that her opportunity to escape might have arrived. At this point she didn't think she could be worse off on her own than she was with the tribe. However, she was given an old mule to ride. Even the poorest old man or youngest child was better mounted than she.

At night around the fires, people talked of the powerful spirit who dwelled in the mound and of the medicine that had been sought and received there, cures for those who were sick, great power in battle and the hunt, even resurrection of the dead. Little Wolf told Cassandra one afternoon, stopping briefly to chat before continuing his excited rambling up and down the line of march, that his father would seek a vision on top of the highest mound where the powerful spirit dwelled, a vision to direct him in his new duties as war chief.

Cassandra hoped the vision would show Counts Many Coup a herd of buffalo or antelope, even a bear lumbering about in some thicket. Now she remembered fondly the wedding feast served by Bluebonnet at Odell Webber's trading post.

The mounds proved to be an eerie line of cones rising high above the plain. Cassandra found herself believing that a powerful spirit dwelled on the highest of them. Camp was set up by an ancient buffalo trail that ran alongside, and Counts Many Coup left to fast and seek his vision. He was gone three days.

"I come for your council, Long Dancer," said the war chief once they had offered smoke to the gods.

"Did the mound spirit grant you a vision?"

Counts Many Coup looked troubled. "I do not know. When I had fasted two days, a thing came to me, but I cannot tell what it meant. I stayed another night, thinking on it, but I am no wiser."

"Tell me what you saw," said Long Dancer.

"I saw the woman Cass-an-dra. She rose up before me, whirling as if caught in the death winds that come with spring. Then she floated before my eyes like a cloud. I thought she wanted to tell me something but had no words. At last she looked away along the line of her raised arm, then faded into a mist and was gone."

"In what direction did she look?"

"To the northeast. What do you think, my father? Was it a dream—to be disregarded? Or a vision sent by the mound spirit? I have never had a vision with a woman in it."

"No," Long Dancer agreed. "It is strange. Had an animal from whom you receive medicine appeared to you thus, I would say that game lay to the northeast, but a woman?" He fell silent for a time, then asked, "Do you desire her?"

Counts Many Coup shrugged. "She is heavy with child."

"She will not always be."

"She seems to be a woman of power," said the warrior.

"There is no such thing among women in their childbearing years."

"She is not of The People."

"True. I think you must speak to her. Find out what you can. You, at least, know her language. When you have learned more about her, perhaps you can judge."

"Bring Cass-an-dra here," said Counts Many Coup, "and then leave us." The face of his wife flushed with anger, but he ignored her. He had fasted long and now ate hungrily what little Faces A Bear could serve him.

"We will talk," he said once Cassandra was seated in front of him. Noting how thin she had become, even though she was only a few months from childbed, he tore off a piece of meat and tossed it to her. From the sigh that escaped her lips as she accepted it, he guessed she must be as hungry as he, although she had not been fasting by choice. Was Faces A Bear denying Cass-an-dra her share? He frowned, thinking that he would not want to see harm come to the golden-haired woman. Then he put such thoughts aside and began to question her about her life.

She answered willingly, surprised at his interest, but nothing she said seemed to satisfy him. Even with food in her stomach at last, she became more and more uneasy. What did he want of her? she wondered.

"What does your name mean?" he asked. "I have not heard it before."

"Why should you have heard it?" she retorted. Then she remembered that they were speaking in English. "How did you learn English?" she asked.

"My father was a white trader, my mother Comanche. Until I was eight years, I spoke both, then only Comanche because my father died and we returned to the Water Horse. Now answer my question."

"It was the name of a prophetess," she replied. She

could see his glance sharpen with interest. "She fore-told the future, but no one listened," Cassandra added dryly.

"Did her spirits speak true?"

"So the tales say."

"Young women cannot have medicine. Was she old?"

"No, but this was thousands of years ago in a land across the ocean."

"Even so, you are a young woman, living here. How is it that spirits talk to you? Sometimes you speak our tongue; at other times you can't even understand."

Rather than lie, Cassandra remained silent.

"You have foretold the future, yet this cannot be. Spirits do not give visions to young women."

"Maybe the spirits speak through my child," she suggested craftily.

"Ah." He thought about that, then leaned forward and laid his hand against her belly, staring into her eyes. "You and I have Thunderbird eyes," he mused. Suddenly he was on his feet. "It could be. You carry a male child, and a spirit speaks through that child. Yes, the spirit said the child's ghost would haunt us if we killed it."

"Or me," she added.

"Do you remember what you said? It was not in your language."

"I have heard." What a bizarre conversation this was, she thought, but if it got her more food . . .

"I think we will find game to the northeast," said Counts Many Coup. "We will travel to the land of the Thunderbird."

In their trek toward Thunderbird country on the Red River, two things happened. They found wild horses and feasted, butchering and drying what they couldn't eat. Cassandra discovered that horse tasted as good as anything else when you were hungry. Then

Comancheros came into the camp to trade, and one of the things they wanted to trade for was Cassandra.

Because Counts Many Coup refused the first offers, more and more horses and trade goods were added, things his fuming wife coveted. The Comanchero leader said he could get good value trading a white woman with child to the whites. Faces A Bear wanted the beads and pots and needles offered with the horses. Cassandra didn't know what to hope for. On the one hand, becoming an item in trade might be the only way she could get back to civilization. On the other, the Comancheros were a vicious-looking bunch, and the idea of being alone among them made her uneasy.

In the end she had no say in the matter. Counts Many Coup sent them on their way, and her resentment against him simmered. If it weren't for him, she might have been home before the birth of her child. She could hardly contain her fury. Then, to her dismay, she discovered that he knew.

"You think I have kept you from your people," he remarked dryly as she served him his evening hunk of bloody meat. "What I have kept you from is rape, possibly death. You would certainly have lost the child before you ever saw another white face. You might have lost your life."

Remembering the Comancheros, she shivered. He was probably right, although she hated to admit it. If only the *Tanima* hadn't killed Alex, she thought miserably. If Alex were alive, she would have been safe by now—and happy. Even if Counts Many Coup had saved her life, she could hardly bear to look at him. She went back to the fire to take meat for herself and was confronted by Faces A Bear.

"So instead of having the trade goods I wanted," she hissed, "I have an ugly, lazy white slave I never wanted." She knocked the food from Cassandra's hand and then whipped her closed fist across Cassandra's cheek, knocking her into the trampled dust of the campsite. Cassandra curled up to protect the baby as Faces A Bear began to kick her.

As suddenly as it started, it was over.

"Is this how you protect my property?" Counts Many Coup demanded. Faces A Bear drew back in fear. Cassandra herself, although relieved at the rescue, scooted away from him.

"Black Rain!" he shouted. Indians were gathering from other campfires to see what had caused the commotion. The Negro woman, clumsy in the last months of her pregnancy, came to his side. "From now on Cass-an-dra is your servant. She sleeps in your tepee and does your bidding, yours and mine, no one else's." Black Rain nodded. Counts Many Coup glared at his first wife. "Never lay a hand on my slave again. She is no longer yours to command."

Humiliated, Faces A Bear went to her lodge. Cassandra pushed herself slowly to her feet as the crowd dispersed. She would have thanked Counts Many Coup for protecting her—or was it the baby he sought to protect? Whatever his motives, he did not stop to be thanked; he had already followed his first wife into the tepee. Cassandra would not have been in the moccasins of Faces A Bear for anything, not that night. The woman would be beaten.

At first Cassandra could think of nothing but the fact that she was at last to sleep in a tepee where neither rain nor snow could fall on her and where there would be a fire in the fire pit to warm her. She beamed at Black Rain. When Black Rain failed to smile back, Cassandra had second thoughts. Who could blame Black Rain if she saw this as an opportunity to avenge past ill treatment by whites?

Rolled in her buffalo robe that night, Cassandra reasoned it all out and decided that suspicion and fear of her new mistress would not improve her lot. She had to hope for the best—and work. The Negro woman's health was poor. There were many burdens Cassandra could relieve her of while Black Rain awaited the birth of her child.

Cassandra herself, now that she was eating regularly again, felt wonderful—full of energy and now full of hope. Maybe tomorrow would be better. It did no good to look too far into the future or to borrow trouble. She had to survive one day at a time. Maybe she and Black Rain could become friends. From Black Rain had come the precious buffalo robe, and the second wife had never gambled either before or after that night. Didn't that mean she had known snow was coming and found an acceptable way to protect a fellow captive? Cassandra did so want a friend. She yearned for someone to talk to.

Since Counts Many Coup had said she had Thunderbird eyes like his, dark blue she assumed, Cassandra became fascinated with the legend. They traveled toward the Thunderbird's home on the upper Red River where the huge bird was said to have burned his image on the ground, having fallen there, wounded by a Comanche arrow. The creature controlled the storms, of which the Comanches were afraid. The blinking of its eyes caused lightning, the flapping of its wings thunder. Rain fell from a huge lake on its back.

As they traveled north, there were signs of spring, and with it a resurgence of hope, energy, and courage in Cassandra. She made it her business to take good care of Black Rain, scouring the countryside for buffalo chips to feed their campfire and edible plants their stomachs. Cassandra did not consider the endless diet of half-raw meat a healthy one for two pregnant women, so she did her best to vary their menu and was successful enough that Counts Many Coup often ate at their fire, infuriating his first wife.

Cassandra raised and lowered the tepee and tucked the inner lining carefully under Black Rain's mattress

Elizabeth Chadwick

on cold, stormy nights so that the rain could not penetrate their warm haven. She helped in the preparation of robes in which to swaddle the new baby and constructed the papoose board on which the child would sleep by day, propped up near its mother or carried on her back. She made, under direction, the stiff rawhide tube to protect the baby at night when it would sleep between its parents. She made two of each item, one for Black Rain's baby, one for her own, reflecting sadly that her child would have no father sleeping beside it.

Then Cassandra gathered moss to absorb the child's excrement. She collected and ground up dry rot from cottonwood trees to be used as powder when the baby had been cleaned and greased at the end of the day. These preparations seemed bizarre and primitive, but she had given up thinking that she would escape before the birth of her own child, much less Black Rain's, and so she wanted to be as well prepared as she could. What Black Rain didn't know was learned from Summer Cloud, the peace chief's wife, and Wolf Woman, the mother of Faces A Bear, whose advice was grudging at best.

Cassandra's efforts did not go unnoticed or unappreciated. Black Rain's first gesture of friendship, unless the buffalo robe had been one, was an offer to share her pipe and tobacco. Cassandra had never smoked and didn't want to, but she could not turn away from this break in the wall of Black Rain's carefully maintained reserve. Cassandra drew on the pipe, held the smoke in her mouth, unsure what to do with it, then spat it out, causing laughter among the other women.

Black Rain smiled tolerantly and passed the pipe again. The second time, Cassandra, inhaling gingerly, breathed in some smoke and coughed until her eyes ran with tears. Again the women laughed. Black Rain said softly, her first communication in English in weeks, "Get used to it, Cass-an-dra. Smoke is a comfort, which you and I have need of."

Cassandra sighed and tried the pipe again. After that she controlled the need to cough, and they smoked together every day or so. They also began to talk at night, wrapped in their robes, lying in the tepee before sleep came.

"I was born on a plantation down the Brazos toward Velasco," said Black Rain in answer to a question of Cassandra's. "In the colony founded by Mistah Stephen F. Austin long before Texas split away from Mexico."

"The Stephen F. Austin colony," Cassandra repeated, her eyes wide in the dark. "Did you ever hear of a family named Daumier at Devil's Wood?"

"Oh yes, Miss Eloise and Mistah Jean Philippe. Lotsa talk about Devil's Wood. Him always in debt from gamblin', her with the babies dyin'. That Jean Philippe Daumier, he was a bigger fool for gamblin' than you are, Cass-an-dra."

"I only gamble to keep warm and fed," said Cassandra defensively. She had been listening to Black Rain's soft drawl with pleasure.

"Uh-huh," said Black Rain. "If that's so, why din you stop once Ah won you that buffalo robe?"

"I've always wondered about that robe," Cassandra murmured. Then with the echoes of Alex's Southern accent in her ears, she whispered, "Did you ever hear of Eloise Daumier's brother? His name was Alexander Harte."

"Oh yes. That plantation come close to bein' a success when he was around. He took the cotton down river, the money from the commission merchants din' get gambled away. But that Mistah Alex, he was a fightin' fool, always off joinin' up for some war, an' his sistah, Miss Eloise, yellin' after him to come on back 'fore he ever get outa the yard. How come you know about Devil's Wood?"

187

"I married Alexander Harte," said Cassandra sadly.

"You don' sound like a girl from mah home country."

"I married him when he was mustanging out here, but the Comanches killed him."

Black Rain sighed. "They killed mah man too."

"I didn't know they raided so far to the east."

"Din'. Jack an' me run away. Always heard slaves could be free, could they get to Mexico, an' that the Comanches, they wouldn't kill slaves; that was what folks said in the quarters. Our massa, he was Mistah Jefferson Pollard of Pollard's Hill, he wouldn't let us marry. Wanted me for himself to warm his bed an' make him some bright niggers."

Cassandra felt confused and horrified.

"That's what you get when you breed a slave woman an' a white massa—bright niggers," said Black Rain bitterly, "but Ah din' wanna be a breeder for Mistah Jefferson Pollard, so Jack an' me took off for Mexico. Did pretty good till the Comanches caught us. Outfoxed the dogs with pepper on our feet, then stuck to the cricks so they couldn't track us. We knew all the tricks. Jus' din' know the Comanches would kill a slave as fast as a white. Only difference was they din' bother with Jack's scalp since he din' have no soul."

"Oh, Black Rain," cried Cassandra. She didn't know which was more terrible, what had happened while Black Rain was a slave or what had happened after her escape.

Surprised, Black Rain touched Cassandra's arm. "No use to cry for me, Cass-an-dra. Ah'm better off than Ah was."

I'm not, thought Cassandra, mourning Alex.

Black Rain's labor began on a gloomy day in March when Counts Many Coup was away from the camp leading a raid. Preparations were made under the supervision of Wolf Woman, who was a midwife. She instructed Cassandra to dig two pits, one for the birth, one for the preparation of hot water. Then Cassandra had to drive two four-foot stakes in the ground for Black Rain to grasp when her pains became severe. Cassandra was sent to bring in sage and ordered to prepare hot coals. Faces A Bear and her sister, Talking Crow, were also in attendance, but their function was the singing of dreary, monotonous songs.

Now that the time was upon them, Cassandra feared for her friend. Too many of Wolf Woman's patients died. Their babies died as well, and Face A Bear didn't want this child to live. She would probably be happy to see Black Rain succumb in childbirth, although she would lose her servant if Black Rain died. Maybe she hoped to regain dominion over Cassandra through the death of Cassandra's new mistress.

Black Rain lay on her bed moaning. Sometimes in the throes of a contraction she was urged to rise and walk around or to grasp the stakes while squatting over the hole. Night fell, and with it a violent thunderstorm rolled into the encampment, lightning splitting the night sky into jagged chunks. Cassandra went to the door flap to watch and was dragged in by the sisters. Comanches stayed in their tepees during storms.

"It is an ill omen for the child," said Faces A Bear, looking smug. "The Thunderbird is displeased."

What was the woman up to now? Cassandra wondered, her sense of foreboding exacerbated. It was spring; spring brought storms. How could the storm have anything to do with the baby?

Thunder rolled, and the lightning cracked and danced outside, glowing through the walls of the tepee, accompanied by the scream of a horse. Cassandra again pushed the door aside and saw that a returning warrior had been hit by the latest bolt. Talking Crow, looking out from behind her, increased the volume of her doleful song.

189

"A girl," said Wolf Woman, for at last the child came.

"An evil omen," said Talking Crow. "She was born as a warrior of The People died under the arrows of the Thunderbird."

"She is a scrawny child and must be thrown away for the good of the *Tanima*," said Faces A Bear.

Thrown away? Did she mean left out to die? Cassandra heard Black Rain's wail. They wanted to abandon this long awaited child? No! Cassandra raced out into the storm, into the very midst of the warriors whose companion had just died. Awaiting the cessation of the next roll of thunder, she threw her arms out, and with the lightning casting a livid glow over her streaming face and body, she cried, "This child will be the mother of great warriors, sons of the Thunderbird."

The men drew back, amazed.

"What is this you say, Cass-an-dra?" Counts Many Coup asked.

"Your daughter is born. Black Storm. Mother of *Tanima* warriors, even to the last days of The People. Do not let the cowardly women throw her away."

Members of the band began to come out of their tepees, Wolf Woman and her daughters among them.

Summer Cloud had gone from her lodge into Black Rain's and returned with the baby. "It would seem that the Thunderbird has smiled on you again, my son," she said, raising the child to Counts Many Coup.

The baby howled loudly, drowning out even the retreating rumble of thunder. "A lusty girl," said Counts Many Coup. Then he turned to Cassandra, taking her shoulders into his hands as he had once before and staring into her eyes. "The spirits speak again through Cass-an-dra and her child. Does he welcome the birth of his sister—what did you call her?—Black Storm? A good name. Do you agree, Father?" He had turned to Long Dancer, and Cassandra was left with her heart fluttering unaccountably.

"A good name for a mother of warriors," Long Dancer agreed, eying Cassandra curiously. "It is your unborn son who speaks?" he asked Cassandra. "His grasp of the Comanche tongue is remarkable."

Cassandra, of course, gave Long Dancer an uncomprehending look, but she thought, wryly, *A remarkable grasp of Comanche and an increasing flair for the dramatic!*

"Can I hold her?" asked Cassandra, looking wistfully at the baby girl whose body they'd just washed and oiled.

"She wouldn't be alive today if not for you," said Black Rain as she put the baby into Cassandra's arms. "You're her mama too. Sisters are mothers to each other's babies," she added, staring at Cassandra as if to ask whether she acknowledged the sisterhood.

Cassandra felt a greater warmth of heart than she'd known since Alex died. "Sisters," she murmured and leaned forward to kiss Black Rain's cheek. "That's a kind thing to say to your slave," she added, grinning.

"How long you think you get to stay a slave?" asked Black Rain dryly. "If Counts Many Coup will marry a black woman with no soul, he'll surely want to—"

"What do you mean, no soul?" Cassandra interrupted indignantly.

"Tha's what The People believe. Black skin, no soul. But Counts Many Coup, he wasn't interested in souls. He wanted tall sons from a tall wife. An' then marryin' a captive only cost him one horse. Now you, you're tall, an' you'd only cost him one horse. Why, you even got a soul. You're gonna be a bargain once you've had your chile."

Cassandra giggled at Counts Many Coup's matrimonial requirements. Not very romantic. And she'd get a horse to escape on. Which came first? she wondered. The horse? Or the wedding night? Alex's beloved face flashed in her mind, and she knew she couldn't marry the war chief.

"Why the tears?" asked Black Rain. "He's a good enough husband, good lover anyways. Ah could do without Faces A Bear always naggin' me, but mah mama always said the sting gotta come along with the honey."

Chapter Twelve

She felt as if her brain had turned to fire when she recognized the squat, ugly warrior who had killed Benjamin Whitney and left her to die, wounded and helpless. She was incandescent with hate as he stared at her. At her hair. Was he regretting that he had passed it up? Was he planning to claim it now that he had a second chance? No casual visitor to the tribe could scalp the war chief's slave, she reassured herself. It would be almost as great an insult as, say, shooting his favorite horse.

Then she realized that he didn't recognize her. How could that be? Perhaps all whites looked alike to him. And he hadn't known that she was a girl. He'd have been twice as furious about the raw scar on his face if he'd known a female caused it. She was tempted to tell him just to see his expression. Instead she returned to her pelt scraping.

"An ugly man," remarked Black Rain, eying the visitor.

"I have no wish to sell her," said Counts Many Coup.

"I offer many horses for a woman who is in no condition to share my bed," said the fat warrior, who was now called Borrows A Lance by his companions.

It must be a nickname originating from the time he attacked her with a borrowed lance, thought Cassandra, shuddering at the idea of belonging to that man.

"No," said Counts Many Coup.

Cassandra let out her breath in a trembling rush. Luck was still with her, and she owed Counts Many Coup a debt.

"Did you wish to marry him?" the war chief asked later.

"No," cried Cassandra.

Counts Many Coup smiled and then beckoned to Black Rain, who had been released from her tepee once the blood had ceased to flow after the birth of her child. She went obediently to the bed of her husband.

Cassandra, alone in the tepee she usually shared, slept uneasily. She feared Borrows A Lance. Would he try to kidnap her, having failed to trade for her? Such things were done among the Comanches, and once the kidnapped woman had spent a night with her abductor, the couple was considered married. The man made her nervous on Counts Many Coup's behalf as well. Borrows A Lance had been simmering with repressed anger after the refusal of his offer. She had seen that fury before and its results. She would have to watch him on her protector's account as well as her own.

She turned restlessly, the sounds of lovemaking in the next tepee keeping her awake. Black Rain had said Counts Many Coup was a good lover. Cassandra wondered if she had moaned like that with Alex? It was so long since she had made love. She turned again, blinking back tears. How foolish she was to think of lovers, she who was so heavy with child that she could hardly move. It was hard to believe that only a few months ago she had raced up and down a field playing shinny. Now she felt like a washtub on legs, and Black Rain had to take care of her. The child would be born soon, and it must be a huge baby. So many died here— mothers and babies. How would she fare? How would her child fare if she perished bringing it into the world? She turned again, seeking a comfortable position, which she never seemed to find.

The baby kicked. Through two walls of hide, Cassandra heard her friend sigh, and then all was still. She slept at last and dreamed that Alex was alive and she lay in his arms, a slender maiden again, accepting his kiss and wondering what it would be like to know his lovemaking.

"I must speak to you."

"I am busy," Counts Many Coup replied impatiently.

"Too busy to heed the welfare of your stallion?" she retorted. Counts Many Coup owned a pinto that was deemed the best stud in the *Tanima* herd. Cassandra thought he probably cared more for that horse than his wives. "The visitor to the tribe, Borrows A Lance, covets your stallion."

"So? It will do him no good."

"He will propose a race—his horse against yours."

"He will lose."

"He will win by trickery."

Counts Many Coup glared at her. "How do you know?"

"I know," she replied with as much arrogance as he. Actually she knew because she had heard Borrows A Lance plotting with his friend. They were not going to leave the outcome of the race and the bet to chance.

"What trickery?"

"His friend will slip a burr into your saddle pad. When you mount, the burr will be driven into the horse's back, and he will buck while Borrows A Lance goes on to win the race—and your horse."

"I will kill him," hissed the infuriated war chief.

"On what pretext? Until you lose the race, you will have no evidence. If you find the burr beforehand and accuse him, he will lie."

"I will make him swear an oath."

"And if he swears false?"

"Comanches do not swear false."

"It would be easier and more satisfying to trick him at his own game." Although Counts Many Coup frowned, obviously not seeing how it could be done, Cassandra had a plan. "At the last minute, double the bet if he will ride bareback," she suggested. "How can he refuse?"

Counts Many Coup looked surprised, then began to laugh.

"Who has a better horse or rides better without a saddle than you? He will not only lose his favorite horse and others; he will always wonder whether you knew of his deceit, and he will be afraid of your denunciation."

Counts Many Coup laid his hand gently along the side of her face. "You are wise for your years, little golden one. I will do as you say."

Cassandra smiled as he walked away. She could hardly wait to see that fat pig's face when Counts Many Coup demanded a bareback race and won all the horses at stake.

Buffalo Leaper roared with laughter. "You challenge my brother to race you with his horse and yours as the prize? You'll lose your horse, Borrows A Lance. Counts Many Coup rides like the Thunderbird on the wings of a storm."

Borrows A Lance grinned, the scar pulling his mouth into a twisted line. "Do you accept my challenge, Counts Many Coup?"

"Of course," said the war chief.

"My horse against yours. At the signal we mount and ride to the tree over there by the black hill and back."

"Agreed," said Counts Many Coup, "but you'll lose your horse."

"I'll win," said Borrows A Lance confidently. "You

have held your name for horsemanship too long, brother."

"Well then, *brother*, let us sweeten the bet. Five additional horses from my herd against five of yours."

"Good!" said Borrows A Lance. "I would not have asked so many of your horses, but since you offer . . ." The scar flared red as his grin widened.

"And to add to the excitement, we'll ride bareback."

"Bareback?" Borrows A Lance looked confused. "There was no mention of bareback," he stammered.

Counts Many Coup was smiling as his glance flicked across Cassandra. She lowered her eyes demurely. The vicious swine had been neatly speared. Now let him struggle on the lance of his own throwing.

"Bareback," repeated Counts Many Coup. "You are not afraid to ride against me bareback, are you, brother? Saddles are for women and boys."

In the face of the crowd's approval, Borrows A Lance could not refuse. He lost the race by three lengths.

"You were too confident," said Buffalo Leaper, clapping the loser on the back. "Did I not tell you my brother was a horseman like no other?"

Counts Many Coup took the visitor's horse and five from his herd. "You were right," he murmured to Cassandra later. "In the morning there was no burr embedded in my saddle pad. Later there was. When I picked up the saddle and pad after the race, the burr bit into my hand, and his face turned as white as yours. Now, as you said, he will wonder as long as he lodges with the *Tanima* what I knew of his plans. But I do not think he will stay."

"He will stay to make more trouble," said Cassandra gloomily.

"Do your voices tell you this?"

"My heart tells me."

Another band camped with theirs. Games, races, and gambling flourished between the visitors and the

Tanima. Cassadra watched the games with envy, sitting cross-legged, her distended belly resting on her thighs. She dreamed at night of running between the stakes, swinging her curved stick, laughing as she had during the one game she had played. But she awoke to feel her baby kicking. Soon she would be brought to bed with her first child, and then she would be slim again. "Patience, little one," she whispered, patting the bulge made by a tiny, impatient foot. "One of us needs to practice that virtue." How she longed to be free of this burden, to hold Alex's son in her arms.

But then her impatience died, and fear took its place. A woman from the visiting band went into labor, and her child, a daughter, was born dead. Cassandra listened to the mother's mourning wails. She had not cried out during her pains, but grief overcame her stoicism. "Oh, Lord, don't let my baby die too," Cassandra whispered. Now she was afraid and would have kept the baby in her womb, where it was safe.

This pain was worse than what she had suffered from the lance wound. They made her walk when she wanted to lie on her bed and moan. They wrapped her hands around the stakes and told her that if she managed to stay alive until morning, her soul could find its way to the land beyond the sun where the game was plentiful and no storms came to mar the peace of grassy meadows.

"I'm not going to die," she muttered, then tore her hands from the stakes and went back to bed.

"She will not do as she should," complained Wolf Woman. "How can the baby come when she will not squat over the hole so it can fall out?"

Black Rain bathed Cassandra's face and sent for Summer Cloud, whose medicine was powerful.

"You must go to the stakes," said Summer Cloud, "so your child can be born."

"There is a special place in the afterlife for women

who die in childbirth," said Faces A Bear, "as good as that reserved for a warrior who dies in battle."

"I won't die," grated Cassandra, "if only to keep myself out of your miserable Comanche heaven."

Fortunately, Faces A Bear didn't understand, although she recognized the anger and backed away. "What can one do for such a woman?" she asked.

Black Rain, frantic with worry, took Cassandra back to the bed and bathed her face. The birth was taking too long; such labors ended badly. A medicine man with otter power was sent for. He drew an otter tail down Cassandra's stomach, then leapt through the tepee door, after which the child should have come. It didn't.

"The baby is too big," said Wolf Woman.

They put hot rocks at her back. Cassandra thought she was in her mother's house, curled by the hearth, reading Virgil. She mumbled about Dido and Aeneas. Black Rain, the only one who understood her, didn't know who Dido and Aeneas were but understood that Cassandra was hallucinating.

They fed Cassandra hot soup to strengthen her. She thought she was in church taking communion, and mumbled, "Forgive us our sins." Black Rain understood the prayer and prayed to the Christian God for the first time since her captivity, tears sliding silently over her cheekbones.

"Now the baby comes," said Summer Cloud, and the women dragged Cassandra to the pit and the stakes.

"A boy," said Faces A Bear enviously.

Cassandra mumbled, "No boys. Mama teaches only girls."

The dreary songs changed to reluctant songs of rejoicing. Wolf Woman cut the cord and wrapped it until it could be hung on a hackberry tree, where it had to remain untouched until it rotted. That way the boy would live to old age, untouched by misfortune. Cassandra drowsed, then awakened mumbling when the pains started again. "I think the professors steal the teacups," she said.

"What is this?" asked Black Rain, alarmed.

"Only the afterbirth," said Wolf Woman.

"I think not," muttered Summer Cloud. "Get her up. Another baby comes."

"Unnatural," keened Faces A Bear. "We must conceal this or bring shame on our lodges."

"We can slip the babies outside the village," suggested Talking Crow. "I will take the boy now. Then we can smother the next one and say he died. That way no one will know of her shame."

"It must be done," Wolf Woman agreed.

Cassandra mumbled about teacups, then screamed.

"A girl," said Summer Cloud.

"Here. Give her to me," said Faces A Bear urgently.

Black Rain waited for Cassandra to forestall them, but Cassandra was asleep. Summer Cloud looked undecided.

"We dare not kill the boy," Black Rain stammered. "He will come back to haunt us. Don't you remember what she said at the scalp dance the first night she was here?"

"The boy has spirit power," Summer Cloud agreed. "Even from the womb, he spoke through his mother."

"Two babies are unnatural," Wolf Woman insisted, although she looked uneasy. "We must—surely, we must—"

"Would you bring a powerful ghost back to haunt the *Tanima*?" demanded Summer Cloud. "You seek to retain the power of your daughter over her husband and care nothing for the welfare of The People. Give me the boy!"

Wolf Woman handed him over, her eyes clouded with fear. "What of the girl?" she asked.

Summer Cloud shrugged. "Faces A Bear can throw her away."

Black Rain, remembering that Cassandra had saved her daughter, cried "No!" and snatched the baby from the first wife.

"The second baby *must* be thrown away," said Summer Cloud. Her daughters-in-law nodded. "Its presence will bring ill luck on the tribe," added the medicine woman.

Black Rain glanced at her friend and fellow wife, then at the baby in her arms, a frail, pretty child. "If we throw her away, her brother will resent it. He will be a man of great power and will avenge his sister's death."

"You know nothing, black woman," snapped Faces A Bear. "You are without a soul and bring evil by your very—"

"Silence, daughter," said Summer Cloud and turned once again to Black Rain. "It is your love for your white sister that clouds your thinking, Black Rain. Even if it were not so that twins are bad medicine, the girl child you hold is fragile and might not live. Were we to keep her, she would drain the mother's milk that should have nourished her brother."

Black Rain again looked at Cassandra, but there was no help there. Her sister slept like a dead woman. What arguments could she use now when everything that Summer Cloud said was according to tribal custom and even made good sense? As many babies as died among the *Tanima*, this girl might well prejudice her brother's chances at life. What would Cassandra want? That both children live, of course, but how? Then Black Rain thought of a solution. "There is a woman in camp whose breasts are full of milk and who weeps for the loss of a daughter." Black Rain looked hopefully at the medicine woman. If the solution came from her....

"Ah yes," said Summer Cloud. "That is sometimes done. If we give the girl to Singing Bird—"

"No!" Faces A Bear cried and reached out to take

the baby from Black Rain, who stepped back quickly, tightening her hold.

"Be silent, daughter," said Summer Cloud. "Your plan is wise, Black Rain. The boy cannot blame us for his sister's death because we will have saved her. The grief of Singing Bird will be assuaged because she will have a baby to fill her cradle board. And the ill luck that follows twins will be averted because the second child will not be among the *Tanima*. Take the girl child to the lodge of Singing Bird and her husband."

"I will do it," said Faces A Bear.

Her mother-in-law stared narrowly at the first wife, then said, "Black Rain will do it." She glanced at Cassandra. "The afterbirth comes." Summer Cloud waved Wolf Woman over to minister to the mother, who barely stirred. Summer Cloud wrapped the boy in soft rabbit skin and placed him in the cradle board. "Cass-an-dra will stay in her bed two weeks."

"That is for me to say," Wolf Woman objected.

"You, who put the welfare of your daughter above the good of the tribe?" Summer Cloud asked disdainfully. "You will throw the afterbirth into running water."

"I know what to do." Wolf Woman muttered sullenly.

Summer Cloud turned to Black Rain, who waited in the doorway with the second baby in her arms. "Your sister will taste no meat lest she bleed excessively. Sage must be burned each day to purify the tepee. When the period of confinement is up, she will rise and go to bathe in running water."

Black Rain nodded submissively.

"Now take the girl child to her new mother."

Satisfied that she had saved both of her friend's babies, Black Rain left. Tomorrow morning she would speak to Counts Many Coup. Perhaps they could get the girl back now that her death had been averted.

* * *

For three days Cassandra slept, waking to nurse her son and sleeping again. Then as she stayed awake for longer periods, she looked around the tepee, puzzled. Black Rain's heart sank, and she stayed outside as much as possible, unable to face the questions to come if Cassandra remembered the night her children were born.

"Where is the other baby?" asked Cassandra on the fourth day, finally realizing that only one baby was brought to her for nursing. Black Rain was lying on her mattress, ready to sleep. "Another was born. I remember the pain. Is someone else caring for it?" She knew that Comanche families took in other children eagerly. "Was it a girl or a boy?"

"A girl," mumbled Black Rain.

"Where is she?"

"Gone."

"Gone where?" asked Cassandra, alarmed.

"Gone, Cass-an-dra."

"I heard her cry."

"They wanted to throw her away—Faces A Bear, Wolf Woman, an' Talkin' Crow," Black Rain replied, resigned to telling the story.

"Throw her away!"

"Leave her outside the camp to die. It's the custom with twins. They think havin' twins is unnatural an' brings evil luck. Even Summer Cloud agreed."

Cassandra made a sound of bewildered pain.

"They let you keep the boy because Ah reminded them he has spirit power. They were afraid of his ghost if he died because of them."

"And my daughter? They left her out to die?" Cassandra's eyes filled with tears.

"No, Cass-an-dra. Ah said the boy wouldn't want his sister killed, but Summer Cloud—she said keepin' the girl might hurt the boy—not enough milk for two."

"I have enough," Cassandra cried. "Where is she?"

"Gone," Black Rain replied sadly. "Ah got them to

203

give her to Singin' Bird. You remember? The woman of the Wasp band whose child died. She had milk. Ah thought Ah could talk Counts Many Coup into gettin' her back when Faces A Bear wasn't around." Black Rain couldn't bear the look of hope on Cass-an-dra's face. "But the next mornin' they were gone—the whole band."

"Which direction?"

"South, but my sister, you have to face it. You may never see her again." Cassandra had gone gray. "Ah did what Ah could. She's alive."

"Faces A Bear did this," said Cassandra.

Black Rain sighed. "An' her mother, Wolf Woman, an' Talkin' Crow. They wanted to kill the boy too." Black Rain rose to kneel beside Cassandra's bed. "Ah'm so sorry."

"I don't blame *you*." Cassandra lay still with her son at her breast, sucking contentedly. She looked down at him and murmured, "But I will be avenged. Faces A Bear will rue the day she saw my face."

"Cass-an-dra, she's the first wife. There's nothin' you can do."

"I will find a way."

"Girl babies are soon forgotten among the Comanches. Maybe you can forget."

"You have a daughter. Would you forget her so soon?"

Black Rain looked at the baby lying among the robes of her bed. "No," she admitted.

"Maybe we'll find her again," said Cassandra, the tears begining to flow again.

"They wouldn't give her back. Singin' Bird—Ah could see the love in her eyes when Ah put the baby in her arms."

According to custom, Cassandra stayed in her tepee after the birth, and the confinement made her desperately restless, wild with grief and rage. She looked at her son and thought of the daughter she had never seen. "What did she look like, Black Rain?" she asked again and again.

"She was tiny. Perfect, but real small, smaller than her brother."

"What color were her eyes?"

"Blue, but in the way of babies. They might not have stayed blue."

"Her hair? What color?"

"Hard to say. Just a fuzz." Black Rain hated the questions. They made her feel guilty. They made Cass-an-dra sadder. "You must stop thinkin' about her. She's gone."

"She's alive," cried Cassandra.

"Maybe," said Black Rain cautiously. "Babies die."

"If she were dead, I'd know it. The woman who took her—Singing Bird. I did not know her."

"She wept for the death of her own child. She took your daughter gladly. She had milk. The baby prob'ly has a better chance with her new mother."

Cassandra turned away, thinking, *They went south. If I could go out, I might to able to see them. One can see for miles on the plains, and my eyes are good. If only I could see them.* She propped up the cradle board.

"What are you doin'? It's taboo for you to—"

"I will leave now," said Cassandra, tucking her son into the cradle board.

"You can't. It's daylight. You'll be seen."

"I cannot go at night. How could I see the march south of the Wasp tribe if it is dark?" To a blouse she had won in the hand game, Cassandra laced her summer skirt, which fell in an uneven hem to her ankles. She had no fancy beaded peplum to wrap around her waist. Pulling on her moccasins, she hung the cradle board from her back and slipped through the stiff hide door of the tepee.

No one noticed as she walked from the village toward a hill crowned by a lightning-blasted tree. She

Elizabeth Chadwick

stood straight, tall and strong beside the tree's twisted, blackened limbs, her son in her arms, and stared to the south. Nothing moved there but hundreds of miles of grass, rippling like a golden sea. Her daughter was gone, lost in that endless prairie. For the first time Cassandra believed that she would never see her again. How could she find the child on that trackless plain? Her baby might die out there, unbaptized among a heathen people.

Cassandra dropped to her knees in the high grass and gathered prairie flowers until she had a sizable bouquet. With no holy water to serve her purpose, she tossed the flowers in a wide circle, letting the wind catch them and waft them south, saying with her face raised to the sun and the blue sky, "I christen thee Alexandra." Then she bowed her head. "In the name of the Father, the Son, and the Holy Ghost. Amen."

Watching the flowers swirl away in the wind, she whispered, "Go with God, Alexandra. May your foster mother love you dearly and the Lord give you good health and happiness. Should your luck be ill and your life short, your father will find you in heaven."

After that she took her son from the cradle board on her back and laid him in the grass. With no baptismal water but her tears, she made the sign of the cross over him and whispered, "I christen thee, Benjamin." She finished the ritual, then sat back and wept as the baby dozed beside her.

"Cass-an-dra, you weep for a child who now has a family and a mother to take care of her, should she live."

Cassandra looked up at Counts Many Coup, whose silent approach she hadn't heard. He did not seem angry that she had broken the birth taboo by leaving her tepee. "I have said good-bye to my daughter. I loved her. The *Tanima* do as much for their loved ones."

"You did not know her; nor could you have kept

206

her, not without bringing ill luck on the tribe. Black Rain thought of the only alternative short of exposing the baby." He drew Cassandra to her feet. "You owe your sister thanks for her quick-wittedness. Now your daughter has a new mother who will cherish her, and you have a male child who may well survive. Put your grief behind you." He then lifted the cradle board and studied Benjamin. "A fine boy. It is cause for rejoicing. Now the time has come that you have a husband again."

There was a long silence during which he studied her as if she were a source of puzzlement to him. "I have two wives already and should probably give you to Broken Nose, who is as my brother and who needs a woman to lighten his sadness for a wife who died."

Cassandra's heart clenched. She didn't want to marry Broken Nose. Oh God, she didn't—

"But there is a bond between us such as I have never had with a woman. Even from the first time you looked into my eyes it was as if—as if we recognized one another."

Cassandra had the same remembrance of that first moment. There had been recognition. She had thought he was Alex. She looked into his face and still saw there the echo of her first love.

"A warrior expects to protect a woman, and I have protected you. He does not expect a woman to protect him, yet you have been my ally—both in the vision world and the real." He frowned, as if he did not know what to make of such an unorthodox relationship, but finally he said, after another silence stretched between them, "I will bring a horse to your tepee when your period of confinement is over."

Cassandra took the child from him, her heart beating very hard. Was that what she wanted? To give herself to this man? If she married Counts Many Coup, he would provide protection for Benjamin and for her, so in truth, she had little choice. Cassandra nodded, her face as serious as his.

"Good. Now, return to your tepee before the others find that you have flouted the ways of The People."

She walked slowly back alone, the cradle board slung from her shoulders. Because she was thinking of what marriage to Counts Many Coup would mean, she did not notice that she was being followed. As a wife with her own horse, she would have the means to flee. Counts Many Coup was frequently absent, hunting and raiding. When next he left, she would flee.

A burly arm clamped around her throat, cutting off her wind and her plans. The baby, pressed between them, howled. Cassandra recognized her captor as Borrows A Lance. Did he mean to kill her or kidnap her?

"Swine!" she snarled in Comanche. "I'll never belong to you." Even as the power of her insult—for swine were taboo—sank into his dull mind, she had reached behind her, into his breechclout, and twisted.

Borrows A Lance screamed, and his grip on her throat loosened enough for her to sink her teeth into his forearm and wrench away. She ran, panicked for a minute, then realized that she had run away from camp, not toward it. Just as she thought of swerving, she saw ahead of her the shields, which the warriors hung at least a half mile from camp to protect them from greasy hands and menstruating women, either of which could disperse their spirit power.

She remembered the shield of Borrows A Lance very clearly. How many times had she seen it in her mind's eye, painted with its buffalo symbols and scalps, decorated with feathers, stuffed now with the papers that had cost her father his life? Her lips drew back in a grimace, and she screamed to call attention to herself and him, for she could hear his clumsy steps behind her. She would rouse the whole camp and have his shield before he ever got near her. Then as she neared them, Cassandra saw that the shields were all covered. She couldn't tell which was his after all.

Glancing over her shoulder, she saw that he had changed course and headed for the end of the row. Had he fathomed her plan? Was he going to protect his shield? Of course, his would be the last, since he was the newest warrior to join the band. She veered in front of him, risking capture, and still got to the end of the row before he did. He roared a protest as she snatched his shield from the mesquite bush where it hung and, panting, turned with the shield in her hands and spat on it. Then she dashed it to the ground.

Still ten feet away, he stopped, aghast. "Look what this white woman has done!" he cried to the people who were gathering.

"She is taboo," they whispered. "She should not be out of her tepee."

"I have contaminated your shield, Borrows A Lance," she hissed. "Your buffalo magic is gone."

"She must be punished," cried Borrows A Lance.

"I am the property of the war chief," said Cassandra, seeing from the corner of her eye that Counts Many Coup had strode into the crowd. "This man sought to rape me because Counts Many Coup refused an offer for me and because he won all the horses. This cowardly warrior sought his revenge by stealing a woman instead of acting the man as he should."

Borrows A Lance cried, "The woman lies. She must be punished for contaminating the shield of a warrior."

Murmurs of agreement ran through the crowd. Cassandra could see the fury in the eyes of Counts Many Coup but did not know if it was directed at her or the fat warrior.

"How did I know which shield was his?" she asked, her voice soaring over the mutterings of the crowd. "The shields were covered."

They stirred uneasily. Borrows A Lance shouted,

"Do not listen to her. She speaks with the crooked tongue of the whites."

"The Earth Mother led me to his shield that I might be avenged. Borrows A Lance has broken the laws of The People."

"She lies!"

"He killed my father, an unarmed old man who was a guest at his fire. He did this because he was greedy. He wanted to stuff this shield with the papers my father carried. Now the Earth Mother has taken from him his buffalo magic."

Borrows A Lance retreated a step.

"Look at the scar on his face. He tells you he got it from a brave warrior with hair like winter grass. He got it from me, a woman with hair like winter grass. How can a man call himself a warrior of The People when he counts coup on a maiden?"

"She lies," mumbled Borrows A Lance.

"You know his name. He borrowed the lance of a brave man who died after counting coup, and as he tells you at the victory dances, he drove that lance through the shoulder of the white warrior with hair like winter grass. Behold his wound in my shoulder." She pulled the neckline of her blouse aside and exposed the scar. "He has broken the laws of hospitality and lied in the warrior's circle."

Borrows A Lance had fallen silent. The mutterings of the crowd fell away.

"No matter what happens to me, I will be avenged for my father's death, because Borrows A Lance will die on his next raid." Cassandra figured that if he was as frightened as he looked, he probably would die if he ever exposed himself again to danger.

The *Tanima* drew away from Borrows A Lance as if he, as well as his shield, were contaminated. Cassandra, left untouched by those who moments earlier had cried for her punishment, turned her back contemptuously on her enemy, hitched the papoose board into a more comfortable position, and strode back to Black Rain's tepee. Benjamin, calmed by his mother's voice, had stopped howling and fallen asleep.

"Did the Earth Mother speak to you?" Counts Many Coup asked as he fell in step beside her.

She debated. He did not believe that women had medicine, and Cassandra did not want her future husband to think her a sorceress. Husbands held the power of life or death over their wives. The only thing that kept a Comanche from killing his wife if he wanted to was the perception that if he earned a reputation as a wife killer he might not be able to get another. "I'm not sure how I knew," she replied, choosing her words carefully. "Maybe he told me."

"*He* told you?" exclaimed Counts Many Coup.

"His fear when he saw where I was headed. I knew a moment of panic when I saw that the shields were covered," she replied honestly. "Then I saw him change directions, and I knew which was his. But now my father's death will be avenged, and that is as it should be. My father was an old man, a man of peace and wisdom who loved The People, and he was unarmed, a guest at the campfire of Borrows A Lance. Such a father should be avenged."

"You spoke Comanche again," said Counts Many Coup. "Speak it to me now."

"I learn," she said and mumbled a few ill-pronounced phrases.

He shook his head. "That is not the voice I heard before. Spirits must be at work."

"Bettah to be a wife than a slave," said Black Rain. "You'll be given a Comanche name—"

"How did you get yours?" Cassandra interrupted.

Black Rain laughed. "Ah cried for days after they killed mah lover an' took me prisoner. They were always lookin' to see if my tears were black, an' they called me Black Rain—even before Counts Many Coup married me."

"And you don't mind if he marries me too?"

"The more wives, the more hands to share the work," said Black Rain pragmatically. "But Ah'll miss you when you get your own tepee."

"Will I have my own tepee?" asked Cassandra, forgetting that she meant to use her bridal horse to escape.

"Sure, an' a better share of the food, an' hides to make clothes, so you don't have to gamble for what you need."

"I like to gamble," said Cassandra, grinning.

"Ah know that," said Black Rain, grinning back. "Just don't you go gamblin' mah stuff away."

"Can I do that?" asked Cassandra.

"Oh yes, but Ah tan your backside if you do. Second wives can beat third."

"And first can beat both," said Cassandra, sighing.

"But you'll still be bettah off, an' he's not gonna pass you up—not a tall woman that won't cost him but one horse an' don't bring along in-laws to be supported.

"He's gotta support Wolf Woman an' Turkey Feather an' the youngest girl, Little Antelope, who's not married yet. You din' know that? You've gone hungry 'cause his game went to their fire. Now you get your share, an' you got no parents for him to support. He's not gonna pass you up, not with hair like that an' medicine."

"Who says I have medicine?" asked Cassandra uneasily.

"Any fool can see that. When's he bringin' the horse?"

"When my confinement is up," said Cassandra, wondering whether she could actually give herself to him. Well, it wasn't as if she had a choice.

Chapter Thirteen

Pausing at the door of the tepee, Cassandra looked out longingly toward the prairie, where seas of grass fed the millions of animals that roamed there, where flowers bloomed, the same flowers she had seen last year when Alex rescued her. Now that she was no longer taboo, having had the ritual bath in running water, the war chief would come for her. *Oh, Alex*, she thought, *if only*—but if onlys wouldn't get her through this night, and there were things to be thankful for, she reminded herself. Benjamin, for one, her sweet baby. And there was food—not just game, but plums in the thickets beside the streams, and grapes, their thick vines climbing everywhere, haws and persimmons. Later there would be pecans and walnuts if they moved east. She and Benjamin wouldn't go hungry.

And she had a friend to talk to in the dark hours of the night. Thank God for Black Rain, who was even now, unfortunately, sewing beads and making fringes on Cassandra's clothes in preparation for the wedding night. Cassandra didn't want to be a bride again. The first time she was bedded had been awful, and *then* she'd been with the man she loved. Tonight—well, she wouldn't think about tonight.

"Come," said Black Rain. "You must get ready. First, we'll clean the baby an' put him in his night cradle."

"Is he going with me?" asked Cassandra.

"Of course."

Black Rain unwrapped Benjamin from his cradle board, where only his face peeked out, that and his penis, which stuck out between the laces and endangered anyone so careless as to walk behind Cassandra. "Stop daydreamin'," said Black Rain, "an' hand me the oil." Benjamin gurgled as Black Rain cleaned him up and patted on powder made from rotted cottonwood. "Here, feed him," she said, thrusting the baby at Cassandra. "You must be ready when he comes."

"We've time," Cassandra mumbled.

"Ah'll lay out your clothes."

Cassandra shut her eyes and tried to blank her mind.

"You gonna use paint?" asked Black Rain.

Cassandra started to say, "Of course not," having always considered that Comanche custom grotesque. But she reconsidered, suddenly seeing the paint as a barrier between herself and reality, something to hide behind. In her beaded, fringed deerskin dress, with her face hidden under the macabre paints, she'd be a different person, not Alex Harte's widow but a Comanche squaw. She would do what she had to do.

The baby's mouth relaxed as he drifted into sleep. What a beautiful child he was, she thought, love for him flushing through her heart as she looked at his tiny face. His eyes were changing; he would be dark eyed like his father, maybe black haired as well. And Alexandra? Did a Comanche woman named Singing Bird look down at Alexandra and thank the Earth Mother that her adopted daughter would be dark eyed and black haired like The People? Blinking back tears, Cassandra prepared Benjamin for the night, then put on the clothes Black Rain had laid out.

"It'll be fine," said Black Rain. "You'll see. Counts Many Coup is a good man to lie with."

Cassandra set out the paints, which were made from clays and juices of weeds and berries. Which colors should she use? Her hand hovered over the black— war and funeral paint—but she knew that would be unwise, so she chose blue and smeared it onto her eyelids.

Black Rain nodded approvingly. "That brings out your eyes," she observed.

Cassandra was tempted to wipe it off. She didn't want to "bring out her eyes." If she looked dreadful, maybe he'd stay away from her after the obligatory consummation. He already had two other wives, one from his own people, whom he must like even if she was plain and cruel, and Black Rain, who was a fine person and beautiful. Cassandra snapped up the olive green. That should make an ugly combination. She smeared it around her eye sockets and over the bridge of her nose. Now she looked like a gaudy owl, and the Comanches didn't like owls; they considered them birds of ill omen. "There, I'm done. How do I look?"

"Well, he'll be surprised," said Black Rain doubtfully.

He was. Cassandra could see it on his face when he passed the reins of the horse to her, a graceful white mare with great, soft eyes. She almost regretted her bizarre effort with the paint pots. He needn't have given her such a fine horse. Black Rain passed the baby to her, squeezing her shoulder in a brief, encouraging gesture. Then, following demurely with the bridle of the white mare in one hand, the baby, encased in his stiff rawhide sleeping tube, on her arm, Cassandra went with Counts Many Coup to his lodge, where he waved casually toward the fire.

A reprieve. He expected her to fix him a meal. She'd forgotten all about food. Propping the baby up carefully, she set to work.

When Cassandra had fed him and done every cleaning-up chore she could think of, she stood indecisively in the center of the tepee. Counts Many Coup was sprawled on his bed, which occupied the place of honor opposite the door. A fine bed, she thought distractedly, elevated six inches above the floor with raw-hide webbing that supported a great thickness of robes, but Cassandra didn't want to occupy it.

It had been a warm day, and Counts Many Coup wore only a breechclout and moccasins. She wished that more of that smooth, bronzed skin were covered. He was not as dark as his fellows, but dark enough to look different and frightening to her. And he had watched her every move for the last fifteen minutes or so.

"You have been with a man before," he spoke into her confusion. "What is it you wait for?"

"I don't know your—your customs," she stammered.

"Customs between men and women are much the same among all people, I would imagine," he said dryly. "Take off your clothes and come over here."

"May—maybe I should wash off the paint first."

"Why do that? I am pleased that you have made yourself beautiful for me."

Her eyes widened, and she turned to see if he was being sarcastic, then was shocked when he came up off the bed in one smooth, quick motion and cupped her face in his hand, turning it toward the fire. "You are very beautiful. The blue and green paints become you."

Having meant to be unattractive, she now felt confused.

"And your hair has always been an amazement to me." He lifted up a strand and let it slide through his fingers.

She could imagine that it was, as he'd said, "an amazement." Faces A Bear had hacked if off again, and today with no moisture in the air, it fell straight, and probably ragged, around her face. She hadn't seen herself in months, but she knew she must look strange.

"Although my father was white, he had no such hair

216

as this." He bent forward and laid his face against hers.

His skin was so smooth, she thought in surprise. Even though she knew the warriors plucked their beards with bone tweezers, she had not expected his face to be so silky.

"Come." He drew her toward the bed. Cassandra turned off her mind and let him undress her. When he removed his own garments, she didn't look. When he urged her down beside him on the robes, she stared up into the dark reaches of the tepee and widened her eyes as if to let the darkness flood her consciousness.

"You are as supple and shapely as a young faun," he murmured, stroking her breasts lingeringly.

"As golden as ripe fruit in sunlight." His hands brushed her thighs with a light, slow touch.

"As warm and sweet on the tongue as honey from the hive." His mouth caressed hers as he slid between her legs and entered her with a smooth, sure stroke.

Cassandra, who had kept her mind blank and distant, was caught unprepared and swept away on a slow, dark flood of feeling. The liquid churning in her loins spread and spread with each stroke of his body until she was drowning in her own frenzy. The sweetness of his words and the seduction of his smooth, powerful body was like a moon-force to which she was the responsive tide, sucked up onto an unknown shore.

When the passion had receded from her heart and limbs, Counts Many Coup, propped on an elbow, looked down at her, amused, and murmured, "Your responses were those of a maiden surprised by rapture, my golden wife."

She flushed and turned her face away. How could she have responded so hotly when she still loved Alex and had taken another husband only out of necessity?

"Why do you turn away?" he chided. "I am pleased with you, Cass-an-dra. You are a woman of power, although how that can be I do not know, and of passion. You will bring me great pleasure and tall sons."

No, her heart cried. *No sons*. She wouldn't.

"Since our passion was such a surprise to you, we must have more so that you may grow accustomed," he murmured, turning her into his arms. "Put your hands on my back."

She touched his taut skin, her fingers against the long muscles. Her breasts flattened against his warm chest. He stroked her again, sending bursts of delight across the surface of her skin like the rolling balls of lightning she had seen skimming the seas of prairie grass.

"Our gods give us this pleasure that we may bloom in our years of strength."

He mounted her, and she could feel the tickle of his long braid as it rubbed across her breast.

"You bloom for me, Cass-an-dra, my golden moon-flower. You open your petals in the night."

It was true, she thought. She was open to him, then closing around him like a flower. The fire built inside her, licking relentlessly at her control until she burst into mindless flame and wrapped her legs around him.

"You understand me now, do you not, Cassandra?" he asked later when she lay spent in his arms. "Even though I speak to you in my own tongue."

With dismay she realized that she had betrayed not only Alex, but herself. All the while Counts Many Coup had been speaking in Comanche, and he knew she understood.

"I have forgotten an important thing," Counts Many Coup said one afternoon as they walked along a path to the stream, she with a buffalo paunch in which she would carry back water. He had been away on a raid, and she found herself glad to see him. "I have not given you a name."

Then she glanced at him resentfully, not wanting a

Comanche name, although she knew he would have his way. She might never hear her real name again unless she escaped, which was not as easy as she had thought. Faces A Bear watched her all the time. But the tribe was moving southeast—toward the settlement line, as well as in the general direction taken by Singing Bird and the Wasps. Maybe—

"I will call you Sees The Future."

Did that mean he now believed that she, a mere woman, had medicine? Just that afternoon she had heard that Borrows A Lance was dead, killed and scalped in a brush with another tribe. *I am a woman of great power*, she thought, then giggled when she realized that she was beginning to believe her own pretending.

"I am glad to find you so happy, Sees The Future," he said with formal solemnity, although his eyes were dancing. "Now you may share that happiness with your husband."

Before she could fathom what he had in mind, he tugged her off the path and in among the trees. Surely he didn't mean to make love here. "You are the war chief," she stammered as he grasped the fold of his breechclout and pulled it loose.

"A war chief can suffer from heat in his loins as well as any other man," he replied, pulling her down into the soft grass and sliding her skirt up onto her thighs, "although I fear that you and I, Sees The Future, act more like young lovers slipping under the tepee wall than a war chief and his beautiful third wife."

He nuzzled his mouth and nose against her neck. "Your skin has the scent of flowers," he murmured. "Are you ready for me, or must I court your welcome while someone on the path may turn aside and find me like a stallion in rut?"

In answer she raised her hips, and he groaned. "Hush," she murmured, even as she drew him in. How had this happened? she wondered, trembling with hunger for the culmination of the feast to which he led her. She gasped and tightened her arms. She had found that she liked him and wanted his good opinion. And she craved his lovemaking. His touch ignited her like the flash of gunpowder. She groaned as his thrusts drove her to mindless joy.

"You are a lusty woman," he remarked as he rolled onto his back, taking her over on top of him.

When she looked down at him, blue flowers poked out beside his head, echoing the color of his eyes, which blazed at her from a bronzed face. Again she had the sense of *déjà vu*. He did look like Alex, except for those eyes.

"Why so sad, golden flower?" He threaded his fingers into the silky strands that fell down around them. "Did I not please you? If you say I didn't, I shall make you swear an oath, and the gods will punish you for lying."

"Women don't swear oaths," said Cassandra.

"They do if I say so." He raised his hips sharply, and she gasped. "Again?" he asked and rolled so it was she who lay on the green grass blades of early summer among the blue flowers.

The war chiefs set the time and place of the summer hunt and sent out runners to scout for a temporary camp that offered both timber and water. In the main camp, excitement boiled like broth in a buffalo paunch filled with hot stones. Racks were built on which the meat could be dried. Mules and pack horses were rounded up to carry the hunting tents, tools, and weapons. And Cassandra learned that Counts Many Coup intended to take *her* with him, not Faces A Bear as would have been customary.

The first wife was incensed, Cassandra depressed. She had thought that she could escape while her husband and his vigilant wife were away from camp.

Even though her heart ached at the thought of leaving him, she would have done it. Even though she dreaded the long, dangerous flight that lay ahead of her. What if her milk failed, or the food gave out, or they were caught, she and Benjamin? And there was Alexandra—somewhere to the south. If Cassandra left the *Tanima*, she might lose forever her chance of getting her daughter back. She had gone over and over every reason to go, every reason to stay, until the indecision clouded her days and left her wakeful at night. The news that *she* was the companion her husband had chosen was almost a relief. Black Rain advised her to go.

"How else can you be sure of getting skins for your tepee?" she asked Cassandra. "And if you stay, Buffalo Leaper can have you."

"What do you mean?"

Black Rain shrugged. "Brothers share wives."

"They're not real brothers."

"They're sworn brothers."

Cassandra couldn't face being shared with Buffalo Leaper, so she stopped trying to think of strategies that would keep her at home.

Before they left, a hunting dance was held, huge fires built to light the festivities, drummers and singers gathered to lead the way. Cassandra became part of a long line of women who faced a line of men. "You have to choose a partner," Black Rain hissed.

"I don't want to," Cassandra whispered back.

"Go on. Choose Counts Many Coup." Black Rain gave her a push, and, mimicking the other women, Cassandra crossed the space to her husband and joined the dance. As far as she could tell, there were no religious implications, just high spirits over the beginning of the hunt. Soon she was swept up in the euphoria, laughing and stamping to the drums, singing with the singers, happy to be young, healthy, and full of life. Even the scowls of Faces A Bear could not dim her happiness.

221

When the dance broke up and the *Tanima* headed toward their lodges to sleep, Counts Many Coup took her to his tepee and tumbled her onto the robes piled on his bed. "You dance with the grace of an antelope," he whispered to her as he pulled her blouse and skirt away. "The heat I feel for you is a sign."

A sign of what? she wondered, pressing against him, eager for his hands and the weight of his body.

"There will be great feasts and rejoicing after this hunt, just as the warrior feasts on his woman and rejoices in her body after a successful war party."

She kneaded the smooth shoulders looming above her and drew his mouth down. She had never thought of lovemaking as a rejoicing, but it was.

Cassandra stood among the trees where the temporary camp had been set up and watched the huge half-circle of hunters spread out on the plain below. Within the line of men the buffalo grazed, unaware of their danger because the wind was against them and because they could hardly see from beneath their thick hair. Counts Many Coup raised his hand, and the hunters advanced until they had closed the distance and begun to circle the herd. Some of the shaggy giants escaped, but most were driven inward, cows and calves in the center, bulls circling protectively until they became confused and stopped.

Then the killing began, each man riding up from the rear and sending an arrow into the right side of his target. Then his horse, which he rode bareback with his knees thrust under a rope, swerved away from the horns of the wounded buffalo. Counts Many Coup used his lance, holding it slanted down across his body and driving it with both hands toward the heart. Cassandra's breath stopped when she saw the huge bull try to turn and charge, but the war chief pressed the lance home, the bull fell, and she let the air flow into her lungs once more. What if his horse had stumbled? What if the animal had completed the charge instead of falling?

When the killing stopped, the butchering began. Cassandra and the other women took tools down to the plain, and later pack horses and mules onto which the meat, bagged in the hides, was loaded for transport to the temporary camp or the permanent camp. Every hunter knew or thought he knew which buffalo were his kill. If there were disputes, Counts Many Coup decided. Some carcasses were assigned to the old and to families that had no hunters. This too he decided.

Next the women cut the meat into thin strips for drying; scraped the flesh from the hides, which would be tanned later; and fed the hunters. While the women slaved, the men ate, laughed, and bragged about their hunting feats. Cassandra had never worked so hard or laughed so much. And Counts Many Coup seemed inexhaustible. Every night, whether he had hunted or feasted that day, he made love to her, and she was surprised at how much she liked having him to herself. It was a strange, bloody, primitive idyll played out under the hot summer sun on wide, grassed plains and in hunting tents—a life for the young, the courageous, and the vigorous, and she gloried in it while it lasted, regretted that it was over when it ended.

"And you wouldn't believe how many he killed," cried Cassandra enthusiastically.

"Why wouldn't I believe it? Who do you think had to flesh all those hides and dry the meat?" Black Rain retorted good-naturedly. They were talking in Comanche now that Cassandra felt safe enough to give up her pretense.

"Well, I did some of it out at the hunting camp! Didn't Faces A Bear help you here?"

"Does she ever? Anyway, she's been busy, she and Elk's Tooth."

Cassandra's euphoria subsided as she thought of Faces A Bear and her family. And Alexandra, whose tiny bones might have lain scattered somewhere to the northwest if Faces A Bear had had her way.

"Maybe next time I tell you that you're going to have a good time, you'll believe me," said Black Rain.

"I always believe you," Cassandra retorted, pulling her mind away from her bitter anger and smiling fondly at her friend and fellow wife. "How is Black Storm?"

"Heavy," said Black Rain. "Pretty soon that baby'll need her own horse. That or she'll break my back."

"Well, he wanted tall children," said Cassandra, laughing.

"He give you one?" asked Black Rain.

"Of course not," snapped Cassandra.

"Too early to tell anyway, but many babies get born nine months after a hunt." Black Rain resumed her work on a tanning solution. An impressive pile of hides awaited their efforts as a result of the summer hunt. "There's a double-ball game this afternoon. Want to play?"

"Which game is that?" Cassandra asked. She had been gurgling to Benjamin while she pounded another root.

"The one with the crooked stick and the thong."

"Oh, I've been dying to try it." All through the last months of her pregnancy, she had watched the game and imagined herself racing down the field, tossing and catching the thong, flinging it around the goal post.

Black Rain stopped rubbing tanning solution into the buffalo hide and studied the sky, which had dark-

224

ened perceptibly as they talked. Heavy, gray clouds were rolling in from the north, blotting out the sunshine and casting shadows over the camp. "We may not be playing after all," Black Rain remarked, "not this afternoon anyway."

Cassandra too glanced up. "Perhaps it will pass," she said. She did so want to play. Her legs and arms tingled with anticipation. The exercise would allay her restlessness.

"Oh, it'll pass, but not before we've been hit by a bad storm," Black Rain predicted. "I never minded the rain back on the Brazos," she added. "It made the melons and yams grow, and we got more to eat, but here..." She shook her head. "You ever seen a flood come up out of nowhere in some little creek you could have walked across ten minutes before? Or a wind that can pull a tree up by the roots?"

Cassandra eyed her nervously, remembering the hailstorm that she and Alex had survived. Had it been only a year? Not much longer surely, but it seemed like half a lifetime, and Alex's face was beginning to fade in her memory.

"And the lightning here on the plains seeks you out."

Cassandra nodded, overcome with gloomy foreboding. "The night Black Storm was born it killed a warrior."

"And you used it to save my baby. Well, we'll be safe, you having Thunderbird medicine."

"But, Black Rain, I don't have—"

"We'll play double ball tomorrow." The second wife smiled cheerfully and bent forward to slap more tanning mixture onto the hide. Then she took up a smooth stone and rubbed it over the surface. "We'll be the best pair a players they've ever seen," said Black Rain. "Those Indian women have short legs, and they're not too fast."

"I remember," said Cassandra, grinning and thinking once more of the game. She wasn't afraid of

Elizabeth Chadwick

storms. When the thunder sounded, they'd take the babies and go into the tepee until it was over. Maybe the storm would pass by with just a bit of rain. Maybe it wouldn't rain at all, and they could still play. "I can hardly wait to—"

She broke off because suddenly she was surrounded by people—Counts Many Coup, his face expressionless; Wolf Woman and Turkey Feather; Talking Crow and her younger sister, Little Antelope, who looked terrified; the brother, Elk's Tooth, and his wife, Falls In Water. The whole of Faces A Bear's clan formed the circle, and Faces A Bear herself, eyes flashing with malice, confronted Cassandra and said, "I accuse her."

Of what? Cassandra wondered anxiously. Her hair, although it had grown again, was not in braids. She had fastened it at the back of her neck with a thong, although she could feel it coming loose and curling in the heavy air that weighed its storm warning on the senses. Cassandra's eyes flicked questioningly to Counts Many Coup.

"My brother Elk's Tooth knows of this thing. My sister Little Antelope as well," said Faces A Bear.

Cassandra's eyes darted to the youngest sister, a sweet girl whom Cassandra had counted as a friend. Little Antelope's arms were crossed defensively over her waist, her hands twisting in the fringe on her sleeves, and Cassandra knew that whatever it was, it would be a false accusation. Why would Little Antelope let herself be used? Had she been threatened by her older sisters or her mother? Cassandra wouldn't put it past them.

"This woman has been unfaithful. For the honor of our lodge, she must pay the price."

Unfaithful? Surely they weren't saying that she'd been with another man? That was ludicrous. She hadn't even wanted to be with Counts Many Coup— well, at first she hadn't. Now—she felt the color staining her cheeks when she thought of their lovemaking.

226

"See!" cried Faces A Bear triumphantly. "Her shame is painted on her face."

"What defense do you make, Sees The Future?" Counts Many Coup asked.

"Did she see *this* in her future?" Faces A Bear interrupted spitefully. "That she would be found out?"

"F-found out in what?" stammered Cassandra.

"A woman who has been unfaithful to her husband knows it," said Faces A Bear contemptuously. "Lies and feigned innocence will not save you, Cass-an-dra."

"Use her Comanche name," snapped Counts Many Coup.

His wife bowed her head, trying to look submissive. "My sister Little Antelope, tell us what you saw."

Little Antelope's fingers clenched over the fringes, her pale brown skin turning white at the knuckles. "I saw—she—she—and Borrows A Lance—"

"Who?" Cassandra demanded incredulously. A woman accused of adultery could be killed by her husband, but Cassandra's terror was overcome by fury. Borrows A Lance—that fat, vicious swine?

"Speak, sister. Do not let the white woman frighten you," Faces A Bear commanded.

They had chosen him because he was dead and could not contradict them and because of the insult.

"In the wood by the—by the—" Little Antelope was stumbling on.

"He's dead!" Cassandra interrupted.

"Let her speak," said Counts Many Coup.

"I—I can't," wailed the girl and burst into tears.

"She can't speak because someone has forced her to lie," said Cassandra. And maybe the girl, who was smitten with Scarred By A Woman, had been easy to convince because she was jealous of Cassandra. Buffalo Leaper's son had made a nuisance of himself on the hunt, mooning over Cassandra, and Little Antelope had watched it sadly. Counts Many Coup, on the other hand, had laughed and teased Cassandra about her admirer. He was not laughing now.

"She can't speak because she is afraid of the sorceress," Faces A Bear retorted. "No matter. My brother knows all and will tell."

The testimony of Elk's Tooth would carry weight. Her word against that of a respected warrior? It might be hopeless, she thought, shivering. Did Elk's Tooth, who had been a candidate for war chief, hope by embarrassing Counts Many Coup to replace him? The roll of thunder echoed through the camp, and the others shifted uneasily.

"Maybe we should wait until after the storm," Elk's Tooth muttered.

The sky overhead was dark now, and lightning flickered in the clouds. *He is afraid of the storm*, Cassandra thought, calculating how that might be to her advantage. "My name has been blackened, and now my detractors want to go to their lodges without saying why. Am I accused of consorting with a man whom all know I hated? A man who killed my father? A man who is dead and cannot speak for himself? What kind of sense does this make?" She turned to Counts Many Coup. "Do you truly believe this of me?"

"We will hear what Elk's Tooth has to say," said Counts Many Coup.

"I saw her lying among the trees," said Elk's Tooth, glancing aside as the lightning flickered again, "with—"

"I was never among the trees with Borrows A Lance," snapped Cassandra. "The only time he touched me, I twisted his man's parts until he screamed—" mouths dropped open at this revelation "—and then I ran away from him."

Elk's Tooth's eyes flicked again to the lightning.

"Elk's Tooth speaks with a crooked tongue and then looks with fear to the flashing eyes of the Thunderbird," said Cassandra. "Let him swear an oath. Let him say before us all, 'May the lightning and thunder take my life if this thing be not true.'"

Thunder rolled and crashed. Elk's Tooth broke into a sweat, although the air had turned cold with the coming storm. "Let him bare his chest to the lightning and take his oath," she demanded as a bolt speared the ground at the edge of the camp. "Swear!" she demanded.

"No!" Elk's Tooth turned and strode away, leaving his sister white-faced in the eerie half-light.

Before another participant in the drama could move or speak, Counts Many Coup had laced his fingers into the hair of his first wife. "So you talked your brother and sister into lying for you? Now, wife of my youth, maybe you would like to take up the fate you planned for Sees The Future," he snarled. She cringed away from him. With his fingers still entwined in her hair, he dragged Faces A Bear, stumbling and whimpering, to her father. "I return her to you, Turkey Feather. Deal with her as your honor dictates. She is my wife no more."

Faces A Bear let out a wail of despair.

"I will not have a liar in my bed," said Counts Many Coup, unmoved by her grief.

No one stirred. Little Wolf, who had watched the whole scene with stunned apprehension, gasped a tiny sob that went to Cassandra's heart. *Poor child*, she thought. *Will he have to leave his father's lodge as well?*

Counts Many Coup flung his ex-wife at the feet of her father and stepped back, reaching out an arm to draw his son to his side. "Sees The Future is now your mother, Little Wolf." He turned to Cassandra. "Pack your things and take your two sons to her tepee," he instructed. "It is now yours." He pushed the frightened child into her arms. She nodded and turned to obey. Rain began to fall, breaking the tension as the group dispersed to their lodges.

Now Faces A Bear has lost her child, Cassandra

thought, *just as, because of her, I lost my daughter*. She hugged Little Wolf and, sweeping up Benjamin from his resting place by the door, took the two children into the tepee.

"I will miss you, my sister," said Black Rain.

"We will be together every day," Cassandra responded, "and now our lives will be easier."

Chapter Fourteen

"Throw it to me," called Black Rain, and Cassandra whipped the thong into the air with the curved end of her stick and sent it flying. Black Rain scored the final goal, and the women of the victorious team hugged each other, laughing as they left the field.

"You are the best players I have ever seen," said Little Antelope. She no longer harbored any jealousy, for Cassandra had arranged what Little Antelope wanted most, marriage to Scarred By A Woman.

"You and Black Rain seem to read each other's minds when you play," marveled the girl.

"We are sisters," Cassandra replied, putting her arm around Black Rain's shoulder and leaning on her hard enough to stagger them both.

"Sisters?" Little Antelope giggled. "You and Black Rain are as night to day."

"Which one am I?" asked Black Rain.

"You're day, silly," Cassandra teased. "I'm the one who's wide awake at night."

"So it would seem," Black Rain agreed, "since I so often find *my* husband awake in *your* bed."

Little Antelope, sensitive to sexual innuendo now that her marriage day was set, blushed. The other women walking around them were laughing heartily at the byplay and laughed harder when Cassandra promised, "I'll send him to you as soon as he returns from the hunt." Actually, she thought their husband divided his favors pretty evenly.

"No, sister," retorted Black Rain, "I'll send him to you once I've worn him out. We all know you white-skins can't stand too much heat."

"Poof!" scoffed Cassandra. "You're the one who left the game panting for breath and wet with sweat."

"True enough," Black Rain agreed. "It's too hot for double ball."

"It's never too hot for double ball," Cassandra objected.

"Sees The Future would organize a game if the snow lay as deep as her horse's withers," said Falls In Water.

"No, I wouldn't. I'd stay in my nice warm tepee and gamble." She wiped her face on her sleeve and bent to take Benjamin from Calling Dove, who had begged to watch him while her mother and Cassandra played. "Let's play the hand game tonight," Cassandra suggested, "while the men are away and we need cook only for ourselves and the children."

Black Rain groaned. "My sister, if once we start, you'll want to play all night and win everything we own."

"If I do, I promise to lose it all back tomorrow."

"And I'll lose two nights sleep instead of one in order to recover my wardrobe," Black Rain complained.

"I want to play," called another of the women. "Come to my tepee tonight."

"Only if my sister will play," Cassandra insisted. "We're a team—unbeatable, that's us."

Falls In Water laughed. "Even I can tell when you two have passed off to each other. Black hand on white."

"We'll have to do something about that," said Black Rain. "Which one of us shall change color?"

"We'll take it in turns," Cassandra suggested.

"Can you truly change your color?" asked Calling Dove.

"Truly, little one, I can't," Cassandra replied, "nor

can Black Rain, and we look so handsome together that we wouldn't if we could."

The two women walked back to the camp arm in arm, reliving the more exciting moments of the game and wrangling amicably over whether or not they would gamble together in the long twilight of the August evening. They shared a tepee again while Counts Many Coup was away with a war party, Cassandra having begged him not to pass them over to his brother, Buffalo Leaper.

"It is our custom," Counts Many Coup had replied.

"He's not your true brother."

"He's as much my true brother as Black Rain is your sister."

"I married you. I only want to share your bed."

"And I yours," he muttered, sliding his hands under her clothes.

Cassandra had glanced aside hurriedly to see if the children were asleep. She felt constrained by their presence, but she went to him willingly. Sometimes his glance alone, across a campfire or on the path to the stream, set her aflame. She begrudged his time away on raids and in Black Rain's bed, although that jealousy shamed her and she concealed it under the banter so common among the women. Her hands went to the thong around his waist, and in seconds she had stripped away his one piece of clothing and knelt to remove his moccasins.

"You are in a hurry, Sees The Future?" he asked, amused.

"In just a few days you will be gone again," she replied, sliding out of her own clothes.

"How do you know that? Does a voice tell you my plans?" he asked, frowning.

"Your eyes tell me your plans. Your restlessness tells me that you want to take your lance and ride out."

"And what tells you what I want tonight?" he teased.

Laughing, she put her hand on the signal of his passion and let herself be pulled down onto the bed. "If I keep you awake all night," she whispered, "maybe you will be too tired to call a war party."

"No true Comanche wife would want such a thing," he muttered. "Now I must tire *you* out so that you will sleep the night away instead of distracting me from my duties."

Cassandra gasped at the power of his entrance and wondered whether he was truly irritated with her. He was usually a gentle lover for so violent a man, but tonight he did indeed seem bent on exhausting her.

"If you wound my back," he cautioned when her nails dug into his muscles, "there will be much laughter tomorrow."

Cassandra tried to relax.

"Still, you need not go to sleep yet," he added, slowing to a maddeningly tantalizing pace. "Shall we do this through the night after all?"

She turned her head and looked at the corded muscles of his arms. *He probably could*, she thought as she strained up to him. He could play her like a fish on a line until she was dying for release. He had done it before, whispering things into her ear that increased her heat without bringing culmination. Where had he learned to make love like this? she wondered. Were all Comanche men so talented? She lifted her hands and brought his mouth down to hers, then slid her fingers over his shoulders and straining arms. She stroked his smooth waist and stomach, and he groaned into her ear, "You overcome my good resolutions."

"You have resolved to drive me mad," she whispered back, "but then what will you do with a crazy wife?"

"Drive her back to sanity on some other night."

"Do not leave me mad," she begged and wrapped long legs around his hips.

"There is little I can refuse you, my golden spider, when you entangle me thus."

Her breath came in gasps, and her body clenched with ecstasy, as did his, but the next day, as she had known he would, he called a war party, and the men flocked to join him. *He is like Alex*, she had thought, *always anxious to be away on some adventure, always willing to put himself at risk. No matter the difference in race or in culture, I have fallen in love twice with the same man.* "Don't go," she had begged before they slept, but he had turned his face away from her, and she knew that she had offended him.

When at last she fell asleep, her dreams were stained with blood and shadowed by violent death. She awoke trembling, tears salty on her lips. Turning on her side, she studied her husband in the dim predawn light of the tepee. He was a powerful man, skilled in warfare, unparalleled in horsemanship, a man who believed in himself and his spirits. Why then should she fear for him? Others believed that she could see into the future, but Cassandra knew that to be untrue. This sudden gloom was not premonition; it was just the natural lowering of spirits that sometimes plagued her before her monthly flow.

Counts Many Coup stretched and turned. "Why do you study me as I sleep?" he asked.

She smiled at him in the half-dark. "What woman would not awaken with lustful thoughts when so renowned and handsome a warrior sleeps beside her?"

He laughed and whispered, "It must to be a brief lust. Will that satisfy you?"

Brief because today he leads a war party out, she thought. She quelled the returning impulse to beg him, just this once, to forgo the raid. *It is only my foolishness*, she told herself, and opened her arms.

"What do you think of, sister?" Black Rain asked, bringing Cassandra back to the present.

Cassandra sighed. "How long will they be away this time, do you think?"

"Ten days," Black Rain guessed. "Are you missing him already?" The war party had been gone only two. "Enjoy your leisure," Black Rain advised.

"How can I when you say it is too hot for double ball and you don't want to play the hand game in the cool, shadowed hours of evening?" Cassandra retorted, laughing. She was resolved to recover her good spirits.

Gaunt from months in the saddle, hair uncut, clothes in rags, the two men lay on the ridge and watched the Comanche war party. "They're headin' home," said the older of the two. "Got their dead with 'em."

His companion focused a field glass on the group of mounted Indians.

"You wanna follow 'em?"

He nodded. They'd heard rumors from Comancheros of a blonde woman in the area. Of course, they'd heard rumors before, rumors which had come to nothing. Seven months without a solid reason to think she was still alive. Alex had almost given up hope, but even without hope he couldn't give up searching.

"What is it, Cass-an-dra?"

Cassandra awoke at the touch of Black Rain's hand on her shoulder. "Nothing," she mumbled. "A dream."

Black Rain chuckled. "You ate too much antelope stew." Then her eyes narrowed because Cassandra hadn't smiled. "Of what did you dream?"

"Death."

"Whose?"

"I don't know," Cassandra replied, trying to shrug off the lingering shroud of fear.

"Dreams don't foretell the future. A warrior's vision might, but a woman's dream—" Black Rain stopped uneasily. "You've never seen the future in a dream, have you?"

"Never," Cassandra assured her.

"What are they doing now?" asked Alex.

Bone scratched the thin white stubble on his chin. "Gettin' ready to parade into the camp."

"If I have to watch one more damned scalp dance—"

"More like a funeral procession is my guess. For someone important too. A chief maybe. Or some special warrior. Ever seen Comanche women mournin' their men?"

Alex shook his head.

"Well, it ain't a sight you're ever likely to forget."

It was like a ghastly repeat of her first day—the grim procession of warriors, their faces painted black, the wails of the women—except that now she was truly one of those mourning women. Now she would shriek and tear her clothes and skin in searing anguish instead of a pretended woe calculated to earn herself a blanket that had belonged in life to the deceased. Now she would give away the possessions of the dead instead of taking them.

She stared down at his body, the smooth bronze skin, the long muscles, the bloody wound in the chest on which she had laid her head so many times after lovemaking, the blue eyes, now closed in death, that once had looked so deeply into hers when he first said there was a bond between them. A bond now blown asunder by the weapons of her own people. His medicine, which was to have protected him from the white man's bullets, had failed. Why, oh why, hadn't he listened when she sought to keep him home? *I am indeed a Cassandra*, she thought bitterly. *A prophetess to whom no one listens. I didn't even believe my own premonitions.*

"They had guns such as I have never seen," said Broken Nose, "guns that fired many shots instead of one."

The rangers, she thought. Her husband and his party must have come upon the rangers with their repeating Colts.

"Counts Many Coup died as he lived—with great bravery. We lost many warriors, but he killed four of the enemy himself, one with a lance."

So he had raced into the face of his enemies instead of taking cover and attacking them with arrows.

"Then the horse of his brother's son, Scarred By A Woman, fell, and Counts Many Coup rode into the heaviest fire to rescue him because he was afoot."

Cassandra remembered riding across the front of a prairie fire to scoop Alex from the talons of death. In her mind's eye she could see Counts Many Coup leaning from his horse to extend his hand to his nephew. But she and Alex had survived; Counts Many Coup had died. She couldn't believe it.

Even with that terrible wound, he should rise and beckon her toward their lodge, scooping up Little Wolf, snatching a banner of meat from a stick planted by their campfire, smiling at her with hot eyes that told her of pleasures they would share when the sun had set and the children slept.

"He was a great war chief and my brother." Broken Nose looked as if he might weep himself.

Cassandra's tears had already blurred her eyes so that she could hardly see the body of her husband. She heard the wails of the women around her—Black Rain, who had lost a husband as well; Summer Cloud, who had thought of him as a son. Cassandra heard her own voice join the lamentation, but no crying out that came from her throat could match the grief that wrung her heart.

"It's her," said Alex. "Look at the hair. It has to be her."

"Be quiet!" hissed Bone. "They may have scouts out, an' if whites killed that chief, we sure don't wanna git caught here."

When he had been prepared for burial, it was Black Rain, as first wife, who sat behind him on the horse and held his body on its last ride. Cassandra thought she could not bear it—to be deprived of that last embrace. They were all gone—her father, Alex, her daughter, and now Counts Many Coup, and not one of them had she been able to hold one last time before they disappeared from her life.

Counts Many Coup had the funeral of a great warrior, having died the death that he would have chosen. The women mourned wildly, Cassandra among them. Many horses were given away. They, his family, gave and gave until there was nothing left, and still they mourned. The customs that had once seemed so strange now seemed understandable to her, as if by giving everything away they could give away their grief as well. As if by exhausting themselves in mourning they would cease to miss the one who had gone. *I have become one of them*, she thought as she dropped onto her bed the third night after his funeral.

"How the hell are we going to get her out of there when she's sharing a tent with that black woman?"

"We're gonna bide our time," Bone replied. "Cassie's all right. She doesn't seem to be in any danger, an' there's no use us puttin' her at risk by doin' something stupid."

* * *

"No!" said Cassandra. "I will not be given to Buffalo Leaper." They were speaking in English so they would not be understood by anyone who heard.

"Cass-an-dra, it's the custom for the brother to take the widow into his—"

"Are you going to his bed?" Cassandra asked.

"He won't have me," said Black Rain. "He's appealed to his father, the peace chief, sayin' he doesn't want a woman with no soul."

"Oh God." Cassandra groaned. "Do you think I could convince him that whites too are without souls? How is it you're so lucky?"

"It's not lucky to be without a hunter," said Black Rain, her face very serious. "An' Ah'm not sure you can refuse him."

"I know," said Cassandra dispiritedly. "I've only put him off. I said I can take no man while my heart still mourns for Counts Many Coup. But I'll never be the wife of Buffalo Leaper. How long do you think I would last under Talking Crow's fist? She hates me because of her sister." Cassandra shivered and stared into the fire. She knew what she had to do, and there was no time to waste. "Black Rain, we have to escape. Will you come with me?"

Black Rain shook her head sadly.

"But we're sisters," Cassandra cried. "I don't want to leave you behind."

"Where are you goin'? To Devil's Wood an' your first husband's people? Cass-an-dra, if Ah go back into slave country, Ah'll end up a slave again."

"No, you won't."

"An' Black Storm, who was born free, would be a slave. Pollard would want me back, an' he lives right down the river from Devil's Wood. If he didn't whip me to death for runnin' away, he'd—"

"Black Rain, I wouldn't let that happen. We wouldn't have to go to Devil's Wood. We could take ship to Massachusetts, where Negroes can be free."

"You might be able to go to Massachusetts, but if we made it out of Comancheria, we'd be in Texas, an' Ah'd never get outa Texas. Any white man who saw me could claim me, an' not a thing you could do. The law's against us. An' Cass-an-dra, much as Ah love you, Ah'd rather be dead than be a slave again. If you go, you'll have to go alone."

"Oh Lord!"

"An' you're right to be afraid. You'll be runnin' for your life, you an' the baby. Think about it, Cass-an-dra."

Cassandra stared at Black Rain with tears in her eyes. "What will you do here, Black Rain? If Buffalo Leaper doesn't want you, how will you and Black Storm survive?"

Black Rain sighed and switched back into Comanche. "Broken Nose will ask for me. Already he appears in my path like a lovesick young brave. He has mourned long for the wife he lost last year, who was my friend. Now he is ready for another wife, and he loved Counts Many Coup as a brother. He will ask Buffalo Leaper for me before the new moon has waned, and Buffalo Leaper will be glad to discharge his obligation to his dead brother. It will be well with me, but for you, my sister, I am afraid. You have set yourself a task that would be hard for a man, and I fear they will come after you when they find you gone."

"But I will go," said Cassandra. It broke her heart to leave Black Rain and Little Wolf and all the friends she had made among the women, but especially Black Rain. "Will my going cause you trouble?"

"It might if we continue to share a tepee. If you move back to your own, I can't be held responsible."

"I'll do it now."

"Have you thought this out? If you're going, you must store up supplies for a long journey."

"What would I need?" Cassandra whispered.

241

"Pemmican. Dried meat. Water. If you do not drink, your milk will dry up and the baby will die."

Cassandra's heart twisted in fear. She was going to expose Benjamin to the most danger of all. Babies were so fragile. And if they were followed and had to hide, the child might cry and get them both killed. If they were caught, the Comanches might toss Benjamin into the air and impale him on a lance. Or see how many arrows could be shot into his body before he fell to earth. She had heard such tales. And the things they would do to her. Oh God, how could she—

"...supplies for the baby," Black Rain was saying. "Moss and cottonwood powder. Extra rabbit skins. You cannot take the night cradle, so you must be careful not to roll on him when you get a chance to sleep."

Cassandra remembered the long ride after her capture, day and night in the saddle. Then, she had been tied behind Counts Many Coup and could sleep. This time she would have to stay in the saddle continuously with *no* sleep, few stops, and little food or water, yet somehow care for the baby. How would she ever manage? If she even got away from camp.

"Black Rain, if I am caught and they kill me, they will spare Benjamin—because they think he has spirit power." That realization hardened her decision to attempt escape. "Would you—would you bring him up? If I die, would you—"

"Oh, Cass-an-dra, how can you even think of this thing? Stay, my sister. You defeated Faces A Bear. You can handle Talking Crow as well."

Cassandra shook her head. She knew she would have left before now if it had not been for Counts Many Coup. His death was the turning point. "Promise me, my sister. If I die, you will be a mother to Benjamin."

"I promise," said Black Rain, her eyes bleak.

* * *

"The child in the cradle board must be mine," said Alex. "My own child, and I've never seen it. I don't even know whether it's a boy or a girl."

"I think she's moving to that other tepee. If she is, we'll go after her tonight."

In the afternoon Cassandra packed a hide bag with supplies and pushed it under her raised bed. A silly hiding place. Anyone who wanted to could find it. Anyone who suspected her. Faces A Bear. The woman blamed Cassandra for her disgrace. And her husbandless, childless state.

Little Wolf, stepchild of Cassandra's heart, would have to be left behind when she escaped. Would Black Rain take him? Cassandra hadn't even thought to ask and was ashamed of her lapse. Still, he would be better here than with her on the dangerous journey she planned. He was a heavy sleeper and would not hear her slip away tonight, but in the morning when he awoke, she'd be gone. Would he understand? Poor child. He had lost his mother and his father and now her. And she couldn't even say good-bye. Cassandra blinked back stinging tears and picked up Benjamin.

As if he sensed her turmoil, the baby was fussy. All day he had cried to be fed earlier than usual and failed to drift into sleep at accustomed times. Was he sickening? She pictured her son falling desperately ill during the flight and dying because she dared not stop to care for him.

"I will cook tonight," said Black Rain when the evening meal drew near. "Feed your baby. He frets."

"I did. Less than an hour ago."

"Feed him again. A satisfied baby sleeps soundly."

Alarmed, Cassandra flashed a glance at Black Rain, but the woman was already at work. Did she know Cassandra would be gone by morning? Cassandra felt like weeping again. She couldn't even say good-bye to this woman to whom she felt closer than any other. Should she make good her escape, Black Rain needed to be able to say truthfully that she had had no fore-knowledge. As they ate together, Cassandra slanted dismal glances at her friend. Then at the end of the meal, unable to help herself, she kissed Black Rain's cheek, something she rarely did. "Good night, my sister," she whispered.

Black Rain stared into her eyes.

We are of one height, Cassandra thought. *And one heart. How unfair it is that I cannot take her with me.*

"I am free here," said Black Rain, her eyes filled with regret. "Do you understand how important that is?"

Cassandra nodded, but in truth she did not understand. Women were not free among the Comanches. A wife could be sent away or even killed by her husband. But perhaps Black Rain was right in saying she dared not return, even briefly, to slave country. "You will be the first wife again," Cassandra agreed, smiling through tears.

"So I will, and Broken Nose will be a good husband, not as good as the one we loved, but ..." She shrugged in helpless regret for Counts Many Coup, whom they had shared.

Their hands, which had been clasped, fell apart, and each went to her own lodge. Cassandra called Little Wolf from his play and hugged him one last time before she tucked him into his bed, noting sadly how he clung to her. Buffalo Leaper or Broken Nose would be his father now. No Comanche child went without a family to cherish him.

Remembering Black Rain's words, Cassandra put Benjamin to her breast one last time, and he fell into as deep a sleep as Little Wolf's. The bag with her meager preparations lay hidden under the bed. Nothing remained but to wait, to stay awake and wait for the camp to settle and the moon to set. She was so tired, worn out by the tension of the day. What if she fell asleep as she had done the last time she planned an escape? Well, this time she wouldn't. The hours crept by, and Cassandra, fighting to keep her eyes from closing, counted them second by second, measuring by the even breathing of the children.

She kept watch by holding the hide door open just an inch. Her hand ached with tension by the time the moon finally disappeared below the far, flat horizon. Then, heart racing, she eased the bag from beneath the bed and rose silently to lift her son, still encased on his day cradle board. He murmured and settled back into exhausted slumber as she put him on her back. Sliding silently through the door, she eased it shut again and made her way from the shadow of one tepee to the next. Even the dogs were asleep, but that could change in a minute. Still, they knew her, and she carried meat to silence them if they barked. A yap or two would not rouse the camp, but a great commotion would. *If only they let me pass*, she thought.

"She's left the tepee!" exclaimed Alex.

"Calm down. They don't have outhouses," Bone replied. "She's just gone to the woods, which, believe me, is a piece of luck." Bone rose. "You keep watch while I waylay her before she returns to camp."

Alex waited anxiously, wanting to go after them but knowing he could never move as silently as Bone. If he let his impatience prevail, he could get them all killed.

She reached the edge of the camp and slipped in among the trees, avoiding the path. It was so dark now that each tree was just a looming black shadow on a black background. If she stumbled or fell, she would wake the baby. If the night-ranging youths were about—but she had heard nothing of them. For all the hours of her vigil, she had strained to interpret each noise in the sleeping camp. With luck they were all abed. Then she heard whispers and froze. Young lovers, she decided at last. Some boy had scratched on the tepee wall of a girl he admired. Or an older girl had lured a shy young boy out for a night of dalliance. Cassandra had smiled while she watched these youthful trysts being arranged all during the summer. How ironic if she, who had lost the two men she loved, should be caught by young lovers. Stepping silently, her arms aching from the weight of her saddle and supplies, she skirted the murmuring couple, then tried to return to her original route.

Oh Lord, she wondered after a few minutes, *am I going in the right direction? I thought I could find my way to the herd blindfolded, but I was wrong. They'll find me in the morning, lost, and know what I've tried to do. They'll—*

Suddenly she saw the edge of the wood and, creeping into the shadow of the last trees, whistled once, then again. In minutes her white mare, whom she had taught to respond to her signal, cantered away from the drowsing herd. That trick was the only good thing to come from her association with Pinto, Cassandra thought as she stood trembling at the wood's edge. If someone saw the mare break from the herd, she would have to fade back into the woods and pray the animal didn't follow her.

Heart in her mouth, she scanned the darkness as the mare slowed, approaching the trees more cautiously. Cassandra saw and heard nothing suspicious so, trembling, she whistled again, just the faintest sound. In seconds the mare was nuzzling Cassandra's hand and allowing herself to be led in among the trees. Cassandra saddled her, tied the bag of supplies to the saddle, muffled her hooves with skins, then swung astride, Benjamin still asleep on her back. She could hear the sound of the shallow creek and guided her horse slowly toward it so that they could continue in water where she couldn't be tracked.

Or so Cassandra hoped. Still, she was terrified. She wanted to pull out on the plain and ride as fast as the horse could carry her, but that would have been a mistake. Even in the darkness, the white of her mare's coat would shine. She needed to get further away before she rode in the open. Was that why Counts Many Coup had picked a white horse as a wedding gift? Her heart clenched at the thought of him.

I'll go crazy with fear and grief if I don't stop this, she told herself. But still she followed the creek. A mile from here she could come out on rock and leave no trace of her departure from the water. It seemed hours before she found the place and listened to the mare's feet tap against stone. In minutes they broke free onto the plain, and Cassandra was fleeing for her life.

"What happened?" Alex's heart clenched when Bone returned alone.

"Damned if I know. I lost her in the woods. But then when I broke clear, I saw someone on a white mare heading east. Alex, I think she's runnin'."

"Escaping? Are you sure it was her?"

"No, I ain't sure, but we've got to follow."

"But what if she's still in camp?"

"You see her go back to her tepee?"

"No."

"If it don't turn out to be her, we'll come back, but if it's her runnin', we daren't lose her agin. For that matter, if they follow her, we gotta be damn sure we catch up to her first."

When the faint glow of sunrise lightened the sky to the east, Cassandra breathed a sigh of relief. She faced the light so knew that she had chosen the right direction. When the Comanches first took her, her sense of direction would have been too poor to make that

choice at night or on a cloudy day. How much she had
learned in those months.

Allowing the mare, which she had ridden hard
through the night, to slow, she twisted in the saddle.
Behind stretched the dark, empty plain. If there were
riders, she could not see them. With any luck, no one
had yet missed her, and when they did, they had to
look for track, which she had taken great trouble to
conceal. Maybe they'd decide she wasn't worth the
trouble. God willing.

Clinging to the trotting mare with her knees, she
shifted Benjamin into her arms to nurse. Far ahead
she could see dimly variations in the flat landscape.
Hills? Trees? Water, she hoped. She had been sparing
with her supply, but it wouldn't last forever. Nor
would her food. She'd have to find fruit and nuts, trap
small animals, catch fish. She had no weapons with
which to hunt. Only twisted rawhide, a fish hook, a
knife, a fire stick, the knowledge she'd accumulated
living in a primitive society, and determination. She
would fend for herself and Benjamin. She hadn't survived this long to give up now.

"It may take time, my love," she said aloud to her
son, "but we'll get back to civilization." In Texas she'd
find towns and ships that connected the Republic with
the United States. She could gain access to her inheritance in Massachusetts. She'd get back home. But
not until—her heart ached at the thought—not until
she'd tried to get Alexandra back. Oh God, Alexandra.
Even now she was riding away from her daughter.

But there were men who traveled into Comanche
territory. She remembered Captain Hays, Alex's
friend. She'd find the Texas Ranger and beg him to
go after the baby. Surely, he'd do it for Alex. Surely,
no Texan would want to leave a white baby out there.
The rangers might well be the white men who had
taken Counts Many Coup from her. Let them at least
return her daughter. They owed it to her. If they

wanted money to find Alexandra, she would pay them. Why had she not thought of that before?

Cassandra shifted her son onto her shoulder and patted his back. The mare's gait had lulled him to sleep, his little head resting loosely against Cassandra. She bent to brush a kiss on the baby fuzz that covered his skull, then shifted him into his cradle board and transferred him to her back. The whole east was ablaze with the coming day when she dug her heels lightly into the mare's sides. She glanced over her shoulder to check her back trail. Nothing. No, wait. The light was still dim to the west, but something— Cassandra swallowed. Were there riders coming over the curved horizon? It couldn't be. She kicked the mare harder, and the drumming hooves matched the frightened beating of Cassandra's heart.

Trees or hills or something floated ahead, but how far? With the sun rising into her eyes, she could not tell, but she had to get there. She had to reach concealment. Knowing the tired mare could go no faster, Cassandra counted to five hundred before she allowed herself to look back again. *There's no one there*, she had told herself over and over again. *Just shadows in the dim light. Tricks played by tired eyes*. And she was tired. Weary beyond belief.

How little sleep she had had since they brought home the body of her husband. Little sleep, much worry, great fear, unbearable tension. It all weighed upon her shoulders, yet she must look again. When she turned her head, the shapes of the horsemen were clear. And closer. Much closer. Coming fast. Faster than her poor, tired mare could ever hope to run, but Cassandra kicked her hard and leaned forward to whisper encouragement in her ear. In vain. There was no greater speed in the horse, whose sides were lathered.

Again she looked back, and the horsemen were closer yet. *Oh God*, she prayed. *Stop them. Don't let them catch us*. But when she looked again, they were gaining, bent low over their horses' necks, and the trees ahead were as vague and distant as ever. *Let them be some other Indians*, she prayed. *Indians who will take us captive but not kill us because we ran away*. When she looked again, they were within a hundred yards of her and shouting, yet she could not see them for the tears in her eyes or hear their anger because her ears thundered with the sound of the mare's faltering hooves and labored breathing. *Oh Lord, save Benjamin*, Cassandra prayed, and then a dark hand grasped her reins.

Her horse was dragged to a stop, and she looked, terrified, into the face of her captor. The world tipped, spun, and faded away.

Book III
The
Planters

*August 1845 to
June 1846*

Chapter Fifteen

When Cassandra came to, she lay across the saddle of a moving horse, Benjamin no longer hung from her back, and she was afraid to open her eyes because she remembered what she had seen. A ghost. Could it have been some manifestation of her terror and desperation? Alex was dead. She had heard the description of his slaying and seen his scalp, yet the man who stopped her horse had Alex's face.

"Cassandra, I know you're conscious."

She kept her eyes tightly closed, trembling at the sound of a voice from the dead.

"I'm sorry we frightened you so badly, but we had to catch up with you."

He sounded so real. *I don't believe in ghosts*, she told herself. When a young warrior on a vision quest had come running into camp saying that he was pursued by malevolent spirits of the dead, she had laughed and shouted, "Begone, spirits!" The young man had given her a horse in gratitude for saving his life, but there had been no ghost, only empty air, his hallucination brought on by fasting, sleeplessness, and superstition. She too had been sleepless. Could what she saw have been a result of—

"Please, open your eyes."

I have to, she thought and edged her lids up. Just a little. So little that maybe no one could tell that she was looking. What she saw through her lashes was Bone, riding beside her, Benjamin sleeping peacefully in the cradle board on his back. Bone? She had assumed that he was dead too. She lifted her eyes to the man who held her in front of him. He still looked like Alex.

"We've been outside that camp for three days, waiting for a chance to rescue you. Couldn't believe it when we saw you leave your tepee and slip into the trees," he said.

"I thought you were dead," she whispered.

"Dead? Why would you think that?"

"They were counting coup and told of killing white men. I saw—I saw your scalp," she stammered.

"Dear God, Cassie." His arms tightened around her.

When they reached the trees, they stopped to change horses. Cassandra knelt by the stream to sluice off the paint she had used to conceal her skin in the darkness, the blue and olive colors that Counts Many Coup had thought so beautiful. With her face dripping, she turned back and studied the land, now touched with rose by the new day.

Silently she said good-bye to Little Wolf, who had filled so many hours with his chatter, and to Black Rain, her sister. Lastly, she bade farewell to a life that she would never know again and to Sees The Future, who had learned to live day by day, savoring the happy days and waiting for the rest to pass.

"We have no time to linger, Cassandra," Alex broke in quietly. "If there's pursuit, we have to outdistance it."

Cassandra nodded and bowed her head over the water once more to wash away the last vestiges of the old life, a smudge or two of paint and a fall of tears. Only her white mare remained.

After two days on the trail, Bone announced that they were being followed. Cassandra wasn't surprised. No doubt, Buffalo Leaper headed the pursuit of a runaway wife he had never possessed. Alex had hardly spoken to or touched her once she mounted her own horse. Even in their dire circumstances, she thought he could have shown her some affection. Benjamin he approached with wariness, as if he were afraid to touch the baby. Didn't he believe that Benjamin was his son? she wondered resentfully. Her sense of isolation and foreboding became more painful than her physical condition, although she ached in every muscle and joint.

They slept in their saddles, keeping an eye on one another, eating what supplies they had with them, stopping only to drink, tend the baby, and switch to the other three horses. Cassandra sometimes wanted to give up and sleep. The idea of lying down, even on the bare ground, seemed the most desirable of luxuries, even better than hot food, although her stomach ached with hunger, or cold water, although between stops thirst parched her throat.

On the fourth day they left the plains and entered a country of cedar-covered hills and grassy valleys. Bone shot a wild turkey and built a fire beside a creek.

"Have we lost them?" Cassandra asked eagerly, her mouth watering at the smell of cooking meat. She wanted to suggest that they throw the bird into the fire Comanche-style and drag it out when it had charred, but she was ashamed to reveal how primitive she had become.

"They're no more than three hours behind us," said Bone. "I spotted five, maybe six men from the last hill."

Cassandra, who had been nursing Benjamin, stiffened, and the baby whimpered. "Then why have we stopped?"

"They're gonna catch us," said Bone, "unless we trick 'em." He cut a piece off the roasting bird and passed it to her on the tip of his knife.

Cassandra laid the meat on a leaf so that she could

tear pieces off and eat as she continued to nurse the baby. With greasy fingers, she reached into her pouch and passed out fistfuls of grapes that she had picked at the last stop. Her stomach had lurched when Bone announced so calmly that they would be caught. Still, she ate.

Alex, who had been collecting and piling stones by the fire, squatted down by Bone and cut himself a portion. "Better explain the plan to her," he suggested.

"We'll split up," said Bone. "Make blanket marks like we slept here. Leave the fire to burn itself out. I'll head southeast takin' two horses loaded with rocks so the track will look like we're all along. You'll head up the creek two or three miles, come out on rock an' gravel an' hide out in some caves Alex and me know of. Even if they're not fooled by me an' my horses, I don't think they kin track you. Stay long enough so you know they're not around, then head east to the Brazos."

"What about you, Bone?" Cassandra asked anxiously.

Bone laughed. "Ain't no Indian alive kin catch up with me, missy. Alex, if you'll jus' finish gatherin' them rocks, I'll set here an' have a few words with yer lady since I ain't like to see her agin."

As Alex disappeared into the trees, Bone said, "Guess there ain't two folks in the world I think more of than you an' Alex."

"Then come with us," she urged. "We can fight them off."

"No, Miss Cassie. We'll do it my way, an' that's not what I wanted to talk to you about anyways."

"What, then?" Cassandra felt like weeping. She was so tired and didn't really see much hope for any of them. She almost wished that Alex hadn't found her.

"You blamin' Alex for what happened to you?"

She stared, surprised, into the skeletal face of this enigmatic man who had always been so kind to her.

"You mean because I was taken by the Comanches? Of course not."

Bone sighed. "He blames himself. Never seen a man more et up with guilt."

Cassandra's heart sank. "You're saying he only tracked me because he felt responsible?" She had wondered why Alex seemed so distant.

"No, ma'am, I don't mean that. Alex Harte loves you. He blames himself that he din' send you back to his sister. Pro'bly blames himself for ever marryin' you, but he did it outa love. No question a that. Now he pro'bly figgers you hate him 'cause a all the things that happened to you an' 'cause it took him so long to find you."

"Why did it take so long?" She didn't mean to criticize, but she had wondered.

"No hep for it," said Bone. "Them as took you, they split an' split agin, 'til we lost your trail. We'd never a come across you, 'cep we run into some Comancheros who seen a blonde woman. So we kep' goin'. Alex wouldn't give up."

"Were the others killed—Nicodemus and Pinto?"

"Nope. They wouldn't go."

Cassandra was shocked—not that Pinto had refused, but Nicodemus? He hadn't cared?

"It ain't gonna be easy fer you, Miss Cassie," Bone warned, "when you git back among white folks."

Why not? Cassandra wondered.

"Jus' you remember he loves you, an' he wouldn't give up 'til he got you back, an' he holds himself responsible."

"But Bone, he's not—"

"Yer right, he ain't to blame, but it's what a man thinks, not what's so, that makes him act the way he does."

Before Cassandra could say anything else, Bone had risen, stripped the last of the meat from the turkey bones, and divided it. Within minutes they were mounting. Cassandra leaned from her saddle to kiss Bone on the cheek. He and Alex clasped hands. Then, wordless again, Bone guided the two rock-laden horses away from the camp. Alex and Cassandra urged theirs from the heavily trodden ground of the camp-site into the water.

Oh God, we're trapped here, she thought, edging back from the cave entrance with the baby in her arms. Co-manche voices drifted up to her. She had been sleeping when Alex nudged her, then took the three horses out to graze, hidden in the woods above the cave. Before leaving, he whispered to Cassandra that he would take a position outside from which he could shoot down on the pursuit if need be. Then, without giving her a chance to object, Alex took both her eight-shot rifle and his six-shot, leaving her with two loaded revolvers. "Don't move from this spot," he said as he left.

She shivered and rocked the baby, hating the cave with its cold dampness that ate into her very bones and its evil smell. Creatures had died here. If she had to die, she didn't want it to be in this place. Benjamin stirred, and she cuddled him as she thought of running toward the entrance where a mist of dim light filtered in. Surely, it couldn't be more dangerous in the warm sun-shine than in this dank hole where she was all alone and trapped.

The voices were closer. She could pick up a word now and then. How could Alex leave her alone? He said he'd draw them off if they realized they'd found their quarry. Draw them off? He'd be killed, and then what were she and Benjamin to do? In a bag around her neck was a piece of paper on which he'd written that she and the baby were his wife and son, his heirs. She was to keep going east to the Brazos, he told her, then follow the river south to civilization. If anything happened to him or if they were separated, she was to make her way to Devil's Wood Plantation. When he said it, she'd still thought the Comanches had followed Bone. She'd never imagined ending up in this dark, evil . . .

There—that was the voice of Buffalo Leaper, brother of Counts Many Coup. He must be just below. Did he know she was here? Had he spotted Alex? With effort she stilled the rasp of her frightened breath and strained to listen. Benjamin stirred, disturbed by her tension, and she rocked him. *Mustn't tremble*, she warned herself. *If Benjamin wakes and cries*—

"I told you the other trail was theirs," said one of the warriors.

"It was a trick. Only one horse carried a man."

Buffalo Leaper again. If she ran out, Alex could escape. She'd say that Alex had left her, deciding she wasn't worth losing his scalp for. But Alex wouldn't do it; he'd never leave her behind. She'd only accomplish a momentary relief from tension and then his death, possibly her own. She bit hard into her lip.

"No one came this way," argued one of the warriors. They had stopped right below her.

"If it were you, wouldn't you have done this?" asked Buffalo Leaper.

"A white woman wouldn't be so smart," said the first speaker contemptuously.

"There were three riders before they separated," Buffalo Leaper said.

"How long do we chase after the woman?" demanded the third man. "There was a deer track in that valley. We should—"

"Until the sun is at its highest point," Buffalo Leaper interrupted. "I too tire of this fruitless journey. If we have found no sign by then, we will turn back and see what luck Elk's Tooth has had on the other trail."

Elk's Tooth? The brother of Faces A Bear was on their trail as well? Cassandra trembled, then went stiff with fear, for Benjamin had whimpered. She yanked her blouse down and put him to her breast.

"Did you hear something?" asked one of the men.

"What?" The other laughed. "Do you fear an ambush?"

"If Elk's Tooth finds the woman, you will not see her again, Buffalo Leaper. Elk's Tooth hates her for demanding that he swear an oath."

"A man who lies on his oath is food for the gods," muttered Buffalo Leaper. "Why should she be falsely branded a faithless wife? You two take the other side of the creek."

The voices were fading upstream. They would continue to search until noon, then return. Cassandra leaned back against the damp wall of the cave and closed her eyes, which had been straining toward the thin light at the entrance. Where was Alex? Would they find him as they searched for sign? Or the horses—they might find the horses. She dared not go to warn him. The conversation among the Comanches might have been a ruse to lure her out. To fool Alex. Had he understood what they were saying? She had no idea if he understood any Comanche. Why, oh, why hadn't she thought to ask? She and Alex had said practically nothing to one another in the days they'd been together.

Cassandra wanted to creep to the mouth of the cave. Just one look at the sun would tell her how long she had to wait until Buffalo Leaper and his companions passed back down the stream. The minutes crept like hours, and there were no sounds but the mysterious rustlings in the cave. What creatures dwelt in caves? she wondered. Bats? Crawling things? Bears? Just thinking of it made her want to scream. And the light, already dim, seemed to be fading, yet it couldn't be night. Benjamin was still sleeping soundly in her arms. He would have awakened to be fed again if night were approaching. Each new thought increased her panic until she knew she had to do something, yet there was nothing she could do but wait.

Think of something else, she commanded herself. She tried. In her mother's school the students had memorized poetry, pages of poetry, books of poetry.

"Of Man's First Disobedience, and the Fruit/Of that Forbidden Tree," she began. *Paradise Lost* was the longest poem she knew, and the most apt; each time she found her own little bit of paradise, she lost it. "... whose mortal taste/Brought Death into the World, and all our woe,/with loss of *Eden* ..." She chanted the verses in her mind, hour after hour, not caring what she skipped over or misquoted, soothed by the rhythm and flow. "... Awake, the morning shines, and the fresh field/Calls us, we lose the prime—" Voices intruded at last. How many hours had it been? The light had disappeared entirely at the cave mouth.

"Nothing," called one of the warriors.

"Nor we," called another, "and the storm is coming."

"There is an overhanging ledge not far from here," said Buffalo Leaper. "We'll try for that."

"How can she have disappeared? I know she was not with the other horses."

"The Thunderbird took her and the child."

"And the extra horses? Were they carried off too?"

"It could be so," said Buffalo Leaper. "She has those eyes. Even my brother's were not so dark a blue."

"Women do not have magic. You just want to get back to your tepee and your other wives, Buffalo Leaper."

Buffalo Leaper laughed, the last sound she heard from the Comanches before their voices faded, washed out by distance, thunder, and lightning. Minutes later, dripping with water, Alex dragged the three horses into the cave.

"Pray God, they're gone for good," he muttered. "I understood that they were going upstream and then returning, but that last conversation was beyond me."

"They're gone," said Cassandra. "They think the Thunderbird took me, so they're returning to camp."

"The Thunderbird? What does that mean?" His

shape sprang to light in the fire he had started, and his shadow danced eerily on the cave wall.

"I am a woman of power," Cassandra muttered, "with Thunderbird magic."

Alex turned to stare at her. "What are you talking about, Cassandra? Were you that afraid?" he asked, startled by her strange answer.

"I'm getting used to fear," she mumbled.

"Oh, Cassie." He laid his hand over hers. "If I have anything to say about it, you'll never know fear again."

Why does he never hold me? she wondered.

Late the next afternoon, they came to the Brazos.

"Does that mean we're almost—" Cassandra stopped because she wasn't sure where they were going. "Where are we headed, Alex?"

"Devil's Wood."

What an ominous name. It brought to mind gloomy forests and mythological monsters. Of course, the plantation might have been named Devil's Wood for perfectly innocuous reasons, although Cassandra couldn't imagine what they might be. Slavery was the explanation that occurred to her, and it was certainly an evil institution, but she doubted that Alex's family would agree. He didn't. Not that the name mattered. She and Alex were simply seeking a haven from which they could plan their future.

"How far is it?" she asked.

"Hard to say. Two hundred miles or more, I'd guess."

Cassandra tried to conceal her dismay. They were still in the wilderness and hadn't encountered another person since the Comanches passed by. And now to learn that she was still two hundred miles from safety, perhaps more!

"We'll camp here tonight."

Alex had shot a deer earlier in the day, butchered it on the trail, and packed the best of the meat on the third horse. Cassandra studied the campsite he had chosen and began to gather wood. While the strips of meat roasted over the fire on sticks, she washed roots she had dug, then cooked them in the ashes, after which she produced mustang grapes gathered while Alex was butchering his kill. Not a bad meal, she thought. Alex, she noticed, was watching her curiously.

"How many things you've learned," he murmured, almost to himself. "I hardly know you anymore."

Nor I you, thought Cassandra. *Time was when you couldn't keep your hands off me.*

As she pulled down her blouse and tucked Benjamin against her breast, she could feel Alex's eyes on her. "Am I so ugly?" she asked sharply.

"Why would you ask me that?"

"Because you stare at me."

"You're more beautiful than you ever were, Cassandra."

"I doubt that, although I'll admit that I haven't seen myself, except distorted by running water, in months. I don't even know how many months I've been—away."

"Over eight, and you're very beautiful—as golden and lovely as sunshine." He stopped abruptly. "What is it?"

"Nothing." Counts Many Coup had said much the same thing. She swallowed hard, confused and miserable.

"And your body is fuller, more womanly."

"That's a miracle," she muttered.

"Why a miracle?"

"Because I went hungry often enough." The stricken look on his face made her wish she'd watched her words.

"Do you want to tell me about it, Cassandra?" he asked, reluctance and unhappiness edging his voice.

Bone had warned her that Alex was guilt-ridden. Now what was she to do? If she told him about the bad times, he'd feel worse, and he didn't deserve to. He'd done more than most men would to get her back. And the good times? How could she tell him about Black Rain? He would never understand how she had come to think of an escaped slave as a sister; he'd probably consider it unnatural—or illegal. And Counts Many Coup? Alex didn't know she'd been married.

"Cassandra, you don't have to talk about it. I want you to be happy again, to forget if you can." He reached out and touched her hand where it cupped Benjamin's head against her breast. "I want you to have a good life," he finished awkwardly. "You and Benjamin."

And what about you, Alex? she wondered. *Do you expect to have a good life with us? Do you even love me anymore?*

"You're white folks," faltered the slender young woman who had greeted their arrival with a leveled musket.

"Sorry to frighten you, ma'am," said Alex. "I'm Alexander Harte, and this is my wife, Cassandra, and our son."

The woman was staring, puzzled, at Cassandra's Indian clothing and the baby on the cradle board.

"I just got them back from the Comanches," Alex explained.

"Oh Lord," exclaimed the young woman, letting her firearm slide down. "Oh, you poor thing." She stared at Cassandra with round-eyed pity.

Cassandra felt the same for the young woman with her straggling hair, her sticklike limbs, and her belly bulging in pregnancy, three grubby children already clinging to her ragged skirts although she was little more than a child herself.

Pathetically glad to see another white woman, Tillie Batts ushered them into the one-room cabin and sent the oldest boy for his father. Cassandra looked around with dismay. Dirt floor. Smoking clay and stick fireplace. Gaps in the log walls that would leave the family freezing come winter. One bed in the corner made of poles thrust through the logs and lashed together on a single crooked leg. These people lived worse than the Comanches, thought Cassandra. Later, when she had been served a meal of salt pork, corn bread, and, as an extra treat because they were guests, molasses, she decided that they ate worse too.

"Was it terrible for you?" Tillie whispered as her husband was bragging to Alex about his corn crop. "Being captured by those red devils?" Tillie added when Cassandra failed to understand the question.

"Well, I learned to make a tepee," said Cassandra, hoping Tillie would drop the topic.

"Had some neighbors to the west," said Rufus Batts. "Indians got 'em. Scalped 'em—man, woman, an' child. Lucky yer alive, missus. Course, maybe you don't feel that way."

What did he mean by that? Cassandra wondered.

"What's the news on statehood?" Alex asked quickly.

"Been offered. That's what a feller said 'bout a month ago. There's a convention meetin' down to Washington."

"D.C.?" asked Cassandra.

"No, ma'am. Washington on the Brazos. They's decidin' whether to accept er not."

"Be damn fools if they don't," Alex muttered, frowning.

"Yep," Rufus Batts agreed. "I come here figgering to be back in the union in no time atall. Heard tell there's a General Taylor from the States down on the Rio Grande keepin' the Meskins out while the Texas fellas decide whether to join up."

"I hope you folks can stay a few days," said Tillie eagerly. "Ain't had no woman company in I don't know when. You're right welcome," Tillie added hopefully. "Oughta be a real treat for ya, sleepin' in a bed an' all." The Battses, in a fever of hospitality, had offered their own bed.

"I appreciate your hospitality, Mrs. Batts," said Alex politely, "but we'll have to move on tomorrow."

"No call to hurry off," said Rufus. "There's good land just west of us. Mayhap you'll want to settle here."

"I've got a place downstream," said Alex vaguely.

"Whereabouts?"

"Above Brazoria."

"Slave country?"

Cassandra watched the disapproval close down like a hood over their host's thin-cheeked face. Minutes later, the Battses joined their children in the loft, and Cassandra found herself tucked beside her husband in the corner bed. This was as close as she'd been to Alex since the rescue, yet he turned away from her and went to sleep while she thought about what it would be like to lie in his arms again.

He didn't seem to want her anymore; perhaps he suspected that she'd had an Indian lover. She turned restlessly, and Benjamin, lying between her and the wall, whimpered in his sleep. Cassandra pulled him into the curve of her body and thought about babies. She could be carrying another child—a baby fathered by Counts Many Coup. How long had it been since her last monthly flow? She had no idea because her life had ceased to have months.

If Alex made love to her tonight or tomorrow night or any night soon and she were to find herself with child, she'd never know who the father was. Maybe that's why he hadn't touched her. He was waiting to see. And if she was with child, what then? Would he abandon her? Or keep her from a sense of duty but resent her—and the new baby? Tomorrow they would follow the Brazos south to an uncertain future, and Cassandra was afraid.

Bride Fire

* * *

She awoke before dawn when Benjamin stirred. The two of them were curled in Alex's embrace, and Cassandra lay still and savored the hard warmth of his body, remembering all the nights when she had lain with him under open skies where the stars were scattered like raindrops caught in lantern light. All her love for him came rushing back with the close familiarity of his body, and she trembled under a quick surge of desire. As if he sensed what was happening to her, his arms tightened, and she felt his lips against her shoulder. Then the baby kicked, and Alex loosened his hold, muttering something about the joys of fatherhood. Stretching, he sat up and looked down at them.

"I want to be off by first light," he said quietly. "We're no longer welcome here."

It was true. The last thing Rufus Batts said to them was, "I don't care for slavers." His wife, however, looked sad to see them go.

"My slaves live better than they do," Alex muttered once they were beyond the clearing and the straggling cornfield with its careless scattering of stumps.

Cassandra glanced at him sharply. "They may not live well, but they're free. Slaves aren't."

"Not everyone cares about freedom. Sometimes a full stomach and a roof over your head is what counts."

"I was a slave, and hungry or fed, I cared about being free."

"Oh Lord, Cassandra, I'm sorry." His face twisted with pain. "Can you ever forgive me for what you went through?"

"I don't have to forgive you, Alex," she replied steadily. "What happened wasn't your fault, and Benjamin and I got through it."

"You may not blame me," he muttered bitterly, "but I blame myself. I knew I shouldn't let you stay out there."

"Alex, I didn't want to be sent—"

Elizabeth Chadwick

"It wasn't a matter of what you wanted."

She gave him an indignant look.

"Or what I wanted. You should have gone back, and I—well, what's done is done. From now on I'll make sure you're safe, both you and Benjamin, safe at Devil's Wood."

"Alex, I don't want to live on that plantation. You know how I feel about slavery."

"I don't care much for it myself, Cassandra, but that's the way things are. You'll get used to it."

"I'll do no such thing! And how's your sister going to feel about your plans? And your brother-in-law, what will—"

"Cassandra, they wouldn't have a plantation if I hadn't fought with Houston at San Jacinto. They sided with Mexico, so they'd have lost the place. Devil's Wood is half mine, and there's a lawyer in Brazoria looking after my share."

"If you hated it before—"

"I didn't hate it. I just got sick of trying to keep my brother-in-law from gambling away the profits and my sister from nagging me to stay home and run the place. Still, it's my home, and we're going to live there."

"I don't even like the name. It's—it's—"

"—the result of something my sister said when they first arrived. She told Jean Philippe she hadn't married him to come to some hellish frontier forest and he was a devil for expecting her to live there. Jean Philippe named it Devil's Wood to spite her."

It sounded like a terrible household, and somehow or other she had to convince Alex that there were other places where they could live safely. They could even go back to Massachusetts. She had a house there, and money. Had she ever mentioned that to Alex?

"Is he asleep for the night?" Cassandra nodded, tucking the robe around the baby. "Come here then."

268

Alex was sprawled on his blankets beyond the flickering light.

Hesitantly she walked over and dropped down beside him. What now? Was she going to get another lecture on accepting plantation life and the institution of slavery?

"Are you ready to resume married life, or do you need more time?" he asked softly.

Startled, Cassandra looked down into his eyes, which seemed intent but expressionless. He certainly looked neither loving nor passionate. "You—you want me?"

"Of course I want you."

"Even though—though—"

"Though what?"

She studied her clasped hands. Now she had to face issues she'd rather have avoided. If she said nothing about the possibility of a child and there was one, maybe he'd think it was his. On the other hand, Alex could count as well as anyone and—

"If you need more time—"

"Maybe I do," she sighed, "but not for the reason you think." She had to tell him the truth. "If we make love tonight—" She stopped, biting her lip. "Alex, after Benjamin was born, I became the third wife of the war chief. I shared his bed." She watched her husband's face twist with pain. "What if I'm with child?" There was a long silence. "I could be, and—and if I am, and we—well, we'd never know—"

"—whether it was mine or his," he finished bluntly. "Do you think you're with child?"

"I don't know."

Alex sighed. "No, I don't suppose you do. I had to tell you the last time."

"Yes," said Cassandra sadly, "and this time I don't even know the month, much less the days. I don't know whether it's summer or fall."

"Almost fall," he said absently, and the silence

stretched again while Cassandra's unhappiness and resentment grew. This wasn't her fault. It wasn't anyone's fault. Couldn't he see that? At least she'd been honest. She could have lied through her teeth and kept on lying.

"Maybe we don't want to know," he said, interrupting the tumble of her thoughts. "If you're willing, we'll just make love tonight and take what comes."

"Is that what you want?" she asked wonderingly.

"Who's to question us?" he replied. "It's not as if I'm blonde or red-headed or even blue-eyed. Whatever child you bear is bound to look something like one of us."

She stared at him, astonished, and then began to laugh.

"Now that's a sound that does my heart good," said Alex and tipped her mouth up to his. When his kiss sent her head reeling, he pulled her to her feet and inspected the attachments of her soft doeskin dress. "If I can get off the pieces I can see, will there be more underneath?"

Laughing, Cassandra guided his fingers to the lacing at her waist. The long, fringed skirt dropped around her ankles, and Alex lifted the loose blouse over her head, then held her away so that he could admire her in the firelight.

"Do you know how many times I dreamed about you, waking and sleeping, while I was trying to find you?" He pulled her down beside him on the blanket, and she began to take his clothes off. "Sometimes it was so real, I'd wake up expecting to find you in my arms." He ran his palms over her breasts and along the curve of her waist. "But my dreams were never as beautiful as the real thing. Look at you," he marveled as he stroked the curve of her stomach. "I've wanted you so long, I'm almost afraid I'll wake up and find this is just another dream."

"Oh, Alex," she sighed and stretched out against

him. He was tougher and harder than ever, and the hair on his body felt strange to her. She brushed her fingertips against his chest and shivered. The light abrasion of his beard as he kissed her was subtly exciting. She had got used to the smoothness of Counts Many Coup's body and the grace of his lovemaking. Alex was—what? So overpowering. His thighs against hers were rough and rippling with muscle, pressing her legs apart.

Suddenly she couldn't wait to be penetrated. She was wild with hunger, and he responded, rolling onto her and filling her again and again until she turned liquid inside, and, peaking explosively, still wanted more. And Alex had waited. He lifted her again up the long hill to rapture, making her shudder and float free as she savored the long spasm of his love. Then, as they lay together, Cassandra thought for the first time that everything would work out, that somehow they would overcome whatever they had to face.

"Well, sweetheart," said Alex, as he rose on an elbow and peered into her face, "I think you've learned something besides tepee-making since I last saw you."

She stiffened and flushed with outrage. *How could he?* she thought furiously and was about to turn on him when he added, laughing, "I'm not complaining, mind you. *I've* got you now, and by God, I intend to enjoy you."

"Alex!" she cried, scandalized. Wasn't he even jealous? She sat up hastily and reached for her clothing.

"Uh-uh, sweetheart," he warned, flipping the skirt away. "We have a sleeping baby, an empty forest, and a fire that should be good for another hour or so. Let's not waste it putting our clothes back on."

"I have to check on Benjamin," Cassandra muttered.

"Benjamin's fine. Now come back here, you lusty wench." He circled her wrist with the fingers of one hand and drew her back down. "I adore you, Cassie."

271

"You do?" Lusty wench? Was that a compliment? she wondered nervously. Tomorrow he might think back on all this and be furious.

"I loved you before, but I always thought I was too old for you. Now, however—" he grinned at her "—I do believe that you've grown up."

"Oh." She smiled and allowed her lips to be drawn to his. Being considered grown up was fine. Of course she was grown up! She slid her hands over his shoulders. Being grown up was more fun than being a scared girl.

Chapter Sixteen

Their next shelter seemed luxurious compared to the Battses' log hut. Quentin and Euphemia McEwen had built a dog-run cabin, two rooms attached by a roofed open area and fronted by porches piled with farming gear, boots, eager hounds, and McEwen children. The family, which included Quentin's brother Robbie, lived surrounded by corn and cotton fields hacked out of the forest, and the brothers were preparing to raft their newly harvested cotton crop down river to a gin at Washington. They offered to barter lodging, river transportation, ammunition, and rations for the horses, and Alex agreed after some obligatory haggling.

The wife, Euphemia, a sturdy, pigeon-breasted little woman who ruled her family with grim rectitude, looked more disapproving than sympathetic when she heard that Cassandra had been an Indian captive. Eyeing Benjamin suspiciously, she remarked that he looked Indian.

"He looks like Alex," snapped Cassandra. "Born among the Indians, not conceived there." Euphemia's glance was so sharp that Cassandra wondered if the woman could read her mind and her growing suspicion that she was again with child, this time with no surety of who had fathered the baby.

Looking more sour than ever, Euphemia said, "And where were you and Mr. Harte married, if I may ask?"

"Webber's trading post on the Trinity," Cassandra replied resentfully.

"There be no men of God there for marryin' folks."

"We were married by bond," Cassandra mumbled, "then later by a priest down toward San Antonio."

"A papist?" exclaimed the woman, horrified. "That be not marriage, not in the eyes of God."

"Well, it is in the eyes of the law," snapped Cassandra, who had had her fill of the nosy, judgmental woman. But then she remembered that they had never acquired the necessary license to make either marriage legal.

If Cassandra could have chosen, they'd have left the next morning. However, Alex preferred river travel, and Mrs. McEwen would not let any of them go until they had attended the Sunday camp meeting

Cassandra agreed, as she had not been to a service in over two years. However, her pleasure dissipated when she realized Euphemia McEwen's purpose. "Brother, these two have been living in sin," stated Mrs. McEwen once she had dragged them forward to the preacher.

Cassandra gasped with indignation, while Alex looked mildly surprised.

"Best you marry them before their immortal souls are lost."

"Certainly," Brother Craigie agreed, tucking complacent thumbs into the pockets of a frock coat that hung like a sack on his skinny frame.

"We've already been married twice," said Cassandra angrily, "once by bond—"

"Marriage by bond is an invitation to fornicate," the preacher declared, "but no marriage in the eyes of God."

"—and once by a priest," she finished, glaring at him.

"A papist? Are you papists?" He looked more offended than Euphemia McEwen had the day before.

"By all means, marry us again," said Alex, who had started to laugh. "You can't be married too many times, right, Cassandra?"

"Marriage is a holy sacrament, not a cause for levity," said Brother Craigie piously.

"Marry away then, Brother," said Alex, still grinning.

And so they were married a third time—a fourth for her, Cassandra thought sardonically, if she counted accepting the white mare from Counts Many Coup as number three. *I'm becoming a professional bride.*

"Do you?" snapped Brother Craigie, for she had missed the last question.

"Yes," she snapped back.

None of the party approved of the long kiss that Alex gave her at the end of the ceremony. The preacher muttered a warning about curbing unnatural lust, at which Cassandra wrapped her arms around her three-time husband and kissed him back ardently. If the onlookers disapproved of the kiss, Cassandra disapproved of their service. It was appalling—all the shouting, the loud repetitive singing, the sermon laced with grim threats—she wondered how the poor children in attendance could ever sleep at night—and finally the flood forward to the mourning bench of worshipers who wanted to confess their sins and be saved, which involved being dunked in the muddy Brazos and fished out spluttering but presumably clean of soul.

When it was all over, Euphemia McEwen said coldly, "You didn't go forward to confess your sins."

"What sins?" Cassandra demanded.

"Fornication with him." She nodded toward Alex, who was discussing cotton crops with the McEwen brothers. "And God knows what you did with the Comanches."

"*I* did?" Cassandra was incensed. "I was a captive.

275

I did nothing but try to keep myself and my child alive."

"You're still wearing Indian clothes."

Cassandra had noticed how rudely all the women stared at her. "I have no others. Do you expect me to go naked?"

"You've an evil tongue, young woman, and an evil past."

And you've an evil mind, thought Cassandra. *How many, like Euphemia McEwen, will treat me with loathing?* she wondered uneasily. *Surely not many.*

Cassandra was aghast when she saw the rough log raft, lashed together without means of steering. The McEwen brothers would pole it down river to the gin at Washington, then sell the logs and make their way home as best they could. Since the deal had been made, Cassandra had no option but to step aboard, sure that she and Benjamin would drown before they ever arrived at Washington on the Brazos.

Once away from the gloomy influence of Euphemia, the McEwen brothers proved to be merry companions—too merry. They were hardly past the first bend in the river before they had broken out a jug of moonshine. Cassandra was appalled to find her safety in the hands of men who expected to survive a trip in such a flimsy craft while they disabled their own faculties with hard drink.

"Stop worrying," Alex whispered in one of the intervals when he was not taking a turn at the poles. "Many a man has made his way safely to the gulf in such a raft as this."

"How many women and children survived?" she muttered.

Alex chuckled and replied, "I'm not going to let you drown, Cassie. With any luck you'll soon be sleeping on a feather bed and wearing a white woman's dress."

"How will you get me a dress?" she asked. After the

reception her Comanche clothes had received at the camp meeting, she didn't want to meet Alex's sister wearing them.

"I know people in Washington. I can barter or get credit if necessary."

Cassandra wondered what the styles were like now. How long it had been since she'd worn anything but men's clothes and doeskin dresses.

As Alex had promised, she slept on a feather bed in the house of Arthur Wall, a friend from one of Alex's military adventures. Although delighted with the bed, she felt lonely because Benjamin was put in a cradle. He, however, didn't seem to mind at all and slept as soundly as ever.

Mrs. Wall took Cassandra in hand by sending for a seamstress and having two dresses from her own wardrobe made over. This involved taking in seams and adding flounces to the bottom of the wide skirt, which was held out with petticoats and hoops made of plaited straw. A corset was produced as well, the constriction of which made Cassandra appreciate the ease and simplicity of her Comanche clothes. She sighed and allowed herself to be adorned with long side curls for a dinner party given in their honor, to which many notable Texans had been invited, men who had come to draw up the new state constitution. Some she had even heard of—Mr. Tom Rusk, Mr. Pinckney Henderson, and Mr. Van Zandt.

Cassandra listened intently to the provisions that were being written into the constitution, the most interesting of which was that married women would retain title to their own property. "Shocking," Alex had said, grinning, and she wondered if he'd truly resent not having free use of her Massachusetts inheritance. She might need it someday, she thought gloomily. She'd been feeling queasy, although it could well be the result of the rich food to which she was unaccustomed.

"And slavery, Mr. Henderson?" she asked. "Will Texas still countenance slavery?"

Alex gave her a warning frown, and she let the matter slide, wishing she could go upstairs, unlace this benighted corset, and crawl in between the clean sheets.

"When will you be moving on to Devil's Wood, Alex?" asked Tom Rusk.

"Tomorrow I reckon. I've passage on a keelboat."

Cassandra came out of her reverie and gazed at him. He hadn't said a word about leaving so soon. Her stomach fluttered at the thought of meeting his sister. How many days were they from Devil's Wood?

"Lord, man," said a planter from the Columbia area, "couldn't you wait for a riverboat? A keelboat's no fit transportation for a gently bred woman."

He made a half-bow in Cassandra's direction, and she almost laughed aloud. Obviously the man didn't know where this particular gently bred woman had been the last year. She doubted that a keelboat, whatever its drawbacks, would prove any more dangerous or uncomfortable than a raft shared with the McEwen brothers, nor the boatmen any more drunken. Robbie McEwen had reeled off the edge five miles above Washington and had to be fished out of the river, an exigency his older brother seemed to find hilarious.

"A keelboat!" cried Mrs. Wall. "Well, I must find you a parasol to protect your skin from the sun, my dear."

How does she think my skin got this color? Cassandra wondered. *Not from using parasols.* She tried to imagine the reaction of, say, Talking Crow if Cassandra had shown up to scrape a buffalo hide carrying a parasol to protect her delicate skin from the sun.

"What were you laughing about at dinner?" Alex asked later.

"Oh, nothing," Cassandra replied. She tried not to remind him of her life among the Comanches. Its results might be something they'd have to face all too soon.

"You look mighty delicious in that dress," he murmured, running a finger from her chin to her cleavage. One of the two dresses Mrs. Wall had provided was a rose silk that left Cassandra's shoulders bare. She had to wear a shawl to conceal the lance scar. "Not a man at the table could take his eyes off you, sweetheart."

"Including you?" she asked.

"Especially me." He bent and placed his lips where his finger had been. "Since we'll be traveling with the keelboatmen for the next few days, maybe we'd best make the most of this time alone."

Cassandra, melting against his black-clad figure, was agreeable. She began to unbutton his brocaded silk waistcoat. The formal clothes became him. She found exciting the thought of the fierce man who awaited her beneath the gentlemanly broadcloth. Alex was a more savage lover than Counts Many Coup had ever been, and she, having been enticed into sensuality by her Comanche husband, now appreciated the passion of the man who had reclaimed her.

However, when Alex slept, Cassandra lay awake, thinking of her conversation with a Captain Ralph Hawkins, former Texas Ranger. The man had marveled that Alex had found her. "Is it so hard?" she asked, thinking of Alexandra.

"Near impossible, ma'am," said the captain. "Many a woman and child have been taken by the Comanches, and few are ever seen again. The usual outcome is the death of those who've tried to retrieve them."

Underlying her newfound happiness with Alex was always the thought of her daughter. If she told Alex what had happened, he would go after Alexandra, and the result? Cassandra would lose him too—in the hope of rescuing a child who might already be dead. She turned away and stifled her tears. What was she to do? She loved him so.

The keelboat was a long, narrow affair, pointed at both ends with a huge rudder for steering and a small cabin that contained rudimentary furniture, windows, and a fireplace, but not, unfortunately, much room for a woman dressed in a full-skirted, pale yellow day gown. Cassandra could hardly get through the door to the cabin, where Alex insisted she stay, isolated from the rough crew. The dirt that greeted her inside boded ill for the light-colored fabric. She had little hope of arriving at Devil's Wood looking even moderately neat and respectable.

The trip proceeded with one alarm after another as they maneuvered around snags and sandbars, low-hanging branches and logjams, and the further downstream they drifted, the more morose Alex became.

"How soon will we get there?" she asked.

"Soon enough to keep Jean Philippe from gambling away the fall crop if we're lucky," he muttered. "I'll probably have to take it down river myself."

"And leave me?" she asked uneasily.

"Well, my sister can hardly be worse than the Comanches. At least you'll be safe and comfortable at Devil's Wood and have help with Benjamin."

"Does your sister have children?" Suddenly Cassandra realized how little she knew about her new sister-in-law.

"She had six," said Alex. "Two died at birth. One was scalded to death when he was two or three. She lost one to yellow fever when they were in Galveston on business, one to scarlet fever at home, and the last in the runaway scrape."

"Oh, my God," said Cassandra, thinking of her own grief at the loss of Alexandra, who might still be alive. Eloise Daumier's children were in their graves.

"She blamed me for Miranda," said Alex bitterly.

"Said if, instead of joining Houston after I escaped at Goliad, I'd gone with her when they had to flee ahead of the Mexican army that Miranda wouldn't have died."

"What happened to the child?"

"Drowned when they were trying to ferry across a river in flood."

"Oh, Alex, that's terrible."

"Yes, it was terrible. The runaway scrape was a terrifying time for all the women and children. Eloise at least had her husband with her, and she wasn't afoot or without resources."

Six children, all dead. Couldn't Alex understand how desperate and irrational his sister must have been when she lost her last child? Cassandra thought again of her lost daughter and the danger to Alex if she told him. The fields and forests flowed by her unseeing eyes as she decided, finally, that telling could only add to his guilt and her fear.

After leaning over to check on Benjamin, who was asleep in a basket, she stared out the window again. Everywhere they passed, cotton was being harvested, black men and women bending in the fields to pluck out the fluffy balls. The weary cadence of their songs wrung her heart. Some of the fields were bare, just an occasional touch of white clinging to the withered plants. From time to time they passed docks and gins, which Alex identified for her, and houses set back from the river on bluffs or hills or among groves of trees. The luxury of the plantation mansions offended her as she compared it to the hard, unpaid labor of the slaves who supported it. How could Alex stomach this system? And how would Cassandra ever be able to live with his sister, who had married to get this life, and his brother-in-law, who wasted the efforts of others in gambling and profligacy?

Two days passed, and Cassandra no longer tried to entice her husband into conversation. She didn't

Elizabeth Chadwick

really want to hear any more about Devil's Wood, and
Alex obviously didn't want to talk about it. The only
comforting thing he'd told her was that they wouldn't
have to live in the same house with the Daumiers.

"I used the overseer's place before I left," he said
grimly, "and I intend to move back into it. Since I do
an overseer's work, I might as well get the privacy of
the overseer's house. I suppose that will embarrass
you."

"Why would it?"

"It's a cabin. Logs, just like the big house, but there's
only two rooms. You won't like it."

"It's bound to be better than a tepee," Cassandra
retorted dryly. How dared he think of her as some
mincing miss who had to be pampered? She'd lived
the same life he had for months, and a harder life than
that afterwards.

"Remind me once in a while, if I forget, that you're
nothing like my sister," he muttered, then grinned
shamefacedly and leaned over to kiss her.

"What the devil!" exclaimed Alex.

They stood on the dock, staring up the hill at the
splendid new white Greek revival mansion with its
columns and galleries.

"Been some changes, Marse Alex," said the old black
man who had moved slowly across the boards to greet
them.

"Not where it counts," Alex muttered. "You've got
a magnificent new house, but you haven't got the crop
in."

"We's gittin' there. Ain't no hurry."

"They won't think that if it rains," Alex retorted.

"Well, you been away," said the old man. "Don't
never go as well when you ain't here."

Several black children scrambled to carry the news
that Alex had returned, and before he and Cassandra
could climb the bare hill to the house, a small woman

282

in black appeared at the door and waited, making no move to greet them.

When they had mounted the steps, she said, "I can see that you've come home poorer than you left, Alex."

"Wrong as usual, Eloise," he replied. "I'm richer by a wife, a son, and enough land to start my own country."

What did he mean by that? Cassandra wondered.

"Where?" asked the sister sarcastically. "Out among the buffalo and savages?"

"Exactly. Where's Jean Philippe? I can see that he's neglecting the important things, as usual."

"Jean Philippe is dead," said Eloise. "He was killed almost two years ago." Then she turned and swept into the house, black skirts brushing the door frame.

She never even looked at me, Cassandra thought.

"It would seem," said Alex dryly, "that we've arrived just in time if my sister is bent on building herself a rich woman's house while she leaves the fields unharvested."

This certainly wasn't what Alex had led her to expect, thought Cassandra as she sat at the long rosewood table with Alex, Eloise, and Mr. Cutter, the overseer. Mr. Cutter was another unexpected facet of life at Devil's Wood. Because Mr. Cutter actually *was* the overseer, he had first call on the log house which had formerly been home to the Daumiers, and Cassandra and Alex had to live with Eloise in the new plantation house. The old overseer's cabin had been put to some other uses, as Eloise had smugly informed them when Alex followed her through the big doors that afternoon and ordered that his few belongings be taken to the cabin.

The plantation house amazed Cassandra. She had thought her family lived well in Cambridge, but this—this was an example of unfettered spending and some almost unnatural avidity for luxury. Under Cassandra's ill-fitting slippers was a velvet carpet. Blue damask curtains hung at the windows. To her right, behind Eloise, stood an immense, elaborate marble-topped sideboard, and above their heads hung a brass chandelier from which the light of glowing candles filtered through showers of crystal prisms. There were armies of silver, china, and candles on the table. And on her left sat Alex, who had been more surprised at the changes than she. He seethed as black servants moved silently about the room serving the first course while a child in a homespun shift stood behind each of the four diners fanning the humid air.

"Don't you think, Cassandra, that you're a little overdressed for a simple family dinner?" Eloise asked with delicate derision.

Cassandra, who had been sampling the soup, an oyster bisque, cunningly seasoned, looked up at her new sister-in-law and caught the gleam of malice in her eyes. "I have three dresses, Eloise," Cassandra replied sharply. "The one I wore today, which is being washed, this one, so kindly provided by Mrs. Arthur Wall—" Cassandra touched the deep bertha of the rose gown—"and a doeskin skirt and blouse. Perhaps you would have found the Comanche outfit more suitable for this *simple* family dinner?"

A smile quirked Alex's lips. "Tomorrow the seamstress can begin on a wardrobe for you, Cass."

Devil's Wood had its own seamstress? she marveled.

"Sarah is still here, I presume?"

"No," said Eloise. "She's dead."

Cassandra could have sworn there was a ring of satisfaction in Eloise Daumier's voice.

"How did she die?" Alex's voice became sharp.

"She just died," Eloise muttered defensively.

"Well, you can tell me yourself, or I'll ask around until I find out." When Eloise didn't reply, he said, "Joseph, get Aunt Heppie in here."

The middle-aged slave who had been serving vegetables mumbled, "Yes sir, Marse Alex," and moved slowly out of the room. Eloise glared. Mr. Cutter cleared his throat and helped himself to the buttered turnips. He was a short, stocky man, sandy-haired with a freckled, kindly face.

"Somethin' wrong with yo dinnah, Massa Alex?" asked the heavy woman who came into the room, as calm as the whites were tense.

"Aunt Heppie." Alex rose from his chair and hugged her. Then he stood back and said, "Now, tell me what happened to Sarah."

The woman glanced at Eloise, absolutely no expression on her broad, black face. "Cut her wrists," said Aunt Heppie. Alex's dark face paled. "When Massa Jean Philippe die, then Sarah gonna be sold away, but not her chillun. Sarah, she weep for her babies she neber see no more. Then she cut her wrists."

"You couldn't have sold them with her?" Alex asked, turning angrily on his sister.

Eloise seemed frozen with some rage that Cassandra didn't understand. "Jefferson Pollard didn't want the children, and you could hardly expect me to give away four valuable slaves."

Jefferson Pollard? My God, thought Cassandra. That was the man from whom Black Rain had escaped, and now he was responsible for tearing a mother from her children and the resulting suicide. Alex seemed angry too, although he must have seen such tragedies before.

"I can't believe you'd sell any of our people to that vicious bastard." When Eloise failed to answer, Alex snapped sarcastically, "Nobody's said what happened to Jean Philippe. Did he cut his wrists too?"

"Now Alex, Miss Eloise she don't want to talk about—"

"Cutter, this place is half mine," said Alex, "and a lot of expensive changes have been made since I left."

"To fight a war," Eloise began bitterly, "that you'd no business—"

Elizabeth Chadwick

"I worked harder on this place than your husband ever did," snapped Alex. "And I put the profits back into the plantation instead of gambling them away."

"You never put any of your *own* money in. Everything you got from Father you lent to Sam Houston in '36 when we needed—"

"—money to pay off Daumier's debts," said Alex coldly.

"And what did you get back?" she retorted.

"Land," said Alex, "lots of land that Jean Philippe couldn't gamble away. Now, what happened to him?"

"He was killed in a duel."

"Was it over a woman or debts?"

Cassandra was beginning to feel a little sorry for Eloise. That was a cruel question to ask, and she found the hostility pervading the room appalling.

"Who killed him?"

"Jefferson Pollard," Eloise mumbled.

"The man killed your husband, and then you agreed to sell him Sarah? You know his reputation with women."

"It was hardly my concern," said Eloise. "I'd have been glad to see the last of her, but as it happened, Jean Philippe lost her in a game of chance and refused to pay up. The duel—"

"—was over Sarah," Alex finished for her. "Pollard must have been furious when she killed herself."

Eloise shrugged. "His wound mortified, and he died himself within a week."

"Good riddance," Alex muttered.

Cassandra thought, *If only we'd known he was dead. Black Rain could have come home with me.*

"That damn Jean Philippe!" Alex burst out.

"Now, Alex," soothed Cutter. "Daumier's been gone these two years."

"Well, that's half of two years' profits that didn't get gambled away," said Alex, "but obviously you've been spending every penny of your half on this house,

286

Eloise. The question is, have you been spending my half as well? Colby Robinson was supposed to keep his eye on you two."

"The agreement was that your half of the profits had to be put back into Devil's Wood, Alex." His sister laid her fork on her plate with careful precision. "This house and its furnishings are part of the plantation."

Alex's face tightened with fury when he realized that his sister had used his money to aggrandize her lifestyle. "You *knew*, Eloise, that the agreement had nothing to do with high living. By God, you're as bad as Jean Philippe."

"I have a right to a decent life," Eloise cried. "You weren't here when I was struggling, when this was all a wilderness and we had to live off wild game and the corn crop failed and the children died and—"

"No one says you've had an easy life," Alex agreed, "but you knew he was a bastard when you married him."

"Well, the house is built and furnished," said Eloise more calmly, "and there's nothing you can do about it. Even Colby couldn't find anything in the contract to stop me."

The room hummed with tension.

"Cutter, why aren't the picking teams out?" Alex asked, turning abruptly to the overseer.

Cutter flushed uneasily and pushed the last of the food on his plate in a nervous circle.

"We've other uses for the hands right now," snapped Eloise.

"Other uses! What's more important than getting the crop in?" Alex demanded. "If the rains catch you with the cotton still in the fields—"

"Oh, it's not going to rain," said Eloise impatiently, "and the grounds need landscaping. There are things that have to be done right now. The house can't be seen to advantage without gardens and lawns."

"We'll start picking tomorrow," said Alex.

287

"You'll do no such thing."

"If you try to interfere, Eloise, I'll take you to court over your theft of partnership funds. You'll never be invited anywhere again as long as you live."

Eloise turned pale. "I have an important visitor coming. I can't entertain properly if—"

"Who'd be fool enough to visit during picking?"

"Horace Waverly," said Eloise, as if announcing a visit from the president of the United States.

"An English author," Cassandra murmured when Alex looked puzzled and frustrated.

"Well, if it were Sam Houston himself," said Alex, "we'd still go into the fields tomorrow. It'll be Christmas before we get the crop ginned, baled, and shipped down river. What were you thinking of, Cutter, to—"

"I make the decisions," Eloise interrupted, "not Mr. Cutter, and I wanted my landscaping finished. Why, I have slips and bushes and seeds from some of the most important people in Texas, your precious Sam Houston included. I'm going to have better gardens than Emily Perry." Eloise began to list the contributors to the prospective beautification of Devil's Wood and appealed for Cassandra's support on the importance of repaying all these gifts by getting the gardens in place.

"Cassandra hasn't heard of Emily Perry, much less any of the others," said Alex dryly, "so you're wasting your time with all that name-dropping, Eloise."

"Never heard of Emily Perry?" exclaimed Eloise. "She's Stephen F. Austin's sister."

"I've heard of Stephen F. Austin," said Cassandra. She was looking at a pie wedge just set in front of her and wondering if she could eat another bite. She felt dazed with food but hadn't wanted to slight Aunt Heppie's cooking.

"Everyone's heard of Stephen F. Austin," snapped Eloise. "Where in the world are you from?"

"Cambridge, Massachusetts," Cassandra replied.

"Her father was a professor at Harvard College."

"A professor?" Eloise's low opinion of professors was blatantly obvious. "And you were in Massachusetts, Alex? Was there a war in the North I haven't heard about?"

Alex offered a brief history of his last three years.

"How dreadful," said Eloise, staring at Cassandra as if she were a distasteful exhibit in a doctor's office. Cassandra had once felt the way Eloise looked when shown a preserved human organ by a professor of medicine.

On that dubious note the dinner ended, and Cassandra retired with Alex to their lavish bedroom with its beautifully carved furniture. The giant four-poster bed stood so high off the floor that a three-step stool was needed to climb in, and the whole structure was draped with canopies, curtains, and netting, the last to defend the occupants against mosquitoes. One of the slaves, a light-skinned girl named Mellie, had offered this information before dinner while she helped Cassandra into her rose gown. Cassandra had wondered what Mellie would think had she known that Cassandra herself had recently been a slave.

"Alex, maybe you and your sister would get along better if you weren't so hard on her," Cassandra suggested once they were ensconced together in the bed. "She *has* had a terrible life. Why shouldn't she want to make it more comfortable and more beautiful if she can afford to? She's lost her husband, her children—"

Alex sighed. "You're too softhearted, Cassandra. She married him knowing exactly what he was. My father warned her against Jean Philippe; so did everyone else, but Eloise wouldn't listen. As for what she's done here, it's madness. She should have been putting the profits into the plantation, not the house. She should have been expanding, which we couldn't do while Jean Phillipe was alive."

"But, Alex, maybe Eloise doesn't want a bigger plantation."

"Frontier economies depend on expansion. In Texas you either expand or you lose what you have. Only a woman would think otherwise."

"Only a *woman?*" Furious, Cassandra rolled away toward the edge of the bed. Instead of protesting her abrupt exit from his arms, Alex grunted, turned over, and went to sleep, leaving her even more angry. And uneasy. Eloise and Devil's Wood were already coming between them, she realized unhappily. For a long time she lay on her back, staring up into the draperies above her. Eloise had insisted that Benjamin be put into the nursery under the care of a nursemaid. Cassandra missed his baby noises in the night, missed being able to reach out to touch or cuddle him. And now, perhaps inadvertently, Eloise had come between Cassandra and Alex. She felt lonely and isolated, convinced that this was an evil place from which she should take her husband and child as soon as she could. Yet Alex, she knew, felt compelled to stay. For her sake, ironically enough.

Chapter Seventeen

"I made that dress myself while I was a Comanche captive. It was the highlight of my wardrobe," Cassandra added with a rueful grin.

"I bet you looked mighty fine in it," said Mellie, her young face alight with interest. "All those beads an' fringes. Did you like bein' with the Indians?"

Cassandra remembered Black Rain, who had escaped from a plantation thinking Indians wouldn't hurt Negroes. Was young Mellie dreaming of such an escape?

"They can be very cruel," Cassandra warned.

"Did they hurt you? Oh, Miss Cass—Cass—an—"

"Try Cassie," suggested Cassandra. Her conscience rebelled. She had been trying to prevent the girl from running away, and what right had she to do that? Freedom at risk was better than safe slavery; she had said as much to Alex.

Cassandra spent the day closeted with the seamstress, Gemmalee, and her small coffee-colored assistant, Esther. They studied back issues of *Godey's Ladies Book* and various fabrics on hand in the plantation storehouses. The supply of silks, cottons, fine wools, and laces was impressive.

"Missus, she only order black since Massa die," explained Gemmalee. "These here left ober from before."

"How about this style?" suggested Cassandra.

Gemmalee's face tightened with alarmed indecision.

"What is it?" Cassandra asked.

"Well, ma'am, it's—it's just that Miz Eloise—she done used that one herself."

Cassandra nodded. Gemmalee feared Eloise's anger should Cassandra insist on having a duplicate dress made. "Just let me know when we see something of hers, and we'll pass right over it. How about this one?"

The seamstress's relief and gratitude were embarrassing as they settled on the first project, a dress of white India muslin with blue silk facing. It featured full sleeves, a very full skirt, and a large square collar. At least it should be reasonably cool, Cassandra thought, fanning herself with the fashion book as little Esther began to pin together the bodice pieces Gemmalee had cut out.

"How long does this weather last?" Cassandra asked.

"Ain't that hot," said Gemmalee, surprised. "But it do cool off startin' next month," she hastened to add, as if contradicting Cassandra would earn her a reprimand. Later she eyed Cassandra and asked, "We need to put in the wider seams?" When Cassandra looked blank, Gemmalee explained, "So's we kin let yo dresses out in comin' months."

Cassandra went very still. Was that a confirmation of her own suspicions? And how could Gemmalee tell? Cassandra had seen no obvious sign, and she had looked at herself in a mirror just that morning. How strange it had seemed. Her own reflection. She was indeed golden—both her skin and hair. "Maybe," she replied evasively, then squeaked because Esther had nipped her with a pin.

"Oh, Miz Cassie, Ah'm so—"

"What have you done, you clumsy little beast?" cried Eloise, who had entered unnoticed.

Her hand was already raised to the frightened

twelve-year-old when Cassandra stepped quickly in front of Esther and said, "She did nothing, Eloise. I had a cramp in my leg." Cassandra stayed between Eloise and the girl. "Pin the back, will you, Esther?" Cassandra could feel the girl's hands shaking and suffered several more pinpricks, but she kept her expression unmoved.

Eloise, frowning, went to a dainty spindle-legged chair with tapestry upholstery and sank down. "I can't imagine where Mr. Waverly is. I expected him several hours ago, before supper. And Alex, why hasn't he been in?"

"I suppose they're busy in the fields," said Cassandra. Gemmalee was industriously basting the skirt.

"Why did you choose white?" asked Eloise. "The season is almost past."

"It doesn't feel past to me," Cassandra muttered, "and white looked so cool—especially after wearing deerskin."

"Oh yes, your Indian experience. I've heard many women would rather die than be taken alive by Indians."

Cassandra stared at her sister-in-law. Was that a criticism? "I didn't have much choice. I was knocked unconscious and came to to find myself tied on a horse, a captive. Are you saying I should have committed suicide the first chance I got?"

"Well, I'm hardly in a position to say what you should have done, Cassandra. I don't know what happened to you, but I've heard that white females are— ah—dishonored."

"You're not a Christian, then?"

"Certainly I'm a Christian," retorted Eloise indignantly. "If you're implying that it's uncharitable of me to mention such things to you, you might remember that I am, after all, your sister-in-law. I felt you might need another woman to—to unburden yourself

Elizabeth Chadwick

to since there are some things you could hardly discuss with your husband.''

And you'll use whatever I say to make trouble between us, thought Cassandra angrily. Then she sighed. *Now I'm being uncharitable*, she admitted. *If I knew Eloise better, I might well want to talk to another woman.* "I just meant that suicide is not an option for Christians,'' she said quietly. "As for what happened—''

"Yes, do tell me about it, Cassandra.''

"Young Esther here's a bit young to hear—''

"She's a slave,'' snapped Eloise, "and a clumsy one at that. Leave the room, girl.'' Eloise gave the child such a look that Cassandra caught her breath with dismay. What could little Esther have done to earn such hatred? The child scuttled out of the room, leaving the dress bodice still pinned to Cassandra's body.

"Well, Eloise,'' said Cassandra, much less willing to make allowances for her sister-in-law after the scene with the seamstress's little helper, "at the first stop, my legs were numb when I was pushed off the horse, and I stumbled into a young warrior. He was about to scalp me when the man I was later forced to marry stopped him.''

"Marry?'' breathed Eloise, horrified.

That admission had been a mistake. Maybe if her revelations were shocking enough, Eloise would forget about the marriage. "I had no food except for a piece of bloody, raw antelope liver and little water, no warm clothing, and nothing to sleep on or in during the whole trip. We were on horses almost constantly for days, and I was terrified of losing the baby. Then when we finally got to camp, I was poked with burning sticks, tied to a scalp pole, threatened by everyone in camp—''

"Cassie, Lula say the baby cryin'. Say maybe you come nurse him.''

"Mellie, how dare you interrupt our conversation, and as for the baby, Lula should have sent to the quarters for a wet nurse as soon as Mister Alex and his wife arrived."

"But Cassie say—"

"Who gave you permission to call her Cassie?"

"I did," said Cassandra, who had noticed for the first time the resemblance between Mellie and Esther. The girls had the same light skin and features.

"I do not encourage such familiarity, Cassandra," said Eloise angrily. "If you're going to live here, you'll have to learn our ways."

Ah, but I'm not going to live here, Eloise, thought Cassandra grimly. *Not a minute longer than it takes me to convince my husband we'll be better off elsewhere.*

"Now, tell Lula to send for a wet nurse, Mellie."

"Excuse me, Eloise. I do not want a wet nurse. I intend to continue to nurse my own baby."

"White women do not—"

"I'm the mother, and I'll do as I please."

Fuming, Eloise whirled and stamped out. The two black women were staring at Cassandra as if she had just breathed fire into the face of a dragon.

"A fine day's work," said Mr. Cutter. He had taken his straw hat off as the two men entered the wide main hall. "Easy to see the hands are glad you're home, Alex."

Eloise and Cassandra, who had been keeping one another uneasy company in the drawing room, turned simultaneously when they heard the voices. Cassandra looked at her husband and felt her heart speed up. He wore a wide-brimmed, low-crowned hat, loose trousers, and knee-high riding boots, and he was shirtless, the sweat glistening on his chest and arms. *My God*, she thought, *he's so handsome.*

"Really, Alex," cried Eloise, "must you come in looking like a common field hand?"

"I've been working like one, so I don't see why not."

"What if Mr. Waverly had been here? He'd have been horribly shocked."

"Obviously he's not here," said Alex sarcastically, "so why are we—"

"But he might have been! He was supposed to be!"

"Joseph," said Cassandra softly, her eyes still caught by the picture her husband made as he stood in the doorway, the low afternoon sun streaming in behind him, "could you have someone see to a hot bath for Mr. Alex?"

"Yessum, Miz Cassie," said Joseph.

Alex shot Cassandra a hard look and stalked toward the staircase. Surprised and confused at his unfriendly expression, she trailed behind. In their room he snapped, "You evidently find me offensive too."

Blinking with surprise, Cassandra stood mute for a moment. Then a slow smile lifted the corners of her mouth, and her eyes glowed with mischief. "Actually, Alex," she murmured, "I think you look absolutely tantalizing. Would you like to make love before or after your bath? I'm agreeable either way." At his stunned look, she burst into peals of laughter and added, "In fact, agreeable hardly covers how much I—"

Before she could finish, Alex had swept her into his arms, muttering, "Minx," and kissed her hungrily, the sweat on his chest and arms soaking into the yellow dress.

Poor Mellie will have another overnight wash-up job, thought Cassandra but found she didn't really care about the condition of her dress, not as long as Alex kept kissing her. Her head was whirling, and he had already covered her breast with one large hand when a timid knock at their door stopped him.

"Oh hell!" muttered Alex. "If that's my sister—"

"It's probably your bath," said Cassandra. "Do you think we could tell them to go away?"

"Are you that eager, sweetheart?" he asked. He looked both pleased and amused.

Cassandra pressed against him, feeling dizzily lustful.

"You realize that we'll have to send them away before I can get undressed," Alex murmured. "Considering the condition into which you've got me, I can hardly let anyone assist at my bath."

"Assist in your bath?" What did he mean by that? "If you need any assistance, *I'll* give it." She remembered Black Rain saying her master had wanted her in his bed. Surely Alex wasn't intimate with the slave girls.

"Will you?" Alex murmured, eying her speculatively. "In that case, let them in. Maybe I can wait to get you into bed after all, if you're going to give me a bath."

Still thinking of all the pretty young girls around the place, like Mellie, for instance, Cassandra went to the door. A tub was carried into the room, then hot water from kettles was poured in, linen towels and soap laid out, until finally Alex waved the various helpers away.

"Do people really give you baths?" Cassandra asked.

"No sweetheart, not since I was a toddler. I gather you didn't mean that offer seriously." He had begun to drag off his boots, then his trousers, and finally his drawers as Cassandra watched.

"Yes, I did," said Cassandra, and she walked over to take up the cloth and soap that had been left on a small table by the tub. She had decided to give him a bath he'd never forget. Then if he ever decided he wanted a woman to bathe him again, it would be Cassandra, not some young slave girl. Alex stepped into the tub and slid down in the warm water, his knees bent up level with his shoulders. She began with his face, her hands gentle and caressing.

"Do you do this for Benjamin?" he asked, leaning his head back and closing his eyes.

"Um-m, h-m-m," she murmured, stroking soap onto his neck and shoulders.

"Lucky baby."

Cassandra rolled up her sleeves and reached into the water to rub his back all the way down onto his hips. Then she washed his chest and finally his legs, running the cloth down between his knees and thighs. Alex opened his eyes and stared at her until she looked up into dark, interested depths. "Stand up," she murmured.

" 'Fraid I'm in no proper state to do that," he replied.

"We *are* married—quite a few times, when you think about it. So many times, I'm not sure *what* our legal status is." Cassandra was chuckling, but Alex frowned. "Now, don't be a sissy," she teased. "Stand up."

"What for?" he temporized, the lazy, speculative look back in his eyes.

"Oh, more washing," she replied, grinning mischievously. "Then I'll rinse you off." She nodded her head in the direction of two more water kettles.

Alex rose, dripping, from the water. He was wonderfully tall, she thought with pleasure. She circled behind him and washed his buttocks with such care that she could feel the muscles tense. Then, murmuring, "Almost done," she circled again, rubbing the soap onto her hands rather than the cloth. She looked straight up into his eyes, smiling, as she finished off his bath.

"You'd damn well better hurry with the rinsing," he muttered, "you little tease."

"Did you like your bath?" Cassandra asked innocently as she poured the warm water over him.

"Just a little too much," he replied, "as you're about to discover," and he whirled and lifted her into the air, empty kettle and all.

Somehow the kettle got left behind, while Alex and Cassandra ended up in the middle of the huge four-poster amid a tumble of damp bedding. Alex kissed and caressed her so thoroughly that at last she begged him to stop the preliminaries.

"Sure you're ready?" he teased.

"I was ready when the door closed behind us."

"Good," said Alex. "Since I've had a hard day, you can do all the work." At which he rolled onto his back and lifted her on top of him. Although unused to innovations, Cassandra found herself deliciously filled with the condition she had created. She gasped and closed her eyes, thinking that if she just stayed where she was, the excitement would carry her over the top. However, Alex had other ideas for which he gave her expert guidance. If her energy flagged, he spurred her on, pulling her forward so that he could kiss her breasts, lifting her hips and easing her down so that she learned to pleasure herself and him, touching her intimately when she was already wild with excitement, until, both of them frenzied, he arched, and she cried out and collapsed against his chest.

"Now," said Alex, whispering into her ear, when he had given her a few minutes to still her racing heart and catch her breath, "I'll give *you* a bath."

"Alex," she said dazedly, "I don't think I have enough energy for a bath."

"Not even if I do all the work?"

"Especially if you do all the work."

Alex's delighted laughter filled the room, almost drowning out the sound of knocking at their door.

"Marse Alex," called a timid voice. "Do Ah take away the bath water now?"

"No," Alex shouted back.

There was a short silence. "Miz Eloise, she say come down to dinnah."

"No," said Alex loudly.

"But I'm hungry," Cassandra whispered.

"Tell Aunt Heppie to send ours up," Alex called out.

"Yes, sah." The footsteps receded.

"Now about this hunger of yours," said Alex. "Just how did you mean that, sweetheart?"

"The bishop arrived last night," hissed Eloise, "and where were you?"

"In bed," Alex drawled. "You want any further explanation?"

Eloise flushed angrily. "Well, he's holding services this morning, and he expects the Nigrahs to attend. I told him I preferred separate services, but—"

"He'll have to do without me and Cutter and the field hands. We're picking, and we'll continue until—"

"Alex, it's a great honor to have the bishop. I don't know how many times I've invited him without—"

"Eloise, have you lost your mind entirely? You leave the cotton unpicked to plant bushes and flowers. You invite English authors—" Eloise's face drooped in disappointment at the reminder of the nonappearance of her literary prize. "—and Episcopalian bishops to visit when you should be—"

"Alex," Cassandra interrupted gently, "if it's Sunday—"

"You don't even know what day of the week it is?" Eloise exclaimed rudely. "How barbaric!"

"We didn't *have* days of the week in *Comancheria*," snapped Cassandra, "and I'm about to agree with you, Eloise. I think we should all attend services, especially the slaves. In this situation we bear a special responsibility for their souls. It's certainly of paramount importance—"

"—to get the damn crop in so we'll all eat this winter—including the slaves. We can worry about their souls once we're sure we can fill their bellies." With that Alex nodded to Cutter, who had been calmly eating his ham and hominy, and the two men left.

"What will Bishop Andress think?" wailed Eloise. "What will the neighbors think?"

Cassandra looked at her curiously. Eloise didn't seem to care about the religious opportunity that had presented itself, only about how this slight to the bishop would affect her social standing. Cassandra herself wasn't an Episcopalian, but she looked forward to the service, which she anticipated would be more to her liking than Brother Craigie's fire-and-brimstone orations.

In fact, Cassandra found the service very comforting. Bishop Andress was a gentle, scholarly man who gave a learned and intricate explication of the Bible verses chosen for that Sunday, and Cassandra, who had been so long away from either church or scholarship, could have wept with happiness to listen to the good man. She did, however, think the sermon held little for the household slaves who sat in back. The bishop made a few remarks for their benefit, gentle admonitions to obey their masters, work hard, and live virtuously. *He shouldn't even approve of their servitude*, she thought despairingly, and wondered how things were ever to change if good men like Bishop Andress and Alex weren't morally outraged by slavery.

Eloise served the bishop a sumptuous meal, apologizing profusely for the absence of her brother. Cassandra engaged him in a discussion of textual interpretations in the Bible. She found, to her delight, that he knew Greek, Latin, and Hebrew, and had done research of his own in his student days.

"What an amazingly fine education you have had, my dear," he said at one point, which earned Cassandra an angry glance from Eloise. Still, angry glances could not dim Cassandra's glow of happiness. She might have been back in her mother's parlor, sitting among the scholars and contributing now and then to their discussions, delighting in the sharpness of her own mind and the intriguing ideas of those around her. After all those months on the plains she had almost forgotten the pleasures of the mind.

What books did the library here at Devil's Wood contain? she wondered. She'd have to start reading again. And there was Benjamin's education to consider. Then she stopped herself with a smile. Benjamin was not quite of an age to be educable. Nursery songs were more to his liking, and he got plenty of those. From Cassandra, from all the black girls and women who wanted to sing to him, even from Alex, who had been caught singing "Come to the Bower" to his son, the ballad that had so embarrassed Cassandra at Odell Webber's trading post.

"Has your baby been christened, my dear?" the bishop asked.

All Cassandra's happy thoughts disappeared, and she turned to him with anguish, remembering Benjamin's baptism, when she had christened her absent daughter. She longed to ask the bishop if that baptism counted, but she could not bear to speak of it, certainly not in front of Eloise. "Since there was no one else to do it, I christened him myself," she replied.

"You are a good Christian mother," said the bishop, leaning forward to pat her hand. "Not all would realize that they could themselves dedicate a child to God. Still, if you would like, we can have a formal christening when Alex returns. Not that your own was not sufficient," he added, "but your husband might like to be present."

Why not? thought Cassandra, touched by his kindness. *I've been married four times. It can't hurt to have Benjamin christened twice.*

"I'll be the godmother," said Eloise.

Cassandra couldn't very well refuse, but the idea made her uneasy.

Alex was enthusiastic when he returned from the fields. "Lancelot," he said, "it's good to see you again," and he clapped the bishop on the shoulder. "Have you claimed a host of souls for Christ since we last met?"

"More, I hope, than you've sent on to their reward," replied the bishop, smiling whimsically.

Cassandra was astounded. She had never heard anyone address a clergyman so familiarly, but the bishop didn't seem to take offense. Eloise did. She glared at her brother until he was told of the proposed christening and said, "By all means, Eloise shall be godmother." His sister's face lit with happiness. "And Cutter shall be godfather. Will you do it, Jonah?"

"I'd be honored, if Miss Eloise thinks it proper," said Jonah Cutter. "He's a beautiful boy is little Benjamin."

Cassandra could see that Eloise did not think it proper for an overseer to stand godfather to her nephew, but Alex gave his sister a hard look and muttered something to the effect that maybe they didn't need godparents after all. Eloise closed her mouth, and Benjamin was christened in the drawing room with all the house servants in attendance.

Then Alex, saying, "I've a favor to ask of you, Lancelot," rushed the bishop off to the study for a conference. Cassandra took the baby up to bed. When she returned, Alex and Bishop Andress joined the ladies once more, Alex announcing, "Lancelot has kindly agreed to come back to Devil's Wood to hold services in October."

Eloise was delighted, as was Cassandra, not only because she liked the bishop, but because she had been harboring the sad suspicion all day that her husband, with whom she'd never really discussed religion, might be an unbeliever. That he would work in the fields on Sunday and force his servants to work then too . . . But now it seemed that he was sorry to have missed the service. She beamed at him.

"In fact, I think we might make it a party," said Alex. "The cotton should be mostly picked by then.

We'll invite all the neighbors." His eyes were twinkling. So were the bishop's, which surprised Cassandra. She wouldn't have thought the Reverend Lancelot Andress a man much given to parties. Eloise began to make plans immediately.

"You and I can discuss the party later, Eloise," said Alex cheerfully.

Cassandra felt a bit left out. Wasn't she to be in on the preparations?

It became immediately apparent that Eloise had no intention of including Cassandra. In the kitchen, Aunt Heppie and her minions were embarking on the preliminary tasks, such as dipping petals and leaves in egg yolk and then sugar and storing them in tin boxes for later decoration of cakes. When Cassandra offered to help, Eloise said, "Do you know how to cook?" and of course Cassandra didn't since Eloise wasn't interested in a good recipe for pemmican. Eloise repeatedly sent her off to Gemmalee and the production of a decent wardrobe.

After several such days, Cassandra rose early one morning, nursed Benjamin, and turned him over to Lula, his day nurse. Then, having had her breakfast, she commandeered a horse and sidesaddle from the stable boy so that she could ride out to the fields. She was wearing her white muslin dress with the blue silk facings, hardly a suitable riding costume, and after so many months riding astride, she hated the sidesaddle, but she couldn't very well ride bareback in her Comanche skirt and blouse.

She followed the road that led to the quarters, a cluster of one-room log houses where the slaves lived. There she found a gang of children hauling breakfasts of corn bread, molasses, and bacon to the field workers, who had been picking since before dawn. Cassandra spent an hour giving rides to astonished, giggling black children and their loads of food. Only when Mr.

Cutter discovered her was she forced to dismount and sit decorously under a tree watching the workers as they poked their fingers into the open bolls and pulled out the cotton, which they then thrust into long sacks, eventually taking their filled sacks to a large wagon to be weighed.

Mr. Cutter explained that it took about fifteen hundred pounds of cotton to fill a wagon, which made up to one bale. "We're gettin' about a bale to the acre," said Mr. Cutter, "which ain't bad. Not bad at all." He pushed his straw hat back and nodded with satisfaction.

"Now, a good field hand, he'll pick two, maybe three hundred pounds a day. But if you'll look over there, working down that third row, that's Abraham, the really big fella. Abraham's a prime hand. Known Abraham to go five hundred pounds in a day. Did it last year an' got his name in the paper. Course, Abraham can't read, but I read it to him. He was real proud. I'll tell ya, Miss Cassie, I wouldn't trade Abraham for ten boys twice his size."

"Hard to imagine anyone twice his size," said Cassandra. Abraham must have weighed two hundred pounds and stood well over six feet. he was taller than Alex. One of the hands had begun a song, and the others picked it up, a slow, sad cadence through which a note of longing echoed. What did they long for? she wondered. Anything but what they had, she imagined. Alex was wrong when he said a full stomach could be more important than freedom.

"Those outside things that hold the cotton—"

"Bolls," said Mr. Cutter.

"They look sharp."

"They are," Cutter agreed. "Pickin' cotton makes for sore fingers and backs. I'm always glad when it's over. Here, boy, take the water that way. They're lookin' mighty thirsty over 'round Abraham."

A child carrying a water bucket and gourd dipper

obediently changed directions and, passing Cassandra
under her tree, smiled shyly and said, "Mornin', Miz
Cassie."

"Good morning, Zekey," Cassandra called back, recognizing one of her passengers. Both the child and
Jonah Cutter looked surprised that she knew the boy's
name.

"Abraham, he'll win himself a fine new shirt this
year, the way he's pickin'," said Cutter.

"How's that?" asked Cassandra.

"Oh, I always figger a prize is worth two whippings
for gittin' better work outa the hands. Alex started the
prizes years ago. Then they stopped after he left in—
when was it?—'42 or so. Never could keep track of
Alex's wars. Anyway, when he took off the last time,
Daumier dropped the prizes an' the work fell off, so
when I come to work here, I started 'em up. Turns out
real good."

Cassandra nodded. It made sense to her.

Another day, Alex, discovering her interest, took her
to the gin, which was in a three-story wooden building. On the top floor they stored seed, the middle floor
contained the gin, and the lower floor was devoted to
baling. Slaves unloaded the cotton from the wagons
and hauled it upstairs to the gin room where one man
spread it across the metal saws which combed the
seeds out. Cassandra watched, horrified because the
man kept turning to grin at her and bob his head.
Each time he did it, she was afraid he'd lose a finger
to the vicious-looking teeth that tore into the cotton.

The seed-free fibers tumbled into a room below,
where slaves raked them into baskets. These men had
white fluff stuck all over their sweating bodies and
looked like giant bunnies to Cassandra. Of course, she
didn't say that, since Alex was explaining the whole
process to her in serious detail. The bunnies carried
their loads to the press, which was a giant tree-trunk
screw that compounded the loose cotton into a bale-

sized box beneath. Mules drove the wooden beams attached to the screw, and on the mules rode giggling little boys.

"Isn't that dangerous?" asked Cassandra.

"Maybe," Alex replied, grinning, "but I did it a time or two when I was a boy, and you can be sure Benjamin will want to when he's old enough."

Benjamin won't be here, thought Cassandra with determination. *Not Benjamin, not me, and not you, Alex.*

Chapter Eighteen

With Eloise preparing for the party and Alex busy in the fields, Cassandra explored, trying to take in the magnitude of operations at Devil's Wood, which was like a principality, self-sufficient except for a few imports. The slaves lived in the quarters in one-room log cabins, Eloise in her mansion, Cutter in his log house. Devil's Wood had its own brick kiln, carriage house, stables, barns, stock pens, smithy, and shoemaking facility. In a sewing house were spinning wheels, looms, and dying tubs.

A separate kitchen house fed both black and white, although the difference in diet shocked Cassandra when she saw the black children being fed at midday from a trough and tended *en masse* by one woman instead of their own mothers. Adjacent to the kitchen house were vegetable and herb gardens and a poultry yard. There were brick cisterns to catch rainwater, again a luxury not available to the slaves. The inhabitants of the mansion had a necessary house built over a ditch in the yard, while the slaves used the woods. She peeked into a small hospital building, now empty. Evidently illness had to wait upon the cotton harvest, as did all activities except the kitchen's.

She wandered farther afield and came upon a small fenced graveyard. Here she found the graves of Jean Philippe Daumier and five of his children. Only in death, she thought, were black and white equally unfortunate, for the slave graveyard, which she had seen

arlier in her wanderings, was filled with children's
raves as well.

Cassandra walked from one small, carved headstone
o the next, reading the names and dates and fighting
he impulse to run back to the house, to check on
Benjamin, to hold him in her arms. But then Eloise
must have held her children and thought them safe,
yet here they lay. Etienne Daumier, 1823; Juliette,
831. Those were the babies that died at birth. Alexander, 1825–1828, and Jean Pierre Daumier, 1827–
831—the boys who had died of scalding and of scarlet
ever. Miranda, 1829–1836, the little girl who had
drowned during the escape from Santa Ana's army.
Only the one who had died in Galveston of yellow fever
ay elsewhere. And where was Alexandra? Had she too
died like all these children, her grave unmarked and
orgotten on some Comanche trail south? *Oh God, let
her be alive*, Cassandra prayed. *Let me find her*.

"Why are you here?"

With the tears still on her cheeks, Cassandra looked
up at Eloise, who sighed and extended her hand. "You
and I are the only ones who ever cried for these children," said Eloise sadly, "but tears never help. After
the tears have dried, the little ones are still dead." She
glanced at the graves. "Miranda isn't even beneath
that headstone. We never found her body. Did Alex
tell you?"

Cassandra shook her head.

"And Blanche—she's buried in Galveston. I took her
with me when Jean Philippe and I went to sell the
cotton. I wanted to keep him from gambling away the
profits, and I did. That year we bought more slaves
and built outbuildings, but I lost Blanche. With yellow
fever, they bury the dead the same day because of the
contagion. I couldn't even take her home." She passed
her hand wearily before her eyes as if to wipe away
the memories. "It's a bitter thing to be a woman," she
muttered.

Cassandra's heart ached for her sister-in-law "They're with God now, Eloise," she said. "They're happier than we are."

Eloise turned, brows drawn together. "I don't believe in God. If there's a God, why are all my children dead?"

Cassandra was stunned at the anger that fueled that bitter outburst.

"God is something men thought up to make women more miserable." Eloise turned and walked down the hill.

Cassandra spent most of her afternoons with Gemmalee, being fitted for gowns and lingerie and helping with the sewing. When free from other duties, Mellie and Esther joined the circle, and as they became used to Cassandra's presence, they talked more freely. Fascinated, Cassandra listened to tales of magic remedies that protected against diseases and spells; of a ghost who walked the roads down river and was as tall as a tall oak and blacker than deepest midnight; of Ondine the slave catcher who saw to it that no slave at Devil's Wood ever got to go visiting because that's the way Miss Eloise wanted it; of corn shuckings and broomstick weddings; of Saturday-night breakdown dances in the moonlight where the slaves danced pigeon wings and jigs, the jubo and the three-star gallop. Abraham was the champion jigger, being able to dance long after his competitors had dropped with exhaustion or disqualified themselves by spilling the water in the cups on their heads.

"Abraham's a fine man," said Mellie wistfully.

"Well, he ain't for you, girl," Gemmalee warned. "Miz Eloise ain't neber gonna let you an' Esther hab no men."

"I don't wan' no man anyways," said little Esther.

"Miz Eloise done heard Ruben been kissin' an' huggin' with Cora's Daisy," said Mellie soberly, "an' she

Bride Fire

had Ruben drug up here an' tole him if'n she ever heard he got any girl with chile, she turn him over to Ondine."

The three shivered and glanced at Cassandra. Who was Ruben? Cassandra wondered as she took another careful stitch along the line of lace she was sewing to the hem of a petticoat. She didn't look up or act as if she were listening, lest they stop talking.

One day Alex appeared unexpectedly in the sewing room with a length of white silk and another of blue so beautiful it took the women's breath away. "Bought these off the river boat. Now let's look at those fashion books," he commanded, dropping the fabric into Cassandra's lap. "I'm here to pick out your gown for the party in October." He examined each colored print. "This one," he decided after careful study.

Cassandra put away her sewing and rose to look over his shoulder. He had chosen a beautiful gown with a blue underskirt and a five-flounce white overskirt with blue embroidery along the edges of each flounce. The tight-fitting blue basque was topped with an off-the-shoulder white bertha embroidered in blue. Cassandra sighed. "The lance wound would show," she said regretfully.

Alex frowned. Gemmalee came to look as well. "Mighty pretty dress, Miz Cassie," she murmured. "Insteada that bertha, Ah could make a stole outa that white silk an' drape it right across yo hurt shoulder down to the other sida yo waist. We could embroider it, maybe put on some blue rosettes fo' fastenin'. Reckon it'd look real fine with yo' golden hair an' all."

"There you go, love," said Alex, rising and pushing the open magazine into her hands. "You girls start that dress right now." He bent forward to kiss Cassandra on the mouth, chucked his sleeping son under the chin, and was gone before she could respond.

"Fine man, that Marse Alex," said Gemmalee. "Now we best start the dress like he say. Mellie, you can do

311

the embroidery, lessen you wants to do it yoself, Miz
Cassie."

Cassandra grinned. "Mellie's a finer hand with an
embroidery needle than I."

Mellie blushed shyly and came to look at the picture.
"Oh, my," she murmured, "ain't that fine? You be the
most beautiful woman on the Brazos, Miz Cassie."

Horace Waverly finally arrived at Devil's Wood,
coming up river on a steamboat two weeks late and
throwing the household into a fever of activity under
Eloise's delighted supervision. The Englishman explained that he hadn't seen any need to hurry since
no one else in the area seemed to. Alex gave him a
look of profound contempt and left the table. After
that, his picking activities kept him away from the
house almost continuously, infuriating Eloise, who
feared that Alex might refuse to attend her party in
the author's honor the following weekend.

Her first sight of Mr. Waverly astonished Cassandra.
He wore an elaborate velvet frock coat and matching
beret, which topped gray-blond curls that fell to his
shoulders. She soon discovered that the ever-present
velvet beret covered a large bald spot on the top of
his head. While she and Eloise were strolling with him
in the only section of ornamental gardens yet planted,
an oak branch snatched the concealing headpiece
from Mr. Waverly's gleaming pate, sending Cassandra
into spasms of swallowed glee. In fact, she found Mr.
Waverly an all-around source of great amusement,
although she politely concealed her desire to laugh
aloud every time he opened his mouth.

Horace Waverly took an immediate liking to Cassandra once he found out that she had, as he put it,
"a bit of education" and had read some of his essays
and a book of his poetry. Without ever asking, he assumed that Cassandra had been impressed with his
work and favored her with amazing lectures on the

breadth of his own education and reading, making grand if general references to authors both classical and modern and assuring her that education in England was far superior in every way to any available in the new world.

For the most part, Cassandra delighted in his ridiculously inflated opinion of himself. Although he claimed to have by heart whole volumes of prose and verse, he never actually quoted anyone but himself. He talked Homer, but recited his own sentimental stanzas on her namesake, the unfortunate prophetess Cassandra.

One of Mr. Waverly's favorite literary topics was the decline of modern literature, excluding his own contributions, of course. He particularly disliked novels, denigrated the works of Jane Austen, for instance, and disallowed Cassandra's spirited defense of *Pride and Prejudice* by remarking that ladies did tend to see more merit than was allowable in the scribblings of their own sex. He declared the novels of Sir Walter Scott mere trivia compared to "the great poetic works of yesteryear," and he had hardly a good word to say for any dramatist that postdated Terence and Plautus. Cassandra drew nonsensical opinions from him on Shakespeare and Ben Jonson and repeated them to Alex when they were in bed at night. Even Milton was dismissed by Mr. Waverly as a "religious fanatic and therefore no gentleman."

"He's hilariously pompous, Alex," she coaxed one night. "You must come home to dinner and listen."

Alex, Cutter, and the hands had stayed out after dark that night, picking cotton by torchlight because Alex feared that storms were looming. "I can think of better things to do when I finally get out of the fields," he muttered.

"Better things? But, Alex, you're too tired," Cassandra murmured teasingly when he bent over to kiss her throat.

"Never too tired for you, sweetheart," he replied, his lips traveling deliciously to her earlobe.

Cassandra shivered with the spiraling excitement he always drew from her and thought lightheartedly, *What more could a woman want? A silly man to amuse her by day and a lover to give her joy by night.* Then she reached up to her husband and thought no more of the English guest.

The one thing that seriously disturbed Cassandra about Horace Waverly was his attitude toward the young female house servants. Although he had brought a manservant with him, he petitioned Eloise to send one girl or another to him to wield the curling iron that produced his long curls. Once, he had asked for Mellie, and Cassandra saw the girl emerge trembling from his door. When Cassandra asked if anything was wrong, Mellie fled down the hall. After that, Cassandra always commanded Mellie's services herself when Mr. Waverly's hair was in need of attention.

Then on a Tuesday late in September when the air was heavy with the promise of rain and all within the house were restless in the hush that preceded the storm, Mr. Waverly caught Mellie on the upstairs gallery and backed her against the wall where the shadows concealed them. Cassandra heard the girl's cry and ran out, but Eloise heard it too, so both women saw Mellie in Mr. Waverly's arms.

"Slut," cried Eloise, her face white with fury. "You'll be whipped for this."

Mr. Waverly dropped his arms and stepped away, leaving Mellie to face Eloise's hysterical fury.

"I won't have this going on in my house," Eloise cried. "When Cutter gets through with you, there'll be nothing left to entice a white man."

"But, Miz Eloise, Ah din'—"

"I know you. The sin is in your blood."

"Oh, marvelous!" cried Mr. Waverly, watching the

scene avidly. There was a soft roll of thunder, and suddenly the rain began to fall, isolating the house from the surrounding landscape in a wall of falling water. None of the people on the gallery even looked at the storm.

Cassandra shot Waverly a horrified glance and stepped into the fray. "Eloise, Mellie's done nothing wrong."

"Stay out of things you don't understand."

"The man pursues all the girls."

"This one led him on."

"Indeed," Mr. Waverly affirmed. "I do believe she did."

"He's lying," Cassandra said softly. "Can't you see that? You mustn't punish her for his—his—"

"I'll do just as I like," Eloise hissed. "This is my plantation."

"And Alex's," Cassandra reminded her. "And I am Alex's wife. I won't have it."

"You? You're telling me what to do?"

"Yes," said Cassandra.

Eloise laughed softly and looked out into the sleeting rain. Then she turned back to Cassandra. "You have no power here. Why should you? You're good for nothing—except maybe breeding. You're with child again, aren't you?" Eloise's glance flicked down Cassandra's body. "How do we know it isn't some half-breed brat?"

Cassandra paled and backed away from the woman, whose eyes shone with malice. She heard Waverly, who had brought this upon them, titter with excitement.

"Don't you ever—ever tell me what to do again, Cassandra. Do you understand me?"

"What's going on here?" Alex demanded. He and Cutter had come in dripping water onto the wide oak planks.

"Your *wife* has been trying to tell me how to deal with my servants."

"She wants Mellie whipped," cried Cassandra, "and Mellie's done nothing."

"God, Eloise," snapped Alex, "when will you learn? If you don't like the girl, sell her. But keep in mind that you won't get a good price if she bears whip marks."

"I don't care about the money."

"You never did," Alex muttered.

Horrified at the inhumanity of the conversation, Cassandra looked from her husband to his sister.

"She's been flaunting herself, and I'll have her whipped for it." Eloise pinned the overseer with a sharp glance. "Cutter." The one word was a command.

Cutter gave Alex a long look, then walked over to Mellie, who was crying, and took her gently by the arm. "Come along, girl," he murmured.

Cassandra watched them go, unable to believe that Cutter was actually going to carry out that order and that Alex was going to allow it.

"Will you escort me down to supper, Mr. Waverly?" said Eloise, all her fury dissipated by Cutter's acquiescence.

"Gladly, madam," said Waverly with relish. "I find I have an appetite."

Cassandra sped toward her room, with Alex calling after her. She slammed the door and threw the bolt. Her breath came in gasps as she tried to control the tears that welled at the thought of Mellie's fate.

"Cassandra, open this door."

She heard him rattle the handle. Mellie was going to be whipped, and he hadn't moved a finger to stop it. Cassandra leaned her cheek against the wood, feeling the vibration as he brought a powerful fist down upon it. "You didn't care about anything but the price she'd bring," Cassandra whispered against the heavy oak.

There was a moment of silence. Then Alex cursed and said to her through the barrier, "Of course I cared, but the only argument that might move my sister is an indirect one. You should keep that in mind if you want to make any changes here." Then Cassandra heard the tread of his boots going down the hall. Was he going to his supper now that the rain had halted the picking? She couldn't deal with what he had said, the gist of which was that Eloise had to be tricked into common decency.

Right now Mellie was suffering the bite of the whip, and Cassandra remembered all too clearly how it had felt that first night in the Comanche camp. Cassandra herself had withstood her ordeal because she had been full of hope and fury. But what was there to give Mellie courage? She had nothing to hope for and no child to protect.

The thought of Benjamin reminded Cassandra of the viciousness of Eloise's attack on herself. *You're with child again, aren't you? How do we know it isn't some half-breed brat?* Eloise had said. Cassandra began to cry. Who was to protect her—and the children, for she *was* with child again, just as Eloise had said. Not Alex; he hadn't reprimanded his sister for her vicious words. Cassandra huddled on the wide bed, shaken by weeping as she acknowledged that, just as she had been unable to protect Mellie, she might be unable to protect her children.

"Hush yo cryin' now, Miz Cassie."

Cassandra, who had heard the whispers outside her door and ignored them, suddenly found herself rocked against a broad, comforting bosom as if she were a child.

"You gonna make yosef sick, an' all fo' nuthin'."

"For nothing?" Cassandra looked up into Aunt Heppie's kind, dark eyes and inhaled her comforting fragrance of baked bread and cinnamon.

317

"Nobody gonna lift a hand to young Mellie, no, ma'am."

"But—"

"Cutter don't beat no one. He jus' let Miz Eloise think he do. He taken young Mellie down to de quarters, an' she have her a lil holiday an' visit with her friends while she s'pose to be healin' up. Miz Eloise, she think Cutter done what she say, an' ever'one happy."

"Happy!" exclaimed Cassandra.

"Yessum. Dis be a pretty happy place since ole marse die an' Cutter come. Course don' nobody wan' work up here in de house—ceppin' me. Ah been with Miz Eloise since she a young bride, an' Ah unnerstand her pain—marryin' dat bad man an' losin' all dem younguns. Better if young Mellie an' lil Esther din' live here, but it cain't be heped."

"Why does she hate them so?" asked Cassandra.

"Dey ole marse's chillun."

Cassandra's eyes widened.

"You din' know de white men, dey find dey comfort down in de quarters. Dat what start all de fuss today, dat Waverly's lustin' after Mellie, jus' like ole marse lusted after Sarah all dem years ago."

Sarah. Cassandra shivered. That was the woman who had killed herself rather than be sold away from her children. And Jean Philippe—what kind of man would gamble away his mistress of many years and make no provision for his children, no matter what their color?

"Ever' time Miz Eloise see dem light skins, she 'member he turn away from her fo black Sarah."

"It's not their fault—what their father did."

"No, ma'am. Now, what Ah done tole you, dat a secret. Long as Miz Eloise think she runnin' dis plantation, she happy, an' we all got a good life. But Ah tole you a secret don' no one want to git around." She looked sharply at Cassandra, who nodded.

"I won't tell," she promised.

"Even when you real mad at Miz Eloise?"

"Even then."

Aunt Heppie, satisfied, started toward the door, saying, "So you don' cry no mo. Ain' good fo yo chile."

"Oh my God! Benjamin!"

"He comin' right in fo his suppah. Won' hurt him a bit to wait. Ever'one been singin' to him, an' dat chile does love music. But Ah wasn't talkin' 'bout Benjamin. You got yosef a second chile to look out for."

Cassandra's hand went to her stomach. Everyone at Devil's Wood seemed to know that she was pregnant.

She watched Aunt Heppie slip away and wondered how the black people could think they had a good life here.

Cassandra had a second visit late in the afternoon—from Mr. Cutter, who sat down on her sofa when invited, turning his hat in his freckled hands and looking very sad and uncomfortable. Cassandra would have liked to reassure the man, but she dared not break Aunt Heppie's confidence. What if Mr. Cutter took offense over the revelation of his secret and stopped his kindhearted deception? Cassandra would never be able to forgive herself.

"Now, Miz Cassie," Jonah Cutter began at last, "I hear from Gemmalee an' them that you been cryin' your heart out over Mellie, an' I just wanted you to know that I never laid a hand on the girl. I reckon you'll think I'm a deceitful man, foolin' Miss Eloise the way I do, but the fact is that I know, if she took the time to consider, she'd never want to bring hurt to a soul."

Cassandra doubted that, but she didn't contradict him.

"It's just that she's been so hurt herself, you see. Miss Eloise is a fine woman, but she was married off to a man who never deserved her an'—an' treated her bad. It's turned her bitter, it has, but given time—"

319

he clenched his blunt fingers over his hat brim "—given time, maybe she'll get over all those years of pain and sadness."

My goodness, thought Cassandra, *he's in love with her*. "Aren't you afraid she'll find out what you're doing?"

"Oh, no." Cutter smiled. "I just tell her I do the whipping down where her gentle woman's heart won't be torn by the cries."

Good lord, thought Cassandra. *Can't he see that a woman who'd order a whipping doesn't have a gentle heart? And doesn't Eloise see the contradiction of his words?* "I think it's you who have the gentle heart, Mr. Cutter."

Cutter blushed and rose, his fingers still clenched on the brim of his hat.

Cassandra's last reassurance came from her husband late that evening when she had already fallen asleep. "Cassie," he said softly, having climbed into bed beside her and cupped his hand over her shoulder. She stirred and, blinking her eyes sleepily, looked up into his face, which was illuminated by the light of the candle he had left burning on the bedside table. "Did you cry so much for little Mellie?" he asked, touching her puffy eyelids. "Had I known, I'd have come back sooner. No one laid a hand on her, you know." Alex smiled wryly. "I went stomping off to rescue her, only to find that Cutter never uses the whip."

"I know," said Cassandra. "But you mustn't tell Eloise," she added hastily.

Alex sighed. "My sister inspires the strangest loyalties. If I were Cutter, I'd go elsewhere. The man's a first-rate overseer and could find another place easily."

"He loves your sister."

"Nonsense," said Alex. "Cutter's too smart for that."

"No, truly, I think he loves her."

"Well, poor Cutter's misfortune is our gain here at Devil's Wood."

"Perhaps if she could come to love him too, it wouldn't be a misfortune," said Cassandra.

"Eloise would never love Jonah Cutter. She thinks she's too good for him, more the fool she. And his love, if it exists, isn't the misfortune I meant. Jonah had his own place in the old days, small—twenty slaves at most, but a fever wiped them all out—his wife, his children, his people. He lost the place just before my late brother-in-law got himself killed."

Cassandra, who had been thinking of Cutter's tragedy, turned her thoughts to Jean Philippe Daumier. "Do you know why Eloise hates Mellie so?" she asked.

"Of course," Alex replied. "I was here many of those years when that bastard was keeping Sarah down in her own cabin in the quarters. Poor girl. She never wanted him, but she had no choice."

Cassandra shook her head. Devil's Wood was an evil place, just as she had once feared. How could Aunt Heppie think they had a good life here?

"Don't tremble like that, love," said Alex. "It has nothing to do with us—all this old history. There wouldn't have been any trouble today if it weren't for that Englishman. My fool sister thinks she's got the prize guest of the year, but I reckon there'll be at least ten people smarter and better read than him at the party next weekend."

"Will there?" murmured Cassandra. "Will there indeed!"

Alex studied her speculatively, then leaned from the bed to blow out the candle. Whatever was on her mind, he could see that it had chased away her dark thoughts.

Cassandra stayed awake late into the night, and at first she *was* distracted by a plan that had formed in her mind, a plan to pay back Horace Waverly, who had stirred up trouble and then watched the distress of others as if it were an entertainment staged for his benefit. Remembering the scene on the gallery reminded her of what Eloise had said to her. Obviously Alex hadn't heard, and she should tell him. He couldn't protect her and the unborn child if he didn't know that Eloise had attacked them. Cassandra shivered as she realized that she was afraid to remind Alex that they might become parents of a half-breed baby.

How little people back East understood the difficulties of life here on or close to the frontier, where people of so many different backgrounds and races came together. Black Rain had escaped Sarah's fate only to fall into the hands of the Comanches, who tolerated her color but thought she had no soul. Counts Many Coup, who was himself a child of a mixed marriage, was accepted by the Comanches because of his prowess in battle, but his choices of a black and then a white wife had been looked at askance in the tribe. What would Black Rain's daughter face, being the child of another mixed marriage? Cassandra wondered. Buffalo Leaper wouldn't have Black Rain because of her color. Would Broken Nose cherish his wife's half-breed daughter? And how was Alexandra, a white baby among the Comanches, being treated?

Cassandra shivered. She herself now carried a child who might be part Comanche. Even with Alex's support, this baby's future looked bleak when people like Eloise were prepared to scorn him. But not as bleak as the prospects of Sarah's children. Eloise hated them, and they had no chance of escaping her malice. Even their fellow slaves, Cassandra had noticed, treated them differently. The Comanches, for all their violence, were more tolerant than any other race. Their captives had a chance to become members of the tribe—wives or warriors. Cassandra had had their trust and then betrayed it. Ironic that Eloise might be the one to exact the Comanche's revenge.

It was all so hurtful and confusing—the way people

treated one another, and Cassandra, caught in the middle, wanted to *do* something, make things *better*. But she had no idea how to go about it. She hadn't been able to help Black Rain, and now she couldn't help herself—much less anyone else. What good were lofty principles when there was no way to implement them? The only plan she could see any hope for involved Horace Waverly, and giving him his comeuppance would hardly be a moral triumph. It would, however, be thoroughly satisfying, she decided, and felt more cheerful. On that note she turned over and slept at last.

Cassandra stood by the rosewood piano studying the party that swirled around her—a small one according to Eloise, only twenty carefully selected guests. Eloise seemed to take as much pleasure in the people she excluded from this literary weekend as she did from those who had been invited and had accepted. Cassandra herself expected the party to be a success. As far as she could tell, there was hardly a guest who didn't find Horace Waverly an obnoxious, condescending popinjay. Cassandra had made it a point to chat privately with the guests whom Alex had identified as very well read in one field or another, and now the time had come to put her plan into action.

She clapped her hands to get the attention of the group, and sending a gracious smile in the direction of Horace Waverly, announced, "With Eloise's permission, I have a delightful proposal to make in honor of our distinguished guest." Waverly beamed at her while smoothing down an errant curl. "As you all know, Mr. Waverly is not only an author of great talent, but a product of the unparalleled excellence of the British university system."

Although several of the guests winced, having been exposed to Waverly's tactless comparisons of education here and abroad, Waverly himself preened.

Elizabeth Chadwick

"Therefore," Cassandra forged on, "for his entertainment, and truly because we can't resist showing him off—" she sent a glowing smile in his direction, trying not to notice that her husband was choking with laughter "—various ladies and gentlemen in attendance this evening have agreed to join me in a quotation contest." The author's smile faltered.

"Each of us who have some little knowledge in one area or another will offer a quotation to be identified. Naturally, our dear Mr. Waverly, who is so knowledgeable in *all* areas; will be offered the first chance to play." Waverly was trying hard not to look aghast but failing rather noticeably. "Should we be able to stump our author, which hardly seems likely, other guests are welcome to take a guess at the quotation."

Cassandra curtsied, sweeping out the delicate green skirts of her new gown, which had been whipped up by Gemmalee and Esther, working hours into the night, although Cassandra had protested that she didn't need a new gown, certainly not at the expense of their rest.

"Miz Cassie," said Gemmalee, "ain't a soul at Devil's Wood, not a black one anyways, who wouldn't work all night every night for you, not after how you took up for young Mellie." And that was that. The dress had been made, and Cassandra treasured it.

The guests were all clapping with pleasure at Cassandra's suggestion, although none but Alex had any idea of the outcome she anticipated. Horace Waverly, looking deathly pale, took a huge gulp of his wine and essayed his usual condescending smile.

The first person to offer a quotation, Cray Williamson from Galveston, quoted from Plutarch's Lives—in Latin.

Horace Waverly, with all the guests watching him expectantly, fanned himself with a palmetto fan and declared, "I'm afraid, my dear fellow, that your *accent*

324

has me completely baffled. Where *did* you learn your Latin?"

"Plutarch. The life of Julius Caesar, isn't it, Cray?" said Alex briskly. He received a round of applause, and Arthur Wall from Washington on the Brazos, who was taking a weekend off from work on the state constitution, offered a few lines from the *Iliad* in "the Queen's English, if you please, Waverly."

"Vaguely familiar, dear boy," said Horace Waverly, who was beginning to sweat. "Must be an unknown translation—from the Greek possibly. Did you translate it yourself?"

Arthur Wall's eyebrows went up.

"Why, Mr. Waverly," said Cassandra, "I do believe you're trying to make us look good. Pray, don't hide your light under a bushel for our sakes."

A wealthy cotton factor from Velasco, Caldicott Barrett, called out the work, and Alice Williamson of Galveston identified the character who had spoken the lines.

"Well now," said Cassandra, "here's one you can't pretend to miss, Mr. Waverly." She gave him a passage from *Paradise Lost*, thinking as she recited of what a comfort Milton's epic had been to her as she waited in that cave, praying that the Indians would pass on by.

Horace Waverly hadn't a clue, but a planter from south of Brazoria had. It took only a few more rounds until no one bothered to wait for the Englishman. The quotations and identifications flew across the circle, and when the party broke up several hours later, Cassandra was congratulated on having proposed a marvelous game.

Eloise looked somewhat confused as she too received their thanks for a delightful weekend, and she was stunned to discover the next morning that Horace Waverly had departed without so much as a farewell to his hostess or a note of thanks. Cassandra caught

Elizabeth Chadwick

her husband's eye across the breakfast table and smiled. It wasn't much recompense for what the treacherous Mr. Waverly had put Mellie through, but it helped a bit. And Cassandra didn't mind the chagrin of her sister-in-law either, although she never explained to Eloise that the game had been a trap to expose the pretensions of an obnoxious guest.

Chapter Nineteen

As October advanced, the gin ran continuously, and field hands picked the last of the cotton. Corn fields were harvested, vegetables picked or dug, winter crops planted between the cotton rows. In the kitchens, Aunt Heppie supervised the preserving of fruits and vegetables even as she continued preparations for Alex's party. Cassandra watched it all and took notes on whatever she thought might be useful once she had lured Alex away from Devil's Wood.

Out in the yards, mounds began to rise, each containing turnips, beets, or potatoes. The vegetables were piled in a deep hole on a bed of sand, then covered with tepees of cornstalks, followed by successive layers of grass, straw, and dirt with only a small crawl hole left open so that a child could wiggle in to retrieve the food when it was needed during the winter. As the number of stockpiles grew, the yard assumed a curious appearance, and Cassandra remembered her father talking of mound-building Indians.

She wondered what he would have thought of his grandson and namesake. Benjamin was thriving. One day as Cassandra sat with Eloise, her sister-in-law cried, "Look," and the two women, who were rarely comfortable with one another, beamed at the baby. Lying on his stomach, he had raised his head and shoulders from the floor and looked about the room for a minute or two before flattening out again. Alexandra, who would be spending all her time in a cradle board or night roll, would not have the chance to do that, Cassandra thought, but how much of the world she would have seen from the back of Singing Bird. If she was still alive. Cassandra's heart clenched at the thought of her lost daughter. She didn't even know what Singing Bird had named the baby.

"What a smart one he is," said Eloise. "Only five months and pushing up already." She bent to pick him up.

I must try to think better of her, Cassandra promised herself. *If good people like Aunt Heppie and Mr. Cutter can love and understand her, I can too.* Except for Sarah's children, Eloise was kind to the black youngsters. She monitored their health regularly and often gave them sweets. Why couldn't she be kinder to the adults? Cassandra wondered. At least she and Eloise had one thing in common, they both loved Benjamin.

During the corn harvest Cassandra took food to Alex; he had grown thinner of late, which she attributed to his long hours in the fields and the many meals he skipped. She was picking her way along a corn row when she stopped, arrested by the face of an older boy. When he looked up at her, she called, "Are you Mellie's brother?" The boy scowled and turned sullenly back to his work. Cassandra continued on her way, but she was sure that must be Ruben, the boy Eloise had warned to beget no children.

"Miss!"

She glanced over her shoulder to see that he had straightened and was staring after her.

"Thanks," he called.

"For what?" asked Cassandra.

"For Mellie," and then he turned away.

Mellie was working in the house again, embroidering the white flounces of the dress Alex had picked out, and now Cassandra, who sat sewing with them, was included in the conversations. They were all curious about her experiences with the Indians and about her life in Massachusetts, about anything outside their very circumscribed world, for Devil's Wood slaves weren't allowed off the plantation.

"We played a game we called shinny," Cassandra recalled one afternoon. "It was so much fun. I'll have to teach you some Sunday."

A trio of dark eyes looked at her in astonishment.

"You'd love it," Cassandra assured them. "We'll need to find sticks and a ball."

"Cassandra." Eloise stood in the door. "Will you come into the sitting room, please?"

What now? Cassandra wondered as she followed Eloise.

"Have you no sense of propriety? Black and white children may play together, but adults maintain a proper distance. You talk to those girls as if they were friends."

"They are," said Cassandra. "I've felt so uncomfortable with the situation here, but now—"

"What situation?"

"Slavery. I hate it. It's a great relief to feel comfortable with people I see everyday."

"You're not supposed to feel comfortable! You're supposed to act properly and not give them dangerous ideas."

"You consider a game for women a dangerous idea?"

"When a white woman proposes to join in," said Eloise. "You'll have us all murdered in our beds."

"By whom?" Cassandra couldn't believe she was having this bizarre conversation. "I don't know how you can stand to live this way, Eloise. It's terrible to enslave people. Think of the children—."

"What about the children?" Eloise demanded. "They're fed and cared for. They're a lot better off than children in the North, who work long hours in factories and never have enough to eat."

"It's true that many children up North live a terrible life," Cassandra admitted, "but, Eloise, they have hope. They know that someday they can make something of themselves if they work hard enough." Eloise snorted. "No it's true. But these children have nothing of their own, and they never will."

"Only my brother would be fool enough to bring home an abolitionist," Eloise muttered.

As she stood at the top of the stairs, the whole puzzling sequence of events finally made sense to her. The bishop hadn't been invited because Alex had missed the service last month, but for another purpose entirely, and the celebration wasn't in honor of the newly completed state constitution—it was in honor of her and Alex. Cassandra looked down at the flowers, the guests, and her husband awaiting her below, and she knew that she was about to attend her own wedding—her fifth, but this time Alex was making it absolutely legal.

Feeling a bit of a fool and yet deeply touched at all the trouble he had gone to, she started down the steps. When she reached the hall below and took her husband's arm, they walked together into the drawing room where the bishop, smiling benevolently, awaited them in front of the ornate marble fireplace.

"This time I have the license," Alex whispered. She smiled into his eyes, and the ceremony began.

Cassandra leaned, breathless, against the wall of the gallery. She had been dancing for hours. Every male guest had claimed a dance with the bride, until finally Alex rescued her and led her into the cool air of the late October evening. "I'll get you some wine, shall I?" he offered, and she nodded gratefully. The midnight supper would begin soon, but in the meantime she was thirsty—and tired, having been up late the night before with Benjamin. Some bride, she thought, amused. One child upstairs and another on the way. She rested her hand a moment on her stomach, which she thought had rounded a bit. Was the baby Alex's? Oh, she hoped so. She loved him so much, and Counts Many Coup was part of the past. She tried not to think of him.

"I can't tell you how embarrassed I was."

Startled, Cassandra drew back into the shadows as Eloise came through the doors with another woman.

"Of course, Alex never had the slightest consideration for the proprieties, but still, I wouldn't have expected him to advertise the fact that they were never married."

"Perhaps he just wanted to give her a lovely wedding," said the other woman. "They can't have had anything very impressive out on the frontier."

"They can't have had a wedding at all," said Eloise. "Who would have performed it? No, Alex doesn't care that much for parties. He'd never have insisted on this one if his conscience weren't hurting him."

"Living in sin all this time!" clucked Eloise's companion. "And a baby too."

"Yes, that's the sad part," Eloise replied. "Poor little Benjamin. He was obviously born out of wedlock."

Cassandra blinked back tears. How could Eloise say something that would hurt Benjamin? The two women strolled off toward the end of the gallery, where they stopped to talk to several more ladies. Was Eloise spreading her tale among all the guests? Cassandra shivered and slipped back into the house, wondering if she should tell Alex? But she couldn't. Not when he'd been so pleased with his surprise and gone to so much trouble. Only to have it backfire like this. Perhaps he wouldn't hear the talk. He wasn't one to listen to gossip, nor was anyone apt to repeat this particular story to him.

Putting on a brave smile as he came toward her, she

accepted the crystal goblet. Soon the wedding supper would begin, with the beautiful cake produced by Aunt Heppie and the toasts to their happiness. Cassandra gritted her teeth, set her empty goblet down, and joined her husband in the next set. Perhaps the dancing would lighten her heart.

"It's traditional for the bride to receive her own servant at the time of her wedding."

"You want to give *me* a slave?" she exclaimed.

"Well, as I said, it's traditional, but I don't—"

"All right," said Cassandra. She had remembered Mellie. She could at least get the girl away from Eloise. And Mellie had brothers and a sister. "I'll take four."

"Four?" Alex looked bewildered. "First you snap at me for suggesting one, and now you want four?"

"Am I asking too much? Well, I have money of my own. I'll buy them from you."

"I didn't mean that. Of course, if you want four, I'll—" He paused, frowning. "Any particular four?" he asked suspiciously.

"I want Mellie, her sister, and her two brothers."

"Cass, you don't want Ruben. I see what you've got in mind, but Ruben—well, he's—"

"—difficult? I don't doubt it. Maybe a little kind treatment will—"

"All our people are well treated."

"Not by your sister they're not. And certainly not her husband's children."

Alex sighed. "They're yours," he agreed.

"Thank you." *Why am I being snippy with Alex?* she asked herself. *It's Eloise I'm so angry at. I ought to tell him what she's been saying. I really should.*

But she didn't. Instead she gave herself up to the joys of the wedding night, which was much more successful than their first. They didn't reappear until the next afternoon and took a barrage of teasing from the guests and an angry scowl from Eloise, which Alex never noticed.

"Four!" cried Eloise. "She's not worth one."

"That's enough," snapped Alex.

"Well, it's the truth. She doesn't know a thing about running a house. Can't cook. Can't—"

"Enough!" roared Alex.

"And she brought no dowry."

"If you mean I have no money, you're wrong," said Cassandra angrily. "My parents left me well provided for."

Eloise's glance sharpened with interest. "Good. We can use it." She turned to her brother. "I've been thinking we should plant cane. We can use her dowry, if she really has one, to finance it."

"Are you mad? The machinery's expensive, and we'd need twice as many slaves."

"Not a penny of mine will ever be spent on buying human beings," said Cassandra coldly.

"You have no say in the matter," said Eloise. "When you married Alex, control of your property passed to him."

"You should familiarize yourself with the new constitution, Eloise. In Texas a married woman retains control, so, as I said, not a penny of mine will be spent on slaves. My parents would turn over in their graves at the very thought."

"And I have no intention of raising sugar cane, so that's an end to the matter," said Alex.

Cassandra felt almost guilty at her lighthearted happiness. They were returning home from a weekend hunting party at a neighboring plantation, and she had had such a wonderful time. All the ladies had been kind and friendly, especially an amusing young woman from Velasco named Effie Barrett. Perhaps Eloise's cruel gossip had not spread, after all. The

Elizabeth Chadwick

gentlemen had been friendly as well, exclaiming over
Cassandra's riding and her skill with a rifle.

"Ah'd never have believed a Yankee girl could ride
like you, Miss Cassandra," said Caldicott Barrett, Effie's husband, at the end of the first day's hunt. "She's
a pure wonder, isn't she, Alex?"

Alex, grinning, had replied, "You should see her riding down wild horses if you want to see a pure wonder,
Cal."

Oh, it had been such fun! she thought exuberantly.
Eloise hadn't gone with them, and when they'd received the invitation, Gemmalee had worked all week
to produce a handsome riding costume. Benjamin,
newly weaned, had stayed home in the nursery, adding to Cassandra's sense of gaiety and freedom. It
wasn't wrong, she assured herself for the hundredth
time, to enjoy a few days away from the baby, although she could hardly wait to get home and see him.

The most important thing, however, had been her
meeting with Captain Ralph Hawkins, the man who
had told her at Arthur Wall's dinner party months ago
that white captives were rarely rescued. The captain
was about to accompany an expedition to Comanche
country in an attempt to make peace on the western
frontier because trouble with Mexico was anticipated
to the south when Texas became part of the union. As
soon as she heard of his mission, she thought of Alexandra. Why could he not make inquiries as they
sought out Comanche bands? Only on the last day had
she gathered the courage to take him aside and beg
his help.

"I haven't told Alex," she had explained, "and you
mustn't. I couldn't bear it if he died trying to find her,
and you said yourself the rescuers die more often than
the captives are rescued. But as you are going anyway—" Her voice broke with anxiety. "I could pay
you. I have an inheritance and—"

"Poor lass," Hawkins had said. "God's given you

334

trials aplenty, from what Alex tells me, and e'en he doesn't know the half of it. Of course, I'll look for your babe."

Cassandra's tears had fallen at his kindness, and the gruff ranger had patted her shoulder. "Don't hold too much hope, lass," he'd warned. "'Tis not so likely I'll find her."

"Singing Bird was the woman to whom they gave her," Cassandra had said eagerly, unwilling to heed his warning. "A woman of the Wasp band."

"Aye. Southern Comanches. I know the tribe."

At that point, their *tête-à-tête* in a sheltered rose arbor had been interrupted by their hostess, who gave them a surprised look, but Cassandra had been too exhilarated to care. *He'll find her*, she thought exultantly as she and Alex rode up to the door of Devil's Wood. *But I can't leave here until Hawkins returns*.

"Cassandra was the toast of the hunt," Alex informed his sister as they entered the hall.

"What does that mean?" Eloise snapped.

"Why, it means she's the best horsewoman in Texas," he replied. Cassandra dropped her riding hat and whip on the little marble-topped table and leaned over to look into the framed mirror. She tucked a straying gold lock into her chignon and smiled at the reflection of her husband behind her. "Not to mention a prime shot," he added.

"You were riding?" exclaimed Eloise.

Cassandra turned to glance at her sister-in-law. "Of course. It was a hunt weekend."

"You're with child. How could you be so irresponsible?"

"I'm not going to lose it," said Cassandra defensively.

"Are you sure that you're with child?" asked Alex quietly.

"Pretty sure," Cassandra admitted, realizing too late that she should have said something to him. It was

Elizabeth Chadwick

a problem she hadn't wanted to face, so she hadn't.

"You'll have to stop riding," said Eloise.

"I'll do no such thing," Cassandra retorted.

"Perhaps she's right, sweetheart." Alex frowned. "If I'd known, I'd have thought twice about going on this hunt."

"What's that supposed to mean? I rode the first six months while I was carrying Benjamin and occasionally after that. I hardly think a weekend of hunting when I'm three or four months along is going to make much difference."

"You have no sense of responsibility or decorum," Eloise charged.

"There's nothing wrong with my sense of responsibility," Cassandra retorted, "and as for decorum, I'd like to see you try to maintain it in a Comanche camp."

"We won't quarrel about this," said Alex calmly. "Cassandra and I can discuss it later. In the meantime, I need to have a word with Cutter."

Alex headed off toward the plantation office, and Eloise murmured, "Three or four months, did you say?"

Cassandra felt a prickle of dread run up her spine. What had her impulsive tongue led her to admit?

"If you're four months along, it's not Alex's."

"Yes, it is," said Cassandra and walked away.

"You might be interested to know," Eloise called after her, "that while you were away from home endangering your second child, I sat your first up for the first time."

Pausing at the foot of the stairs, Cassandra closed her eyes. A milestone in her son's life, and she'd missed it. And she was missing all the milestones in her daughter's life. Oh God, Captain Hawkins had to find Alexandra. She glanced back at her sister-in-law. How smug Eloise looked. As if, by staying home, she'd won Benjamin as a reward for virtue and responsibility.

Shaking her head, Cassandra started upstairs. She was being silly.

"I don't think you're irresponsible, sweetheart," he protested. "I just don't want you to take any risks. I've never forgiven myself for—"

"Alex," she chided gently. She was so relieved that he had been thinking of her welfare rather than supporting his sister, and he didn't seem to have noticed her slip about the number of months she'd been pregnant. After all, as irregular as she was, she might only be one month along. Wouldn't that disappoint Eloise?

"We had a wonderful time, didn't we?" she asked wistfully.

"God, yes," Alex agreed. "It was almost as good as mustanging. Damn cotton," he added.

"If you hate being a planter, why don't we leave?"

"No, Cass. This time I'm making sure you're safe and well cared for. I won't take any more risks, love."

"But, Alex, you don't like it here."

"We're staying."

"Then for heaven's sake, do something else while you're here."

"You mean try sugar cane?"

"No, that sounds worse than cotton." She could see that he agreed. "What about animals? Some of the men were talking about the money they had made from their herds."

Alex nodded thoughtfully. "I could breed horses."

Satisfied, Cassandra snuggled down beside him. If he got interested in horses or cattle, there were better places to raise them than Devil's Wood, places where he wouldn't have to deal with his sister. Once the baby was born, they'd leave. But gracious, what would she have done if he'd agreed to leave immediately? She hadn't been thinking straight, not when Captain Hawkins would be bringing Alexandra to Devil's Wood. And in the meantime she'd try to think of other things. A horse-breeding operation might be an opportunity for Ruben. Now that he belonged to her, she had to see that he learned a trade. Mellie and her sister were accomplished seamstresses and passable ladies' maids. Randall was too young yet to train, but Ruben—Ruben needed a new direction.

Cassandra struggled into wakefulness, aroused by distant screams and shouts. "Alex?" She listened again, then nudged him forcefully. "Do you hear that? What can it be?"

"Coming from the quarters," he mumbled. Then he sat up abruptly. "Damn. It must be fire." He threw back the quilt and slid, naked, to the floor. Cassandra followed him. "No, no, sweetheart, you stay here," he ordered as he fumbled into his trousers and grabbed up a shirt.

"I'll do no such thing," Cassandra retorted, dressing as fast as he because she ignored her corsets and pulled a simple, loose day dress over her nightclothes. By the time they left their room, Eloise, wearing a voluminous nightgown and ruffled cap, was poking her head into the hall, and the night nurse Delilah, carrying a very excited Benjamin, was peering from the nursery door.

"What is it?" Eloise asked.

"That's what I'm going to find out," Alex replied and headed for the stairs with Cassandra at his heels.

"Oh Lord," Delilah moaned. "Sure to be fire."

"Cassandra, there's no need for you to go. Alex and I can—" Eloise stopped talking because Cassandra was already halfway down the stairs.

"What the devil's going on?" Alex demanded when they discovered a crowd of slaves wailing and shouting as three white men tied Joseph, the butler at the main house, to a pole in the center of the clearing.

"Who are those men?" Cassandra whispered to Mellie.

"Slave catchers," replied her brother Ruben, who stood behind Mellie with his hands resting protectively on her shoulders. "Ondine and his men."

Cassandra noticed that all the slaves were dressed, although it was long after midnight. She had never seen the men who held Joseph captive.

"What are you doing on my land?" Alex demanded. He held a pistol, one of the revolving Colts he had carried on the frontier, and the leader of the three white men, a burly fellow with overlong black hair and strange, dark circles under narrow eyes, had raised his hands placatingly. The backs were covered with coarse black hair, even down onto the knuckles, and Cassandra shuddered at the sight of him.

"No need to take offense," he began.

"I do take offense. Untie Joseph before I put my first bullet into your gut."

The other two backed away but left Joseph tied. "I caught them holdin' one of their secret meetin's," said the leader. "I've your sister's orders to keep her people on the property an' in their cabins at night."

"It was jus' a worship service, Marse Alex," said Joseph. "Ah da preacher. You know Ah been saved dese many years an' got da call to bring others to Jesus."

"And you know night meetings are forbidden," cried Eloise. "Ondine was doing what I asked," she said to Alex. "I won't have them making voodoo curses and plotting—"

"For God's sake, Eloise, don't talk nonsense. Joseph's no voodoo priest. I reckon he's a better Christian than you or I." Alex turned to Ondine and said, "Off my land."

"Your sister—"

"My sister is not holding the gun. I am." He pointed it at Ondine's chest, and the leader jerked his head to the two followers. In seconds their horses' hooves were drumming on the river road. Alex shoved the pistol into the waistband of his trousers and drew a knife to slash Joseph's bonds.

"You've undermined my authority," cried Eloise as soon as they reached the hall and took off their cloaks. "Surely you don't mean to allow secret meetings where they'll plot against us and—"

"Don't be ridiculous, Eloise," said Alex brusquely. "We're not going to have a slave rebellion at Devil's Wood."

"If it weren't for Ondine, they'd all have run away."

"As close as you keep them caged, it's a wonder they haven't," Alex muttered. He had entered the drawing room to pour himself a brandy. "I don't want the likes of Ondine laying a hand on my people."

"I own half," snapped Eloise, "and everyone uses him."

"Eloise," said Cassandra quietly, "you don't want them attending services on the few occasions when you have any, and I take it that you haven't offered them the use of the church building on Sunday when you're not using it. When are they supposed to worship?"

Eloise flushed. "Not in secret night meetings. It's dangerous. And causes illness. Mr. Pettigrew at Dower Grove told me that he never got a decent day's work out of hands who'd been holding noisy, all-night prayer meetings."

Cassandra drew a calming breath. "The constitution guarantees freedom of religion."

"It's a nice thought, sweetheart," said Alex from the chair where he sprawled, snifter in hand, "but not one that would hold up in court."

"I don't see why not," retorted Cassandra. Here she tried to be reasonable with Eloise, and did he back her up?

"They're not citizens," he pointed out.

"Just like a man," she snapped. "Giving me some coldhearted legal mumbo jumbo. They're souls. Just ask Bishop Andress if you don't believe me. He insisted that everyone—not just whites—attend his service, and if you and Eloise intend to deny people on this plantation freedom of worship, I don't. I'll hold services myself. In the church."

Having made her pronouncement, Cassandra flounced toward the hall.

"You're not wearing petticoats!" Eloise called after her, scandalized.

Cassandra was both furious and worried. Now that she'd committed herself to holding a worship service, she had to wonder just how she'd go about it. She hadn't even taught Sunday school at home. Kindly Bishop Andress might be horrified to hear that a woman, unordained and unprepared, was preaching in his diocese. And what would her prospective congregation think? Those thoughts got her out of her dress and up the three steps to her bed, where she snuggled under the quilts. Alex followed her after several minutes and pulled her comfortably into the circle of his arms. "I've never made love to a lady preacher," he whispered. "If I promise to come to your service, will you let me try it out?"

"Making love?" she asked, turning to him and circling her arms tightly around his waist. "I'd be delighted. We lady preachers need all the loving reassurance we can get."

"Count on me," said Alex as he began to remove her nightgown. "I'm a great supporter of the church."

"Funny," murmured Cassandra. "I hadn't noticed that." He had captured one nipple, and the rush of heat that followed his attentions sent all thoughts of sermons and religious freedom fleeing from her mind.

She'd led them in a hymn, which hadn't gone too well because she was the only one who knew the words. Even Alex only hummed along. Once they noticed, the congregation politely joined in the humming, leaving Cassandra the sole singer. And there were no hymnals, not that a hymnal would have helped. Only she and Alex could read.

Then she'd said a prayer, and everyone had said, *Amen.* After that, feeling a bit desperate, she had read a Bible verse and begun to explain it. Although the black faces in front of her were attentive, and her particular friends gave her smiles of encouragement, Cassandra didn't think she was really creating much of an impression on her audience. Therefore she hurriedly concluded her explication and said, "Now, fellow Christians, I think we'd all like to hear from Joseph." He *was* their preacher, or so he had said the night Ondine broke up the prayer meeting. Why did everyone look so surprised, including Joseph? "Joseph, would you care to give us a sermon?"

Joseph rose hesitantly. "Yes, ma'am," he mumbled and took the lectern while Cassandra went to sit beside Alex.

"Good thinking," murmured Alex as Joseph folded his hands on the high stand and made his opening remarks.

Cassandra herself thought it turned out very well. Joseph certainly had a style all his own, and although she'd never attended a service quite like it or heard such singing—very rhythmic and lively—she thoroughly enjoyed herself and shook hands with everyone in attendance afterwards, with Joseph at her side.

"Preachers and elders always do it," she whispered to Joseph as she insisted that he join her at the door. "It's so everyone can tell you what a fine sermon you preached, which you did, Joseph. If you don't mind, I think it might be best if you continued to conduct the services."

"But Miz Eloise—"

"Oh, she won't attend, do you think? But I will, so

she should be happy. I'll take a Sunday school class."

Joseph looked dubiously toward Alex, who said, "Sounds good to me. I enjoyed your sermon myself, Joseph. Bishop Andress was always a bit too erudite for my taste."

Cassandra shot her husband a disapproving glance. It was hardly proper to criticize the bishop. After all, Joseph was no more an ordained minister than Cassandra. Bishop Andress could take offense and veto the whole Sunday-service scheme. And what must Joseph think of Alex criticizing the bishop? Maybe Joseph didn't know what *erudite* meant and had missed the tenor of Alex's remarks. Cassandra certainly hoped so.

"Annabel told me she caught them in the rose arbor," Eloise said spitefully. "He was touching her shoulder."

"What the hell were you doing alone with Hawkins?" Alex demanded.

Cassandra's indignation disintegrated into panic, but the sight of her sister-in-law's triumphant smile steadied her. "I had a favor to ask of him," said Cassandra, lifting her chin defiantly.

"What favor I'd like to know?"

Good heavens, could Alex be jealous of a man almost old enough to be her father? Cassandra wondered. But then Captain Hawkins *was* rather handsome. "He's going into Comanche country, and I left behind loved ones when I escaped." Which was certainly true.

"Loved ones!" echoed Eloise with exaggerated horror. "Well, I don't see why you had to be alone with the captain if your purpose was to send messages."

"Don't you?" Cassandra stared at her coldly. "Well, Eloise, I've found out the hard way that people have no sympathy for women who've been taken by Indians—as if having been tortured, terrified, starved, and enslaved makes us some sort of sinners." She noticed that her scowling husband had turned pale. "You yourself, Eloise, make cruel remarks about me to your friends. Did you think I haven't heard the things you say about me?"

"I don't know what you're talking about," Eloise said quickly.

Cassandra muttered *liar* under her breath, and Alex frowned at her. Later, once they gained their own rooms, he demanded, "Just what loved ones are these to whom you're sending messages?" His face was dark with anger. "Your war chief husband?"

She looked at him with surprise. This was the first time he'd mentioned that aspect of her life. "He's dead, Alex," she said coldly. "He died as he lived—in battle." *He died as he would have wanted to die*, she added silently. *I can always console myself with that thought*. "I managed to escape with Benjamin shortly after his funeral. Otherwise, I'd have been passed along to his brother."

"Oh God, love, I'm sorry." Alex looked conscience-stricken.

One more day I've kept the secret of his daughter from him, she thought. *One more day I've kept him alive.*

Chapter Twenty

"We'll get a better price if you take it to Velasco yourself," said Eloise.

"All right," Alex agreed wearily. "If the *Mary Elaine* makes it here within the next week, I'll try to strike a deal with Captain Wiggins. If not, I can hire keelboats."

"I'll go with you," Cassandra offered enthusiastically, for she thought taking the baled cotton to market sounded like a wonderful adventure. And she'd have Alex to herself. Lately Eloise always came up with some new task to keep him away from home.

"You can't," said Eloise, "not in your condition."

"I feel fine."

"If you fall ill on the river, what will you do? One would almost think you want to lose this baby."

"I don't," Cassandra protested, trying to ignore just a shadow of unease in the back of her mind. Eloise had said nothing more about the matter of paternity, and Cassandra had been hoping her sister-in-law regretted having raised the question, but here it was again, the hint that...Cassandra shook off the thought. She wanted the new child—no matter what.

"Maybe you shouldn't, sweetheart," Alex temporized.

"It would be irresponsible for you to go," Eloise insisted, "not only because of the baby, but you never do your share here at Devil's Wood."

You never let me, Cassandra thought resentfully, but

she didn't want to quarrel with Eloise again. As it was, she had to endure her sister-in-law's scowls every Sunday because of the services in the little church. And maybe she *should* take the safest course and stay home. With Alex gone, she could concentrate on learning about domestic matters. She'd add pages to her housekeeping notebooks.

Therefore, while Alex steamed down to Velasco, Cassandra watched the women dipping candlewicks into beeswax and melted tallow. She attended soap-making sessions at which grease and lye were heated in giant kettles. She visited the weaving room and was taught to work the looms and spindles. She learned which berries, barks, and clays made good dyes. And she made notes on all of it, something of which Eloise was unaware because Cassandra avoided her.

Cassandra now knew how laundry was done, although she didn't relish the long process of scrubbing the clothes with homemade lye soap, boiling them in gigantic witches' caldrons over wood fires, scrubbing yet again, rinsing in several different tubs, and finally fishing the garments out on broomsticks to be wrung by hand and hung to dry. And ironing—Lord, there were all kinds of irons—and all hot. She'd burned a finger trying to produce a wearable ruffle.

Outside, she observed the men mending fences and planting hedges of bois d'arc, which she recognized as a tree prized by the Comanches for arrow-making. Here at Devil's Wood it was planted to create hedges through which the free-ranging stock could not penetrate to the corn fields. Vast quantities of wood were chopped for the winter woodpiles, and winter clothes were handed out to the workers. Cassandra made note of the quantities needed.

When the pecans fell, the woman and children went out to harvest them. Cassandra tagged along, gathering nuts with the workers and singing the gathering songs. The men hunted to provide meat for the larders now that the weather was cool enough for its preservation. Since the slaves were allowed no firearms, they carried the pine torches that were shone into the deers' eyes to immobilize them, after which the masters shot the quarry. With Alex away, Cassandra hunted with Cutter once or twice.

The slaves also ran trap lines to catch small animals, and they fished. In fact, during her first real confrontation with Ruben, Mellie's brother, Cassandra insisted that he take her fishing after Sunday service. Although reluctant and resentful, he had mellowed a bit, and she found, to her relief, that she liked the boy. He was quick-witted and even humorous when he chose to let down his guard.

And she was beginning to learn about tending the sick, for she followed Aunt Ginger, the laundress and midwife, as she cared for people down in the quarters who had fallen ill or been injured. For more serious medical problems, a doctor who lived twenty miles away in town was kept on retainer by the plantation to treat blacks and whites alike, something that Eloise had pointed out to Cassandra. "Do your precious little factory children up North have such good medical care?" she asked.

Cassandra wasn't sure that good medical care could be expected from a man who carried leeches around in a jar, although she knew that bleeding with leeches was considered an efficacious treatment for many ailments. She personally thought she'd rather trust her health to Aunt Ginger's home remedies, garlic and rum for the children in the spring, herb infusions and evil-smelling poultices, some of which were taken from Eloise's family household book. It held recipes, cures, and all sorts of domestic information.

Cassandra had become quite familiar with that book during many afternoons spent in the plantation kitchen with Heppie. It was an impressive building with a stone fireplace big enough to roast a steer.

Dutch ovens, in which pies and cakes could be cooked on hot bricks, were built into the sides of the chimney. The fireplace itself held iron cranes that allowed Heppie to swing her pots out when she wished to tend them and to move them from hotter to cooler parts of the fire. Trivets, spiders, and three-legged pots were used to cook food over raked-out coals on the hearth. There were spits for roasting and long-handled spoons for basting, long tables with bread boxes beneath, and pie safes to protect the food from flies, and more kitchen utensils than Cassandra had ever imagined.

And then there were Eloise's recipes, which Cassandra read and copied. "Maybe I could actually cook something myself, Aunt Heppie," Cassandra suggested one day. "Not that I've never cooked," she added defensively. "I cooked all the time in the Comanche camp."

"Honey, gatherin' a few grapes an' roots an' hangin' some meat over a fire till it ain't quite so bloody, dat ain't cookin'. Don' know how you survived; jus' da food be enough to kill a body." Heppie shook her grizzled head. "An' as for you cookin', any time you take a mind to, you're more'n welcome to hep. Lord, we got us a heap a work come December. Miz Eloise, she ain't much on religion, but she do like Christmas, so we be runnin' day an' night to celebrate da baby Jesus' birthday."

On one cold November afternoon while Alex was still away, Cassandra, tired of her domestic studies and the strain of avoiding Eloise, walked along the river road, gazing over the bluff at the turbulent brown water and dreaming of the time when she and Alex would have their own home. Her daydreams were cut short when she heard the dull thud of hooves coming around the bend, then saw a dark-clad mounted figure and finally a pale face with stubbly chin and long hair. It was Ondine, the slave catcher.

He pulled his horse up just a foot from her and,

looking down menacingly, said, "I hear you're holding services now for the Devil's Wood slaves."

"Yes," said Cassandra. She had to back up a step because he had edged the horse sideways toward her.

"I don't like things that interfere with my business."

"Does religion interfere with your business, Mr. Ondine?" she asked, raising her chin bravely to show that she was not afraid. Again she had to back a step because the sweating horse, at the urging of its sinister rider, had moved closer still. Behind her she could hear the rush and suck of the river.

"People who don't know how things are supposed to be in slave country interfere with my business."

She could smell him, a sour, unwashed odor, but she dared not back another step, not with the riverbank so close. Alex and Cutter had discussed whether the river road would hold when the water ran in full spate. They said the banks caved in from time to time, taking sections of the road with them. The rusty, black skirts of Ondine's frock coat were so near her eyes that she could see the weave of the cloth and the damp hair on the horse's flanks. Surely Ondine didn't mean to—

"You better remember what I said, Miz Harte."

The voice itself was dark with threat, and Cassandra's heart pounded in a heavy rhythm that echoed the dangerous rush of the water behind her.

"Best watch them banks. They're soft." Then as abruptly as he had appeared, he cantered away, leaving her shivering, her feet sinking into the rain-soaked earth of the shoulder. With great care she picked her way back to the middle of the road and turned toward home.

In December Alex returned, bringing a beautiful set of leather-bound books for Cassandra. "In case you want to have another quotation contest," he explained, grinning as he presented them. "Folks are still talking about it."

For Eloise he produced a handsome black bonnet in the new, closer-to-the-face style. "Emma DeLaine of Velasco assured me that bonnet is in the height of fashion," he told his sister, who was as excited as a girl and gave Alex an affectionate smile, the first Cassandra could recall between brother and sister. For Benjamin a brightly painted rocking horse was carried up to the nursery. The baby adored it and crowed with laughter when his father made the blue and red horse rock. However, Eloise objected when Alex proposed to hold his son in the wooden saddle.

The riverboat on which he came up river brought a hold full of supplies for the plantation—flour, sugar, coffee, tools, fine fabrics, and liquors, all the things they did not grow or make for themselves, but that was not all. The reason for his prolonged absence was the purchase of a fine stallion and two thoroughbred mares.

"What were you thinking of, Alex?" Eloise demanded. "You've wasted our money on those creatures and then failed to purchase either the velvet for draperies or the china I planned to use at the Christmas ball."

The aura of good feeling died a quick death. "You've plenty of china, Eloise, and I've not noticed that we have any undraped windows or tattered hangings. As for the horses, I intend to increase our herds."

"I haven't agreed to any such thing."

"You don't have to agree, Eloise. For three years you spent my money on frivolities to which I never agreed."

"It's important in our circles to entertain well," said Eloise. "Just because you've a wife more savage than civilized—"

"That's enough of that," Alex commanded. "And as for your china and velvet draperies . . ."

Cassandra lost track of the argument as the accusation that she was "more savage than civilized" hit home. That was both cruel and untrue, and she resented it.

When she began to listen again, Alex was saying, "It's good land, and we'd be fools not to take advantage of the opportunity to buy. Statehood will bring in swarms of immigrants, and land prices will soar; they're already—"

"It's miles from here," Eloise interrupted. "And who would run it? You? Are you planning to neglect your obligations here to go haring off on some new scheme?"

Alarm shot through Cassandra. She wanted to leave Devil's Wood, but remaining in slave country was not the future she had in mind.

"No, Eloise, I'm not planning to leave. Cutter can run the new place, and I'll run this one."

"Acting as overseer again? Coming in shirtless and sweating like a field hand? Have you no conception of how a gentleman should act? Planters are men of leisure."

"Planters may act like they're men of leisure, but if they're any good, they work damned hard. You do yourself, Eloise, so don't try to tell me about gracious living. It's just another example of the hypocrisies on which the cotton economy is founded, only slightly less foolish than the moral justifications for slavery."

"What are you saying?" Eloise gasped.

Cassandra wanted to hear his answer as well.

"I mean that the next time someone quotes scripture to me in defense of slavery, I may just tell them what I really think."

"What *do* you think?" Cassandra asked. She had always been so disappointed that Alex supported the "peculiar institution," as they chose to call it in Texas.

"The reasons for slavery are purely a matter of economic necessity, and I don't want to hear any of your moral arguments against it, Cassandra," he replied testily.

"Well, I absolutely refuse to consider the purchase of another plantation," said Eloise. "We'd have to go into debt, and I've had enough of debt. What if it failed? We could lose Devil's Wood. We could lose everything." Her voice had risen hysterically.

"Cutter's a fine overseer. Nothing he manages is going to fail."

"His own plantation failed."

"Because everyone died. If everyone dies here, we won't care one way or another what happens to the land, will we? And as for my embarrassing you by acting as overseer, I was thinking of making Abraham overseer."

Eloise's face turned gray.

"Before you go into hysterics again, let me point out that Ashbel Smith left his place in the hands of a slave overseer this year, and Old Peter turned a record crop, and Uncle Billy at the Biggum plantation in Brazoria County is another who did a fine job."

"Never," said Eloise. "You'd be asking for revolt. We'd all be—be murdered in our beds. Why, in—in '41 to the east of us, they had to—"

"I remember, Eloise," said Alex, "but believe me, you worry too much about such things. Our people wouldn't—"

"You don't know that," she cried. "There's someone down there in the quarters right now plotting against us."

"Eloise!"

"There'll be no slave overseer on my place. Never. And I won't sanction buying another plantation."

"I agree with Eloise," said Cassandra, who was afraid that buying another plantation would tie Alex more tightly to this area, when she had her heart set on leaving as soon as the new baby was born. "If you buy another place, you'll have neither the time nor the money to carry out your stock plans, Alex, and I do think they'll bring you more pleasure and satisfaction, very probably bigger profits. Isn't the market for stock more stable than that for cotton?"

Although Alex had been frowning when Cassandra began to speak, he was simply looking thoughtful when she finished. *I've won for now*, she thought and turned to Eloise to say, "That bonnet really becomes you, Eloise. Marjorie Henson is going to be livid with jealousy when she sees it."

The thought of a livid Marjorie Henson evidently drove business concerns from Eloise's mind, for she rose from the black horsehair sofa to try the bonnet on in front of the ornate, gilt-framed mirror that hung above a carved walnut table in the drawing room.

Once Alex had left, Cassandra asked, "How can you stand to live here, Eloise, if you're in such fear of a revolt?"

"What choice do I have?"

Again Cassandra felt that sharp pang of sympathy that made her feelings for Eloise so confusingly ambivalent.

"What do you think would happen, Cass, if all the slaves were set free?" Alex asked.

"Why, they'd be a lot happier; that's one thing," she replied. "They'd have the same opportunities to make something of their lives that everyone else has."

"A lot of them would starve, or at least end up worse off than they were before. They're used to being taken care of. None of them can read or write, and their skills are minimal. The price of cotton won't support a decent wage for field workers, so we'd all end up hungry." Alex frowned. "I reckon emancipation could turn out to be a real social and financial disaster for the plantation economy and all its people."

Cassandra had no reply. In truth, she could imagine, now that she thought about it, all the terrible problems that might ensue. The well-meaning people who preached emancipation where there were no slaves to amalgamate into a free society never envisioned those problems. Still, the difficulties inherent in emancipation didn't excuse continuing slavery. Over the next days as she began her cooking lessons with Aunt Heppie, Cassandra considered solutions. After the production of her first pie, she decided that if she and Aunt Heppie were to compete for a job as cook to some family, Cassandra would be the worker to go hungry and jobless. They threw the pie away, and Cassandra tried again the next day.

"Don't you feel discouraged, chile," said Aunt Heppie. "You'll neber be a great cook like me, but we'll git you to da point where you won't poison Marse Alex."

"It wasn't that bad!" said Cassandra defensively.

Alex got to sample her second effort—in the privacy of their room.

"What do you think?" Cassandra asked anxiously.

"It's—ah—interesting," said Alex, laying down his fork. "What's in it?"

"Apples," Cassandra snapped. Maybe she'd try cakes tomorrow. The pies didn't seem to be going very well. It was that pesky crust. Hers always stuck all over the rolling pin, making jagged holes in the finished product, which Aunt Heppie considered unacceptable.

"Ain't no pies with holes comin' outa mah kitchen," she declared.

"This is dreadful custard," said Eloise. "Do you think Heppie can be ailing? She's served several dishes of late that aren't up to her usual standards."

If I had any conscience whatever, I'd admit that Aunt Heppie didn't make this miserable custard, thought Cassandra, feeling disheartened. *Maybe I just wasn't cut out to be a cook. I should have been a teacher like my mother and father. I do well enough in Sunday school,* she thought, *although it would help if the children could read*.

Cassandra's eyes widened. No education and no skills with which to earn a living, Alex had said. In her excitement she completely forgot about exonerating Aunt Heppie. "I have the most wonderful idea!" she cried. "I want to start a school. I can use the church and—"

"For whom?" Eloise demanded, her face registering a hysterical dread that Cassandra had seen before.

"The slave children," Cassandra faltered. Good Lord, did Eloise think that education, as well as religion, fostered violence? "Just a few hours a day. Think of how nice it would be for them, and it would give me something worthwhile to do. You know you're always saying, Eloise, that I don't do enough around here."

"I said no such thing," Eloise exclaimed. Her hands were trembling. "And I counted on you to help with the preparations for Christmas. There's all the cooking and decorating, and the ball."

"What ball?" Alex demanded.

"We'll need presents for our people, toys for the children. I thought you might make those, Cassandra. The little ones do so look forward to their Christmas gifts."

Cassandra hadn't known that Eloise gave the slave children Christmas gifts, but she might have guessed.

"And this is Benjamin's first Christmas. It's such a special time. I remember when Miranda—" Eloise faltered. "Children love Christmas," she finished in a choked voice.

"Eloise, of course I'll help." Cassandra rose immediately and went to her sister-in-law, their differences forgotten. How difficult it must be for Eloise, remembering all those earlier Christmases when her children were alive.

Having been put in charge of children's Christmas gifts, Cassandra settled on rag dolls for the girls and enlisted Gemmalee and Mellie to help. For the boys, she inveigled Alex into the purchase of real marbles when he was off on stock-buying trips. She'd noticed that the black boys played marbles with great enthusiasm, but they had only mud balls. She and her helpers would make pretty bags to hold the Christmas marbles. And candy. She and Aunt Heppie could make candy for each child.

"*You* gonna make candy, Miz Cassandra?" asked Heppie, her broad face wrinkled in lines of doubt.

"Well, surely there's some kind that's not so hard," said Cassandra, hurt at Aunt Heppie's lack of faith.

"Oh, Miz Cassie, don' you worry. Dey chillun gonna like whatever dey git jus' knowin' you done made it yo'sef."

Cassandra sighed. She'd rather the children liked their candy because it was tasty.

When she learned that the house was decorated every Christmas with holly branches and evergreen boughs, she volunteered to lead the collecting expedition, and Eloise didn't protest. Cassandra had anticipated a lecture on the responsibilities of impending motherhood. Instead she was allowed to choose her own helpers, and she elected Ruben and Mellie. Ruben suggested that his young brother and sister be included.

"Randall kin climb a tree better'n a squirrel, an' Esther—well, she'd enjoy the outin'," he finished lamely.

"Of course we'll take them," Cassandra agreed enthusiastically, "but Randall's too little for sawing off limbs up in trees."

"Yessum, but he kin climb for the mistletoe—you know, for Christmas kissin'."

"Oh, yes. Does it grow in trees?" The four of them deluged Eloise for three days running with holly, evergreens, and mistletoe. On the fourth they took Abraham along and brought back the huge Christmas tree and the Yule log.

"Choosin' jus' the right Yule log, Miz Cassie, that's mighty important," said Abraham. "Long as the log burns, the holiday lasts an' folks don't hafta work."

"Really?" Cassandra was enthralled with the idea. "You mean we all do for ourselves between Christmas and New Year's? In that case, poor Alex is going to start 1846 feeling terribly bilious."

Mellie started to giggle. "Don't you worry, Miz Cassie," she said reassuringly. "Marse Alex ain't gonna hafta eat yo cookin'. The house servants takes turns with the chores an' cookin' an' such."

"Has to be colored folks 'round to keep wettin' down the Yule log, else Christmas might end the very next day," said Esther. Ruben gave her a squelching look, but she shot back, "Miz Cassie ain't gonna tell, are you, Miz Cassie?"

"Of course not," said Cassandra, hardly listening. She had discovered an odd thing while the greenery expeditions lasted. As busy as Eloise was, Cassandra always found her in the nursery when they returned with a new load. Eloise seemed to take a greater interest in Benjamin every day, and he *was* an enchanting child; Cassandra could hardly blame anyone for wanting to spend time with him.

The tree was hung with popcorn strings, cotton balls, and homemade ornaments and lighted with candles. Cassandra thought it more beautiful than anything she'd ever seen.

On Christmas Eve, both the slaves and the family opened presents. Alex gave Cassandra an emerald necklace and earrings so lovely they took her breath away and a fine chestnut mare, which dimmed her high spirits. The horse reminded her of her life with the Comanches. She remembered the white mare that had been her wedding gift from Counts Many Coup. How she had come to love him! Yet it wasn't a disloyalty to Alex because they were so alike, adventurers both of them. If Counts Many Coup had been set to running a plantation, he'd have hated it as much as Alex did. But Counts Many Coup was dead. Given the precarious lives of the Comanches, they might all be dead, and this child she carried the only one to carry on his line—if the child was his.

She thought of Little Wolf and Black Rain. Cassandra missed her so. There was no friend to whom she could talk as she had talked to Black Rain. No companion with whom to share games and chores and laughter. What was Black Rain doing now? *I must do more for the people here*, Cassandra thought, *since I can do nothing for my friend. After Christmas*, she vowed. *After Christmas, I'll think of something.* Her last thought was of her baby daughter. *Oh God, let Hawkins bring her home to me*, Cassandra prayed.

"Why do you look so sad, love?" Alex asked. "It won't be long before you're riding again, although I suppose giving you a horse might not have been a very good idea."

"It's a beautiful horse," she assured him. "I love it."

On Christmas day there was a great feast—oysters brought up from the gulf, turkeys stuffed with Aunt Heppie's famous dressing, roast pork and all manner of vegetables from the plantation gardens, white flour biscuits and preserves, plum pudding, cakes, and pies. The different dishes were as numerous as the guests.

"A feast fit for a king, Eloise, Cassandra," said Paul Grafton of Fair Acres as the desserts were being served.

"Most kind of you, Paul," Eloise replied, "but I'm afraid Cassandra had no hand in the cooking. The poor girl's education has been sadly neglected in that area, although no doubt her cooking skills might be appreciated in a Comanche camp. She tells me she knows how to make pemmican and dry meat."

Cassandra could feel the uneasy shifting of the

guests around her. Her captivity was never mentioned, so this sudden change made her uneasy. Still, they had been getting along well enough lately, so Cassandra smiled at her sister-in-law. "I have a holiday surprise for you, Eloise," she said cheerfully. "You know your grandmother's famous recipe for Christmas apple-cherry cream cake? Well, I've made it for you."

A beaming Aunt Heppie carried the cake in and put it down before a very pale Eloise. Cassandra crossed her fingers under the table. She'd made the blasted recipe four times before she finally got it right and hoped those trial runs would insure that the fifth attempt proved edible.

Eloise cut the cake and passed around slices to the guests. "I suppose we must try it," she said, smiling thinly, "since Cassandra has been so brave as to have it served."

"You first, Eloise. I made it for you."

Eloise took the first bite as if she expected to be poisoned. *Oh well*, thought Cassandra, *one can hardly blame her, given my record up to now.*

"Very nice," said Eloise.

Cassandra's heart sank. Never was a compliment offered with less enthusiasm.

"Why, sweetheart, this is excellent," said Alex from his end of the table.

"It is?" Hesitantly, Cassandra sampled her slice. *It is good*, she thought. So what was wrong with Eloise?

After dinner when darkness had fallen, Cassandra headed toward the stairs to fetch Benjamin for the fireworks.

"Just a minute, Cassandra," Eloise murmured. She closed her hand over Cassandra's wrist with enough force to cause a bruise. "Step into the sitting room, please." Once the door had closed behind them, Eloise turned on her and hissed, "Where did you get that recipe?"

359

Elizabeth Chadwick

"Why, from the household book," Cassandra replied.

"*My* household book? The book that has been kept by the women of my family for three generations?" Eloise demanded. "You had no right!"

"But, Eloise, I'm part of your family."

"Don't you ever—ever touch that book again. Heppie must have showed it to you." Eloise's fists were clenched at her sides. "I'll have her beaten. I'll sell her."

"Eloise, that's crazy." In truth, Eloise *looked* crazy. "Heppie's been with you all your life. How was she to know that you'd be angry? And how will you ever explain to your friends why you sold Aunt Heppie?" If any argument would deter Eloise from taking her fury out on the cook, that should be it, but Eloise didn't even seem to hear.

"You're never to touch that book again, never to use my recipes, never to go into my kitchen. Do you hear?"

"I hear." Cassandra watched Eloise sweep from the room. *I'll never understand her*, Cassandra thought wearily, *much less make a friend of her.* Cassandra went upstairs to get the baby. If they didn't appear soon on the gallery, Alex would come looking for them. She was still shaking so badly as a result of the confrontation that when she found Alex, she handed Benjamin to his father at once.

All the adults and younger children were gathered on the gallery, while the older children, black and white, circled excitedly around a supply of hog bladders that had been filled with air and hung to dry. Once attached to sticks, the bladders were thrust into the huge bonfire and exploded. Soon the air was filled with loud bangs and the delighted shrieks of the children, none of whom was more enchanted than Benjamin.

For Cassandra, however, the rite held no pleasure. Each explosion further frayed her nerves, and her mind was filled with Eloise's hostility. Once the children were put to bed, there would be a grand ball. Cassandra dreaded it. How was she to pretend, when she saw Eloise, that nothing had happened? The woman hated her; she didn't even consider Cassandra a member of the family.

"You're not feeling ill, are you, sweetheart?" Alex asked with concern as he turned the baby over to Delilah.

Cassandra shook her head. She could easily plead indisposition and concede the field to Eloise, but why should she? She'd been looking forward to the ball. She tipped her chin up and smiled at her husband. "I'm feeling very well," she replied.

"Good, because I intend to have a bigger share of your dances than I did at the wedding."

Cassandra slipped her arm through his and went with him into the drawing room, which had been hastily cleared of furniture during dinner, the carpets taken up and chairs set out around three walls, while an orchestra made up of talented slave musicians from various plantations clustered near the fourth.

"It's customary for the owner and his wife to dance the first dance alone," said Alex, bowing and offering his hand. Cassandra curtsied and allowed herself to be swept away, but all the while she could feel Eloise's eyes on her, hostile and malevolent, reminding her of Faces A Bear, who had stared like that while Cassandra and Counts Many Coup danced the night before the summer hunt. She shivered, remembering the fate planned for her by Faces A Bear. Did Eloise hate her that much? What were *her* plans?

"Are you cold?" Alex asked.

Cassandra shook her head and smiled more brilliantly. As the evening progressed, she danced with all the gentlemen, chatted with the ladies, and sipped from her crystal goblet of syllabub, a delicious mixture of eggs, milk, wine, and spices. She had copied the recipe out of Eloise's now forbidden household book. Cassandra wondered if the guests had noticed that Eloise never spoke a word to her the whole evening. Each time Cassandra felt her sister-in-law's unfriendly eyes upon her, she had another glass of syllabub until she felt quite giddy and didn't mind at all that she was being snubbed.

Cassandra's wine-induced euphoria took a sudden downturn when she was heading for the stairs and a necessary visit to her room. When she stopped dizzily for a moment to lean her head against the wall, she overheard a conversation among several ladies in the sitting room.

"If she's as far along as Eloise says, she shouldn't be dancing."

"Or tippling either," added a second. "It's obvious to me that she's a bit—well—tipsy."

Am I? wondered Cassandra.

"Eloise says there's no telling who the child's father is," murmured the third gossip.

Cassandra stiffened. Eloise *couldn't* have said that!

"She told me the same thing." The speaker's hushed tones were fraught with avid shock. "Poor Alex. What will he do if the babe looks like an Indian?"

"Ship his wife straight back to Massachusetts, I imagine."

"Do you think he'll keep Benjamin? Goodness, what a scandal! One child born out of wedlock and the second fathered by a savage."

A wave of nausea swept over her, and Cassandra ran for the stairs. Dear Lord, what was she to do? In her room she sank into a chair, head in hands, and tried to think. What advantage did Eloise see for herself in precipitating this scandal? Was it pure, unthinking dislike that had motivated her? Possibly. She hated Cassandra and maybe Alex as well. But why would she want to hurt Benjamin, whom she had always seemed to love? Perhaps she was bent on driving them all away and keeping Devil's Wood for herself. If that was the case, she'd be doing Cassandra a favor.

But Eloise kept forcing more and more responsibility onto Alex; if she wanted him gone, why was she letting herself depend on him? Oh, it made no sense. And whatever Eloise's motives, Alex was going to stay here until the baby came, and the next months would be terrible. Cassandra knew she'd be shunned and whispered about as long as she lived at Devil's Wood. A grim prospect.

Downstairs, euphoria prevailed. All expected 1846 to be a banner year because President Polk was about to sign Texas into the union. But Cassandra expected 1846 to be a time of trial, another period to be suffered through, one day at a time. Well, she had learned to do that. Now she would put her expertise to good use.

Chapter Twenty-One

"Bring him to me, Lula," said Eloise, holding out her arms. Obediently the day nurse, deflected from her path toward Cassandra, placed Benjamin in Eloise's arms. "And how is my sweet boy today?" Eloise crooned to the baby.

Benjamin patted her cheek and chortled quite distinctly, "Ma ma ma ma ma ma."

"That's my smart little Benjamin," cried Eloise as shocked tears rose in Cassandra's eyes.

The first time her baby had ever said *Mama*, and he said it to Eloise. How could that have happened? Cassandra knew that Eloise spent time with him, but not that much, not more than Cassandra herself. *I didn't even realize that he'd be talking so soon*, she thought. Then she caught the smug look on her sister-in-law's face and realized that Eloise would have known when to expect his first words. In fact, Eloise must have coached him.

"Aren't you proud of him? He's such a smart boy."

Cassandra stared at her coldly. "Since we're speaking of learning—and teaching—I think it's about time I got my school started," she replied.

"What school is that, sweetheart?" Alex asked as he entered the room.

"The school I'm going to hold for the children," Cassandra replied. She rose and scooped Benjamin from Eloise's arms. "The school I meant to start in December but put off because Eloise said she needed

364

all that help with the Christmas preparations. Well, Christmas is over, and I've been forbidden to enter the kitchen, so I have plenty of time for—"

"Wait a minute," Alex interrupted. "What's this about your being forbidden to enter the kitchen?"

"Your sister was angry because I used your grandmother's cake recipe." Cassandra took grim satisfaction in the thought that she had copies of every one of Eloise's precious Harte recipes, those and all the other items in the household book, the treatments for illness and the instructions for everything else a woman might be called upon to do or supervise in the course of her domestic duties. There were even midwifery instructions. *I could deliver my own baby*, she thought—then realized that might be bit extreme. Still, unknowingly Eloise had provided Cassandra the means to run her own home once she had pried her mule-headed husband loose from Devil's Wood. "She forbade me to look at her household book or cook in her kitchen—ever. I'm barred from domestic activity here, so I might as well make myself useful elsewhere. The church building should do for my school."

"No!" Eloise cried.

"Look, sister of mine, this is my house, and my wife can damn well enter the kitchen and do whatever she wants there. She can burn it down if she takes a mind to, and I don't want to hear any more nonsense about—"

"She wants to educate slaves," Eloise screamed.

"Keep your voice down," Alex snapped.

"She won't need to burn the kitchen. They'll do it for her—the kitchen and the house. The first thing they'll think, if she teaches them to read and write, is that they're as good as we are, that they should be free, that they can take revenge. We'll all be dead before the year is out, our throats slit, our—"

"Calm down, Eloise," said Alex sharply. "There'll be no school."

Cassandra couldn't believe that he was going to side with his sister. Was she to spend these last terrible months before her confinement without the support of her husband? Cassandra rose, feeling besieged on every side. And there sat Eloise, completely calm now, whereas just minutes ago she had been hysterical— Eloise looking smug, thinking she'd won. "Alex," Cassandra appealed, "surely you don't believe her nonsense about rebellion. Education would make them worth more to you, not less."

"You're probably right," Alex agreed.

Cassandra let out a trembling breath.

"But, sweetheart, we'd never hear the end of it from the neighbors. This is a closed society, and what you're proposing—well, it's just not done. You have no conception of the uproar it would cause."

Cassandra took a step away from Alex. "I never took you for a coward, Alex, or a man without principle."

He looked stunned at her words, then angry. "There'll be no school," he grated, "and I don't want to hear any more about it. As for you, Eloise—" he turned to his sister, who was looking very pleased with herself "—don't let me hear that you're treating my wife with anything but the respect she deserves. Do you understand?"

"Yes, of course," said Eloise pleasantly. "However, Cassandra has entirely misrepresented—"

"That's enough. I've had my fill of mediating in women's quarrels. I've neither the time nor the stomach for it."

Women's quarrels? Cassandra's eyes narrowed. "Four of the slaves you don't want educated belong to me."

"Cassandra!" he said warningly.

"And I'll do just as I like where they're concerned." Then, still carrying Benjamin, she turned and left the room.

"Ma ma ma ma ma," said Benjamin, clapping both

pudgy hands to her cheeks as she climbed the stairs.

"You don't know who Mama is, do you?" Cassandra murmured. "But, sweetie, it's not Aunt Eloise."

"Why would we want to?" asked Ruben suspiciously. "Schoolin' kin only git us in trouble."

"If I could educate everyone in the quarters, I would," Cassandra countered, "but I can only do it for you four because—because—"

"—we're your slaves," Ruben finished for her.

"I don't mind learnin' to read," said Esther.

"Me either," Randall agreed.

"Why are you arguin', Ruben?" Mellie asked. "If you be here readin', you don't be out in the cold wind plowin'."

"It'll make us different," Ruben mumbled.

"We are different," said Mellie sadly.

"If you can read and write and do sums, you'll have more interesting work," said Cassandra persuasively. She'd like to have told them that she wanted to prepare them for freedom, but she couldn't make promises she might not be able to keep. If she and Alex never left Texas, she wouldn't be allowed to free them. Black Rain had said the law didn't allow for free Negroes in Texas. And if she died in childbirth—she shivered at the dark thoughts that had plagued her of late—if she died in childbirth, the four children would revert to Alex.

"What interesting work?" asked Ruben.

"My husband is buying stock—horses and cows. You can help with that."

"Don't need to read to take care of horses."

But Cassandra could see that he was interested. "There are books on breeding and treating their illnesses that you'll need to read."

"Why the others need to learn?" he persisted.

"Well—cooking's easier if you can read the recipes."

"Din' do you much good," Ruben retorted.

"Ruben!" Mellie cried.

"Wouldn't you like to be able to read the magazines that we use to make dresses, Mellie?" asked Cassandra, pressing her advantage. "And reading's fun. You know how everyone likes ghost stories. Well, books are full of stories. That one I told at Halloween about the headless horseman, that came from a book."

"Oh, Ruben," cried Esther, "that be a fine, frightenin' story. Even ole Whit don't tell a better story'n that."

In the end Cassandra got her way, and the four children came to her for two hours every day but Sunday.

All during January northers blew across Devil's Wood. On the worst days, white and black alike stayed inside, the men whittling household implements and repairing farm tools, shoes, and harness. The women wove cloth, quilted, knitted, and made baskets. And Cassandra observed and made notes, trying her hand at the various skills when she could. On milder days, plowing teams went into the fields to prepare for February and March when new crops would be planted; fences and outbuildings received repairs; manure was raked across the gardens; and trees and bushes were planted. Alex planned and put down orchards that winter.

The most important activity of January was the second hog butchering. Everyone took part in the event because, after the creatures were killed, they had to be scalded in great iron tubs to loosen the hair, scraped, hung, gutted, and cut up. Cassandra hated the bloody business, but she stayed to watch as long as she could stand it, hoping particularly to learn something about the sausage-making that went on in the kitchen. Finally she had to turn away disappointed, because Eloise stood guard at the kitchen door and Alex had gone on to another chore before Cassandra could get his support.

"I'll git the recipe for you, Miz Cassie," Mellie whispered, "so's you kin put it in your book."

Cassandra hadn't realized that Mellie knew about the notebooks, but, pleased, she smiled at the girl and replied, "Remember every detail you can." Then as Mellie trotted off to help with the grinding, spicing, and packing of the sausage, Cassandra wrapped a cloak around her swelling body and drifted toward the wood beyond the quarters. The cold air was bracing and cleared away all those cobwebs of resentment that association with Eloise spun in her mind.

How far away from childbed am I? Cassandra wondered. Because she had had no way to keep track of time during her last pregnancy, she couldn't compare the changes in her body then and now. She simply had to have patience, learn what she could while she was here, wait for word about Alexandra, then insist on leaving once the baby was born. But, oh, she hated Devil's Wood! She knew that Eloise was continuing to visit Benjamin, although the nurses had become evasive when Cassandra asked. As often as she could, she kept the baby by her side, but you couldn't take a little one to a hog butchering.

"Tired of the blood an' guts?"

Cassandra looked up, startled. Ondine had appeared suddenly on the path in front of her.

"Alex told you to stay away," she stammered.

"Heard you're teaching them bright niggers to read."

Cassandra remained silent.

"Miss Eloise tole you not to do that."

"How do you know?"

"People 'round here got ways a stoppin' things they don't like. Jus' you 'member, an' stop learnin' them niggers things they don' belong knowin'. Else you'll be sorry an' them too."

The man terrified her. His hair was longer and greasier, his face more dissolute and threatening. She

Elizabeth Chadwick

wanted to scream for help but was afraid that if she screamed, he might attack to shut her up.

"Scared, ain't ya? You should be."

As he had before, he turned abruptly and was gone. How had he known where she would be? Did he lurk here every day waiting for a chance to catch her alone? Or had Eloise summoned him? Either way, the situation was frightening. She'd have to tell Alex. However, by the time she returned to the house, Alex had gone down river. He stayed away several weeks and hadn't even said good-bye. He missed her birthday. Feeling dismal and sorry for herself, Cassandra wondered if her birthday would ever be celebrated again. She'd turned eighteen among the Comanches and nineteen with only Eloise for company.

"We're invited to a gala at Johnson's," said Eloise ten days later.

Cassandra thought of the looks and whispers she'd have to endure if she went. Nor would Alex be there to stand between her and the hurtful tongues. Eloise had probably planned this. Why else would she want Cassandra to travel, even a short distance? Heretofore she had insisted that Cassandra stay home because of her pregnancy.

"I don't think I'll go."

"Suit yourself," Eloise replied, "but I plan to take Benjamin. Ellie Johnson will want to see how he's grown."

"No!" said Cassandra and walked away before her sister-in-law could argue. *How dare you propose to take my baby away without my permission? That's what I should have said to her.* Cassandra's thoughts ran hot with suppressed anger. *I'm going to make myself sick if I don't stop this,* she told herself. But she couldn't stop; she was eaten up with suspicion and couldn't sleep until Eloise had left. Cassandra watched over Benjamin every minute lest her sister-in-law spirit him away. Then when Eloise was finally gone, Cassandra chided herself for her foolishness but began to worry that Ondine would come to the house. She took to keeping a rifle by her bed and only put it away when Alex returned.

"Why didn't you say good-bye to me?" she cried, throwing herself into his arms.

"But, sweetheart, you weren't around, and you knew I had to leave."

"I didn't."

"Eloise must have told you."

Eloise. Always Eloise.

"I asked her to mention it to you the day before the hog butchering—that was just before Cutter and I rode off to Baker's Landing."

"She didn't."

"And I told Gemmalee to give you my love when I'd waited as long as I could for you."

"Gemmalee never said anything," Cassandra wailed.

"Sweetheart, are you—"

"I saw Ondine in the woods."

Alex frowned. "What did *he* want?"

"To threaten me."

"About what?"

Cassandra paused. If she told him it was about the teaching, which he hadn't approved of, he might forbid her to continue, and it was one of the few things that gave her satisfaction in this miserable place.

"Cassie, love, are you feeling all right?"

Without thinking, she laid her hand against her swelling stomach.

"What is it?"

"Oh, nothing. He just kicked," she mumbled.

Alex's face lighted. "He kicked? Can I—"

Cassandra smiled at him and took his hand.

"My Lord," Alex breathed, "feel that!"

"I do," said Cassandra, grinning. "Quite frequently."

Elizabeth Chadwick

"I do love you so much, Cassie," Alex murmured and leaned forward for a long, slow kiss. "I don't suppose we could—ah—"

"Make love? I don't see why not."

Laughing, Alex swept her toward the drawing room.

"Alex, not here surely?" she gasped.

"I don't see why not," he echoed and fastened the double doors behind him.

In February when the weather warmed, the vegetable and flower gardens were put in. Cutter supervised the tarring of the corn seed to keep it safe from insects and birds while it germinated in the ground, and then the planting gangs sowed the corn fields. Cassandra took notes. She also kept notes on the progress of her pregnancy, planning, when the baby was born, to count back so that she could tell what symptoms appertained to what months of pregnancy. She wouldn't ask Eloise or anyone else, because she didn't want to reveal the fact that she had no idea when the baby had been conceived. She also made notes on Benjamin's progress so she'd know what to look for with the next child. In February Benjamin pushed himself up into a sitting position and waved his arms triumphantly for the first time.

"Alex," she cried, "he sat up by himself."

"He did that several days ago," said Eloise.

I won't let her get to me, Cassandra vowed silently.

"Statehood will be proclaimed on the nineteenth," said Alex, plucking his son from the carpet before the child fell over. "What a day that promises to be!"

"Well, Cassandra is in no condition to go," said Eloise, "but I'm sure she wouldn't want you to miss it."

"I wouldn't dream of going without her," said Alex, but Cassandra could see that he wanted to be there when the Lone Star flew for the last time in the history of the republic.

Alone with Eloise again, Cassandra thought, feeling miserably disheartened. "Of course you must go, Alex. It's a great moment in history."

"I'll be back by the end of the month," he promised. "Before time to plant the cotton."

"Even if you're not," said Eloise, "Cutter can do it."

Cassandra looked at her in astonishment. Now there was a change of heart. Eloise in past months had been increasingly insistent on Alex's plantation responsibilities. Now she wanted him to take a vacation during the most important part of the cotton-growing cycle.

"I imagine you're relieved to have him away," said Eloise.

"Why would you say that?"

"Because he can't visit the quarters when he's not here, can he?"

"He's down there all the time," replied Cassandra, puzzled. "Why would I object?"

"Well, you're right, of course. It's best to ignore what you can do nothing about."

"What are you talking about, Eloise?"

"The girl he's keeping down there."

Pain cut into Cassandra's heart. "You're lying."

"Have it your way." Eloise put down her sewing, rose, and left the room.

"You're lying," Cassandra whispered. Alex would never do that. He'd felt such contempt for his brother-in-law because of the tragic liaison with Sarah. Cassandra knew Eloise was lying, yet she wept that night. *I don't have enough to do,* she told herself when her weeping had finally abated. *That's why everything bothers me so much. When I was with the Comanches, I never had time for tears.*

The next day she got out all her notebooks and reread them. She had to be ready when it came time to leave.

* * *

373

"Cassandra, Aunt Heppie mentioned that some o
the children are sick down in the quarters," Elois
said. "I wonder if you'd mind having a look."

"Of course," Cassandra agreed.

"Take Mellie with you."

Cassandra and Mellie wrapped up against the chil
north wind and walked down the road to the cluste
of one-room cabins. Even inside the first cabin the
visited it was cold, and there were two children ill.

"That's whoopin' cough," said Mellie. "Ah know
'cause Ah had it."

"Is it bad?" asked Cassandra.

"Bad enough. Lil ones die from it."

"Oh Lord." Cassandra looked down at the two chil
dren under a thin quilt in the one-legged bed, and sh
thought of Benjamin. Would he get it? Cassandr
swallowed hard. She wasn't going to let anything hap
pen to Benjamin, her beloved baby. "We'd best te
Eloise." What had the notebooks said about whoopin
cough? Cassandra was so anxious, she couldn't re
member, but her sister-in-law would know. The
trudged back up to the big house, where Eloise me
them on the gallery. "Mellie says it's whoopin
cough," said Cassandra, moving forward to walk in
side.

"Whooping cough?" Eloise blocked the door. "Ar
you sure?"

Cassandra shrugged helplessly. "They were cough
ing."

"That's what it is," Mellie affirmed.

"Then you can't come in," said Eloise.

"What do you mean?" Cassandra's heart began t
race.

"You've been exposed. Do you want to endange
Benjamin?"

"Well, no, but—"

"I know you'll want to nurse the sick children, s

l have bedding carried down there for you. You and
ellie."

Cassandra was thunderstruck, yet what could she
o? If Benjamin caught the disease through her, she'd
ver forgive herself. Dazed at the swiftness with
hich she had been turned out of the house, Cassandra
turned to the quarters. How long would she be away
om Benjamin? And how long would she be able to
ke care of sick children before her strength gave out?
e had felt much less well with this pregnancy than
r first, ironic as that seemed. Given the degree of
xury in which she lived, she should have felt better.
n the other hand, living with Eloise was very diffi-
lt.

"Ah cain't believe Miz Eloise din' know it was
hoopin' cough," said Mellie softly. "Cain't believe
nt Heppie din' tell her."

Cassandra felt a cold foreboding overcome her. Had
loise deliberately schemed to get her out of the house
d away from Benjamin?

In the next week while they spooned mixtures of
oney, whiskey, and lemon juice into the coughing
ildren, whom they had isolated in the hospital
bin, and took turns keeping watch at night, Cassan-
ra could feel the weight dropping off her as her ex-
austion grew. The only highlight of her day was the
ews that Benjamin remained uninfected, but she lost
ack of the days. One child died, then another, and
e wept with their mothers and thanked God her own
as safe. Each night, she prayed that the unborn child
ould be unaffected by her vigil and the primitive
onditions under which she was living. A good tepee,
hen she had one, had been warmer and better proof
gainst cold winds and rain than these cabins, al-
ough her fellow workers did their best to make her
omfortable.

Then suddenly as she was dozing at the bedside of

a sick child, Alex strode in and swept her into his arm
carrying her away to the plantation house.

"Benjamin," she mumbled sleepily. "I can't
back."

"Get that out of your mind," said Alex. "You
going straight to your own bed."

"But Benjamin—"

"Doesn't have to come into your room until the e
idemic is over."

"I was just protecting your son," said Eloise wh
they came through the door.

"Were you protecting my second child as well?"

Cassandra could see that Eloise wanted to call in
question his claim to the unborn child but didn't da

While Cassandra lay in bed and the doctor w
called to examine both her and the children she h
been taking care of, Alex directed the spring plantin
He ate all his meals in Cassandra's room, and the on
words she overheard between him and his sister we
harsh ones.

In March the weather warmed, and sweet pota
sprouts were planted. Randall told her there was not
ing tastier than a sweet potato cooked in hot ashes
the hearth. Green began to show in the cotton row
and the cultivating crews went into the fields to we
and chop grass. Mr. Cutter suggested buying geese
eat the grass, but Eloise ignored him, and Alex w
away.

Cassandra, who had played shinny during her fi
pregnancy, found it exhausting to climb the stairs a
wondered how soon the child would be born. Too soo
she was afraid. There'd been no word of Alexandr
Also, she and Benjamin, once the whooping cough e
idemic had run its course, needed time to get rea
quainted; he had stopped calling her *Mama*. Had
begun to think of Eloise as his mother during the se
aration? It was a thought Cassandra couldn't bear.

At mid-month Alex came home for a week, and although she was up and about, they ate together in their room. But then he had to leave to investigate a debt of Jean Philippe's that was still contested. "Send a message to Pate Baldwin for me, will you, sweetheart?" he said to Cassandra as he packed his saddlebag. "Tell him I'll be along next week to bid on his gray brood mare." Cassandra nodded and relished his long kiss. His affection did not seem to diminish with her increasing girth. Eloise had lied about his going to the quarters; Cassandra was sure of it.

She walked slowly downstairs to find her sister-in-law and carry out Alex's commission. "I need to get a message to Pate Baldwin at Riverway."

"I don't have anyone free to go," said Eloise shortly.

"When will you?"

"Who knows?"

Gritting her teeth, Cassandra sent for Ruben, who was now Alex's representative in the stables. "The boy's got a natural affinity for horseflesh," Alex had said.

"I want you to take a message to Riverway."

The boy frowned and shifted uneasily from one foot to the other. "You know we ain't allowed off the place."

"That's Eloise's order, not mine. I'll give you a note of permission along with the message for Mr. Baldwin. You'll have to stay there tonight and return tomorrow."

Reassured, Ruben agreed eagerly. For him, Cassandra realized, this minor errand was a great adventure. What a shame his life should be so circumscribed because of Eloise's fears and prejudices.

Late the next morning Cassandra was playing with Benjamin on the upstairs gallery when someone in the yard demanded to see Eloise. She glanced over the rail and saw Ondine below at the foot of the steps.

Elizabeth Chadwick

With him, trussed up on the back of a mule, was Ruben.

"Caught one of your people, Miss Eloise," said Ondine with an ugly grin. "Want me to do the whippin' for you?"

Cassandra sped into the nursery and thrust the baby into Lula's arms, ran down the hall to her own room and then down the stairs, praying all the way that her flying feet wouldn't trip her up. She was across the hall and out the front door to take her place beside Eloise before Ondine could do more than yank Ruben from the mule.

"I went on business for Miss Cassandra," Ruben was saying to Eloise.

"You know the rules," said Eloise, her face cold.

"I did send him," Cassandra protested.

"Everyone knows Devil's Wood niggers ain't allowed off the place," said Ondine. "This one was off."

"With a note of permission from me."

"He tore up my note, Miss Cassandra," said Ruben.

"Take your hands off him, Ondine," Cassandra ordered.

"That's for Miss Eloise to say, not you."

"He belongs to me. I have the ownership papers."

"Ah'd have to see 'em, an' even then—well, it's beginnin' to look to me like you're unnatural fond of this boy. With your man away all the time, maybe you're—"

Cassandra lifted her Colt rifle from its concealed position in the folds of her skirts and leveled it at the slave catcher. "Are you sure you want to slander me?"

Ondine swallowed hard, then put his insolent grin back in place. "Well, I don't reckon you're gonna shoot me," he said, hooking both thumbs in his belt.

"You're wrong. That's exactly what I'm going to do if you don't let him go immediately, and I'll be perfectly within my rights because it's obvious that you mean to steal or damage my property."

"You're 'specially not gonna shoot me 'cause if he's really your property, you might hit him. Probably would. That's if you hit anyone atall." Ondine had thrust the roped boy in front of him.

Swept with a red tide of rage, Cassandra stared meaningfully at Ruben, then pulled the trigger as the boy tore free and darted out of the line of fire. The slave catcher staggered, blood staining the left thigh of his trousers.

"Now get off this plantation," said Cassandra coldly.

"I'm hit," the man gasped.

"Then you'd best hurry before you faint from blood loss, because, Ondine, if you're still on our land in fifteen minutes, conscious or unconscious, I'll kill you."

Ondine dragged himself into his saddle and turned eyes full of hatred in her direction. "You'll be sorry you tangled with me," he promised.

"No, Mr. Ondine, *you'll* be sorry you tangled with me. I'll finish you off if you ever show up here again."

"You're no better than a savage," hissed Eloise when he had gone.

"Were you behind his taking Ruben?"

Eloise backed away because when Cassandra turned to her the rifle turned as well.

"Were you?" Cassandra demanded. "And the insult? Did you put him up to that? If he's your man, warn him. Otherwise, his death will be on your head."

"Ruben, thank God you knew to pull away. I was so furious with that man I pulled the trigger almost without thinking. I might have hit you." Cassandra was now trembling with reaction, whereas during the actual confrontation she had been so angry that it had been as if some part of her stood back watching the incident with grim satisfaction. She had been two people.

Ruben, a grin covering his whole face, said, "Miz Cassie, that was the finest thing I ever seen. You must be the best shot, man or woman, on the river. Why, you put that bullet in his leg without even nickin' me."

"I'm not that good a shot," Cassandra confessed. "I was just too furious to think straight."

"Well, it sure did turn out fine. If I gotta be owned by someone, I'm real proud it's you."

Although she appreciated the compliment, Cassandra was afraid of the fury that had surfaced in her that morning.

Chapter Twenty-Two

In April the children were given doses of sulfur and molasses as a spring preventive, and the men not at work in the fields were set to cutting trees and splitting them into rails while the sap was up. Cassandra made note of the proportions of sulfur to molasses, and even forced herself out to watch the rail splitting in case she should ever need to plan for a fall fence.

When she returned to the house, reflecting that the gallery stairs got longer every day, she heard Eloise saying, "She shot him."

"Cassandra shot Ondine?" Alex sounded skeptical.

Cassandra dropped her wide-brimmed hat on a table and went into the sitting room. "It's true," she told Alex. "I did shoot him. A flesh wound in the thigh, but I'll put the next bullet into his chest if he comes back."

Alex's eyebrows rose in amused interest.

"Then what he said must be true," snapped Eloise.

"And what did he say?" Alex ushered Cassandra toward the sofa.

"No, the straight chair," she murmured. "It's easier to get out of." She sat down and leaned her head against the high upholstered back. "What did he say?" she mused. "Well, first he wouldn't let go of Ruben, although I'd already explained that I sent the boy to Riverway with your message to Pate Baldwin."

Cassandra fanned herself with a pretty fan that matched her yellow dress; she was feeling hot and ill.

Elizabeth Chadwick

"Then he intimated that my interest in Ruben was improper," she continued. "I suppose I shot him for both reasons. Because he was threatening to whip Ruben—with Eloise's approval—and because he'd insulted me."

"You wouldn't have reacted so violently if the insult weren't true," said Eloise. "She dotes on that sullen, rebellious boy, Alex. It's unnatural."

Cassandra's eyes narrowed, but she didn't look at her sister-in-law. She never wanted to look at Eloise again. Alex said soothingly, "You needn't bother to shoot Ondine, Cassie. I can take care of him myself." Then he turned to his sister. "Why does Ondine think he has any call to act for us?"

"He—he acts for everyone," Eloise replied.

"Not for us, not if you did what you were supposed to."

"I own half of this place, and I don't want *my* slaves running away."

"Ruben is not *your* slave. Did you tell Ondine that when he brought Ruben in?"

"She didn't," said Cassandra.

"And you weren't even mildly upset when he insulted Cassandra?" Alex's anger had escalated, and his sister, looking small and anxious now, rose from her seat.

"Eloise, you're treading a very thin line with me. You either act as a sister should, or you'll find yourself with no family left."

Good, Cassandra thought. *She'll never change her attitude, and every move she makes against me will ease my way in convincing Alex to leave once the baby's born.*

The work crews had begun thinning the cotton, and blue skies shone on their labors, while untilled fields lay deep in wildflowers and the gardens planted in February had begun to bloom. From the upstairs gallery, where Alex had a chaise longue placed for her,

Cassandra stared across the river at a swath of blue-
bonnets and thought how nice it would be to take
Benjamin there for an afternoon, to run through the
flowers, laughing. She watched the river boats pass
by and dreamed of sailing away from Devil's Wood
and Eloise.

Eloise had inveigled the bishop into coming for
Easter and was busy decorating the church and inviting the neighbors for the service and a sumptuous
dinner to follow. Increasingly tired, Cassandra intended to attend the service but not the dinner, which
infuriated Eloise. However, Cassandra wouldn't be
bullied into providing a dinner-table target for the
gossips.

Cassandra dropped wearily onto her chaise longue.
From below, the chatter of the guests drifted up as
they strolled on the gallery after the Easter feast. The
service had been lovely, the bishop's sermon on the
Resurrection so touching and full of hope that it had
brought tears to her eyes and enabled her to ignore
the stares of the visitors. Unfortunately, she could
imagine their thoughts, and all her suppositions
spelled misery for her children should she and Alex
stay here at Devil's Wood. But they wouldn't. Very
soon they could leave. Alex's only tie to the place was
his fear for her safety while she was with child, her
only tie the hope of a message about her daughter.

"Miz Cassie?" Mellie called from the open doors.
"The bishop's come to visit."

Although Cassandra felt too weary and ill to welcome callers, she tried to look pleased and told Mellie
to show him out on the gallery.

Much to her surprise, the bishop, when seated,
looked very uneasy. "I thought your sermon so moving, sir," she said quietly. "One of the things I miss
most is the opportunity to attend church regularly."

"Ah, but I hear you have rectified that lack here at Devil's Wood," said Bishop Andress.

Oh Lord, he disapproves of our services, she thought, *but what else can we do if we're to have regular worship?*

"I was so pleased to hear that something is finally being done for the souls of your people."

Cassandra relaxed. At least today she wouldn't be called upon to fight for her principles.

"Actually, Cassandra, it was another matter I wanted to discuss with you." He paused with a sigh.

"What is it, Bishop Andress?" she asked, puzzled.

"I wonder, my dear, whether you and Alex have discussed the problem of the—er—paternity of the child you carry?"

Cassandra started to tremble, and she could feel the flush rising to her cheeks.

"I realize how terrible this must be for you, child, but you are not to blame for what happened during your Indian captivity. Your marriage will be the closer for a frank discussion with Alex, and the problems you face because of the child will be easier to bear when you face them together. You'll find Alex both understanding and—"

"What has she said?" Cassandra interrupted, her voice trembling. "That I've lied to Alex? Alex knows everything there is to know." How could Eloise be so unprincipled as to use the kindly, well-meaning bishop? "Eloise put you up to this, didn't she? Eloise, who spreads hurtful rumors among all her friends so that I have to listen to women calling into question the legitimacy of our first son and the paternity of our second." The bishop looked shocked. "Eloise," cried Cassandra, the pace of her heart accelerating, "who exiled me to the quarters for weeks on the pretext that I was a danger to Benjamin. I'd still be there if Alex hadn't rescued me. She hires Ondine to threaten and insult me and—" Cassandra, near hysteria, doubled forward as pain burst in her lower back.

"My dear child, what is it?"

"Get Alex," she gasped.

She dragged herself up from the soft comfort of the chair and fumbled her way inside to the bed, where she curled up. The baby was coming, and it was too early.

Eloise entered the room with Alex at her heels. "What is it?" she asked.

"The baby," Cassandra whispered.

"I knew it. If you deliver now, it's no child of my brother's."

"Eloise," said Cassandra, pushing up on her elbow, "if I lose this child, you'll pay. The last woman who tried to hurt a child of mine lived to regret it, and you will too."

Eloise backed away, her malevolence turning to alarm.

"It's going to be all right," said Alex soothingly.

"She made the bishop talk to me about the paternity of our baby." Cassandra gasped as another pain hit her.

"*What*?" Alex grasped his sister's upper arm, tightening his fingers until she cried out.

"The first pain came when I realized what she'd done." Cassandra sank back on her pillow, exhausted and frightened. "If the baby dies, it's because she wanted it dead. Why else would she have sent me to the quarters when there was whooping cough down there, and then kept me there when—when—" She stopped as the next contraction hit.

"She's wrong," Eloise cried. "I'd never hurt any baby. Even that half-breed she's trying to pass off as—"

Alex flung his sister across the room, and she staggered, trying to regain her balance. "Someone had to talk to her," Eloise cried, "She can't go on pretending it's your child. Look at her! She's about to deliver, and it's only April twelfth. You can count. If you

385

got her back in August, she's carrying some dirty Indian's—"

"Get out!" Alex shouted.

Eloise stumbled through the door, and he slammed it behind her. Then he returned to the bed and climbed up beside Cassandra, smoothing the tumbled hair away from her forehead and murmuring, "It's all right, sweetheart. It's going to be all right."

"How can you say that?" Cassandra sobbed bitterly. "You don't know what it is to lose a child."

"You're not going to lose it. Now hush, don't cry."

"Even if it lives, the scandal—"

"There'll be no scandal," he murmured and stretched out beside her, drawing her gently into his arms. "I told you months ago that the child will be mine, and no one's going to say anything different."

"Eloise already has."

"Eloise, if she's been talking out of turn, will learn to keep her mouth shut, and you'll be fine, you and the baby. I'll never again let anything bad happen to you."

Cassandra's eyes closed, and she rested her head wearily on his shoulder. It was so good to be in his arms, encircled by his love. No wonder Eloise was always urging him to go away. She wanted Cassandra vulnerable in his absence. *I'll keep him beside me from now on*, she thought sleepily, *and then when the child is born—when the child is—when would that be?* The contractions had stopped. "Don't let Eloise come back."

"All right, sweetheart."

"She'll throw the baby away."

"What?"

"Don't let her near me. Or the baby. Promise."

"I promise."

Cassandra would have nodded, but she was too weary. She couldn't even open her eyes. *Maybe not today, after all*, she thought.

"Alex." He looked over his shoulder and saw his sister again at the door. "You can't stay with a woman in labor."

"The contractions have stopped," he whispered.

"Well, I'll stay with her."

"You'll stay away from her." He lowered Cassandra gently to her pillow. "Now get out, Eloise. And keep your mouth shut from now on."

Eloise glared at him and whirled into the hall, slamming the door. Alex looked down at Cassandra, but she was deeply asleep and hadn't heard.

Never give your enemies power over you. It was something Counts Many Coup had said, and now Cassandra saw the truth of it. Eloise was an enemy. Therefore, since they couldn't leave Devil's Wood immediately, Eloise had to be kept at a distance. To protect herself and her unborn child, Cassandra called Aunt Ginger in and told her that under no circumstances was Eloise to be allowed in the room after labor began.

"But, Miz Cassie, she da mistress."

"Alex knows my feelings. You can send for a doctor; you can tend to me yourself; but if you let her in the room, you'll both have to leave."

"Who gonna birth da baby?" asked Aunt Ginger. "Da truf is, Miz Cassie, once you gits along in yo labor, you ain't gonna care who's here an' who ain't."

Cassandra remembered the first time and feared that what Ginger said might be true, but Alexandra might not have been given away if the midwives hadn't been enemies. "I intend to keep a rifle by my bed," said Cassandra. "No one touches me or the baby but people I can trust."

"Lordy, lordy," muttered Aunt Ginger.

Next Cassandra moved to protect Benjamin. By telling people that he was illegitimate, Eloise had attacked him. Therefore Cassandra called the nurse-

387

Elizabeth Chadwick

maids in and demanded that Eloise be kept out of the nursery.

"Miz Cassie, she do what she wanna do. Nuthin' us say gonna keep Miz Eloise—"

"He's my son, and I won't have her near him. If she insists, you're to come to me—immediately."

Lula and Delilah looked terrified.

"General Taylor's moved south to the Rio Grande," said the guest. "Looks to me like Polk wants a war."

Alex shrugged. "That land's claimed by both countries, and the Mexicans won't negotiate."

"Heard tell some of your old ranger friends are down there scouting for Taylor."

"I heard the same thing," Alex murmured.

Cassandra perked up, wondering if Captain Hawkins was among Taylor's rangers. Alex frowned at her when she asked, but Cassandra didn't care. She yearned for word of her daughter. Why hadn't Hawkins sent a message?

"Last I heard, Hawkins was out on the plains somewhere looking for Comanches," said the guest.

Cassandra nodded and went back to toying with her food and thinking of other things. She had discovered Eloise in the nursery just before dinner. How many other visits had the nursemaids failed to report? Unfortunately, they were in no position to oppose Eloise. They would have to stay here after Alex and Cassandra had left.

"Taylor's got a base at Point Isabel, and he put a company headed by a major named Jacob Brown right smack across the border from Matamoros. Then the Mexicans sent this General Arista across the river. Arthur Wall just got back. He says there's more soldiers than jackrabbits ridin' through the chaparral down there."

"Sooner or later, there'll be shooting," said Alex.

I'll replace the nurses with Mellie and Esther, Cassandra decided. *They'll do what I tell them.*

"Don't you think you're overreacting?" Alex murmured later in the evening when she told him her plans.

"No."

"And this business of not allowing Eloise in the room when your time comes—Cass, honey, that's crazy. You may not like Eloise, but she does know a lot about childbirth."

"Alex, you either give me your word right now, or I'll go into Washington and have the baby at Wall's. I can leave with that man who's staying the night."

"You don't even know when you're due," he exclaimed. "You can't go traipsing around the countryside."

"Your word," she demanded.

"All right," he agreed reluctantly. "Just don't get upset again."

"If you keep her away from me and my children, I won't get upset."

"The Mexicans fired at Taylor's troops on the twenty-fourth," said Alex. "A fellow coming up river from Velasco on the *Savannah* brought the word."

"I think today's the day, Alex," said Cassandra. A contraction had awakened her just before dawn.

"What day, sweetheart? They may have declared war in Washington, but we won't hear of it for a while."

"The day the baby's born," said Cassandra. The pains were coming about every twenty minutes.

"Oh, my Lord." Alex turned pale.

"It's all right," she said soothingly. "Just get Ginger and send for the doctor."

"I can't leave you by yourself at a time like this."

She grinned. "Do you want *me* to go down to the washhouse and get Aunt Ginger?"

"Of course not!" he exclaimed, then realized she was teasing. "How can you joke about it?"

"Because I've done this before."

"Well, I haven't" Alex muttered and went to summon the midwife.

In the next hours, Cassandra realized that arguments went on in the hall beyond her door, but Alex kept his word: his sister stayed outside.

"If I were about to have an Indian brat, I wouldn't want the family to see it either." That was the last thing Cassandra heard Eloise say. Four hours after Aunt Ginger bustled into the room, the baby was born.

"Oh my," said Ginger, "You got yo'self another fine son, Miz Cassie."

"Let me see him," Cassandra whispered. She was so tired. It seemed to her that she'd been tired for months. Aunt Heppie, who had come up from the kitchen to assist at Alex's request, put the baby into Cassandra's arms.

"Look jus' like Marse Alex, ceppin' he got yo eyes," said Heppie.

Cassandra looked down into the startling blue eyes and wondered. They might be his heritage from her, or they might be Thunderbird eyes. What did it matter when he was so beautiful and healthy? Her heart flooded with love for this new child.

"Would you like to hold him?" she asked Alex, wanting to share this special happiness with the man she loved.

"Why, he's small enough to fit in my hand," said Alex, laughing in wonder as he took the baby from Cassandra. "And look at his eyes. I wouldn't have thought any eyes could be bluer than yours, love, but—"

"Babies' eyes change," snapped Eloise. She had slipped into the room unnoticed and peered around her brother. Then she caught her breath.

"Does he look Indian to you, Eloise?" asked Cassandra coldly.

"No," Eloise admitted. "No Indian child, even one just a few hours old, could have eyes that color."

How ironic that Eloise was convinced of the baby's paternity because of a trait he could have inherited from his father. Of course, no one knew, or ever would, that Counts Many Coup had been blue-eyed. And no one would ever know whose child this baby was, Cassandra realized wearily.

"What you gonna name him, Miz Cassie?" asked Aunt Heppie.

"I don't know," Cassandra murmured as she reached for the baby before Eloise could take him from Alex. Because Cassandra was studying her son again, she failed to notice the disappointment that flashed over Alex's face.

"Well, since you've no ideas on the matter," said Eloise briskly, "I think he should be named Jean Philippe."

Cassandra snapped out of her sleepy contentment. "Absolutely not."

"Alex, talk to her," ordered Eloise. "As my husband has no heirs, it's natural that he be remembered in this way."

"I will not have my son named for your husband, Eloise."

"Why not?" asked Alex, his face expressionless. "It might go a long way toward making peace between the two of you, and it's not going to be very pleasant living here if you're always feuding with Eloise."

Cassandra stared at him incredulously.

"Well, what do *you* want to name him?" Alex snapped.

"Justin."

"Justin? Where the hell did that come from?"

"It's a family name." Cassandra was furious with both of them—Eloise for presuming to choose a name,

as if the new baby were hers instead of Cassandra's
and Alex for going along with it.

"Best Miz Cassie git her some sleep now," said Aunt
Heppie. "You git along, Marse Alex, Miz Eloise, an'
you han' me dat baby, Miz Cassie. Cain't have yo
rollin' over on him when you asleep."

"We need a night cradle," Cassandra murmured
Now that Eloise was leaving, exhaustion began to
overcome Cassandra.

"Got a cradle," said Heppie.

"No, no. The rawhide roll. You know." Cassandra
turned on her side and pillowed her cheek on her hand
Justin was a good name. It was the Christian name of
Counts Many Coup. Had she been back in the Coman
che camp, there would have been a rawhide roll to
protect the baby as he slept between her and his fa
ther. She drifted into sleep, thinking of those blue
blue eyes, and the first time she'd seen eyes like that
They'd been in the face of the man who saved her life
the man she'd thought was Alex until she saw the eyes

Cassandra yawned and stretched luxuriously.

"Ah, so you're awake at last, Mrs. Harte."

She looked at the man by her bed and realized he
was the doctor. *Does he ever arrive in time to deliver*
baby? she wondered. "Aunt Ginger?"

"Right here, Miz Cassie."

"Where's the baby?"

"He with his wet nurse, Miz Cassie."

Cassandra struggled into a sitting position.

"Here now, Mrs. Harte, you must lie down. You're
exhausted from your ordeal and need your rest," said
the doctor.

"Who ordered a wet nurse?"

"Why, Mrs. Daumier made the arrangements. I as
sure you the woman she chose is quite healthy and
suitable. I've already examined her."

"I want Justin in here this moment."

"Please lie down, Mrs. Harte."

"What's going on now?" Eloise asked as she entered the room. "I could hear the fuss all the way down the hall."

"Mrs. Harte seems to object to the idea of a wet nurse," said the doctor.

"Cassandra, you cannot nurse another child. You're much too pale and thin," said Eloise.

"If I'm pale and thin, it's because you tricked me into going down to the quarters, knowing those children had whooping cough, and then wouldn't let me back in the house."

Both the doctor and Eloise looked embarrassed at that blunt accusation. "For heaven's sake, Cassandra, gentlewomen do not nurse their own babies, and if you won't think of the proprieties, think of your son. What's he to do if—if you're not here?"

"That won't be a problem, since I have no intention of being separated from him." Cassandra threw back the sheet and began to move toward the edge of the bed.

"Mrs. Harte, what are you doing?" cried the doctor.

"I'm going to get the baby," replied Cassandra, who was feeling with her bare toes for the first step.

"Miz Cassie, you cain't git outa bed," cried Aunt Ginger.

"Get the baby!" Dr. Mills ordered. "We can't have her wandering up and down the halls when she's just given birth. If she wants to nurse the child—"

"No!" cried Eloise.

"Mrs. Daumier, I must beg to disagree with you. Both mother and baby will fare better if Mrs. Harte is not upset. Here, Mrs. Harte, let me help you back to bed."

Once Mellie had carried the new baby into the bedroom and placed it in her arms, Cassandra allowed herself to be settled against her pillows.

"Has *she* been in the nursery, Mellie?" Cassandra asked.

"No, ma'am, only to bring in the wet nurse."

"Stay away from the children, Eloise," said Cassandra. Eloise's face turned bright red, and the doctor gasped. "Why don't you all go away? Ginger, where's Alex?"

"He be along any minute. I send Esther for him."

"Then who's watching Benjamin?" Eloise demanded. "You turned out experienced nurses, Cassandra, for these two who know nothing about babies, and—"

"It's none of your concern, Eloise. I don't want you around the children unless I'm in the room."

"I think we'd best leave," said the doctor. "Mrs. Harte needs to get some sleep."

"What's his birth date, Alex?" she asked.

"April the twenty-sixth."

She watched Benjamin pull himself to his feet, using his father's trouser leg, and she burst into tears, thinking that she'd missed all this with Alexandra, the first sitting up, standing, speaking.

"Cassandra, what is it?"

"Now don't you worry, Marse Alex," crooned Aunt Ginger. "New mothers, they sometime be sad an' tearful."

"I don't know when Benjamin's birthday is," Cassandra wept. "We'll never know what day he was born because I was with the Comanches."

"Oh, sweetheart." Alex, who had been somewhat distant since the confrontation over the new baby's name, picked up Benjamin and walked over to drop a kiss on Cassandra's cheek. "Benjamin isn't going to mind."

"Of course he'll mind." Cassandra handed Justin, who had finished nursing, to the midwife. "He'll never have a real birthday. How can he have birthday parties when—"

"Now, Miz Cassie, jus' you stop yo cryin'. Dat chile's about a year ole, so what you do, you an' Marse Alex pick yosef some nice day in May you bof like an' give it to lil Benjamin fo his birfday. Be jus' fine dat way."

"Sounds reasonable to me," said Alex. "How about the fifteenth? That's midway through."

"All right," Cassandra agreed, sniffing, "but I wish I really knew."

"He stood up and I wasn't there?" Eloise turned pale. "You didn't even tell me?"

Eloise had come in with Alex after dinner when Justin was three days old. "If you weren't keeping me away from them. I wouldn't have missed it. It's unnatural."

"What are you talking about?" Cassandra thought Eloise was acting very strangely. "It's not as if they're *your* sons." As soon as she'd said it, she realized that Eloise did sometimes act as if Benjamin and Justin were hers.

"I'm going to be Justin's godmother."

The christening was to be two days hence.

"No, you're not," said Cassandra calmly. "You've told everyone in the county that he's a half-breed—"

"But I know he's not."

"—so I'm certainly not going to let you stand godmother to him."

"I'll assure everyone—they'll only have to look at him to—"

"I've already asked Effie and Caldicott Barrett."

"They have to get back to Velasco."

"They've agreed to stay."

"I christen thee Justin Whitney Harte," said Bishop Andress, "in the name of the Father, the Son, and the Holy Ghost." Little Justin stared with large blue eyes as the bishop sprinkled water on his head, but he didn't cry. Justin rarely cried, Cassandra mused, but then Benjamin hadn't cried either when she had christened him beside that lightning-struck tree. When the group in the little church bowed their heads to pray, Cassandra prayed for all her children, especially Alexandra, who was out there somewhere, waiting to be rescued. Why, oh why, didn't Hawkins send word? He'd promised.

"Don't cry, sweetheart," Alex whispered. "No one's gossiping."

But he was wrong. Although Eloise pointed out to all the guests the baby's strong resemblance to Alex, Cassandra heard the women whispering about the child's dark skin.

"Of course, he has Cassandra's eyes," said Eloise desperately, "but his dear little face, just like Alex's when he was a baby."

"Goodness, Eloise, that's been thirty years or more," said one of the women. "How can you remember what Alex looked like?"

I don't care, thought Cassandra. *As soon as I'm stronger, we'll leave. Maybe after Benjamin's birthday. Hawkins will have brought Alexandra back by then.*

At least the men weren't gossiping. All they could talk about was the war with Mexico. Rumor had it that General Taylor was marching toward a confrontation with General Arista and had called on Texas for four regiments, two horse and two foot.

Cassandra had been wrong in thinking that the men weren't talking about her and her child. Word had gotten back to Alex that a young sport from a plantation near San Felipe de Austin had said that the baby, except for the mother's blue eyes, looked like an Indian to him. "Harte's got a cuckoo in his nest and horns on his forehead—buffalo horns," had been

the exact words quoted to Alex and the cause of his
determination to challenge the man.

"You'd risk your life in a duel with some stupid
young popinjay?" Cassandra cried, aghast.

"If you were a Southern lady," said Eloise, "you'd
realize that a Southern gentleman has to defend his
honor."

"If Alex dies—"

"I'm not going to die, Cass," said Alex impatiently.
"I'm just going to teach that fool to curb his tongue."

"He was just saying what your sister told everyone."

"I didn't," cried Eloise. "I told them how much the
baby looks like Alex."

"Not before he was born. Before he was born you
were saying—"

"Cass, you don't know who started the gossip. Why
do you accuse Eloise?"

"Because I heard her."

"You must have misunderstood," said Eloise.

"I don't know how the hell I'm supposed to run a
plantation when I spend half my time mediating between you two," said Alex bitterly.

Cassandra worried every minute for two days, terrified that he might have issued the challenge without
telling her and that some morning she would awake
to find him gone. How could he think of letting another
man take a shot at him, maybe kill him? In less than
two weeks it would be Benjamin's birthday, the date
she had set in her mind for convincing Alex that they
would all be happier away from Devil's Wood, the date
by which she was sure word would have come from
Captain Hawkins.

Two nights in a row, before the matter of the duel
came up, Cassandra had dreamed that a man on horseback arrived at the great double doors of Devil's Wood
and presented her with a beautiful, one-year-old baby
girl. Cassandra felt herself getting stronger every day,

more optimistic, and both of her sons were thriving. As soon as Alexandra arrived, they'd be ready to travel—if she could just keep Alex from fighting this foolish duel.

But then suddenly it didn't make any difference, because a man stopped by on the night of May third, and Alex left the next day. The cotton was budding in the fields, the time for leaving was so close, and Alex announced that he was going—alone.

"Taylor needs every Texan he can get," he said.

"You can't go," Cassandra cried, panic-stricken, knowing with a terrible gut-wrenching surety that he'd die if she allowed him to fight this war. The ominous sense of *déjà vu* was upon her. She'd had this same appalling premonition before Counts Many Coup led his last war party out of camp, but then she had ignored her own fears. She hadn't tried hard enough to keep him home. And he'd died, just as she believed Alex would.

"It's war, Cassandra."

"War? How can you talk about war? You have a wife and two children." *Three children*, she thought.

"All the more reason to go. A man who won't fight for his family is a pretty poor man."

"That war's not about safety. It's about land and who gets some godforsaken strip of desert down on the border."

"Well, it's our godforsaken strip," Alex muttered.

"You'll be killed!" She couldn't believe it. She'd forgone the chance to get Alexandra back in order to keep Alex safe, and now he intended to go off and get himself killed for some patch of worthless Mexican desert.

"Cassandra, you're overreacting," said Alex. "I won't be killed." He tried to put his arms around her, and she jerked away.

"Alex, believe me, I *know*. If you fight in this war

you'll die. You'll never come back." Her eyes were filling with tears.

"Cassie, sweetheart, that's crazy. I've been in more fights than I can count, and nothing's ever happened to me."

"Alex, I beg you—"

"Alex has never passed up a war in his life," said Eloise. "Did you really think he'd start because of you?"

"Stay out of this, Eloise," Alex snapped, his face flushed. "I'll be back before you know it, sweetheart."

"What about Benjamin? What about Justin? They're so little. If you don't care about me, think of your sons. They won't even remember you. It'll be as if they never had a father at all. Do you want that? You missed the first months of Benjamin's life—"

"Cass, that's not fair. You know I—"

"Now you'll miss all the rest. And for what?"

"If you can't understand—"

"Understand? I understand that you don't care enough—"

"Cassandra, I have an obligation. This is my state, my country, my fight. And those rangers down on the border are men I've fought with before. They're like brothers. I can't let them down."

"Let them down?" she echoed bitterly. "They can die just as easily without you as with you, Alex. But the children and I—how are we to live without you?"

Alex sighed impatiently. "I'm not going to die, Cassie. I'll be home before summer's end. You'll see."

Cassandra saw, as clearly as if she were back in the Comanche camp, the warriors bringing back the corpse of her husband. How could she face it again? To see Alex—cold in his own blood. "Please, Alex," she whispered.

"You're wasting your breath," said Eloise.

"Sweetheart, if you were asking anything else of me, you know I'd—"

She felt a great hopelessness sweep over her. He wasn't going to listen. "I'll never forgive you if you leave," she whispered. The tears were streaming down her face. "You can't. You just can't go."

But he did, and Cassandra watched him ride away, leaving her where she had never wanted to be. All her plans, her months of patient waiting, and he'd left without her. He wouldn't be here for Benjamin's birthday—the date he'd chosen himself. He'd never see his daughter when she came home. If she came home. *I might as well have sent him to look for her*, thought Cassandra bitterly. *And I never kissed him good-bye. We never made love again*. She wept inconsolably.

Chapter Twenty-Three

Word spread along the river that a battle had been fought on the Rio Grande, and Cassandra, terrified, wondered if her husband had arrived in time to fight with Taylor's army? Had he been killed? She couldn't imagine life without Alex, while he, obviously, could easily enjoy life without her.

"He's fought in every skirmish and war since '32 when he first came to Texas," said Eloise. "And now that you've besmirched his name—"

"Be quiet, Eloise."

"I suppose he married you because you were the only white female out there."

"He married me because he loved me. Do you really think he'd have spent nine months tracking me through *Comancheria* if he didn't?"

"You were carrying his child. What else could he do? But now, Cassandra, it's time that you repaid him by considering the welfare of his children."

"I am. I'm keeping *you* away from them."

"But that's wrong. They love me," said Eloise, "and I love them. Surely you can see that they'd be better off with me."

"What are you talking about?" Cassandra had the chilling premonition that the motives behind Eloise's baffling hostility were about to be revealed.

"As long as *you're* here, Cassandra," said Eloise in an unusually gentle and reasonable tone, "Justin will be an outcast. People will remember your Indian captivity and the shadow on his birth, but if you leave—"

"Without him?" Cold fingers crept up Cassandra's spine. Was that what Eloise wanted?

"And Benjamin. With you here at Devil's Wood, people can't forget that he was born out of wedlock, but if you leave, they will." Her smile radiated kindness. "And I'll take good care of the babies. You know I will."

She wants my children!

"And you have to consider Alex. He'll be fighting duels for the rest of his life if you don't go away."

She's been planning to get rid of me all along, and I never realized it.

"Benjamin and Justin will inherit Devil's Wood when Alex and I are gone, but you hate it here, Cassandra. You know you do. You'll be so much happier in Massachusetts among your own kind."

Happier without Alex? Without the children? Did Eloise really believe that?

"If you think about it, you'll see that I'm right."

When had she settled on this plan? When she first decided that Justin wasn't a half-breed? Or maybe the first time she held Benjamin in her arms.

"Please, Cassandra. You must do the right thing. For everyone's sake."

Cassandra stared at her sister-in-law, too stunned to answer.

Docked at Harte's landing, the *Mary Elaine* brought news of a second battle between Taylor and Arista. Cassandra went weak with relief because there was no word of Alex's death. However, the messenger who came to the house bore a special message for Cassandra. "Ma'am," he said, "Captain Ralph Hawkins bade me tell you he'd found not so much as a rumor among the Comanches. Didn't say what he meant, but I suppose you'll know. Not so much as a rumor, he said, and he was sorry for it."

Cassandra's heart sank. She did understand the message. No one knew of a white baby given to a Comanche woman named Singing Bird a year ago. From the upper gallery she stared bleakly at the riverboat which had brought such disheartening intelligence. Her daughter seemed farther away than ever, and her husband still in danger.

I've got to get Alex away from that war, Cassandra decided when she'd thought over the news from the southern border. And then suddenly, now that she was no longer tied to Devil's Wood by the hope of word about her daughter, Cassandra knew how to secure the safety of her husband. If she could lure him away from the border, her premonition of his death would be voided. She had seen him dying in battle. If he fought no battles, he'd live, and her plan would solve the problem of Eloise as well.

She hurried down to the stables to consult Ruben, then held whispered conferences with Mellie, Esther, and Randall. "You don't have to go with me," she told each of Sarah's children. Eloise wanted her to leave? Well, she would, but she'd take the children, all six of them if they were willing.

"You can stay here. If Alex doesn't come for us, we'd have to go to Massachusetts, and you might not like it there." But Cassandra didn't believe that her husband would let her go. He might have foolish male notions about wars and the obligation to fight in them, but he did love her. He would come after her. Nor did she believe that her four black children would want to stay behind. As for Alexandra, once she had access to her inheritance, Cassandra could hire people to search for the baby.

"How we gonna git away?" asked Ruben.

"We'll be on the *Mary Elaine* when it leaves tomorrow morning," said Cassandra.

"You got any money, Miz Cassie?" asked Mellie. "Mus' cost a lotta money to go on the big boat."

Money was a problem. "I'll use Devil's Wood credit," said Cassandra, hoping that Captain Wiggins would agree. "Once we get to Velasco, I'll use my own." Again she hoped that would be possible. She had very little money on hand.

"Miz Eloise not gonna let us go," said Randall.

"We'll pack and leave after she's asleep." Cassandra still had a sleeping potion the doctor had given her after Justin's birth. Eloise would sleep deeply tonight and late tomorrow, too late to stop their escape.

"I wanna go," said Esther, her eyes shining. "I wouldn't even mind seein' Massachusetts. What's it like, Miz Cassie?"

"Cold," said Cassandra, shivering at the thought of a life without Alex but praying that wouldn't happen.

My dearest husband,

Since you left, Eloise has insisted again and again that the children can never be safe from gossip unless I leave Devil's Wood. In one respect, I believe that she is right. There can be no life for them here, not when Benjamin is thought to be illegitimate and Justin a half-breed. She was, however, wrong in thinking that I could be parted from them or convinced to leave them in her hands.

Because your conscience dictates that you be away from us in these trying circumstances, I feel it best that the children and I leave. I shall take the boat down river to Velasco and thence to Galveston, where I hope in good time to find passage to Massachusetts. It is my dearest wish that sometime in the future, when your military duties leave you free for family concerns, we will see you again. Until then I remain most lovingly and respectfully yours,

Cassandra Whitney Harte

Alex was a mule-headed man, but if he didn't get the message in that letter, he was more dense than she thought. Cassandra made two copies. One she would leave with Gemmalee to give to Alex if he returned to Devil's Wood. The other she would address to him in care of General Taylor's army and send by whatever means she could find when she was on the boat—if she made it that far. Surely one or the other would get to him and convince him that neither wartime adventures nor mistaken concerns for her safety were reason enough to risk losing his wife and children permanently.

As soon as the boat left the dock, Cassandra's heart lifted. Just being away from the hostile atmosphere at Devil's Wood produced a sense of euphoria. She couldn't believe the escape had gone so easily. A half hour after Eloise drank the coffee Cassandra poured for her, she was yawning. An hour after that, all the servants but Cassandra's had gone to the quarters so that she, Randall, and Esther could pack while Mellie and Ruben carried trunks and packages to the landing. Since she never intended to return, Cassandra took everything that was hers, including her whole wardrobe and all the wedding and baby presents she had received. Before dawn the seven of them were waiting on the wharf to embark. Cassandra simply told Captain Wiggins that she was going to meet Alex, which she hoped would be true. The captain didn't ask her to pay; he assumed that her expenses would be charged to the plantation account.

Where once she had watched the shores of the Brazos passing by with a sense of unease as she was carried down river to Devil's Wood, now she watched

Elizabeth Chadwick

with delight as she steamed away. It was Benjamin's birthday, the fifteenth of May, the beginning of a wonderful new life—or so she hoped.

"You know how long ago they left?" Ondine asked. "Or how they got away?"

"I only know they're gone," cried Eloise. "She's taken the babies from me, and you have to get them back."

"Any horses missin'? A carriage? She didn't walk."

"The riverboat," said Eloise. "She must have taken the *Mary Elaine*. It tied up at our dock for wood yesterday, but it was gone this morning."

"Maybe," said Ondine. "That means she's got a seven-hour lead on me if they left at dawn. Did she have money?"

"No." Eloise looked distraught. "I don't know. You've got to bring the babies back. I don't care about the rest of them. In fact, you're not to let her return. Convince her to keep going. Give her money if she needs it."

"Oh, I imagine I kin see to it she stays away without givin' her nothin'—money anyways," said Ondine, his smile venomous.

"Good. Fine. Just get the babies back. And I don't want the four slaves either. Once you get the babies, you'll have to hire someone to take care of them, a wet nurse for the little one. Nothing must happen to the babies. You understand that?"

"Don't you worry, Miz Eloise. I'll take care of ever'thing. It'll be a pleasure."

"The babies, that's what's important. They're mine."

Captain Wiggins had put her in a luxurious stateroom, assuring her that nothing was too good for the families of the men who were defending Texas and the United States against Mexico. Cassandra didn't

mention that she thought Alex had volunteered in order to indulge his passion for war and to escape the
rigors of life with feuding females. She smiled gra-
ciously and accepted the cabin, pleased to think that
the bill would ultimately be presented to Eloise.

"Oh, you do look beautiful, Miz Cassie," said Mellie.
"Esther, pull out the tray from the black trunk an'
fetch me the net for Miz Cassie's hair."

Cassandra's company at dinner had been solicited
by a number of gallant gentlemen, and she planned
to amuse herself by flirting with them all. She hoped
Alex would hear about every smile she doled out; a
little jealousy would make him think twice about leaving her in the future. "Pin the stole a little tighter,
Mellie. I don't want it to slip and reveal the scar."

"A hundred men gonna lose their hearts to you tonight, Miz Cassie."

"Good." Cassandra picked up her fan and gloves.
"I'll be back before Justin wakes up."

"Don't you worry. We keep him happy with sugah
watah if you not back in time."

Minutes later Cassandra entered the elaborate dining room, fan fluttering. She had seen the Southern
belles plying their fans. There was nothing to it, although why men should be enchanted by a woman
peeking at them from behind a fan, she didn't know.
"Good evening, Mr. Holyrod."

"Ma'am." A planter's son from below Brazoria
bowed deeply. "There's to be a band tonight. I hope
you'll favor me with a dance."

"I'm sure I'd be delighted, Mr. Holyrod."

The more she heard about Velasco, the more Cassandra thought she might extend her stay there so that
she could sample the delights of the place—the oyster
shanties, the bathing facilities, the horse racing, and
the gambling. She'd told the susceptible Mr. Holyrod
that she "just loved gaming," neglecting to mention
that her experience had been gained kneeling in the

dirt, playing the hand game with the *Tanima*. Perhap
she'd prove lucky again and win some money in Ve
lasco. Until she could call on her Massachusetts funds
she'd need it. In the meantime she'd have to stay wit
the Barretts, who had begged her to visit when the
stood godparents to Justin. And the longer she delaye
in Velasco, the easier it would be for Alex to catch up
Always assuming that he wanted to.

"How gallant you are, Mr. Menzies," she murmure
to another admirer who had presented her with a bou
quet of flowers. Where in the world had he got them
Did the captain keep bouquets on board for amorou
gentlemen?

Cassandra lay very still, listening. The stateroor
was dark, no sounds at all, yet something had awak
ened her. "Mellie?" she whispered softly so as not t
awaken the babies. Mellie was a light sleeper, yet sh
didn't answer. Could she have slipped out? Perhap
the sound of the door closing after her had interrupte
Cassandra's sleep. Were she not so tired, she migh
have risen and fumbled in the dark for the lamp. In
stead, she turned in her bed and snuggled down t
sleep again. There was nothing to fear. No one coul
get onto the *Mary Elaine* when it stopped for the nigh
without the posted crewman seeing them, and tucke
under her mattress, easily accessible, was the Colt rif
Alex had given her—how long ago? Just about tw
years. *The further I am from Devil's Wood, the safer w
are*, she thought and closed her eyes.

She slipped back into a restless sleep, dreaming c
rustlings in the darkness, only to be awakened late
by a bloom of light shining through her eyelids and
voice saying, "Reckon I'm ready for you now, Cassie."

Cassandra blinked, and Ondine appeared before he
eyes like an ugly mirage. For a moment she though
she might be dreaming, but then she saw that Melli
and Esther were tied and gagged. So was Benjamir

struggling pathetically against his bonds, his little face red and tearstained. "What have you done to him?" Cassandra gasped.

"He's fine," said Ondine callously. "He ain't happy, but he ain't hurt none. As for the little one—" he glanced at Justin, who was still sleeping in a cradle beside Cassandra's bed "—the half-breed, as long as he don't wake up an' howl, he'll be fine. Miss Eloise, she don't want the babies hurt. She jus' wants 'em back, but she don't care about the rest of you." He gave Cassandra a cruel grin that made her fingers go cold. "Where's the boy? The one I caught a while back when you shot me?" He waved the pistol casually at her. "You're gonna pay for that. You know? You're gonna wish you never set yerself crosswise of Ondine. Now, where's the boy?"

"Gone," said Cassandra. "He ran away when we got to Brazoria." She could see the eyes of Ruben's sisters widen in surprise and hoped that Ondine wouldn't notice. Ruben and Randall had berths in the hold, but she knew Ruben looked in on them periodically during the night. *Let him come now*, she prayed. *All I need is a distraction.*

"That the truth?" Ondine asked suspiciously, then answered his own question. "Yeah, it figgers he'd run away. Even havin' hisself a white woman wouldn't be enough, would it? Too bad I ain't got time to have a sample myself, but then I'm not sure I'd wanna have a woman who don't care what color man she lays with."

Cassandra felt a hysterical desire to laugh. Ondine thought he was insulting her, when in reality he was affording her relief from horror.

"I wasn't sure jus' what I was gonna do with you until I seen all the stuff you got in here. Best thing would be to make it look like you got off at Pate's Landing, an' now I see jus' how I'm gonna do that." He studied the two girls. "Which one a you girls wants

409

Elizabeth Chadwick

to come along with me? No sense my payin' good money for a nursemaid. As for you, Cassie, you better start prayin' 'cause you're goin' overboard."

Overboard? He probably thought she couldn't swim and would drown, but he was wrong. She'd swim to shore and get help. Even if he took the babies, she'd get them back.

"Think I'll take you," he said, pointing to Mellie. "You're the most scairt. So you—" he pointed to Esther. "Over by the trunk." Grasping the girl's arm, his pistol against her head, he dragged her forward. "Now, stand still whilst I open it," he ordered.

Was he looking for money or jewelry? Cassandra wondered.

"All right, climb in."

Trembling, Esther obeyed. Then Ondine slammed the trunk lid closed on Esther. "Good thing the boy took off. Don't have no trunk for him. Gonna be hard stuffin' you in that big un, Cassie."

"What are you—"

"I'm gonna lower you an' all your belongin's an' your other girl down nice an' quiet into the water, an' while you're drownin', this one an' me'll take off with the babies. Pretty smart, hu-u?"

Cassandra thought of being put into the water, locked into that trunk and helpless. Oh God.

"Now you slide outa that bed nice an' quiet like." He came toward her and pointed the pistol at Justin. "Reckon if I gotta kill one a your babies, Miz Eloise'd rather it be the breed. Don' know why she wants him anyways."

With a gun pointed at Justin's head, Cassandra couldn't risk reaching for the rifle, yet it was her last chance. Once she was away from the bed, she wouldn't be able to get it.

"Move," snapped Ondine.

The pistol in his hand wasn't a multishot revolving mechanism; at least she didn't think so. If, once she

410

was off the bed, she threw herself in front of the gun, he couldn't shoot the baby. He'd have to shoot her, and the sound would bring help. It was the only choice she had, short of meekly climbing into a trunk and drowning with Esther while Ondine took the children. She had a feeling that Justin would never make it back to Devil's Wood alive, not in Ondine's care.

"Move or I shoot the kid."

As Cassandra threw back her sheet, the door flew open. Ondine's head swiveled, and Cassandra dove at him, grappling for the gun. When they collided, the pistol flew from his hand. "Get it," she cried to Ruben, even as Ondine's hands closed over her throat.

"Leave the gun or I'll kill her," Ondine rapped out, his fingers tightening. Cassandra's wind was cut off although her lungs still struggled to draw in air.

I've only a minute, she thought desperately. She raised her fingers, clawing for his eyes, and he had to release her throat to grasp her wrists before she blinded him. "Ruben!" she cried and saw that the boy was there, the gun against Ondine's head. She heard the click, but it didn't fire. *Oh God,* she thought. *I could have got to my rifle if I'd known his pistol would misfire.* She threw herself against Ondine, knocking him from his feet so that they both went sprawling. "The rifle," she called to Ruben just before her head hit the stout leg of the bed. Even as the blackness closed in, she heard an explosion.

Cassandra regained consciousness to a cacophony of howling babies, shouting men, twittering women, and weeping girls. Her head ached abominably, worse when she opened her eyes than when she kept them closed. "She's coming to," various voices cried, the sound making her wince.

"Can you tell me what happened, Mrs. Harte?" asked Captain Wiggins.

"The slave catcher," she said weakly. "He was trying to kidnap the babies."

She could hear the horrified voices. "A slave catcher?"..."After white babies?"..."String him up."

"Where's Ruben?" she asked.

"Your boy is in custody, ma'am," said Captain Wiggins. "He shot a white man."

"Esther and I would have been at the bottom of the river, locked in our own trunks, if it weren't for Ruben."

Amid the murmurs of horror, she heard Mr. Holyrod say that he intended to give Ruben a fine reward.

Good, thought Cassandra, *since I've no money to do it. But maybe later I can give Ruben his freedom.*

The last day on the boat, Cassandra met a Major Meredith Ross who was on his way to join General Taylor. To him Cassandra entrusted a copy of her letter to Alex. Major Ross expected to reach his destination within two days. If he did and found Alex immediately, Alex might arrive in Velasco before week's end. In the meantime, Cassandra had begun to feel awkward about imposing herself on the Barretts even though they'd urged her to visit.

Her worries, however, proved unnecessary because she had no sooner stepped off the boat in Velasco than she found herself in Effie Barrett's arms being consoled over her terrifying experience. The news of Ondine's attack had preceded the boat down river and caused a stir in Velasco.

Cassandra and her entourage were whisked by carriage to the Barretts' large frame house, which was already overflowing with guests who had come for the racing season. The wealthy planters drove plow horses hitched to big-wheeled carriages over the muddy, stump-obstructed roads of Texas so that they could race their own thoroughbreds or bet on their friends' horses at the Newmarket Course.

Cassandra was caught up immediately in the excitement. She attended a ball that very night at which she danced and promenaded and sampled the lavish midnight buffet. At dawn the younger members of the group, led by the indefatigable Effie, rode down to the oyster shacks on the gulf for a breakfast feast of fresh shellfish. Cassandra was enchanted by the miles of sand beaches and the gentle rolling breakers that confronted her as she ate oysters and flirted with Mr. Holyrod, who had followed her to Velasco instead of getting off at his own landing.

"He's smitten," Effie assured Cassandra.

"Then he's wasting his time. Alex will arrive any day."

"Oh, my dear Cassie, I pray you won't be disappointed. Everyone knows how Alex loves a war. It's not likely he'll leave before it's over."

He'd better, thought Cassandra, *or he'll have a long journey to get me back.*

"But, my dear, you can stay with us the whole time. We've a bathhouse of our own," Effie revealed temptingly, "and can go to the sea any afternoon. It's *so-o* healthful."

"Miss Cassandra, we're going to have a race on the beach," called Mr. Holyrod. "I hope you'll give me a favor to bring my horse luck."

"Is he a good horse?" asked Cassandra.

"The best," Mr. Holyrod assured her.

"Then I'll do better than a favor, Mr. Holyrod. I'll ride him myself."

"Oh, my dear Miss—" Holyrod stumbled to a stop, unable to find a proper response to such an unusual suggestion. "I wouldn't dream of asking."

"Why, Mr. Holyrod, I do believe you've no confidence in my ability to win for you."

"Not at all, Miss Cassandra, it's just—just—"

Elizabeth Chadwick

Effie Barrett was giggling. "Ronald, you're fairly caught. You'll have to let Cassandra ride or lose her good opinion and that of all the other ladies. Now, what handicap shall Cassandra have since she must ride sidesaddle?"

"I'll do no such thing, Effie. I rode astride for over a year with Alex and then with the Comanches, and I shall ride astride today. Your brother can lend me trousers. He looks to be about my size."

"Oh, what a scandal!" Effie cried delightedly. "We'll be the talk of the town."

Mr. Holyrod looked somewhat reluctant, but the race was set for ten that morning. The feasters left their piles of empty shells and went to summon all their friends while Cassandra assembled her riding clothes.

"Captain Harte, I've a message for you from your sister on the Brazos."

Alex, who had been on patrol with a ranger company, slipped wearily from his horse. "From my sister? Is there no word from my wife?"

"In a manner of speaking, sir. Mrs. Daumier says your wife has taken the babies and run off and you'd best come home at once."

"Cassandra has *left*?" Alex pulled off his hat and wiped his brow. "Left for where?"

"Mrs. Daumier don't know, sir, but she says you'd best get home."

Cassandra nursed Justin, cuddled both babies, and then availed herself of Sam Hardin's wardrobe. She chose fawn trousers, a full-sleeved white silk shirt, a gold and brown embroidered vest, and a wide-brimmed tan hat, plus Sam's best leather riding boots, for Effie's brother had small feet. Thus scandalously attired, she returned to the beach to inspect the horse of Albert Camp, against which she was to race. De-

414

ciding that she might never find a better opportunity to win money, she wagered half of what she had with Mr. Camp, who could hardly refuse to bet on his own horse. Cassandra's offer stirred up a fever of betting, and, the odds going against her, she laid one-quarter of her remaining resources.

She knew that some of the ladies were looking at her askance, but she had had enough of toadying to Southern gentility. "Well, Mr. Camp," she said, "we shall see whether a Southern-bred male jockey can beat a Comanche-trained female jockey. It will be an interesting experiment, will it not?"

She sprang astride her horse, only momentarily disconcerted by the unusual feel of the saddle—so different from the one she had used on her white Comanche mare—then turned the creature's head to the starting line. She could see that Mr. Camp's jockey, a young cousin of his from Columbia, considered it beneath him to race against a woman. *More the fool he*, she thought. *Since he rates his chances so high, perhaps he'll ride a careless race.* Once she'd won this contest, she had variations to propose, tricks she had picked up from the Comanches, things she had practiced with Little Wolf when he was learning horsemanship from his grandfather. Oh, Mr. Camp and his condescending cousin had some surprises in store, and so did those gentlemen who were betting against her.

"The finishing line shall be that flag we've placed down the beach," said Camp, "and you'll start here at the sound of the pistol."

Cassandra crouched in her saddle, having shortened the stirrups. Around her she could hear the shocked twitterings of the ladies and the amused remarks of the gentlemen. "By God," said one, "this may be the best spring season yet. If she does even reasonably well on the beach, we can get her to ride at the track. Think of the novelty!"

"Think of the duel you'd have to fight when her

husband gets back from the war. Alex Harte may not take to the idea of his wife wearing trousers and riding like a man."

"I wish more women would wear them. I've never seen a prettier derriere, nor one displayed to better advantage."

Cassandra, trying to concentrate all her attention on the sound of the starting gun, could have done without the remarks about her derriere. Nor did she relish the idea that Alex might feel called upon to fight a duel. And where was he? She counted off the days and realized that it was too early for his return. Well, in the meantime she'd make some money, which they could put to whatever venture they took on to replace Devil's Wood as a livelihood.

Hadn't Alex's father been a commission merchant in cotton? Caldicott Barrett was a cotton factor and was obviously doing very well since he could support his extravagant young wife in such grand style. Still, if Alex had wanted to be a cotton factor, he could have stayed in New Orleans. Whatever suggestion she made would have to be more adventurous, something that had all the appeal of war but less danger and more money.

The gun sounded, and Cassandra dug her heels into Ronald Holyrod's horse. She leaned forward over the mane, whispering praise in his ear while she urged him forward with her knees and heels. Camp's cousin was already using the whip although he was neither ahead nor behind. Foolish, Cassandra thought. She wouldn't go to the whip unless she was losing.

"Run, you beauty," she whispered into his ear and felt the horse surge. He understood. He was like a good Comanche pony, tireless and all heart, a horse who knew he was part of his rider. She could no longer see the nose of Camp's gelding but never looked back. The flag was ahead, and she dug in her heels, her upper body flattened onto the horse's mane. Then the banner flowed by, no competitor beside her, and she went loose in the saddle, whispering softly, "Beautiful, beautiful horse," as they slowed to a stop and circled back to a throng of admiring sportsmen.

"By God, Miss Cassie, you ride like a goddess," cried one of her young admirers.

"Like a damned Indian," muttered Camp, who was glaring at his discomfited cousin.

"Ah, but I'm not an Indian, Mr. Camp, just a sometime and reluctant guest of the *Tanima*," said Cassandra, "and I do believe you've lost some money to me." Cassandra remembered every bet she'd made and the odds at which she'd made it, and she collected on the spot, laughing with such delight that her debtors could hardly take offense at their losses. "I've two children and four Nigrahs to support while my husband is off defending the country," said Cassandra cheerfully. "Just consider your losses a contribution to the war effort."

"'Twas just a fluke, cousin," she heard the opposing jockey say to Mr. Camp. "She'd never manage it again."

"Why, sir, I'd be more than glad to give you a rematch if Mr. Holyrod is willing to let his horse run again."

"Done," cried Holyrod, who had bet on Cassandra out of gallantry and made a good deal of money. "And we must get Efraim Baines to attend. He's the best judge of horseflesh and riders among the old three hundred." The next beach race was set for the following morning.

"I wonder what Alex will think of all this?" Cassandra murmured to her delighted hostess, Effie Barrett.

"Oh, men never think a woman should do anything but sit home embroidering and having babies. You have to train them as I have Caldicott. I declare, he's almost come to enjoy my outrageous conduct, although when we were first married, he gave me endless dull lectures on propriety. Of course, while we were courting, I was the quintessential demure miss. And speaking of demure misses, our amateur theatrical society is doing *Hamlet* next week. I don't suppose you'd care to play Ophelia?"

"Ophelia's a ninny."

"Well, then, take Gertrude, and I'll do Ophelia, though goodness knows how I'll learn the lines."

"Aren't you leaving it a little late?"

"Our Ophelia eloped last week with a Yankee ship captain who put into Galveston—a Roman Catholic no less. Can you imagine? Oh, dear, you aren't Roman Catholic, are you? For all I know, all Yankees are Roman Catholics. But that's all right as long as you'll play Gertrude."

"Of course I will. I'll even prompt you if you forget Ophelia's lines."

"You know both parts?" Then she answered herself. "Of course you do. Caldicott told me about your wonderful quotation party where you made such a fool of that obnoxious Englishman. And Cray Williamson of Galveston never stopped singing your praises when he passed through. His wife said if more women were as well educated and quick-witted, we wouldn't be relegated to gossip and embroidery."

"I can't say that I noticed Mrs. Williamson doing either when they visited," said Cassandra dryly, but she was pleased. Alice Williamson had been a sharp-tongued, extremely intelligent woman whose good opinion Cassandra valued now that she knew of it. How fine it was to get away from Eloise and her criticism and contempt.

What kind of woman deserts her husband when he's fighting a war? Alex wondered bitterly. He'd been riding for hours, stopping to trade horses wherever he could. Perhaps it was some trick of Eloise's. She wanted him back at Devil's Wood and was using Cassandra to get him there. Cassandra might have gone to visit a neighbor, and Eloise—well, there was no use speculating. He'd find out soon enough, but if this was some ploy of his sister's, he'd—he'd—he didn't know what he'd do.

Chapter Twenty-Four

On the second morning Cassandra raced and won again. She also met Mr. Ephraim Baines, a white-bearded gentleman, hardly her height, thin and dapper. Mr. Baines said, "My dear, were I forty years younger, I should steal you from the estimable Captain Harte. As it is, I shall have to settle for the pleasure of your company during the racing season."

Cassandra became his protégée. They attended the races at the Newmarket Course together, handicapping the horses and betting larger and larger amounts. Without asking, Mr. Baines seemed to know that Cassandra needed the money and advised her knowledgeably. Mornings, he produced other horses for her to ride in the beach races and encouraged her taste for madcap events that involved riding half the course hanging over the side of the horse or scooping up objects while riding at full speed. The impromptu races drew larger and larger crowds as the days went by.

"You're a prodigious fine gambler, Miss Cassandra," said one of the young men. "Are all Yankees so venturesome and so lucky?"

"I learned to gamble among the Comanches," Cassandra replied. "I'd have frozen to death or starved if I hadn't been good at it. Fortunately, I was and won a deerskin wardrobe, a buffalo robe, and dried meat to see me through the winter. Shall I teach you to play?"

"No, indeed," exclaimed the young man. "I've lost

a fair amount in coin to you, dear lady. I've no desire to lose my wardrobe and my dinner as well."

Cassandra looked him over, then laughing replied, "I don't believe your clothes would fit me anyway, sir."

"You're welcome to ride with us, Captain Harte," said the keelboat owner.

"Many thanks, friend," Alex replied, "but a horse is faster—going upstream at any rate."

Ronald Holyrod became sulky as he found his influence superseded by that of Ephraim Baines, a man old enough to be his grandfather. He was especially hurt at an event where the young men and women held auctions, bidding upon members of the opposite sex, who then had to act as slaves to those who won them. Cassandra arrived too late to be bid upon herself, although Mr. Holyrod had been prepared to expend a great deal of money to make her his slave for an afternoon. Then during the ladies' bidding, Cassandra took no part and disappointed him further. He subsequently transferred his attentions to an unmarried lady from Independence.

What could have happened? Alex wondered for the hundredth time. The questions helped to keep him awake when he was swaying in his saddle, exhausted. Had Eloise made Cassandra's life so miserable that she couldn't bear to stay at Devil's Wood? Cass was no longer an easily frightened, thin-skinned girl; it was hard to imagine that his sister could drive her away if she were determined to remain.

Which might mean that he himself had been the cause of her departure. He knew she had not wanted him to volunteer, but surely she hadn't been so angry that she'd leave him—without even giving him a chance to defend himself. What if she no longer loved him? What if she hadn't loved him in all the time since he'd taken her back from the Comanches?

During the long hours as he rode toward Devil's Wood, he realized that he knew hardly anything about her experiences during those months of captivity. His own guilt had kept him from asking. Maybe she resented his lack of concern. Maybe she resented being forced to live in a slave society when she hated the institution. Because it was an institution he himself took for granted, he had never given her feelings on slavery serious consideration.

Or maybe she resented his lack of support in her troubles with Eloise. But he'd been so busy—pursuing success in tasks that bored him. And he'd persevered for her sake. Didn't she realize that? It wasn't fair of her to leave him when everything he'd done had been for her welfare. Except the war, of course. But it wasn't as if he'd left her destitute. Thousands, no, millions of women would be glad to have the easy life he'd given Cassandra. So why had she left him?

Some afternoons when there was no race at Newmarket, Cassandra attended ladies' events, among them an excursion to the Barretts' bathhouse. As she was changing into one of the heavy, all-encompassing bathing costumes, the young lady beside her displayed an object she had crocheted from the hair of her fiancé. "Surely you have something crocheted or tatted from the hair of a loved one," she exclaimed when Cassandra asked about the custom.

"No," Cassandra replied, "but I've been offered a scalp or two." She no longer tried to hide her Comanche sojourn. She spoke of it freely, although many of the ladies professed to be shocked.

"Oh, Cassie, do you have one—a scalp?" Effie Barrett asked eagerly. "How I envy you your adventures."

The young lady who tatted with human hair was staring at the scar on Cassandra's shoulder.

"Even my encounter with a Comanche lance?" Cassandra retorted, touching the scar.

"How did it happen?" Effie demanded, unabashed.

"They killed all in our party and left me for dead. Alex rescued me." Where *was* Alex? Six days had passed since she sent the second note. He should be here by now. Surely he was coming. Surely he cared more for her and the children than he did for that war with Mexico.

Disheartened, she followed the others out to splash around in the water. Once soaked, the cumbersome outfits became so heavy that by afternoon's end, Cassandra felt more like napping than performing the extended toilette necessary for that night's masquerade ball. The banquet featured a whole roast pig, and was followed by dancing to a hired orchestra containing accordions, a piano, flutes, and violins. The champagne, the juleps, and the fine brandies flowed. Then, much to Cassandra's surprise, the kissing games commenced.

"Oh, Cassie, you're not leaving," Effie cried when Cassandra lifted her full hoop skirts and prepared to climb the stairs.

Cassandra shrugged. She had enjoyed the music and the romantic glow of the candles, the cotillions and minuets, even a little innocent flirting, but she had no desire to kiss or be kissed by anyone but Alex. Where was he? Her heart ached for him, and Benjamin continued to ask hopefully for "Dada" each night when she put him to bed before flitting off to another ball. How could Alex have left them?

Alex rode into Devil's Wood late at night, coming through the slave quarters and rousing the people to ask questions.

"She's gone fo sure, Marse Alex," said Joseph. "Her an' the lil ones and Sarah's four chillun. Slipped away

in the night an' tookin' the *Mary Elaine* down river
Das what us figgers."

As Alex led his horse up the road toward the plantation house, Gemmalee slipped from between the
trees and whispered his name. "Got a writin' fo you
from Miz Cassie." She tucked it into his hand. "Don'
tell no one, specially not Miz Eloise. No one know I
had it."

Alex stared curiously at the seamstress. What the
hell was going on here? A message from Cassandra
about which Eloise knew nothing? Which Gemmalee
feared punishment for delivering? He pocketed the
paper, his fingers brushing over the wax seal. "My
thanks, Gemmalee," he murmured. "I'll say nothing."

Once in the house, he lit a candle in an ornate
holder, broke the seal, and read his wife's farewell
note. *I shall take the boat down river to Velasco and
thence to Galveston, where I hope in good time to find
passage to Massachusetts.* How long was it since her
departure? Could he catch her before she set sail for
Boston? She felt that he had left her vulnerable to a
woman who wished to steal her children. Dear God!
How could Eloise have given her such an idea? His
eyes skipped down to the closing. *I remain most lovingly and respectfully yours.* Words. Polite words. Was
she truly his any longer?

"Who's there?"

He looked up the stairs to see his sister, candle held
high, her robes flowing around her small body.

"Alex?" She began to descend. "You took your time.
She's kidnapped the children and run off. With some
man, I imagine."

"Really?" He didn't believe that. "What man?"

"How do I know? I've sent Ondine after them. He'll
bring the children back."

"Ondine?" Alex roared. "He hates her. He's threatened her before."

"He'll get the babies back," Eloise murmured. "I expect him any day now."

"And what do you expect him to do about Cassandra?"

Eloise shrugged. "It's your sons you need to worry about. What kind of life would they have with her here to remind everyone of—"

"—of all the scandal you spread?" Alex could hardly contain his fury. "If anything happens to Cassandra, you'll pay, Eloise. By God, I'll have you thrown in jail."

"She's the one who should be arrested. She kidnapped the children."

"They're her children!"

"They don't need her. I can bring them up."

"So you really did drive her away deliberately?"

"She was supposed to leave the children. She understood that. She—"

"Well, she's gone. You succeeded that far, Eloise. But you'll never see Benjamin or Justin again. Or me either. In about ten minutes I'll leave as well."

"You can't," said Eloise smugly. "You own half of Devil's Wood, and you have your sons' inheritance to think of. You have to run the plantation. Just as I have to raise the babies—so the land can be passed on in the family."

"Not my family—I'm going to sell my half."

Eloise turned pale.

"You're your own worst enemy, Eloise. You could have been friends with Cass instead of trying to drive her away and take her children."

"I deserve children," said Eloise in a faltering voice. "They're my last chance. Once I realized that the little one wasn't a half-breed, I knew what I had to do. I knew they were meant for me."

"By God, Eloise, are there no limits to your selfishness? Look at how many people you've made miserable trying to get what you wanted."

"I don't know what you mean," she cried. "It's other people who've ruined *my* life."

"Nonsense. You married a man you didn't even *like* because you coveted his social position and way of life, and the result was that you ruined his life and your own, not to mention breaking our father's heart."

"Father never loved me."

"He adored you."

"He left his money to you."

"He gave you a huge dowry, which you and Jean Philippe frittered away, you on clothes and high living, Jean Philippe on gambling. Father worked hard for his money. He didn't want to see any more of it thrown away."

"Too bad he didn't live to see you give it to Sam Houston," she snarled.

"No one believed more in freedom than Father. He put his life on the line against the British in New Orleans, in case you've forgotten. And he'd have done what I did and fought against Mexico."

"You had no right. Half of that money should have been mine. Now it's all gone for land I don't want. And if you'd stayed with me, Miranda wouldn't have died."

"Miranda was your responsibility and Jean Philippe's. You wouldn't even have Devil's Wood if I hadn't gone to war, and after that, you'd probably have lost it for debt if I hadn't run it, which I never wanted to do. You married Jean Philippe with the idea of using him, and when that didn't work, you used me. God knows what you'd have done to your own children if they'd lived, and when they didn't, you were perfectly willing to wreck Cassandra's life and mine to get your hands on our children. And what good did it do you, Eloise? You've made everyone close to you miserable, and you've nothing left."

"I have Devil's Wood," she replied, her back stiffening. "And I can take care of myself."

"Can you?" Alex sighed. "Maybe you should consider marrying Cutter."

"Never."

"The man loves you. Why don't you find out what it's like to live with someone who thinks you can do no wrong?"

"I'd never marry an overseer," said Eloise disdainfully.

Alex shrugged and picked up his saddlebags. "The lawyer will get in touch with you," he called over his shoulder.

When he reached the bottom of the steps, he looked back at his sister, who stood in the door of her huge house.

"I'll get what I want on my own," she said.

He nodded and swung astride. What he wanted was Cassandra and his children, and he'd find them if he had to go all the way to Boston.

Fortinbras having spoken the last lines of the play, Cassandra rose breathless from her death scene to take her bows with the rest of the cast. Effie stood beside her, giggling in a fashion most unlike Ophelia, and Hamlet, otherwise known as Effie's brother Sam, who had just that day won an important race at Newmarket, gave Cassandra an exuberant hug. "A salute, fair mother," he cried and kissed her cheek.

"You're supposed to be in love with *me*, not Cassandra," said Effie, pouting as the audience applauded wildly.

"My congratulations, Mrs. Harte," said Cray Williamson, the wealthy Galveston commission merchant who had participated brilliantly in her quotation contest months earlier. "Your Gertrude was magnificent. I could almost believe that you were Hamlet's mother rather than a lovely young girl."

"I am myself the mother of two boys," said Cassan-

Elizabeth Chadwick

dra, laughing. "But I thank you for the compliment, sir."

"With your husband so bravely occupied in the Mexican war," said Alice Williamson, "you must favor us with a visit to Galveston, Mrs. Harte. We leave tomorrow and would be delighted to take you with us. I promise you many new and delightfully learned friends if you will oblige us."

Cassandra's laughter stilled. Alex should have been here by now. He was overdue, perhaps not coming at all. Her heart misgave her. As Eloise had said, and Effie too, he was too much a war lover to care more for his family than his adventures. Hardening her heart, she turned to the gracious Mrs. Williamson and said, "How kind of you to invite me. I should love to pay you a visit if my two children and four servants would not be too much an imposition."

"It's settled, then," said Cray Williamson. "We can delay a day or so for your convenience."

"I would not put you out, sir," Cassandra protested. "Since my Comanche days when I was expected to fold my tepee and be gone in a half hour or less, I have been accustomed to efficient and fast departures. An hour or two should do for me even now."

"An admirable talent, madam," said Cray Williamson. "You must teach it to my wife."

Cassandra smiled at Alice. "I doubt that Mrs. Williamson needs lessons in anything I could teach. I've not forgotten the breadth of her knowledge—nor, I warrant, has the disconcerted Mr. Horace Waverly."

The three of them laughed, for it had been Alice Williamson who finally sent the egotistical English author creeping to his bed.

"Well, Effie," said Cray Williamson when Effie Barrett joined their group, "I have stolen your guest from you. She leaves with us tomorrow."

"No!" cried Effie, taking Cassandra's arm and smiling. "Well, I shall never have as much fun again until she returns. Cassandra will stir up society in Galveston, I promise you."

Cassandra thought of her absent husband and sighed. Tomorrow's move would take her farther yet from him and closer to a ship that would carry her to Massachusetts. Perhaps she had overestimated her power to attract him.

"Aye, 'twas a terrible thing," said Captain Wiggins, "and the man who stood watch that night—I've sent him on his way, but your wife, sir, is a brave and resourceful woman. The dastard intended to lock her and one of her maids into trunks and throw them overboard before he made off with your babes. Mrs. Harte and the boy Ruben got the best of him, and the sheriff has him now, but I tell you, sir, there were gentlemen aboard who'd have hung Ondine on the spot had I not intervened. Mrs. Harte was greatly admired by all the passengers. Why, young Holyrod, you know Bertrand Holyrod's boy, he followed her to Velasco, much in love, I'd say, poor pup."

Alex was glaring, horrified at the danger to his wife and children and none too pleased to hear the tales of her many admirers. Why wasn't she looking after the babies instead of dining and dancing with every gentleman along the river? Where was her sense of responsibility?

Then, chagrined, he realized that he was the one who had laid aside his responsibilities. Cassandra had the children with her and had risked her life for their well-being, while he had gone off and left them because he was tired of planting cotton. At that very moment the captain was telling him how Cassandra had thrown herself in front of a drawn pistol in the hands of Ondine, that she would have died had the weapon not misfired.

"But have no fear, sir, she's safe with the Barretts in Velasco. Mrs. Barrett was waiting at the landing when we docked. She whisked your wife and babes away in the carriage before we'd hardly begun to unload the trunks."

Alex nodded with relief. He'd see her tomorrow. Thank God. And he knew where to find her. He wouldn't have to search the town for his wandering wife, making himself look like a hapless fool in the process.

Cassandra's initial impressions of Galveston were not so favorable. They took a schooner from Velasco, the cool gulf breezes pleasant after the warmth they had left behind, but when they approached the island, Cassandra was appalled to see the wrecks of many ships, masts and bows thrusting forlornly from the water. Then, although Mr. Williamson had spoken proudly of Galveston as the finest deep-water harbor on the coast, excepting New Orleans, the water at the outer bar was only eleven feet, so that they and their baggage had to be taken in by lighter, a transfer which made her fearful for the babies. The island itself was a low expanse of sand barely higher than the surrounding waters of the gulf and making her wonder how it fared during the great storms that rolled in every fall. She'd not be here to find out.

Once ashore, she discovered the city to be a bustling place with many wharfs and with great commission houses along the Strand. Pigs roamed the streets eating garbage, which seemed to be the only method for disposal of refuse. The stench was overpowering—rotting oysters on the beaches and human waste and garbage in the streets and alleys.

Too late, she remembered that Eloise had come here in '39 and lost a child to yellow fever. *What have I done?* Cassandra asked herself and clutched baby Justin as a carriage bore her to the Williamsons' house, a fine place with a walled garden in front and lush tropical plantings—palm trees and flowering shrubs whose fragrance overpowered the natural stench of the town and went a way toward calming some of her fears. Alice Williamson identified bougainvillea, oleander, and poinsettia among other bushes in the garden, although she warned that the oleanders were poisonous. "Don't let Benjamin put the leaves or blossoms into his mouth."

Cassandra shuddered. Alex had better hurry, she thought. As hospitable and charming as the Williamsons were, she'd not stay here long, endangering her children. Alice and Cray had had yellow fever and were immune. In fact, they belonged to a society that provided money and nursing for fever victims, but Cassandra and her children had no such immunity, and Cassandra decided that she would rather not be a recipient of their society's beneficence.

"Of course I can arrange it for you," said Cray Williamson. "Cambridge, you say?"

"Well, the bank's in Boston," Cassandra replied.

"It will take time," said Williamson.

"How much time?" she asked anxiously. Just that morning Benjamin, who was usually so cheerful, had been whiny and restless and she was terrified that he might be coming down with some tropical disease.

"He's teething, dear," said Alice Williamson.

"If you're in need of funds, Cassandra, I'd be glad to advance whatever you need," said Cray, "although I'd heard you won a goodly amount at the races."

Not enough for seven passages to Massachusetts, she thought, but she'd said nothing of her plans to him. She still hoped that Alex would come for them.

"I appreciate the offer, and I did do well gambling," Cassandra replied. "It's just that I should claim my inheritance sooner or later and, with Alex away, I'd like to have my own money."

"Isn't he supporting you?" asked Williamson, frowning.

"Alex is at war," she replied, not quite keeping the resentment from her voice, "and I've six people dependent on me and a sister-in-law who sent an armed slave catcher to steal my children. I'm not likely to look to her for funds should I need them," she added bitterly.

"A slave catcher?" Williamson looked horrified.

"Yes." Cassandra felt no qualms about telling the story. Ondine would pay for his crime, but Eloise would not unless society exacted a price in social ostracism. "He planned to lock me and one of my girls in trunks and throw us into the river to drown. The babies he would have taken back to Eloise along with Mellie, the older girl. My boy Ruben and I fought him off until help came, but by then I was unconscious and Ruben had to shoot Ondine with my rifle to keep him from strangling me."

"Good Lord. Does Captain Harte know of all this?"

"Who can tell?" muttered Cassandra.

"Gone?" exclaimed Alex.

"Why yes, but she was the toast of Velasco, I can assure you," said Effie. "We've never had a better racing season. Cassandra's wonderful fun. She played Gertrude in *Hamlet* and was a stunning success. And Ephraim Baines adores her. They bet together and cleaned out every gambler in town."

Alex, remembering his brother-in-law's uncontrolled gambling, frowned. "Why was Cassandra gambling?"

"I think she needed the money, although, of course, she never said so, and we did all we could for Cassie and the babies." Effie peeped at him with a malicious little twinkle in her eyes. "It is so hard for women whose husbands are off sporting about in the wars."

"Sporting about?" Alex glared at her.

"Oh, we all know you, Alex. You couldn't pass up a

war if your whole family lay abed with the summer complaint and were like to die."

"Cassandra's never had malaria," he grumbled. "I'm the one who has it. And I've never denied her a thing."

"I don't doubt it," Effie agreed. "I'm sure if you forgot to see that she had cash or credit, Eloise would have been most generous."

Alex flushed, realizing for the first time how hopeless Cassandra's situation had been. He had indeed left her penniless, and she had survived with bravery and ingenuity, just as she had survived all the other disasters that had befallen her since she came to Texas.

"And of course all the young men adore her," Effie continued with relish. "Poor Holyrod was quite heartbroken when she took up with Ephraim Baines."

"Ephraim's old enough to be her grandfather."

"But such a gallant gentleman. He took over her races."

"What races?"

"Didn't I tell you? Cassandra raced on the beach every morning. First, her mount was Holyrod's thoroughbred, and she raced against Camp's cousin—and won. She's a magnificent rider."

"No one knows that better than I," he muttered, remembering how Cassandra had ridden across the front of an prairie fire to rescue him. "But it's damn dangerous for her to be racing sidesaddle."

"She rode astride. Sam lent her the clothes, and she did look stunning. All the young men were quite knocked off their feet, and the older ladies—" Effie giggled. "Well, I can tell you, no one ever made a bigger impression in Velasco. Between her racing in trousers and her gambling—I do swear more money changed hands on the beach than it did on afternoons at Newmarket—and her Comanche stories—"

"She told Comanche stories?"

"Oh yes, she said there was no use to keep quiet about it since your sister gossiped about her to everyone. Cassandra was just setting the record straight. We were devastated to see her go."

Alex gritted his teeth. The fool woman had been talking for hours and had yet to say *where* Cassandra had gone, although it had been his first question. "Where is she, Effie?" he demanded once more.

"I don't think I'll tell you," said Effie Barrett. "Find out for yourself. After all, she sent word to you weeks ago, and you've taken your own sweet time coming."

"I knew nothing until I got a note from my sister," said Alex defensively, "and then I rode straight home."

"Put the man out of his misery, Effie," said Caldicott Barrett, who had come into the drawing room in time to hear his wife's teasing refusal. "Cassandra's gone off to Galveston with the Williamsons, but I fear there'll be no schooner going that way for a day or two."

Alex groaned. He didn't think he could take any more of Effie's teasing, nor more time separated from Cassandra, not when he was unsure of whether she meant to leave him forever.

"There's free blacks here in Galveston, Miz Cassie," said Ruben excitedly. "There be one called Major Cary who carried messages for the army durin' the revolution, an' he done bought hissef an' his family free. They do say he's a better shot with a rifle than any white man, an' he own his own livery stable. Ah could do that. Work fo money when I ain't workin' fo you an' buy us all free."

Cassandra sighed. "You don't have to buy yourself free, Ruben. Actually, here in Texas it's not legal for a slave to buy his freedom."

His face fell.

"But soon we'll take ship for Massachusetts, where all men are free, and I'll see that you are, all four of

you, and that you're well educated enough to earn
your own way. If you want to continue to work for
me, you can, but you'll be paid wages."

"They many colored folks in Massachusetts?" asked
Ruben.

"No," Cassandra replied, "but they are all free men.
You'll make a good life, Ruben."

"What about Marse Alex?" asked Mellie, who had
been listening with wide, worried eyes.

"I guess he's not coming," said Cassandra. She was
by now convinced that she had been wrong, that Alex
would not pursue her again as he had when the Comanches took her. Maybe his love for her had died in
those months at Devil's Wood. Maybe he believed
Eloise's original conviction that Justin was not his
son, and he'd decided that he didn't want to be saddled
with a half-breed child and a wife about whom people
told scandalous stories. "I guess we'll have to make
our own way. I shall ask about ship departures."

"Galveston's a fine place," said Mellie wistfully.

"Galveston has much sickness and terrible storms
in the fall. Didn't you see all the wrecked ships in the
harbor?"

"Might be if we leave on a ship, we git wrecked too.
Ah'm afraid of drownin'," said Esther. "Couldn't we
go by carriage?"

"It's a very long way," Cassandra replied. "And expensive. If I don't get money soon from home, I shall
have to sell my wedding presents or, worse, borrow
from Mr. Williamson."

"I could earn us ticket money," Ruben offered.
"Maybe Major Cary give me work in his livery stable."

"An' you could lease me out as a ladies' maid an'
Esther to sew," said Mellie.

Tears rose in Cassandra's eyes. These children
wanted to take care of her.

"Don't cry, Miz Cassie," said Ruben. "Why, in no
time atall we have the money so you kin go home.

435

That where yo mama live? In Massachusetts?"

"She did, but she's been dead four years, and my father was killed by the Comanches."

"They mus' be real mean to hurt yo shoulder like they done an' kill yo papa," said Randall. "May be a good thing we go to Massachusetts. Pro'bly they ain't no Comanches there."

"No," she agreed. "There are no Comanches in Massachusetts." *And no Alex*, she thought sadly, *and no Alexandra*.

"I'd be glad to take you, Captain Harte, but I haven't a cabin unbooked."

"My wife's in Galveston, and I have to—"

"Would that be the lady that set the town on its ear, racing on the beach of a morning?"

Alex gritted his teeth.

"Why, I won twenty dollars on a race where she rode half the course hanging off the side of her horse, no saddle, just a rope. Never saw anything like it."

Alex went pale.

"The other rider never even finished. He fell off on his head, and I hear tell he's still afflicted with fits."

"Maybe you've a bunk below decks I could have." Alex had seen the Comanches hang off the sides of their horses shooting arrows from under, but he'd never thought to hear that his own wife would take such a chance. Dear God, she might have killed herself in some fool prank before he could even get to her. "I'll sleep on deck if need be."

"If I had a woman like that, I'd be anxious to see her again," said the captain admiringly. "She must keep you hopping."

"Yes," said Alex. "It took me nine months to get her and my son back from the Comanches. That's where she learned her riding tricks."

"With the Comanches? Do tell? Well, I guess I'll ave to find you something on board."

"I'd be obliged," said Alex, breathing a sigh of relief. etting passage didn't mean he'd get her back, but it id bring him a step closer.

Chapter Twenty-Five

"Why, Captain Harte," said Alice Williamson when he was shown onto the gallery where she sat reading, "you haven't arrived a day too soon."

"She's still here then?"

"Yes, she is, but packing. Her ship sails in two days' time. Won't you be seated?"

"Ma'am, if you don't mind, I'd like to go straight to my wife."

"Maybe you should at that," said Alice, smiling slightly. "You men think you suffer all the dangers of life with your wars and duels and other foolish adventures, but I doubt you've been through any times more trying than your wife has known of late."

"As I heard it, she's been the toast of both Velasco and Galveston," he muttered.

"So she has. Cassandra's a beautiful young woman, with intelligence and courage as well. I'm surprised you were so eager to leave her at Devil's Wood."

"There's a war," said Alex defensively.

"Can they not fight their latest war without you, Captain Harte? I believe you've served Texas more often than most and might have sat back on your laurels this time."

"I hope I have better luck pleading my case with my wife than I'm having with you, ma'am," said Alex ruefully.

"Up the grand staircase, turn left. You'll find her behind the second door." Alice Williamson went back

her book. She had no doubt that Cassandra would
rgive her adventurous husband. A woman of nine-
en, as deeply in love as Cassandra Harte, could for-
ve a lot, and it was clear to Alice Williamson that
ptain Harte loved his wife.

Alex heard her voice behind the door and flung it
en. At the sound, Cassandra glanced up from the
unk into which she was packing the blue and white
wn she'd worn to her fifth wedding, the one at Dev-
s Wood that had given Eloise so much fuel for the
azos gossip mill. Having abandoned her hopes that
 would come for her, Cassandra was stunned to see
r husband in the doorway.

"If you've a mind to wear it again," he said, nodding
ward the dress in her hands, "I know a judge here
 Galveston who'd be glad to wed us."

Her lips quivered into a smile. "I do appreciate your
oughtful offer," she replied, "but I think I'm beyond
ing a bride at this point."

Alex frowned. "Have you ceased to love me?" he
ked bluntly. He'd turned the matter over in his mind
 many times during this last pursuit of her that the
estion was too urgent for subtle approaches or flow-
y language.

"Why would you ask that? I've never given you
use—"

"You left me," he interrupted, all his shock and hurt
ughening his voice.

"Your sister gave me little choice, Alex," she replied
asonably, but her heart was beginning to flutter
ith happiness.

"I know all that, and I'm sorrier than I can say for
e pain and danger you've endured. But I have to
now. Have you ceased to love me, Cassandra? Alice
illiamson said you're about to leave Texas, which
rely means you're leaving me as well."

"Didn't you get my letter?"

"Not till I'd reached Devil's Wood, and what did
say? That you were leaving but hoped we might s
one another 'sometime in the future.' *Sometime*, Ca
sandra? Is that what a woman writes who loves h
husband? To see him *sometime*? And then you sign
yourself 'respectfully' mine. *Respectfully*?"

His indignation was such that Cassandra began
laugh. "Alex, I love you. My dearest wish was th
you'd follow me as you did before, but I too doubt
your love. You were the first to leave—and don't t
me about that war. I don't want to hear—" To h
astonishment Alex turned clean away from her a
scooped Benjamin off the carpet where he had be
sitting, staring wide-eyed at his father.

"Dada?" he piped questioningly when he was no
to nose with Alex.

"That's right, Dada," his father replied and kiss
the little boy, handing him immediately thereafter
Mellie, who had been hovering at the edge of the co
frontation between her master and mistress. Th
Alex scooped Justin from his cradle, kissed the slee
ing baby, and handed him to Esther. "Take the ch
dren off to the nursery, girls," he ordered.

"But, Alex, there is no nursery. The babies are slee
ing in here with me," said Cassandra.

"Well, take them off somewhere, girls," Alex o
dered and hustled them out the door.

"What in the world—"

"If you don't want to marry me again, you can
least go to bed with me." He pulled her up from t
low rocking chair in which she was sitting.

"It's afternoon, Alex, not night. Soon it will be tin
to dress for the evening meal," Cassandra proteste

"And I've a mind to satisfy my hunger a bit ear
today, my loving and respectful wife." He cupped h
face in his hands, flicking the pins from her chigno
with long fingers as he began to kiss her. "Haven't y

440

an afternoon of love for a man who's been chasing Mexicans through the chaparral?"

"No, but I might find a kiss for a man who could give up chasing Mexicans to chase after his runaway wife."

"Fortunately, you weren't that hard to follow, love. You've left a trail of swooning gentlemen—"

"No such thing."

"—and scandalized matrons in your wake. I fear it will take more than a kiss to pacify me when I consider your activities of late."

"Then I shall certainly try to court your good opinion," Cassandra replied. She unbuttoned his shirt and pressed her lips against his chest, then pulled the edges apart so that she could flick his nipples with the tip of her tongue.

"Where did you learn that?" he growled.

"From you," she replied and ran her nails lightly through the hair on his chest from his collarbones down to his navel, where she slipped her fingers beneath the waistband of his trousers.

"God, Cassandra!" Alex shuddered. "You're a brave woman to tease a man who's been hungering for you so long."

"I *am* a brave woman," she whispered against his mouth, her lips open and tempting.

Alex thrust both hands into her long, silver-gold hair and pulled her head back so that he could kiss her exposed throat. "Undo your dress," he coaxed.

Shivering with anticipation, she slipped the buttons with trembling hands as he followed the bared skin with his tongue and pulled the opened dress to her waist.

"The rest," he mumbled, and she undid the corset strings. Alex suckled her nipples through the chemise until she was no longer able to deal efficiently with her own laces, so distracted was she by the havoc he was creating in her senses. Finally the corset fell away, and he pushed the chemise down, his mouth still at her breast.

Cassandra was trembling, her body anguished with desire. "Let's go to bed," she begged.

"You've changed your mind then?" he asked as he loosened the waist of her gown and then undid her petticoat ties. "Maybe you'd rather get dressed for dinner." She pressed her body against him, and he obliged her by dropping her pantalettes around her ankles and kneeling to run his hands up the inside of her thighs. Cassandra stopped breathing as she felt his finger slip inside. "I think you have missed me," he murmured. He parted her delicately and rubbed his thumb against the sensitive nub of her womanhood, a long finger still inside her. Her legs gave way as the first spasms of rapture tore through her.

"Here, sweetheart," he muttered, taken by surprise at the reaction. "Don't faint." Alex rose from his knees, lifting her out of the circle of discarded clothing that surrounded them, and carried her to the bed. She pulled him down after her, eyes dilated with passion.

"Cassandra, I have to get the rest of my clothes off," he protested and did so in seconds. Even as he came to her, she was arching to meet him, and their bodies merged with the sharp thrust and clutch of unappeased desire. He was like a spear in water, sending ripples outward in a widening circle until first her body and then her mind were caught in the quivering backwash of ecstasy that sucked them both under.

"My God, love," he groaned when the last spasm had trembled into heated exhaustion, "I can't imagine why I wanted to go off to war."

"It was a puzzle to me as well," she replied seriously. "In fact, so many things that happened those last months were a puzzle to me. Why would you take Eloise's part against me?" she asked, knowing that these things had to be put behind them if they were to make a good life together. The loving wasn't enough

hen resentments and misunderstandings remained
nresolved.

"When did I ever do that?"

"When Justin was born. You would have let him be
amed after her husband, and yet you never liked the
an."

Alex's face went still.

"Was it—" she hesitated "—was it because you
ink he's not yours?"

"You didn't care what he was named," Alex mut-
red.

"Of course I cared, and I didn't want it to be the
ame of an immoral ne'er-do-well like your brother-
-law."

"And you didn't want to name him after me either."

"Oh, Alex. Was that it?"

"You've named neither of the boys after me. Didn't
ou think I'd want at least one of my sons—"

The tears were rising in Cassandra's eyes. She
ould never have kept secrets from him, even if she'd
ad the best of motives.

"Well, it's nothing to cry about. If you don't like the
ame—"

"I love your name. I love you, Alex." She sighed.
And we do have a child named after you."

"What the devil does that mean?"

"When Benjamin was born—there was another
aby." Alex looked confused. "Benjamin was a twin,
lex. We had a daughter as well."

"And she died?" he asked, his eyes filling with sad-
ess.

"They wanted to throw her away." Cassandra's lips
ere trembling, the tears spilling down her cheeks.

"I don't understand."

"They think twins are unnatural, and they don't
alue girl babies, and I—I had a long labor. I hardly
emember the end of it, or the argument that followed.

443

The women wanted to leave our daughter to die on a hill outside the camp."

"Oh, my God."

"Black Rain stopped them. She talked them into giving the baby to a woman who had just lost her own, a woman of another band. By the time I was myself again, our daughter was gone."

"You mean you never saw her again?"

"I never saw her at all."

"But why didn't you tell me, Cassie. I could have—"

"—gone after her? Of course, you would; Bone told me how guilty you felt about everything that happened. You'd have gone after her and been killed yourself. I couldn't stand to lose anyone else."

"But, Cassandra, I had a right to know."

"Perhaps, Alex, but you didn't seem to want to know anything about the time I spent with the Comanches. I took my own measures to get Alexandra back and to protect my family. You remember Captain Hawkins. The loved one I asked him to find was Alexandra."

"Oh God, and I suspected—"

"—that I was yearning after Counts Many Coup. Well, as I said, he died, and Hawkins sent word after you were off to the wars that he'd found no trace of Alexandra." She brushed away a second fall of tears.

Alex pulled her gently into his arms. "I am doubly to blame, love—for my jealousy and for my cowardice. I should have made you tell me everything that happened, but I was afraid to hear." He cupped his hand over her neck and rubbed it comfortingly. "My poor sweetheart. All this time—" His voice faded away into anguished silence.

Cassandra nestled her cheek against his shoulder. "Even though she was gone, I baptized her, and named her Alexandra, because, you see, I thought you were dead. Almost from the beginning, I'd thought you were dead. When the war party that captured me arrived at the main encampment, they counted coup, and I thought I saw your—your scalp. I was tied to a pole during the victory dances, and they imagined me very brave because I didn't seem to be afraid. But I wasn't brave. I was just numb with grief. I didn't care what happened to me."

"Oh, Cassandra."

"But the next morning I felt Benjamin move—or maybe it was Alexandra—and I knew I had to stay alive for the baby's sake. Then when I baptized her, I named her after you because I thought, if she died—so many Comanche babies die—maybe you could find each other in heaven if—well, I suppose it sounds silly. But I did so want our poor little daughter to have someone. If she's dead, God will have accepted her into heaven, don't you think? Even though they took her away from me before I could baptize her. He'd know I did the best I could. Don't you think?"

"I'm sure of it, love."

"So it wasn't that I didn't want to name one of our children after you. You understand?"

"Of course."

"And Alex, we can't go back to Devil's Wood. I'm sorry. I know you'll be giving up a lot by—"

"Sweetheart, don't worry about it. I never liked growing cotton. It's boring, if you want to know the truth, and even before my thrice damned sister nearly got you killed, I didn't want to live with her. I just wanted you to be safe."

"Yes, well, I liked mustanging better than plantation life, but it would be hard with two children."

"It would be impossible," said Alex, astonished. "Don't even think of it."

"But maybe we could do something similar."

"Similar?"

"We could raise animals. You'd enjoy that more than growing cotton. Horses, cattle, whatever. I have money, if I can ever get my hands on it. And we can sell the wedding presents. I even have all the money I won gambling, but I don't suppose you know about that."

"I know all about that," Alex snapped. "When did you develop this taste for gambling?"

"Oh, I don't really have a taste for it. I just gamble to keep body and soul together, you might say."

"What's that supposed to mean?"

"Well, with the Comanches I got clothes and food by gambling. I never did get a tepee to sleep in that winter, but I won a good buffalo robe."

"You had to sleep outside the whole winter?"

"Most of it, but it wasn't too bad. I got a blanket right away by being the loudest mourner at someone's funeral." He gaped at her. "And then I began to win at the hand game. Finally I got to sleep in Black Rain's tepee because the number one wife hated me and knocked me down. You might say I became the slave of a slave. Black Rain had been a slave at Pollard's Hill before she ran away and was taken by the Comanches. Strange, isn't it? That her owner, whom she hated, should have killed your brother-in-law over another black woman he coveted? Anyway, Black Rain became the second wife of the war chief."

"Dear God," said Alex, shaking his head. "You were a slave to a Nigrah? And you said the war chief? Does that mean you shared a husband with her?"

"I loved her dearly," snapped Cassandra, "and I'd have taken her with me if she'd have gone, but she said there was nothing back here for her but bondage."

"She was right," Alex agreed.

"And another thing. I intend to free Sarah's children. They can come with us or go to my cousins in Massachusetts, but I intend to set them free."

"I've no quarrel with that," said Alex.

"I'd have set Black Rain free if I could have."

"Maybe she *was* free, Cass. Did she hate her life with the Comanches?"

"No," said Cassandra. "No, she didn't." Cassandra pressed a fingertip against her lip, frowning thoughtfully. "Maybe you're right, and I just didn't understand. But as I said, we can use my money to buy land—"

"We don't need to do that. I've more land out on the frontier than ten men could use."

"You do?" Cassandra did remember him saying something about land.

"We passed through some of it in the area around that cave."

"Why, it's beautiful out there."

"Yes, but it's Indian country."

"I'm not afraid of the Indians, Alex. I was one."

"Well, the frontier's moving west all the time, and with the U.S. Army in Texas, there'll be a market for horses and mules, not to mention beef. Then there's an export market for hides and tallow. You might have hit on a good idea."

"And living so close to the Comanches, maybe we can find Alexandra."

"Maybe."

"And think what an adventure it will be," she added exuberantly. "You won't need to go off to war because—"

"—because I'll have my own sweet adventurer at home to keep me occupied."

"When can we leave?" asked Cassandra enthusiastically. "I'm quite prepared. I have notebooks full of information on how to do all sorts of domestic things. I put my time at Devil's Wood to good use."

"Well, you're probably the only woman in the country who approached life on the frontier in a scholarly fashion," he replied dryly. "Don't you want to have a honeymoon here in civilized comfort before we leave to carve out our empire in the wilderness? Your first honeymoon wasn't all that spectacularly successful."

"Oh, well," said Cassandra airily, "I was just too

young. What do brides know about honeymooning, after all? But now—" she grinned at him "—now I can appreciate the more delightful aspects of that particular field of, ah—study."

"Now that you've reached the ripe old age of nineteen and have become such an apt student? Would you care for another lesson?"

"Right now?"

"Why not? Even empire builders should take time out for education."